Praise for the Writings of Janny Wurts

"Janny Wurts brings an artist's eye for detail and mood to the field of fantasy writing."

—Robert Lynn Asprin

"A gifted creator of wonder!"

—Raymond E. Feist

"A creative flight of fancy into the lives of elves, dragons, wizards and space soldiers from award-winning writer and illustrator Janny Wurts. *That Way Lies Camelot* is your ticket to a world where sorcerers rule the day, and if you look carefully, you'll spot a fire-breathing dragon lurking in the shadows."

—*Boston Herald*

"Thoughtful and moodily satisfying . . . Wurts's pure fantasies are filled with concrete details and have an eerie believability. . . . A compassionate, cynical, smart collection."

—*Kirkus Reviews*

Janny Wurts

THAT WAY LIES
CAMELOT

HarperPrism
A Division of HarperCollinsPublishers

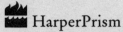

HarperPrism

A Division of HarperCollinsPublishers
10 East 53rd Street, New York, N.Y. 10022-5299

This is a work of fiction. The characters, incidents, and dialogues are products of the author's imagination and are not to be construed as real. Any resemblance to actual events or persons, living or dead, is entirely coincidental.

A hardcover edition of this book was published in 1994 by HarperPrism.

ISBN 0-06-105778-9

HarperCollins®, ®, and HarperPrism® are trademarks of HarperCollinsPublishers, Inc.

Cover illustration by Janny Wurts

First paperback edition printing: October 1997

Printed in the United States of America

Visit HarperPrism on the World Wide Web at
http://www.harpercollins.com

❖ 10 9 8 7 6 5 4 3 2 1

Dedication

To my readers –
the magicians who make all books possible

Acknowledgments

Given that short fiction is not my natural venue; that about every story I ever started on my own grew rapidly into a novel or more, I'd like to acknowledge the following editors, who asked.
Because of them, this collection exists.
Terri Windling, Richard Pini, Bill Fawcett, Rosalind Greenberg, Richard Gilliam, Susan Schwartz; and Rachel Holmen and Marion Zimmer Bradley.

Contents

THAT WAY LIES
CAMELOT

Wayfinder

Ciondo had blown out the lanterns for the night when Sabin remembered her mistake. Lately arrived to help out on the sloop for the summer, she had forgotten to bring in her jacket. It lay where it had been left, draped over the upturned keel of the dory; wet by now in the fog, and growing redolent of the mildew that would speckle its patched, sun-faded shoulders if someone did not crawl out of warm blankets and fetch it up from the beach.

The wind had risen. Gusts slammed and whined across the eaves, and moaned through the windbreak of pines that lined the cliffs. Winter had revisited since sundown; the drafts through the chinks held the scent of northern snow. The floorboards, too, were cold under Sabin's bare feet. She looked out through the crack in the shutter, dressing quickly as she did so. The sky had given her a moon, but a thin, ragged cloud cover sent shadows chasing in ink and silver across the sea. The path to the harborside was steep, even dangerous, all rocks and twined roots that could trip the unwary even in brightest sunlight.

Stupid, she had been, and ever a fool for letting her mind stray in daydreams. She longed to curse in irritation as her uncle did when his hands slipped on a net, but she dreaded to raise a disturbance. The household was sleeping. Even her aunt who wept in her pillow each night for the son just lost to the sea; Sabin's cousin, who was four years older than her undersized fourteen, and whose boots she could never grow to fill.

"A girl can work hard and master a boy's chores," Uncle Ciondo had summed up gruffly. "But you will never be strong enough to take the place of a man."

Yet the nets were heavy and the sloop was old, its scarred, patched planking in constant need of repairs. A girl's hands were better than going without, or so her mother insisted. Grudgingly, Uncle Ciondo agreed that Aunt Kala would do better if an empty chair no longer faced her through mealtimes. Sabin was given blankets and a lumpy cot in the loft, and cast off sailor's clothing that smelled of cod and oakum, poor gifts, but precious for the fact they could ill be spared.

Her lapse over the jacket could not go unremedied.

She fumbled and found her damp boots in the dark. Too lazy to bother with trousers, she pulled on the man-sized fisher's smock that hung halfway to her knees. The loose cuffs had to be rolled to free her hands. She knotted the waist with rope to hold it from billowing in the wind, although in the depths of the night, no one was abroad to care if she ran outside half-clothed.

The board floor squeaked to her step, and the outer latch clanged down as she shut the weathered plank door. "Sabin," she admonished as she hooked a heel on the door stoop and caught herself short of a stumble, "Don't you go tripping and banging, or someone will mistake you for trouble and shoot you in the back for a troll."

Except that no one in her village kept so much as a bow. The fisherfolk had only rigging knives and cutlery for the kitchen, and those were risky things to be throwing at trolls in the dark. Given any metal at all, and a troll will someday do murder with it; or so her mother used to threaten to scare out her habit of mislaying things. Sabin sighed at her failure since her jacket was not hanging as it should to dry on the hook by the hearth.

mightily. Despite her best effort, his head dipped under the flood. He swallowed a mouthful, gagging on salt, while she grunted in tearful frustration. The wave sucked back. He dragged his face free of its deadly, clinging currents with the dregs of his failing strength. His feet seemed fastened to the shoaling sands as if they were moored in place.

Belatedly suspicious, Sabin kept tugging. "Your ankles. Are they in irons also?"

He made a sound between a laugh, a sob, and a cough. "Always."

His floundering efforts managed to coordinate for a moment with hers. Together they stumbled a few yards shoreward, harried on by flooding water. Again the wave ebbed and he sank and bumped against the sand. Panting, Sabin locked her fingers in his shirt. She held him braced against the hungry drag of the sea, desperate, while her heart raced drumrolls with the surf. Something was not quite right, she thought, her stressed mind sluggish to reason. The incoming tide carried no flotsam, not a stick or a plank that a shipwrecked man might have used to float his way ashore. "You never swam," she accused again, as he regained the surface and spluttered.

Weak as he was, her sharpness stung him. He raised his chin, and eyes that were piercingly clear met hers, lit by the uncertain moonlight. "I didn't." His voice held a roughness like harpstrings slackened out of tune. "I begged help from the seaborne spirits that can be called to take the shape of horses. They answered and drew me to land, but they could not see me safe. To lead one even once from the water dooms it to mortal life ashore."

The interval between waves seemed drawn out, an unnatural interruption of rhythm like a breath too long held suspended. Even disallowing for chains his weight was too much for a girl, but it was a spasm of recognition like fear that locked Sabin's limbs and tongue—until those cut-crystal eyes looked down. As if released from bewitchment, she blurted, "Who are you?"

She thought the wind took her words. Or that they were lost in the grinding thunder of the sea as she scrabbled the last yards to dry sand. But when, safe at last, he collapsed in bruised exhaustion, he answered. "I am a Wayfinder, and the son of a Wayfinder." His cracked tone broke to a whisper. "And I was a slave for more time than I care to remember."

He spoke nonsense, she determined, and said so. He was a madman and no doubt a convict who had fled in the shallows to hide his tracks from dogs. A denial she did not understand closed her eyes and her heart against the logic that argued for him: that the road ran high above the cliffs, and those few paths that turned shoreward were much too steep for a captive to negotiate in chains. Had he come that way, he should have fallen, and broken his legs or his neck. Through teeth that chattered, Sabin waited. Yet the refugee stayed silent. She poked him in the ribs with her toe and found he had succumbed at last to the beating the sea had given him; either he slept or had dropped unconscious. The wind bit at wet flesh, made cruel by driven spray. The tide rose still, and the sand where he lay would very soon be submerged. Forced by necessity, Sabin arose. The jacket she had left on the dory would have to serve the old man as a blanket until Uncle Ciondo could be fetched from his bed.

Sabin awakened to sunlight. Afraid of her uncle's gruff scolding, she shot straight, too fast. The blood left her head. Dizziness held her still and blinking, and she realized: Uncle Ciondo was shouting. His voice drifted up through the trapdoor to the ladder, though he probably stood in the kitchen by the stove, shaking a fist as he ranted.

"A condemned man, what else could he be! Or why should anyone have chained him? Those fetters were not closed with locks. They were riveted. We cannot shelter such a man, Kala."

The castaway, Sabin remembered. She pushed herself out of bed, and tripped in her haste over the wet smock she had discarded without hanging last night. From the clothes chest she grabbed her only spare, and followed with the woolen britches every fisher's lad wore to sea. She left her boots. Even if they were not drenched and salt-stiff, they would make too much noise and draw notice.

Masked by the murmur of her aunt's voice, declaiming, Sabin set bare feet on the ladder. At the bottom, the door to Juard's room lay cracked open, beyond the stairwell which funneled the bellow of her uncle's protest. "Kala, that's daft and you know it! He could be dangerous, a murderer. I say we send him inland in the fish wagon and leave his fate to the King's bailiff."

Sabin's uncle was not hard-hearted, but only a sailor, and the sea rewards no man for sentiment. Ciondo would care very little if the rescued man could hear the rough anger in his voice. But as a girl not born to a fisher's trade, Sabin flinched. She tiptoed down the hall and slipped through the opened door, a ghost with mousy, tangled hair and a sail-cloth smock flocked at the cuffs with the rusty blood of gutted cod.

The man the sea had cast up was asleep. Chains lay on him still, looped at wrists and ankles with spare line that tied him spread-eagled to the bedposts. Ciondo had taken no chances, but had secured the refugee with the same half hitches he might use to hold a dory against a squall. Still, the undyed wool of the blankets hung half kicked off as if the prisoner had thrashed in nightmares. His rags were gone. Daylight through the opened shutters exposed a history of abuse, from the salt-galled sores left by shackles to a mapwork of dry, welted scars. He was not old after all, Sabin saw, but starved like a mongrel dog. His skin was sun-cured to teak and creases, and his hair bleached lusterless white. He looked as weatherworn as the fishing tackle on the sloop's decks, beaten by years of hard use.

Aunt Kala's voice filtered through the doorway, raised to unusual sharpness. "Ciondo, I'll be sending no man on to the bailiff before he finds his wits and tells his name! Nor will any needy stranger leave our roof hungry, the more shame to you for witless fears! As if anybody so starved could cause harm while bound up in metal chains!

Now be off! Go down to the beach with the rest, and leave me in peace to stir the soup."

A grumbling followed, and a scrape of boots on the brick. Few could stand up to Kala when she was angry, and since Juard's death, none dared. She was apt to weep when distressed, and if anyone saw her, she would throw cooking pots at them with an aim that could flatten a pigeon.

Cautious in the quiet after the door slammed, Sabin crept to the window. The sun threw slanting bars of yellow through gently tossing pines. Yet if the vicious, tearing winds had quieted, the sea mirrored no such calm. Beyond the spit off the point, the breakers still reared on the reefs, booming down in tall geysers of spray. The surge rushed on untamed, through the harbor gates where the round-bottomed boats rolled at anchor, an ominous sign. Sabin bit her lip. She squinted against the scintillant brightness of reflections and saw wreckage scattered amid the foam: the sundered masts and planking of ships gutted wholesale by the reefs.

No one had shaken her awake at dawn because today the twine would not be cast out for fish. When the wrecks littered the beach, men plied their nets to glean a storm's harvest from the waves. Custom barred girls and women from such labor, lest the nets bring up dead bodies, and the sight of drowned flesh sour the luck of their sons, born and unborn, and curse them to the horror that had befallen cousin Juard, to be taken alive by the sea.

The man on the bed had escaped that fate, just barely. He had come in on a ship that was now ripped to fragments, Sabin knew for a surety. He had not swum; not in chains. And horses did not run in the sea. Unwilling to risk misfortune by looking too closely at the waves, or what tossed and surfaced in the whitening tumble of foam, Sabin spun away from the window. She shivered in the sun that fell on her back, and shivered again as she saw that the man on the bed had awakened. He studied her, his eyes like fine flawed crystal broken to a razor's edge.

"You do not trust me," he said in his rusty whisper. He flexed one wrist, and immediately grimaced in pain.

"My uncle thinks you're a murderer."

He ground out a bitter, silent laugh. "Oh, but I am, though my hand has never taken life."

She frowned, a plain-spoken girl who dreamed, but had always hated riddles. "What is a Wayfinder?"

Riddles came back in answer, as he regarded the beams of the ceiling. "One who hears the sea. One who can read the earth. One who can travel and never be lost."

"I don't understand." She stepped back, and sat on the clothes chest that had once held the shirt she was wearing, when it had been Juard's, and she had spent days spinning thread for her father's loom. Now her hands had grown horny and tough, and fine wool would catch on the callus. But the incessant lapses of attention had not left her; she forgot to mind sheet lines as readily as she had faltered at spindle and wheel. She curled her knees up and clasped her hands to bury that recognition. "Anyone can be lost."

He stirred in the faintest impatience, jerked back by the cut of his chains. "Inland to the east, there is a road, a very dusty road with stone markers that winds through a forest. Beyond lie farmlands, and three villages, and lastly a trader's town. Beyond brick walls are wide sands, called by the desert people who live there Dei'eh'vikia." His head tipped sideways toward Sabin. His eyes now were darkened as gray sapphires, and he considered her as though she should be awed.

She was not. "You could have spoken to someone who passed that way," she accused. "Perhaps you lived there yourself." But she knew as she spoke that he did not. His vessel had broken on the reef, and never sought harbor in these isles. Few ships did, for the rocks gave hostile greeting to mariners from afar.

He looked at her in sadness or maybe pain, as if he had offered riches to the village half-wit who had use for no coin at all. He kept staring until she twisted her fingers together, embarrassed as if caught at a lie. For all his foreign accent, he had pronounced the place name as crisply as the nomads who made the desert their home.

Townsmen and traders slurred over the vowels and called it Daaviki, in contempt for the troublesome native speech.

He perceived that she knew this. He saw also that stubbornness kept her silent.

He looked at her still, his gaze heavy-lidded, almost glazed as a drunk's. The angle of his neck must have pulled at his shoulders and wrists, but he shed any sign of discomfort as he said, "Sabin, outside this room, there is a passage covered with braided rugs. It leads to a stairway that winds around itself twice. Downstairs, to the right of the kitchen lies a door that leads to a springhouse. Purple flowers grow by the path, and seven steps to the left lead to the sea cliff where there is a little slate ledge. You like to sit there on sunny mornings, in what you call your chair seat. But the people who inhabited these coasts before yours used the site as a shrine." His grainy voice was almost gentle as he finished. "They left carvings. You have seen them, when you scratched at the moss."

Sabin jumped up with her mouth opened like a fish. He had been carried into this house, unconscious. Ciondo had brought him through the front door. Someone might have mentioned her name in his hearing, but there was no way he could have seen the springhouse, or have known of her fondness for that ledge. Her aunt and uncle did not know, nor her own mother and father.

"I am a Wayfinder," he said simply, as if that sealed a truth that she realized, shivering, could not be other than magic. Her need to escape that room, and that compelling, mesmeritic gaze came out in a rush of speech. "I have to go, now."

The Wayfinder let his head fall back on the pillow. At a word from him, she would have fled; she waited, tautly poised on one foot. But he made no sound. He closed his eyes, and curiosity welled over her fear and held her rooted. "Still there?" he murmured after a while.

"Maybe." Sabin put her foot down, but quietly.

He did not open his eyes. "You have a piece of the gift yourself, you know, Sabin."

She quivered again, as much from anger. "What gift!"

His hands were not relaxed now, but bunched into white-knuckled fists. One of his sores had begun to bleed from the pressure; he was trying her uncle's knots, and finding them dishearteningly firm. "You came to the beach at my call."

She stamped her foot, as much to drive off uneasiness. "You called nothing! I forgot my jacket. That was all."

"No." His hands gave up their fretting. "You have given your jacket as the reason. But it was my call that caused you to forget it in the first place. When I asked the spirits for their help, you heard also. That was the true cause of the forgetfulness that drew you outside in the night."

"I've been scolded for carelessness all my life," she protested, "and my jacket was forgotten at twilight!"

"And so at that hour I called." He was smiling.

She wanted to curse him, for that. He seemed so smug. Like Juard had been when he teased her; and that remembrance called up tears. Sabin whirled violently toward the doorway and collided headlong with her aunt.

"Sabin! Merciful god, you've spilled the soup." Kala raised the wooden tray to keep it beyond reach of calamity, and her plump face dimpled into a frown. "What are you doing here anyway? A sick man has no need for prying girls."

"Talk to him," Sabin snapped back. "He's the one who pries."

"Awake, is he?" Kala stiffened primly. She glanced toward the bed and stopped cold, her chins sagging beneath her opened mouth, and the tray forgotten in her hands. For a moment she seemed to breathe smoke as she inhaled rising steam from the soup bowl.

Then she exploded. "My fool of a husband! Rope ties! The cruelty and the shame of it." She stepped sideways, banged her tray down on the clothes chest, and in a fit of total distraction, failed to bemoan the slopped soup. "Sabin, run out and fetch our mallet and chisel." She added to the stranger on the bed, "We'll have you free in just minutes."

For an instant, the Wayfinder's cut-crystal eyes seemed to mirror all of the earth. "Your goodman thinks I'm a murderer."

"My goodman is a fool who thinks in circles like a sand crab." Kala noticed that Sabin still lingered in the doorway. "Girl, must you always be idling about waiting for speech from the wind? Get along! Hammer and chisel, and quickly."

Kala had matters well in hand before the last fetter was struck. "You're taking up no space that's needed," she insisted with determined steadiness. "Juard's bed is yours, he's dead and at rest in the sea, and if you care to lend a hand at the chores, we could use the help, truly. Sabin belongs home with her family."

She ended with a strike of the mallet. As the last rivet sheared away, and rusted metal fell open and clanged in a heap on the floor, the Wayfinder raised his freed wrists. He rubbed at torn skin, then looked up at Kala, who stood over him gripping the tools with both fists braced on broad hips. In profile, Sabin saw the stranger give her aunt that same, heavy-lidded gaze that had earlier caused her the shivers.

"He's not lost, your Juard," the broken voice announced softly.

Kala went white. She dropped the tools with a clatter and clapped her palms behind her back to distract bad luck, and avert the misfortune of hearing false words. "Do not spin me lies! Respect our loss. Ill comes of wishing drowned men back from death, for they hear. They rise in sorrow and walk the sea bed without rest for all of eternity."

The Wayfinder cocked up his eyebrows in sad self-mockery. "I never lie. And no such lost spirits walk the sea, nor ever have." At Kala's shocked stiffness, he thumped his marred fist on the mattress in frustration. "Your boy is not dead, only washed up on a beach, as I was."

Aunt Kala turned her back, which was as near to an insult as anyone ever got from her. The Wayfinder glared fiercely, his ice-gray eyes lit to burning. Then his jaw hardened until the muscles jumped and his speech scraped out of his throat. "Your son fetched up on the Barraken Rock, to the west. At this moment, he is gutting a fish with a knife he chipped from a mussel shell."

"My son is dead!" Kala snapped back. "Now say no more, or when Ciondo comes back, you will go trussed in the wagon to the bailiff's. I'll hear your word."

The Wayfinder sighed as though sucked down in a chasm of weariness. "Woman, you'll get no word from me, but neither will you hear any, either, if that is your desire."

"It is." Kala stamped out through the doorway without looking back. "Sabin," she yelled from the threshold at the head of the stairwell. "You'll see that yon man eats his soup, and bring down the tray when he's finished."

But Kala's bidding was impossible to carry out, Sabin found. On the bed, the Wayfinder had closed his eyes and fallen deeply asleep.

The house stayed quiet for the rest of the morning, with Kala beating quilts with a ferocity that outlasted the dust. At noon Uncle Ciondo returned from the beach, swathed in dripping oilskins, his boots caked to the ankles with damp sand. The bull bellow of his voice carried up through the second storey window where Sabin kept vigil over the invalid. "Kala! Where is that man?"

The thwack of the broom against fabric faltered. "Where else would he be, but in bed? The shame on you, Ciondo, for leaving him trussed like the felon he certainly isn't." Smack! went the broom on the quilts.

When only the cottage door hammered closed in reply, Sabin gripped her knees with sweaty hands. She all but cowered as her uncle's angry tread ascended the stairs; bits of grit and shell scattered from his boots and fell pattering against the baseboards as he hurried the length of the hall. The next instant his hulking shoulders filled the bedroom doorway and his sailor's squint fixed on the empty shackles that lay where they had fallen on the floor.

"Fool woman," he growled in reference to his wife. He raised hands scraped raw from his labors with net and sea, and swiped salt-drenched hair from his temples. Then he noticed Sabin. "Out, imp."

Her chin jerked up to indicate the man on the bed. "I found him."

"So you did." Ciondo's grimness did not ease as he strode closer, but he did not send her away. Sabin watched as he, too, met the uncanny gaze of the stranger who had wakened again at the noise. The sword-edged clarity of that stare arrested her uncle also, for he stopped, his hands clenched at his sides. "Do you know that all morning we have been dragging in bits of burst ships? Not just one, but a fleet of them."

The Wayfinder said a touch tartly, "Karbaschi warships."

"So you know them." Ciondo sighed. "At least you admit it." His annoyance stayed at odds with his gesture as he noticed his boots, and the sand left tracked in wet clumps. Hopeful as a miscreant mongrel, he bent and scuffed the mess beneath the bed where Kala might not notice. He dusted his fingers, ham-pink and swollen from salt water, on the already gritty patches of his oilskins. "You were a criminal? Their prisoner perhaps?"

The Wayfinder's lip curled in a spasm of distaste. "Worse than that."

Ciondo straightened. "You'd better tell me. Everything. Our people fear such fleets, for where they go, they bring ruin."

The man propped up by the pillows seemed brown and wasted as stormwrack cast up and dried on the beach. In a whisper napped like spoiled velvet, he said, "I was their Wayfinder. Kept bound in chains to the flagship's mast, to guide them on their raids. When I refused to see the way for their murdering, or led them in circles at sea, they made sure that I suffered. But by the grace of your kindness, no more."

Uncle Ciondo's square face looked vacant with astonishment. "You!" He took a breath. "*You?* One of the *in'am shealdi*, the ones who are never lost? I don't believe it."

"Then don't." The Wayfinder closed his eyes. His

lashes were dark at the roots, and bleached white at the tips from too much sun. "Your wife named me liar also."

"Storm and tide! She'll fling any manner of insult at a man, if she thinks it will help make him listen." Ciondo shifted stance in disgust. "And I did not say you spoke falsehood, but only that I can't believe you."

At this, the Wayfinder's eyes flicked open. Though he tensed no muscle, Sabin felt warning charge his presence that swept the room like cold wind. "Is it proof you want? You shall have it. Leave me blindfolded on any of your fishing sloops, and give me the tiller, and I will set you an accurate course for the spit called the Barraken Rock."

"A wager?" Ciondo covered his uneasiness with a cough. Thoughtfully, he added, "The trial would have to be at night, or the sun on your face might guide you."

"Be it night, or in storm, I care very little," the Wayfinder challenged. "But if I win, I'd have your promise: not a word of my gift shall go beyond this village. Your King, if he found me, would send me back as a bribe to plead for an exemption from tribute. Greedy traders anywhere would sell the secret of my survival. The Karbaschi make unforgiving masters. If they learned I still lived, a warrior fleet would sail to collect me, and killing and looting would follow. If your people have no riches to adorn Karbaschi honor, your houses would burn, and your daughters know the miseries of slavery."

Ciondo went pale, even to the end of his nose that seasons of winds had buffed red. He stepped back from the edge of the mattress and sat, without care for his soggy oilskins, on the cushion by the windowseat. "If you are *in'am shealdi*, then you steered those ships afoul of the currents. Was it you who set your Karbaschi overlords on our reef to drown and then took your chance in the sea?"

The Wayfinder denied nothing, but regarded his wrists as if the weals dug by fetters could plead his testimony for him. A tight-drawn interval followed, broken at last by the rattle of pots in the kitchen; Kala had relented enough to oversee the noon meal. Her industry spoiled the quiet, and forced the Wayfinder to raise his burred voice to be heard.

"Men travel the land, but they do not hear it. They sail the waters, yet they do not know the sea. The Karbaschi warships carve paths of destruction, and the peoples they conquer grieve for slain husbands and sons. But where the Karbaschi stay to settle, they bring cruelties more lasting than death to the flesh. The lands they rule will wither in time, because they are a race who take and give nothing back. Their habit of pillage has deafened them, until they plow up forests for fields and raise towns without asking leave. The rituals mouthed by their priests are empty of truth, and without care for the still, small needs of the earth." Here, the invalid lifted his wasted, leathery shoulders in a shrug. "*In'am shealdi* are actually guardians. We nurture the spirits which the Karbaschi run over roughshod, because they love only the desires of humanity. It is such spirits that show me the way. If I call, they answer, though the Karbaschi ruled my body as a man might course a hunting dog. The guidance given to me in trust was forced to ill use, and inevitably brought the earth sorrow. The day came when I could not endure its pain, or my own, any longer."

The Wayfinder sounded wistful as he finished. "I expected to die in the sea. Since I did not, I should like very much to stay. To live simply, and make use of my talent very little. I wish for nothing beyond your leave to guide your village sloops back to anchorage each night for the rest of my life."

Secure in the belief she was forgotten where she sat on the clothes chest, only Sabin caught the half glance he flicked in her direction. As if his cracked voice informed her, she knew: because of her he begged sanctuary— because of the gift he claimed she shared; and not least, for the sake of Juard *who was dead, who had to be dead, else magic and spirits were real and horses ran wild in the sea.*

If in truth such beauty existed, she would never shed the distraction of dreams but helplessly become consumed by them until the small inattentions that cursed her grew monstrous and took over her life.

Spooked by strangeness that threatened to draw her

like some hapless moth to a flame, Sabin sprang to her feet and fled. Out through the hall she pounded, and on down the stair beyond. Kala called out as she passed through the kitchen, to say the noon meal was waiting. But the girl did not stop until she had left the house, and raced at reckless speed down the cliff path to the place she called her chair seat.

There she spent the afternoon, while the Wayfinder slept. She did not return for supper, though Kala called from the back door to say that their guest had arisen for the meal. By that Sabin understood that her uncle had accepted the Wayfinder at his word; an outsider who spoke false might stay because he was ill and had need, but he would not be invited to table. One supposed that Kala and the stranger had settled their hostilities by not speaking.

At nightfall, when most folk gathered at the tavern, the beachhead glittered with torches. Word had passed round of a wager, and every boy with the sea in his blood turned out to ask Ciondo's leave to man the sloop, never mind that the craft was handy and needed little crew. The commotion as boasts were made and shouted down, and lots were finally drawn to keep the choice fair, enabled Sabin to sneak past and hide under the nets in the dory. Certain she had not been seen, she peered out cautiously and saw the tight knot of men stepping back. They left the Wayfinder standing alone with black cloth muffling his head. He turned unerringly toward the tender that was Ciondo's. If his steps were unsteady due to weakness, the line he walked was straight. He crossed and found the thwart without fumbling, and spoke so no others could hear. "Your good aunt does not know where we sail. I never mentioned to your uncle that I know your cousin Juard to be alive. Before we arrive at the Barraken Rock, I give you the burden of telling him."

"Aunt Kala would curse you for putting your lies in my mouth," Sabin accused from under damp nets, the reek of which suddenly made her dizzy. She was trembling again, and that made her angry, for he sensed her fear, she was certain. She could feel those pale eyes burning even through their veiling of cloth as he said, "But you are not Kala. You are the child of a weaver, and your fears are not ruled by the sea."

"They are when I sit in a boat!" she snapped back, more like her aunt than herself.

He laughed in his broken, rasping way, and because there was no malice in him, she wanted to hit him or scream. Instead she shrank into a tight huddle. Light and voices intruded, and the boat lifted, jostling, to be launched. As the keel smacked the water, and blown spray trickled through her cocoon of nets, she tasted warm salt with the cold. Tears; she was crying. The man seemed so certain that poor, lost Juard still breathed.

Sabin felt the rampaging buck of the surf toss the dory over a swell. The alternative terrified her, that her cousin had rightly drowned, and that this stranger who lured the people laughing to their boats to follow his blindfolded quest was a sorcerer who could swim in iron chains. They might rescue Juard, or else join him, leaving more bereaved families to weep and to curse at the sea.

Sabin rubbed the stinging cheek her uncle had smacked when he found her, and smacked again when she told what the Wayfinder had said of her lost cousin. While the wind shifted fitfully, slapping sails and stays in contrary gusts, and moonlight silvered the wavelets, she braced against the windward rail, away from the men by the binnacle. Their talk grew ever more sullen as Juard's fate was uneasily discussed, and shoreline and lights shrank astern.

"Nothing lives on the Barraken Rock but fishing birds that drink seawater!" cried Tebald over the wear of patched canvas. Young, and a friend of Juard's, his jutted chin and narrowed eyes were wasted.

Blind behind swathes of black rag, the Wayfinder stood serene before aggression, his thin hands draped on the tiller as if the wood underneath were alive.

Darru argued further. "Without a fresh spring, a castaway would perish."

"It has rained twice in the past week," the stranger rebuked. "Oilskins can be rigged to trap water, and the seabirds are plentiful enough to snare." Ciondo's spare smock flapped off his shoulders like an ill-fitting sail, the cuffs tied back to keep from troubling his sores. The linen bindings covering his wrists emphasized prominent bones; a man so gaunt should not have been able to stand up, far less command the muscle to mind the helm. But Sabin could see from where she stood that the sloop held flawless course. The wake carved an arrow's track astern.

Ciondo glowered and said nothing, but his hand strayed often to the rigging knife at his belt.

"We should put about and sail back," Tebald said.

Darru was more adamant. "We should let you swim back, stranger, for your lies."

The Wayfinder answered in the absent way of a man whose thoughts are interrupted. "If I prove wrong, you may kill me."

At this came a good deal of footshifting, and one or two gestures to ward ill luck. No one voiced the obvious, that they could kill him only if malfortune went elsewhere and they lived to make good such a threat.

The night wore on and the stars turned. The wind settled to a steady northeast, brisk and coldly clear. Moonset threw darkness on the water, and the land invisible astern. Once, Darru repeated the suggestion that the wager be abandoned, that the sloop seek return by the stars. He spoke to Ciondo by the mainmast pinrail, but was answered in gruff-voiced challenge by the Wayfinder aft at the helm. "Would you take such a chance, just to keep Juard's doom a clear certainty?"

Darru spun in vicious anger, jerked back by Ciondo's braced hand. "Don't provoke him! He is *in'am shealdi*, or how else does he steer without sight? Find faith in the straight course he sails, or else give the decency of holding your tongue until you have true cause to doubt."

"Grief for your son has turned your head," Darru muttered, shrugging himself free. But he could not argue that lacking clear stars or a compass, no ordinary man could keep a heading hour after hour without mistake.

Night waned. Sabin slept through the dawn curled against a bight of rope. She dreamed of waves and white horses, and the rolling thunder of troubled seas until Tebald's shout awakened her. "The Barraken Rock! Dead off our bow, do you see!"

She opened her eyes to a dazzle of sunlight, and the soured smell of seaweed beached and dried. "Juard," she whispered.

No one noticed. Ciondo stood as a man frozen in place by the foremast stay; the more volatile Darru gave back laughter and cried to his fellow crewman, "Where were you an hour ago when the spit rose out of the sea?"

"Sleeping," Tebald confessed. His awed glance encompassed the scarecrow figure who guided the tiller with a feather touch, and whose eyesight was yet swathed in cloth. The mouth that showed underneath seemed turned up in detached amusement. Tebald leaned down and ruffled Sabin's hair as he passed, his discomfort masked by a shrug.

Peevish and oddly unrefreshed, she tried a kick that missed at his ankle. "Don't do that. I'm not a little girl anymore."

Tebald ignored her as if she were a bothersome younger sister. To Ciondo he said, "The wager's won, I'd say. Your *in'am shealdi* should take off his blindfold. It's probably making him sweat."

"I said so," Ciondo admitted. With one hand fastened to the headstay, he kept his eyes trained on the rock that jutted like a spindle from the sea. "Tell him again if you want."

But with the arcane powers of the helmsman now proven, no one seemed anxious to speak. Sun glared like molten brass off the wet shine of the deck, and the sheet lines creaked under their burden of sail. The pitiless isolation of the sea seemed to amplify the wind, and the mingled cries of seabirds that squabbled and flew above the rock. The deeper shout that was human seemed to rend the day's peace like a mortal blow to the heart.

On that gale-carved, desolate spit, splashing in seawater to the knees, a raggedy figure ran, dancing and gyrating to a paean of reborn hope.

"It's Juard!" Darru gasped. He glanced nervously back at the Wayfinder, ashamed for his unkind threats. Tebald at his side held his breath in wordless shock, and Ciondo just buried his face in his hands and let the tears spill through his fingers.

It was Sabin who moved to free sheet lines when the Wayfinder threw up the helm. While Tebald and Darru roused belatedly to set the anchor, the girl unlashed an empty bait barrel. She stood it on end by the sternpost, climbed up, and as the Wayfinder bent his head to receive her touch, she picked out the knots of his blindfold. The cloth fell away. Hair bleached like bone tumbled free in the breeze, and she confronted a face set level with hers that had been battered into pallor by exhaustion. The eyes no longer burned, but seemed wide and drugged as a dreamer's. She could almost plumb their depths, and sense the echoes of the spirits whose guidance had led the sloop without charts.

"You could hear them yourself, were you taught," the Wayfinder murmured in his grainy bass. Yet before those eyes could brighten and tempt her irrevocably to sacrifice the reality she understood, she retreated to a braced stance behind the barrel.

"The moment Juard can sail with his father, I'll be sent back home. Whether or not there are horses in the sea, I shan't be getting lost behind a loom." Her bare feet made no sound as she whirled and bounded off to help Ciondo, who was struggling in feverish eagerness to launch the tender by himself.

The sloop was met on her return by men with streaming torches. Juard's reappearance from the lost brought cries of joy and disbelief. Kala was fetched from her bed for a tearful reunion with the son miraculously restored to her. For Juard was alive; starved thin, his hair matted in tangles so thick they could only be shorn, and his skin marred everywhere with festering scratches that needed immediate care. The greedy sea had been forced to give back its plunder, and the news swept like fire through the village.

A crowd gathered. Children in nightshirts gamboled on the fringes, while their parents jabbered in amazement. The Wayfinder whose feat had engineered the commotion stood aloof, his weight braced against the stempost of a dry dory as if he needed help to stand up. From farther back in the shadows, outside the ring of torchlight, Sabin watched him. She listened, as he did, to the noise and the happiness, and she alone saw him shiver and stiffen and suddenly stride into the press with his light eyes hardened to purpose.

He set a hand marked as Juard's on Ciondo's arm, and said, "No, I forbid this," to the fisherman who had been boasting the loudest. "You will not be repeating this tale to any traders, nor be offering my service to outsiders. This is my bargain for Juard's life."

Silence fell with the suddenness of a thunderclap. Surf and the snap of flame remained, and a ring of stupefied faces unfamiliarly edged with hostility. "Which of us made any such bargain?" shouted someone from the sidelines.

The Wayfinder's peaked brows rose. "Ciondo is my witness, and here is my warning. For yourselves, you may ask of me as you will. The guiding and ward of your fleet I shall do as I can; but let none beyond this village ever know that I am *in'am shealdi*. Say nothing, or sorrow will come of it."

Finished speaking, or perhaps too weary to stay standing, the Wayfinder strode out of the pack. He left all the village muttering and wondering as he moved in slow steps toward the path. On the chill sands outside the torchlight, Sabin watched him vanish in the darkness under the pines. She did not follow; nor did she feel moved to join the villagers. The waking dream had touched her. Curiosity no longer drove her to discuss the stranger Kala sheltered.

"Was he a felon, to want such secrecy?" one goodwife muttered from the sidelines.

Ciondo replied in indignation, "Does it matter?" Then good sense prevailed over argument, and Kala scolded the gawkers roundly for keeping poor Juard from his bed.

A month passed, and seven days. Juard recovered his health and returned to fishing on the sloop. The Wayfinder who had brought his recovery took a longer time to mend. Kala pressed food and comforts on him constantly, until he complained of her coddling. Unlike anybody else, she listened, and left him alone. His white hair began to grow out its natural color, a golden, honey-brown, until Sabin sitting in her chair seat on the cliffside could no longer pick him out from the villagers who manned the sloops. She saw him seldom, and spoke with him not at all. Winding the skeins of wool and stringing the looms in her father's craft shop in furious concentration, she avoided walking the beach. Since the night she forgot her jacket, she could not bear to watch the combers. She heard them, felt them, even indoors with her ears filled with the clack of shuttle and loom—the thunder of what might be hooves, and the tumble of white, upflung spray that pounded the beaches in procession. She swept cut threads from the floor, and helped her mother bake, and each night begged her sleep to show her silence.

It did not. She misplaced socks and tools, and once, let the fire burn out. The waking world came to seem as a dream, and herself, strangely separate, adrift. She was scolded more often for stargazing, and seemed more than ever to care less.

The Wayfinder laughed in the tavern at night, accepted, but with a reverence that marked him apart. Two boats he saved from ruin when storms caused shoaling off the reefs. Another smack was recovered with a damaged compass after squall winds blew it astray. No one knowingly broke the Wayfinder's faith, but his presence loomed too large to shelter. Sabin understood this, her hands fallen idle over wool she was meant to be spinning. She twisted the red-dyed fibers aimlessly, knowing: there were traders

who had heard of Juard's loss, and who saw him back
among the men. They asked questions. Driven by balked
curiosity, they pressured and cajoled, and won themselves
no satisfaction.

The silence itself caused talk.

Summer passed. The winds shifted and blew in cold
from the northeast, and the fleet changed quarter to follow the shoals of fish. The looms in the weaver's shop
worked overtime to meet the demand for new blankets.
Sabin crawled into bed each evening too tired to blow out
the lamp; and so it chanced that she was awakened in the
depths of night by the blood-dim glow of a spent wick.
This time no forgotten jacket needed recovery from
shore. The restlessness that stirred her refused to be
denied.

She arose, dressed in haste, and let herself out of the
back door. Lights still burned in the tavern, and a few
drunken voices inside argued over ways to cure sharkskin.
Sabin slipped past, down the lane toward her uncle's cottage. Once there she did not knock; every window was
dark. Instead she went on down the cliff path. Her shins
brushed the stalks of purple flowers, dried now, and rattling with seedheads in the change of season. Wind
snatched her clothing and snapped at the ends of her hair.
A wild night, yet again, the kind that was wont to bring
wrecks. She completed the last, familiar steps to the chair
seat, dreading what she might find.

The horizon was clearly delineated under a waning
half moon. Clouds scudded past like dirty streamers, mud-
dling the swells pewter and gray, and against them, like
penstrokes in charcoal, an advancing forest of black masts.
Where peaceful craft would have plied sails, this fleet
cleaved against the wind, lashing up coils of foam beneath
the driving stroke of banked oars.

War galleys, Sabin identified, though the Karbaschi to
her were just talk. The Wayfinder's secret was loose in the
world, and his overlords had returned now to claim him.
Poised to run and rouse the town, Sabin found she could
not move. Her flesh became riveted by a cry that had no

sound, but ripped between the fabric of the air itself to echo and ring through her inner mind.

The vibration negated her scream of terrified surprise, and filled her unasked with its essence: that of rage and sorrow and mystery, and a wounding edge of betrayal.

Dizzied almost to sickness, she clawed at the rocks for a handhold to ward off a tumbling fall. The summons faded but did not leave silence. The grind of the sea overwhelmed her ears with a mauling crescendo of sound. Cowering down in the cleft of the chair seat, Sabin saw the sea roll back. It sucked in white arrows of current off the tide flats until slate, shingle and reef were laid bare. Fish flapped in confused crescents across settled streamers of weed, and the scuttled, half-rotted hull of a schooner turned turtle with a smack in the mud. Fishing boats settled on their anchor chains, and townside, the bell in the harbormaster's house began steadily tolling alarm.

Faintly, from the cottage behind, Sabin heard her uncle's bellow of inquiry as the clangor aroused him from bed. Juard, also, would be tossing off blankets, and stumbling out with the rest.

Sabin did not move. She, who had been born in a village of seafarers, and should have been, *would have been*, one of them, could only stare with her joints locked immobile. She alone did not flee in blind concern toward the beach path to stave off the threat to their boats.

Had she gone, it would not have mattered; the chair seat offered an untrammeled view as the horses thundered in from the sea.

They came on in a vast, white herd, manes tossing, and forehooves carving up arcs of flying spray. The water swirled under their bellies and legs, and rushed in black torrents behind uncountable upflung tails. Wave after wave, they surged in, plowing up weeds and fish and muddy gouts of seabottom, and milling the shells of galleys and sloops into shreds and splinters as they passed. Spars of fishing smacks entangled with snapped off oars and the dragon-horned timbers of Karbaschi shipwrights; the cries of warriors and oarsmen entangled in the flood mingled with shouts from the villagers who saw their fleet and that of the raiders become smashed to kindling at a stroke. The horses swept on in a boil of foam that boomed like a god-wielded hammer against the shore. Spindrift sluiced across the cliffs. Ancient pines shivered and cracked at the blow, and boulders broke off and tumbled.

Drenched to her heels by cold water, Sabin cowered down, weeping for the beauty of a thousand salt-white steeds that reared up and struck at the windy sky. And with that release came understanding, at last, of what all along had been wrong: her heart held no sorrow for the terrible, irreversible destruction that rendered her whole village destitute.

Lights flickered through the pines at her back, as angry men lit torches. Shouts and curses carried on the wind, and the tolling bell fell silent, leaving the seethe of the seas a scouring roar across the reef. Sabin pressed her knuckles to her face. The Wayfinder was going to be blamed. This ruin was his doing, every man knew, and when they found him, they would tear him to pieces.

Pressed into her cranny by a weight of remorse she could not shed, Sabin saw the wild horses swirl like a vortex and turn. Back they plunged into the sea that had spawned them, leaving churned sand and burst wood and snarled bits of rope. Amid the roil of foam, a lone swell arose and broke; one mare spun away and parted from her companions.

Sabin saw her stop with lifted head, as if she listened to something far away. She tossed her mane, shedding spray, then raised up one forehoof and stepped, not into water, but most irrevocably, out onto wrack-strewn sand.

Sabin cried out at that moment, as if some force of nature wrenched her, spirit from flesh. Reflex overturned thought, and she was up and running inland at a pace that left her breathless. Voices called out to her as she reached the lane, people she knew, but she had no answer. The torchlight in the market did not slow her, nor the press of enraged men who gathered to seek their revenge. Scraps of conversation touched her ears and glanced away without impression—the *in'am shealdi* and his vicious, unfair bargain—Juard's life, in exchange for the livelihood of all the village. Boats had been broken and sunk. Folk would starve. The Wayfinder would be made to pay, made to burn; they would pack him off in chains to rot in the dungeons of the King's bailiff. A hangman was too good for him, someone yelled, his words torn through with the sounds of a woman's crying.

Sabin stumbled and kept going, past the cedar shingles of the wool shop where her mother stood on the door stoop. "Girl, where are you off to, there's salvage work to be done, and soup to be fixed for the men."

But the rebuke of her parent was meaningless, now, and had been for quite some time.

Deep darkness wrapped the hollow where the crossroads met the town and the lane led inland through forest. Sabin went that way, her lungs burning, and her eyes streaming tears. The terrible truth pursued her: she did not weep for loss. The village was nothing to her, its hold inexorably diminished since the moment she left a jacket on the beach.

By the stone marker on the hill above the market, the Wayfinder waited, as she knew he would. He sat astride a mare whose coat caught the moonlight like sea-foam, and whose eyes held the darkness and mystery of water countless fathoms deep. She tossed her head at Sabin's arrival, as if chiding the girl for being tardy, and her mane lifted like a veil of spindrift; subsided like falling spray.

The Wayfinder regarded Sabin gravely, the burning in his eyes near to scalding. "You heard my call," he said. "The mare came, and you answered also."

Sabin found speech at last. "You knew I would."

He shook his head, his unbleached honey-colored hair veiling his weatherbeaten face. "I wasn't sure. I hoped you might. Gifts such as yours are needed sorely."

The white mare stamped, impatient. She blew a salty, gusty snort. New tears welled in tracks down Sabin's cheeks, and she reached out trembling fingers and touched the shimmering white shoulder. It was icy as seawater;

magical and terrifying and beautiful enough to bring madness. The words she struggled to shape came out choked. "If the horse cannot return, then neither will I."

"You are both my responsibility," the Wayfinder admitted. "And will be, to the end of my days." He extended his hand, no longer so thin, but disfigured still with old scars. "You must know the Karbaschi would have burned more than boats, and slaughtered and raped did they land."

Sabin felt as if she had swallowed a stone. "You spared the whole village, and they hate you."

He sighed, and the mare shifted under him, anxious to be away. "Oh my dear, it could not be helped. What is a boat? Or a man? New trees will grow and be fashioned into planks, and women will birth babies that age and grow senile and die. But just as this mare can't return to the waves, so an earth spirit that is maimed can never heal. The Karbaschi shed more than mortal blood. I could not allow myself to be captured, however bitter the price."

"You could have died," Sabin said, her gaze transfixed by the horse.

And he saw it was not his exile, but the fate of the mare that she mourned. The two of them, man and girl, were alike to the very core.

A shout knifed the quiet, and torches shimmered through the trees. The mare stamped again, and was restrained by a touch as the Wayfinder said in measured calm, "I can still die. But you must know, the mare should be cared for. She is not of mortal flesh. If I give myself up, hear warning. Your talents will blossom with time. A horse such as this will draw notice and the Karbaschi will send another fleet. Their craving for conquest is insatiable as the ocean is vast, and *in'am shealdi* to guide them, most rare."

She made no move, and her rejection seemed to shatter his detachment. He lifted his head as the noise of the mob came closer. The edgy, unaccountable wariness that every offered kindness had not softened, gentled very suddenly into pity. *"In'am shealdi,"* he murmured in the grainy, musical voice that had commanded the horse from the sea. "This mare left the water at my call, you are right, but her sacrifice was never made for me."

Sabin looked up, stricken. "For my life?" she gasped, "or my gift?"

"Both." His eyes were not cold. Inside the serenity lent by power lay a human being who could bleed. "If you treasure the beauty of the horses, heed this. We are the only ones who know their kind. Others see no more than surf and foam. It is our protection, Sabin, that keeps this spirit-mare alive, our call that lends her substance."

The torches reached the crossroad, and light flared and arrowed between the trees.

"There he is!" someone shouted, and the note of the mob quickened like the baying of hounds that sight game.

To her dream-filled ears, the pursuers uttered no words, but made only a cacophony of vicious noise. The roll of the sea held more meaning, and from this time forward, always would.

Sabin grasped the Wayfinder's hand. Clinging as if to a lifeline, she let him pull her up astride the mare. As the villagers burst into the clearing, they lost their quarry in a half-glimpsed flash of white. The clearing resounded to what could have been hoofbeats, or the enduring thunder of a comber pounding the pebbles of the shore.

The Antagonist

J ensen stepped briskly from the orange-lit access corridor, and a thrill touched him as the confined echo of his footfalls fell away, lost amid the din of Point Station's docking hangar. Through the bustle of mechanics stripped to their thinsul suits, and the cross bracing of gantry arms and loading winches, he found the object of his passion instantly. A smile of predatory satisfaction lit his face. She was exactly as they had described her, in tones that varied from frustration, to thwarted fury, to outright, obsessive longing: ugly, patch-painted, and scuffed, a typically hard-run small-time merchanter. Yet the awkwardly configured spacecraft under Jensen's eager scrutiny was nothing of the sort. His trained mind could admire the artistry with which her weaponry and shielding had been installed without marring her image of innocuous decrepitude. Jensen squared his shoulders, missing the stiff scrape of his ensign's collar. Like the deadly, efficient bit of machinery he viewed, he would use camouflage to disarm his prey. For the *Marity* was the love and the pride of MacKenzie James, a skip-runner wanted on eighty-six Alliance planets for illegal trafficking in weapons, treason, theft, and sale of classified Fleet documents. Piracy was not a trade for the cautious; the Fleet's autonomous diligence ensured that most skip-runner captains paid for their wealth with imprisonment or early death. But "MacKenzie, James," as the criminal files formally listed a man whose true name was only a matter of conjecture, was no ordinary skip-runner.

Mostly he was too good. The captains, officials, and highly placed admirals he had evaded, avoided, and unabashedly fooled in the course of his career made him dangerous, a topic of wild speculation in the barracks and the bars but one most scrupulously avoided in the company of superiors. To Michael Christopher Jensen, Jr., anyone who could engineer the skip-runner's long overdue arrest would gain promotion, accolades, and a reputation of undeniably proven merit. For a young man who had yet to earn "his paint" in battle against the Khalia, MacKenzie James was a piece to be manipulated.

Jensen adjusted the unfamiliar ties of the Freer over-robe he had acquired with some difficulty for the occasion. He looked the part, he knew, with his rangy frame and dark hair and eyes; meticulous to the point of fussiness, he had made certain no detail was out of character. Like many a fringe worlder, Freerlanders liked independence a bit too well to submit to Fleet sanctions; skip-runner captains knew them as a dependable market for illicit weaponry. They were ornery enough, or maybe just proudly stubborn enough, that only the reckless interfered with them in public. Still, as the young officer strode into the chaos of the loading lanes, his palms sweated. His plan might be soundly designed, but he was not quite brash enough to be unafraid. *Marity*'s master had ruined many a promising career before an unscheduled repair stop had delayed him; and though inconvenienced, MacKenzie James would never be caught unprepared.

Especially here; Point Station was a crossroads for the remote boundary of Carsey Sector, a center for commerce and intrigue only sporadically patrolled. Betweentimes, those goods and outbound colonists who were of questionable legal status arrived and departed with all the speed that over-used, outdated equipment could command. The ratchet of the winches was loud enough to drown thought, and the reek of heated machinery a metallic taint in the musty, recirculated air. Jensen made his way cautiously. Ducking a trailing power cable, and wary of stepping into the path of the squat, radio-controlled light-loaders, he noticed the stares prompted by his black-fringed Freer robe. He adjusted his hood, careful to carry himself with the right degree of arrogance. His mimicry seemed effective. A dock worker stumbled clear of his way, and behind the periphery of the hood, someone else muttered, "Pardon, Freerlander."

Jensen buried his hands in red-banded cuffs and kept his steps light, as if he had grown up walking icy, wind-carved sands; nothing less than perfection would deceive MacKenzie James. As *Marity*'s spidery bulk loomed closer, the time for second thoughts narrowed. Now, Jensen no longer regretted that necessity had forced him to include Ensign Shields in his plan. That she drifted just beyond Point's grav field perimeters in the dispatch courier Fleet Command had assigned to the pair of them now offered great reassurance. Though technically his senior, and compelled to collusion by a veiled threat of blackmail, she would not let him down. The moment her courier had altered course for Point Station, the Ensign was committed.

Jensen managed not to trip on any cables as he crossed the apron which separated *Marity* from the adjacent berth. Eyes narrowed beneath the fringe of his hood, he promised that overcoming Shields's reluctance would be the last time he traded upon his father's influence for his own gain. The man who arranged MacKenzie James's arrest could write any ticket he wished and with this in mind, Jensen studied the slots that recessed the studs of *Marity*'s entry lock. The young Fleet officer repressed a whistle of admiration at the evident strength of her seals. No Freer ever uttered anything that resembled music outside of ritual. Such attention to detail was not misplaced, for a moment later he found himself noted by the ferret-quick gaze of the individual who served *Marity* as skip-runner's mate.

The man was typical of the type signed on by MacKenzie James. Young, athletic, and guaranteed to have no ties, he turned from wheeling a cargo capsule that had overlapping layers of customs stamps to mark a conspicuously legal course across Alliance space. The Freer robe drew his attention. An instant later, Jensen found his path blocked, and his hooded features under scrutiny by a pair of worldly eyes.

"You're here to see Mac James," said the mate.

He placed slight emphasis on James, the Mac more a prefix than first name. Jensen considered this idiosyncrasy while returning a nod of appropriate Freer restraint.

The man smiled, suddenly older than his years. His thinsul suit hung loosely over his frame, no doubt concealing weapons. "Godfrey, wherever we alight, and no matter how unexpectedly, you people seem to find us." But his easy manner was belied by the tension in his stance.

Yet skip-runners could be expected to treat strangers with caution. Careful to pronounce the name precisely as *Marity*'s mate had, Jensen said, "Then Mac James is available?"

"Mac's topside." His appraisal abruptly complete, the mate jerked his head for the young officer to follow, then gestured toward the open jaws of the lock.

Jensen took a slow breath, readjusted his Freer hood, and ducked under *Marity*'s forward strut. He set foot on the loading ramp, and quashed a panicky urge to retreat. The burning ambition which held him sleepless each night drove him forward as the mate disappeared into shadow.

Jensen passed the lock. *Marity*'s interior seemed dim after the arc lamps that illuminated Station's docks. His spacer's soles clung lightly to metal grating, the sort that adjusted on tracks to vary storage according to the demands of different cargoes. But as Jensen blinked to adjust his vision, he heard the clang of an innerlock; a cool draft infused the outer hold and by that he guessed that on the far side of that barrier *Marity*'s resemblance to a merchant carrier must end. Only a craft that carried state-of-the-art shielding and navigational equipment would trouble to control its atmosphere while in port.

The mate paused at the head of the corridor and called, "Mac?"

A grunt answered from the ship's upper level, distorted into echoes by the empty hold.

"Company's here asking for you." The mate waved for Jensen to pass him and continue alone down the access corridor. "Ladder to the bridge is there to the left."

Startled to be left on his own, Jensen crossed the threshold of the innerlock with his best imitation of Freer poise. He set cold hands to the ladder beyond. Faintly over the mate's receding footsteps, he heard the muted grind of light-loaders laboring outside of *Marity*'s hull. Then the innerlock hissed shut. Irrevocably sealed off from Station, and isolated amid the hum of the air-circulating system, Jensen recognized the sizzle of a laser pencil cutting through cowling.

"Come to talk, or to tap-dance?" *Marity*'s master called gruffly from above.

Jensen climbed. Sweating under his Freer cowl, he emerged in the windowless chamber of the bridge. Dead screens fronted the worn couches of two crew stations. The controls beneath were sophisticated and new, and somehow threatening without the array of labels and caution signs indigenous to Fleet military vessels. Jensen repressed a slight prickle of uneasiness. The man who flew *Marity* knew her like a wife; his mates without exception were pilots who could punch in and out of FTL or execute difficult dockings in their sleep.

"You're no Freer," the captain's gravelly voice observed from behind.

Jensen whirled, fringes sighing across the top rungs of the ladder. Bent over the far console was the skip-runner half of Fleet command would trade their commissions to jail. Through the dazzle of the laser-pen, Jensen made out a dirty coverall with the clips half unfastened, knuckles disfigured with scars, and a profile equally blunt, currently set in a frown of concentration. Shadowed from the laser's glare by a flip-shield, eyes light as sheet metal never left the exposed guts of *Marity*'s instrument panel, even as Jensen shifted a hand beneath his robe and gripped the stock of the gun hidden beneath.

"Care to tell why you're here?" The laser-pen moved, delicately, and the shift in light threw MacKenzie James's scarred fingers into high relief. With a small start, Jensen recognized old coil burns, from working on a ship's drive while the condensers were activated. The story was true, then, that Mac James had changed a slagged module bare-handed to make his getaway the time he had sabotaged the security off Port.

Mesmerized by the movement of fingers that should by rights have been crippled, Jensen opened, "You run guns," and stopped. The man's directness had rattled him and he had neglected his guise of Freer restraint; but then, Mac James had already observed he was no Freer. Why, then, let him in at all? Taken aback, Jensen was unable to think, except to notice how remarkably deft the scarred hands were with the electronics.

"You're not here to negotiate business." MacKenzie James joggled a contact, applied his pen, then thumbed the switch off. The laser snapped out, and *Marity*'s master swung around, a hulking bear of a man with a spare brace of contact clips dangling from the head strap of his eye shield. He snapped up the plate, revealing a face of boyish frankness entirely at odds with his reputation.

Jensen opened his mouth to speak, and was cut off.

"You're Fleet, boy, don't bore me with lies." Mac James whisked clips and shield from his forehead and threw them with a rattle into the disjointed segment of cowling. "That makes you trouble, unwanted being the least damning complaint I have against you." He leaned heavily on the back of the nearest crew chair, his manner distinctly exasperated. "Don't bother with the gun, I know it's there."

"Then you'll surrender your person without a fuss," said Jensen, his confidence buoyed by the realization that the man he covered was sweating. "*Marity* has skip-run her last cargo."

MacKenzie James raked scarred fingers through a snarl of uncombed hair. "Boy, you've put me in a very bad position, and I'm not known as a nice man."

"That doesn't concern me." Jensen eased the pellet gun from his robe, pleased that his hand was so steady. "Your papers, Captain. Tell me where they are."

MacKenzie James slung himself into the gimballed couch. Light from the overhead fixture flashed on the worn tag he wore on the chain at his neck. The lettering stamped in its surface was ingrained with dirt, legible even in dim light: "MacKenzie, James, First Lieutenant." That rumor also was true, Jensen reflected; or maybe part of it, that a two-credit whore from the Cassidas had gotten herself knocked up, then smuggled herself and her byblow into the quarters of her officer lover. An emergency call to action came through, and when the captain in command had discovered a civilian on board, he had dumped her through the airlock into deepspace as an example. Her lover had subsequently died in action. The kid, who may or may not have been related, had been signed over to some Alliance charity orphanage. Though given a legal name, he never called himself by anything but the inscription on the dogtag, surname first; and harboring no love for the military, he grew up into the most wanted man in Fleet record.

MacKenzie James raised tired eyes. "Boy, if you continue with this, all the wrong people are going to suffer."

Jensen gestured with the barrel of the pellet gun. "Who? Not all your clients are like the Freeborn, who think to beat the Khalia single-handed. The guns you skip-run are as likely to be used by criminals as in defense."

"Godfrey," said MacKenzie James with exactly the same inflection his mate had used earlier. "Nobody informed me I was such an idealist."

Marity shuddered slightly, as if jostled by on-loading cargo. MacKenzie James sighed with apparent resignation and said, "My flight papers are in the starboard vault. Here's the key."

His coil-scarred fingers moved, very fast, and switched on the laser-pen.

Jensen ducked the beam in time to save his eyes. He even managed to keep his pellet gun trained on the patch of sweaty chest exposed by MacKenzie's gaping coverall; but the young officer didn't fire, which proved a mistake.

Hands that by rights should have been ruined flicked a switch, and *Marity* came to life with a scream of drive engines. She tore her gantry ties, stabbed upward with her gravity accelerators wide open and smashed through the closed hangar doors. Jensen was thrown to the deck. He heard the wail of sheared metal as landing struts wrenched off. *Marity* jerked, half-spun, and yanked free, burning outward into deepspace and trailing a tumbling wake of debris. Horrified, Jensen imagined Point Station thrown into wobbling chaos: alarm sirens smothered by the inrush of vacuum, and the light-loaders' magnetic treads plodding mechanically over the dying thrash of the workers *Marity* had sacrificed to rip free.

MacKenzie James sat immobile in his threadbare deck chair. "This craft is fitted with several sets of back-up engines," he admonished. "Point Station personnel and Carsey sector authorities know better than to meddle with us."

"Bastard," Jensen said thickly. He moved gently against the pressure of acceleration, his pellet gun trained steadily on his antagonist. "Your mate was equally expendable?"

"Evans?" MacKenzie James did not change expression as the glare of the laser pencil snapped out. "No Freer ever approached us without elaborate clandestine overtures and a meeting in private. Evans should have remembered."

But Jensen's equilibrium had recovered. The vibration just prior to takeoff, surely that had been the lock cycling closed? Evans in all probability was on board. The control panels on the bridge seemed utterly dead; but with back-up systems, even now the mate might be piloting from a remote station elsewhere on *Marity*. If Evans was at the helm, Ensign Shields was going to have to fly her shapely ass off to keep up. Fortunately her ability was equal to her boasts.

Right now the primary directive was to take control before *Marity* gained enough charge to sequence her FTL drive. Icily composed in the half-light cast by the bridge control panels, Jensen shifted the target of his gun and squeezed the trigger.

The light-pen in MacKenzie's hand shattered. Fragments of casing raked his wrist and drew blood while the expended pellet screamed past his groin and imbedded in the stuffing of the adjacent crew chair.

Mac James moved, but this time Jensen was ready. Before the captain reached cover behind the bridge cowling, the Fleet officer had him cornered. Breathing hard, and sweating beneath his Freer robes, he trained his weapon squarely on the skip-runner's heart. "Roll over. Cross your wrists behind your back. One wrong move, and you're dead."

MacKenzie James grunted, eased his weight off his right forearm, and carefully extended it behind his waist. "You're Marksman Elite?"

"Unfortunately for you," said Jensen, concentrating more on the left hand of his captive than acknowledging the accolade he had striven for, and won with such pride at an exceptionally early age. Gun at the ready, the young officer loosened his robe and retrieved a pair of loop nooses, the thin, cutting type Fleet marines used to restrain everything from murderers to brawlers. He hooked the first over James's upraised wrists and jerked tight.

"Now raise your ankles, Captain." James did so, and the second noose shortly trussed his legs.

Smiling raggedly from triumph and excitement, Jensen locked the ends and began to search the captain's person. The man was tautly muscled, which was unusual enough to inspire caution. Most skip-runners were slender to the point of fragility, the result of long hours lurking in null gravity, their ship's systems shut down to a whisper to avoid notice. MacKenzie James also carried no side arms, only a small knife in a sheath sewn into his boot. Jensen confiscated this, then shoved his prisoner awkwardly onto his back.

MacKenzie returned a cool, appraising stare that, even behind a pellet gun, Jensen found disturbing. "You will tell me where Evans is piloting, clearly and quickly."

The captive smiled with brazen effrontery. "By now I expect what remains of my mate is being bundled up in a body bag."

"Back at Station?" Jensen resisted an urge to step close; even bound, the captain was bulky enough to roll and knock him down. "I'm not a fool, James. If Evans died on Station with the rest of the dock personnel, who guides this ship?"

MacKenzie's grin turned thoughtful. "Well now, I could say with reasonable certainty that *Marity* flies on a hardwired connection between her accelerator banks and her coil regulator. Assuming I don't lie, any fool knows she'll blow when the condensers overheat."

Jensen considered this, unpleasantly confronted by the mulish courage that had confounded so many officers of the law before him. The captain *might* be lying; but his reputation said otherwise, which placed Jensen squarely on the prongs of dilemma.

MacKenzie James stopped smiling. "Don't think too long, boy. Since you so proudly blasted my laser-pen, I'll have to rummage around for my cutter tool to break the bridged circuit."

"Shut up." Jensen needed a second to clear his mind. Somewhere on *Marity* would be a kill switch to cut the drives in the event of emergency; the other fail-safes and override systems would be nonexistent, for skip-runner captains as a rule pushed their machinery over margin. The complication that this ship held to no specs, that she was a jumble of ingenuity and modifications hung together by the cleverest criminal in the Alliance meant Jensen was in too deep. If MacKenzie James were freed to right his bit of sabotage, chances were he would create additional havoc in the wiring, perhaps even contrive to regain advantage.

"I'll take my chances," Jensen decided. But his confidence was forced. If Evans had made it on board, he was now in serious trouble.

With the nooses secured without slack to a deck fitting, MacKenzie James could not roll onto his stomach. Nothing important lay within range of his feet. Certain as he could be that his captive was secure, Jensen sealed the bridge behind him and descended into *Marity*'s service level. Away from Point Station's fields, the descent shaft had no gravity. Already the chill of deepspace seemed to have penetrated its shadowy depths. Jensen drifted in a faint fog of condensation left by his breath, the ladder rungs icy beneath his sweating hands. His feet tingled with the knowledge that at any second a plasma weapon might sear upward and fry him like a fly on a web. The Freer robe swirled and caught at his ankles and knees. Jensen longed to shed the fabric, but dared not. Sewn into the sash was the transmitter that enabled Ensign Shields to track him, and *Marity*, through the deeps of space.

Jensen reached the base of the shaft without incident. Gun at the ready, he barely waited for his soles to grab on the decking before he started forward. His danger now redoubled, for the access corridor extended in both directions; MacKenzie's mate might easily slip into the bridge behind him and set his captain free. The fact that the mate had no key to release the nooses, and that the material of which they were made was extremely difficult to cut offered only slight reassurance. Under Mac James's spoken guidance, Evans might take control of *Marity* from the bridge.

Jensen glanced nervously over his shoulder, then rounded the crook in the corridor near the access door which had first admitted him. Beyond lay the hold, dark except for the blink of the indicator that showed the life-support system which served that portion of the ship was currently switched off. Jensen agonized for a moment in indecision. If the outer lock was sealed, then Evans was surely on board. No sense in crippling his judgment with worry if the man had died back on Station; crisply Jensen punched the stud he found near the hold's double-safetied access latch.

Arc lights flashed on, lancing uncomfortably into

pupils grown adjusted to the dark. Jensen squinted through glare off the port's bubble window. Beyond the crosshatch of struts and decking, the lock was securely closed. Nearby, garishly colored in the severe illumination, lay the cargo capsule Jensen remembered from the apron back on Station. Fear raised gooseflesh at the nape of his neck. Whether or not MacKenzie James had triggered a remote control in the opened pilot's panel, that capsule had not wheeled on board by itself. Skip-runner's mate Evans had assuredly made lift-off, which made light of any sort a liability. Jensen set his hand on the stud to kill the arcs, and stopped, caught short by something bulky that drifted above the grating which floored the hold.

The thing twisted gently in null grav. Jensen made out the limp form of a man, and realized he'd been lucky. The automatic cutoff functions of lift had trapped Evans within the hold. Jensen glanced swiftly at the gauges in the panel by the lock controls. *Marity*'s hold maintained atmosphere, but no recirculation for oxygen. As a safeguard against stowaways and other breaches of security, cargo areas as a rule did not allow manual access to the habitable portions of the ship. Dependent upon rescue from within, *Marity*'s mate was probably hypothermic, for the cold of deepspace would swiftly permeate the uninsulated hold.

Jensen considered, then cold-bloodedly stabbed the light stud off. By now a steady whine pervaded the corridor; *Marity*'s engines climbed steadily toward overload. Evans probably knew the location of the emergency cutoffs, but it would likely take too long to force the information out of him. Jensen quashed his last pang of conscience.

The gloom seemed deeper on *Marity*'s lower deck, and the cold more cutting. Though the breath came ragged in his throat, the young officer clung righteously to his purpose. The mate was a skip-runner's accomplice, a criminal no invested Fleet officer could condone.

Jensen ducked through a companionway. His eyes reflexively traced the layout of cables on the far side. Guided by their convergence, he pressed forward and ascended a small ramp, half-stumbling over the shallowly raised treads. The transmitter sewn into his sash dug into his waist, reminding that he had to succeed, or leave Ensign Shields to answer to Fleet admiralty for diverting a courier from dispatch duty.

The whine of stressed engines rose relentlessly, throwing off unpleasant harmonics. Jensen covered his ears with his hands and hurried blindly forward. The cables threaded through a conduit above a small hatch, and, by the shielded panels, Jensen figured the drive units lay immediately beyond. If he were forced to tear the coils out barehanded to prevent an explosion, he wondered whether the burns would prevent him from manipulating his gun.

But that concern became secondary when Jensen discovered the shielded doorway was secured with a retina lock, inoperable except to Mac James, and maybe his mate. With no alternative left but to fetch Evans, he returned down the access corridor toward the hold.

But when he banged the switch once again, the arcs glared off a vista of empty grating. The cargo capsule lay open in the harsh light, and Evans was nowhere to be seen. With a crawling chill that had nothing to do with sweat, Jensen spun and raced for the bridge ladder. He'd made an idiot's misjudgment. *Marity* was a skip-runner's craft; he should never have assumed her specs would conform to those of a common merchanter.

The rungs themselves hampered, spaced as they were to a design that differed from Fleet regulation. Clumsily shortening his reach, Jensen made more noise than he intended. Above, the gruff voice of MacKenzie James called warning.

"Company, mate. Initiate without cross-check and take cover. I trust your coordinates from memory."

Evans returned a protest, just as Jensen reached the upper level. The shift from weightlessness to induced gravity blunted his speed, yet still he managed to fling himself into cover behind an electronics housing. Aware of him, Evans still did not turn, but lingered to fine-tune something in the control panel. Noosed helplessly to the crew chair, MacKenzie James cursed viciously.

Driven by threat of failure, Jensen raised his gun and fired. His pellet hammered Evans in the back of the head. Instantly dead, the mate pitched forward into the control banks. His body quivered once, and slipped to the deck, leaving vivid smears on the cowling.

Jensen shivered with relief. In the icy clarity of adrenaline rush, he noticed that MacKenzie James said nothing at all; but his steely eyes bored with steady and unsettling intensity into the Fleet officer who had gunned down his mate. He seemed almost to be listening for something.

Jensen discovered why a moment later. *Marity*'s engines died to a whisper. There followed a peculiar hesitation in time, that blurring transition which signalled the drop into FTL.

Jensen knew a chill of apprehension. He had not killed swiftly enough. Now she hurtled through deepspace toward a destination only MacKenzie James and his dead first mate would know. Still, though the ship was untraceable to the courier, Jensen did not lose control. The prize, the skip-runner captain whose capture would gain him advancement, was still at his mercy.

Jensen dug in the pouch sewn into the Freer robe for another round of ammo. His fingers snagged in the fabric; he swore and wrestled them free, while from the deck, MacKenzie James broke his silence.

"Most Freer carry their weapons on a belt across their chests. The pouch is for pills to kill parasites, and the clip on the seam hangs their water skins."

Jensen clamped his jaw tight, methodically busy with reloading. If Mac James chose to make conversation, he would have a purpose other than boredom.

"Godfrey, who's left to shoot but me?" The skip-runner never glanced at the corpse, oozing blood an arm's length from him.

Jensen snapped a fresh round into the magazine of the gun and tried to figure why Mac James might wish to distract him with chatter. Quite dangerously, the stakes had altered. He might hold the upper hand, but the captain was not entirely at his mercy. With *Marity*'s major controls stripped of function and her FTL hurtling her toward an unknown destination, Jensen shoved back the first, creeping stir of doubt. He could defeat the retina lock over the drive access hatch by dragging his captive down below and manhandling him up to the sensors. But disabling *Marity*'s FTL condensers would do no good if he had no inkling of her position. Jensen stepped over the mate's sprawled feet. Most of the screens were opaque, empty of data as the rest of the controls. As he surveyed the opened cowling and tightly racked maze of exposed boards, it occurred to him that Mac James might have prepared his own diabolical sort of defense: *Marity* was probably inoperable by any hand but her captain's. Jensen clenched his hands, rage at his predicament momentarily making him dizzy. He would come out of this on top, with the promotion he was long since due. Freshly determined, he searched out the stop-marker coordinates that glimmered on the navigational board.

The fix was still within Carsey Sector, and surprisingly familiar. That James would wish *Marity* to emerge only hours away from the wreckage he had left on Point Station bespoke unsettling confidence. Jensen hid his hands in his robe, too careful to give way to elation as he identified the fix as Castleton's World, a lifeless planet until recently, when Fleet Command had cut ground there for a large-scale outpost. Two squadrons patrolled there, with a dreadnought in synchronous orbit to maintain security for the duration of the construction.

Jensen turned slowly from the controls, startled to find that MacKenzie James seemed to be sleeping. Ripped with an irrational desire to destroy the man's nerveless peace, the Fleet officer said, "Castleton's isn't the refuge you hoped for, not anymore."

MacKenzie James replied without opening his eyes. "You're not much in the confidence of your superiors, are you, boy? Or maybe the news is too recent, or the planned assault on Bethesda makes Fleet brass too busy to keep current."

The assault on Bethesda was supposed to be top secret. Horrified that a common skip-runner should be party to Fleet secrets, Jensen stiffened. He leveled the barrel of his pellet gun just as the gray eyes of his captive flicked open. They reflected a cold and bloodless amusement that made him ache to pull the trigger.

"Khalia," said MacKenzie James with uninflected plainness. "The new base on Castleton's was overrun, utterly, and stripped of all survivors."

Disbelief made Jensen tremble. Even the hand which held his weapon was not exempt. The captain had to be lying, his words a ploy to provoke a careless reaction. Only Jensen made it a point never to be careless.

Mac James shrugged. "If you aren't going to kill me out of pique, you might want to clear the remains of my mate from the bridge. Because unless you wish to become a slave of the Khalia, I'll need to reconnect some circuitry without tripping over dead meat."

The sheer effrontery of the suggestion undid Jensen's poise. "You think I'm a fool?"

Mac James stirred against the confines of his bonds. "Yes, but how much of one I'm waiting to find out."

Jensen's jaw jerked tight. He pointed his gun to the deck, viciously flipped on the safety, then turned his back on his prisoner. All sensor displays were lifeless; when *Marity* broke out of FTL, no method remained to determine whether the ships which would greet her were Fleet, or enemy; and hell only knew if the defensive shields had power. Jensen felt a detestable sense of helplessness. Mac James had him boxed; not being a hardware man, he lacked the knowledge to hack the electronics back into working order.

Mac James drawled lazily at his captor's back. "The sensors and analog screens are operational, boy, but you'll need to engage the power switch."

Jensen hesitated out of principle. The control panel might possibly be booby-trapped. Yet logic dictated that Mac James would hardly plot murder while still under restraint, not unless he planned to die slowly of dehydration.

Alert for surprises, Jensen hunted among the controls and flipped the appropriate switch. The analog panel hummed to life, and snow hazed the monitor, while the sensors gathered data. Presently, the haze subsided to black, which was normal; no image would resolve until *Marity* re-entered normal space.

Jensen tried the power switches for weaponry, without success. The guidance computer also proved to be dead, and only the watching presence of MacKenzie James prevented Jensen from hammering the panels in frustration. The chronometer by *Marity*'s autopilot alone showed any indicators, the most maddening of which informed that reentry into sub-light at Castleton's was barely thirty minutes off.

Jensen paced. Careful to stay within the perimeters of *Marity*'s artificial gravity, he avoided the congealing runnels of Evans's blood, and also that portion of deck included in MacKenzie's field of view. He dared not give the skip-runner captain his liberty. Yet to risk re-entry near a base under Khalian control without fire power or maneuverability begged the most terrible fate. Not least, a concern the young officer would never have admitted out loud, was the fact he had never seen action against the enemy. Jensen had never doubted his courage. But the possibility of closing with the enemy in a small, converted merchanter like *Marity* frayed his confidence to tatters.

The chronometer on the autopilot clicked over; seven minutes to re-entry. Mac James once again appeared asleep. His behavior seemed inhuman, until Jensen recalled that *Marity* had docked at Point Station forty-eight hours before under emergency priorities. By the grimy, unkempt appearance of the captain's person, he probably had not slept while he effected repairs on his ship. Jensen himself had not rested for nearly as long, but excitement and stress had put him on a jag that precluded relaxation.

At a minute and a half to re-entry, MacKenzie James opened his eyes. The corpse of his mate lay undisturbed on the deck. Jensen stood at the analog screen, his gun clenched in anxious fingers. Beneath the Freer robe, his left hand gripped the keys to the nooses which secured MacKenzie James with white-knuckled indecision.

One minute to re-entry; Mac James quietly recommended pressing the toggle to unshutter the shield generators. Though to do so felt like capitulation, Jensen did not cling to foolish pride. A suspicion crossed the young officer's mind, that more of *Marity*'s systems might be operational than the control monitors indicated. But no time remained to run cross-checks. The buzzer signaled phaseout of *Marity*'s autopilot, and the eerie instant of suspension which heralded transition from FTL to normal space followed after. Jensen watched the analog screens with taut anticipation.

Castleton's appeared as a dun ball, mottled gray at the terminator; the larger of two moons showed as a sliver to dayside, but Jensen spared the scenery barely a glance. The sensors finished processing data, and the screen became peppered with silvery specks; scouts by their formation. Larger shapes nestled among them, unquestionably cruisers, with a third one tucked away behind the mass of Castleton's.

"Godfrey," Mac James observed, his neck craned awkwardly to allow a view of the screens. "They didn't waste time expanding their strike force, now did they?"

"They might not be Khalia!" Jensen snapped.

A buzzer clipped his outburst short. Lights flashed warning on the analog panels, and one of the flecks gained a faint halo of red.

"Well, Fleet or enemy, boy, one of them is about to fire on us." Mac James shrugged irritably at his bonds. "If you like slavery, or maybe even vivisection, just keep sitting there doing nothing."

Jensen raged, uncertain; *Marity*'s sirens wailed with sudden violence, her shields crackling under the impact of a hit.

"Warning rocket," Mac said tersely. "Probably they're provoking to see whether we want a fight. Power up the transmitter, boy."

Jensen hesitated.

"*Do it now!*" barked MacKenzie James, adamant as a Fleet rear admiral.

Another red halo bloomed on the analog screen. Jensen slapped the transmitter switch. The gabble of alien speech that issued from the speaker caused the last bit of color to drain from his face.

"Now listen carefully, boy," said the hell-begotten captain from the floor. "Do exactly as I tell you, or we'll both get our guts ripped out."

"You planned this!" Jensen accused, horror sharpening the immediacy of their peril.

"Yes, now shut the hell up and listen!" MacKenzie said.

The patter of Khalian changed inflection, and a singsong voice in poorly pronounced wording began a demand for the surrender of *Marity* and all human personnel on board.

Still clutching pellet gun and keys, Jensen rubbed his hands over his blanched face.

"You will surrender my ship to the Khalia," MacKenzie James instructed tersely. "But add that you will submit only to a great captain, one who has proven his merit. That one, you will say, is the Khalia cruiser currently in orbit over the night side of Castleton's."

Jensen lowered his hands, incredulity spread across his features.

Before he could draw breath to speak, Mac James cut in, "*Just do it!*"

Instead Jensen spun and stabbed each of the firing studs in frenzied succession. Nothing happened. *Marity*'s weapons remained utterly unresponsive. Furious that his career should be finished without a single rocket fired in protest, and whipped by recognition that no option at all remained to him, Jensen crumbled at last into panic. "Why disable the weaponry, man? Why, if you planned this cruise into an effing Khalian fleet?"

"I probably wanted to commit suicide." Mac-Kenzie's vicious sarcasm jarred like a slap. "Maybe, though, I'll get slavery or vivisection instead."

A shudder shook Jensen's frame as the voice on the transmitter changed from a demand for surrender to threats. Rather than be blasted to vapor, Jensen pressed the toggle to send. He surrendered *Marity* and all on board to the Khalia in a voice he barely recognized as his own. Only as an afterthought did he include MacKenzie James's stipulation: that prize rights and conquest be awarded to one of proven merit, the great captain who cruised the dark side of Castleton's.

The effect upon the Khalia was profound. By their belligerent and bloodthirsty reputation, Jensen expected the enemy would converge upon their prize without delay. Instead, the scout ships clustered tightly to their respective cruisers; as if locked in deadly partnership, the closer pair of warships wheeled and advanced upon the one which even now accelerated from the shadowed side of Castleton's.

"They'll challenge," MacKenzie broke in, answering Jensen's puzzled frown. "Khalian war leaders can't bear to defer without a fight. That lends you a very narrow margin to get this bucket operational. Which means my release, boy, because this is the only break you're going to get."

Jensen rounded upon the captain. "You never intended to surrender!"

Mac James returned a withering stare. Mollified by a knowledge of the enemy not even Fleet intelligence could equal, Jensen thumbed the safety toggle off his pellet gun. Then he took the release key in his other hand, stooped, and unclipped the nooses from MacKenzie James's feet. The man shifted forward to better expose his hands; the noose was soaked with blood. Nerves, or tension, or sheer frustration had caused the skip-runner captain to wrench at his bonds until his wrists tore open. Jensen keyed the catches, a sick clench in his gut causing his guard to slip. In that instant, MacKenzie's elbow hammered upward into his face. A spin and a kick relieved Jensen of his weapon. The young officer crumpled to his knees. Feeling as if every knuckle in his hand were broken, he fumbled to pull the knife he had confiscated earlier.

Mac James reached it first, and tossed it rattling into a corner. Disregarding Jensen completely, he retrieved the fallen gun, discharged the single round into the stuffed seat of a crew couch, then hurled the weapon without ceremony down the companionway ladder. With no break in movement he bent over the opened cowling of the control panel and furiously began to work.

Lights flashed to life under the captain's ministrations, casting baleful light over his frowning features. To Jensen, who moaned through clenched teeth at his back, he said, "Clear Evans out of here, boy. If I trip over him at the wrong moment, some Khalia butcher'll hack off your balls."

Jensen obeyed to buy time, lull the captain into the belief he was cowed. Evans's corpse was already cool to the touch, his bulk limp and awkward to lift. Hampered by his injured hand, Jensen was forced to drag him. Blood from the dead man's shattered jaw smeared the white deck. Dizzied with pain from his hand, Jensen choked back a wave of nausea. He reeled into the nearest crew chair, just as *Marity* roared to life. MacKenzie James crowed over the controls like an elated child. Scarred fingers kicked in the accelerators.

On the analog screen, the first pair of cruisers closed to do battle, scout ships circling to one side like swarms of angry bees. Now and again the bolt of a plasma discharge flicked through the flashes of heavy rockets.

"They're pounding themselves to a pulp," Jensen observed in amazement.

"Better hope they do." MacKenzie twisted a lead, then punched up *Marity*'s screens. "The one who's not joining the cockfight will be on our butt quick, before the survivor calls challenge on him."

"How do you know?" Jensen hated himself for the admiration which colored his tone. "Where did you learn so much about the enemy?"

MacKenzie never glanced up from the controls. "Evans could have told you. Right now, I'm too busy." He flung himself into the adjoining pilot's chair, took the helm, and almost immediately *Marity* veered.

Still nauseous, Jensen sought stability in watching the analog monitor. As the attitude thrusters opened wide, the pared disk of Castleton's fell away, replaced briefly by space sprinkled with fixed stars, and the moving points of enemy warcraft. These were eclipsed in turn by the disk of Castleton's sun; MacKenzie flicked the stabilizers and banged the heel of his hand down, shoving the gravity drive into full acceleration.

Jensen made a sound in protest as several g's of force ground his body against the crew chair. "Out of the frying pan," he managed, before discomfort forced him silent.

MacKenzie James said nothing. His profile seemed motionless as laser-cut quartz in the lights off the monitors as *Marity* picked up speed. Fueled by the gravitational field of Castleton's sun, she gained velocity at a rate that was frightening. Jensen battled for equilibrium. He was not the pilot that Shields was, but he could recognize when safe limits were transgressed. As if his worn old craft did not hurtle full tilt for annihilation in the fires of a star, Mac James sat back and flexed his scarred fingers in a manner that suggested habit. Then, as *Marity*'s course held stable, he shoved forward against the force of acceleration and busied himself again with the circuitry.

"Haven't you done enough?" Jensen demanded, mostly to distract himself from fear. With the Khalia behind, and the inferno of Castleton's star raging forward, what composure he had left was faked.

Mac James pulled a wire from the cowling and unceremoniously stripped it with his teeth. He twisted the bared end into a hook which he clamped to some unseen contact below. Another panel on *Marity*'s control boards flickered to light; satisfaction made her captain expansive. "You're better endowed with luck than brains, boy. You're not going to burn. Just maybe you'll be spared the hell of being bait for Khalia as well."

He added no explanation. But as the third Khalian warship swung to intercept, the captain responded with hair-raising innovation. He spun *Marity* into what seemed a suicidal trajectory toward Castleton's sun. Like some terrible vulture, the Khalian cruiser swung into position, shadowing their descent into the inferno. If Mac James even once tried his drive brake, *Marity*'s occupants would be weasel meat.

Jensen masked fright with bravado. "You're sending yourself to hell, by way of the inferno."

MacKenzie James said nothing. The staccato buzz of an alarm sounded, and the control board transformed to a field of warning lights. Caught in horrified absorption by the star swelling on the analog screen, Jensen almost forgot the Khalian warship until it fired.

The rocket lanced across the screens, violet against the glare of Castleton's star.

"My god," Jensen said angrily. "Do they believe in miracles, or what? They may as well vaporize us, for all that we can stop."

"They think we're what we seem," MacKenzie James said softly. "A merchanter caught without escort." He paused, as if that explained everything. A second Khalian rocket seared across the screens. In the fitful, flickering light of its passage, the captain seemed to recall that the man in the crumpled Freer robe who sweated in his crew chair was not his knowledgeable mate.

"The Khalia believe that we have chosen suicide rather than be captured. They fire to salute our courage, for by their honor code, our action is admirable."

Which fit with the accuracy of truth, Jensen reasoned. With a crushing sense of frustration, he cursed the fact that he could not return the information to his superiors. Surely such knowledge would have earned him a commendation and promotion—but the closing proximity of Castleton's sun foreclosed any chance of survival.

MacKenzie James seemed peculiarly indifferent to the end his own subterfuge had created. Hunched like a bear over his controls, he grinned. "Watch now." But the corpse of the mate which oozed by the companionway showed as much enthusiasm as Jensen. "In a moment, the Khalian ship will brake and pull off, just enough so she'll bounce off the gravity well at a tangent."

"So what," Jensen shot back. The captain was crazy; they'd melt just as handily by hydrogen fusion, but the man acted as if he was ignorant of the fundamental rules of physics.

"Now," murmured Mac James. The Khalian cruiser shifted. His scarred hands moved at the controls, and *Marity* responded with a roar like a Chinese dragon. Jensen was tossed backward as her entire aft quarter opened up into a fireball.

Jensen saved himself from a bruising fall with the hand Mac James had injured. Pain exploded like white heat. His head spun and his vision momentarily went black.

"We're not a merchanter," admonished MacKenzie James from the dark. By the time the officer's eyesight cleared, *Marity* had burned into a new trajectory, a searing arc that would carry her into a parabolic orbit just within survivable limits. This, with an antique mess of a drive unit that ran on explosive propellants—no sane captain would have such a relic on a space-going vessel.

"But the quick acceleration is damned handy in a pinch," the skip-runner captain said brightly. "It's saved my butt more than once."

Mac James stretched in his chair, flexing his fingers in a hellish glare of warning lights and attitude meters. Jensen held his opinion. *Marity* might be safe at present, but only by the grace of surprise. Khalian raiders would be waiting once they rounded Castleton's sun, and even Mac James's famous cunning was not equal to combat against a cruiser.

The skip-runner captain met Jensen's skepticism with a stinging honesty. "Boy, your officer's handbook doesn't list every known fact in the universe. The systems they have are infrared, which happens to be our salvation, because the emissions from that star out there will blind them."

And it dawned on Jensen then, that both of them were going to survive. The Khalia believed they had burned. Once eclipsed by Castleton's star, *Marity could* hammer her way into escape trajectory with her anachronistic fusion rockets, then power down. With her gravity drives turned off, no infrared scope could distinguish her from an asteroid. Hopelessness and lethargy vanished in a breath. The pellet gun which Mac James had carelessly tossed down the companionway became of paramount importance.

Jensen measured the distance to the opened hatch with his eyes. The expanse was wider than he liked, particularly since the Freer robe would encumber him. Still, with Castleton's world and the threat of the Khalia keeping MacKenzie James preoccupied, there might never be a better opportunity. Jensen gathered his courage and jumped.

He completed no more than a step when a weight crashed into his shoulders from behind. He fell heavily to the deck. At once the muscled bulk of MacKenzie James bore him down. Jensen countered with a wrestler's move that should have freed him in short order. Instead the captain anticipated him, caught his wrist, and twisted. Jensen cursed, forced to fall limp or scream with the pain of dislocated joints.

Just shy of injury, Mac James let up. "You're trouble," he said bluntly. And as though he handled a vicious animal, he rolled and jerked Jensen upright. The strength in his hands was astonishing. Very quickly, the Fleet officer found himself noosed and helpless in the coils of his own restraints.

"Also, you talk too much," MacKenzie added. He ripped away the sash of the Freer robe, pausing as his fingers encountered the bulk of the transmitter. A wicked flash of amusement touched his features as he went on and twisted the material into a gag, which he tied expertly in place. Jensen struggled but gained nothing except cuts on the ribbon-thin metal of the noose. Shoved into the nearest crew chair, he glared back as the captain studied him in passionless silence. The directness of the man's gaze unnerved Jensen as nothing had before.

"What chance did you give Evans?" Mac James's voice held a roughness that might have been grief, except his expression showed no feeling at all. The captain flexed his ruined fingers, one after another. Tortured with the certainty his fate was being weighed, Jensen recognized more

than habit in the movement; such ...
restored mobility to hands crippled w ...
driving persistence of the captain's ...
became frightening to contemplate.

Jensen closed his eyes, opened them to ... captain
watching him still. The ambition that ha ...
attempt at his capture withered away to diffide ... he gag
tasted of sweat and desert spice and stale saliva, and the sick
fear in Jensen's gut coiled tighter by the minute.

Aware his captive's composure was crumbling,
MacKenzie James jerked him to his feet and spun him
around. "Evans never did like to kill," he said in contempt.
"For that, you'll leave *Marity* alive."

But reprieve was not what MacKenzie James had in
mind as he hefted his captive through the companionway.
Towed through null gravity like baggage, Jensen had to
writhe ignominiously to keep his face from banging the
bulkheads. The hiss of the lock to the cargo hold spilled icy
air over his skin. Left to drift, the young officer could not
see his captor, but an echoing flurry of footfalls and the
clang of something metallic did little but amplify his apprehension. Then hard hands caught his legs. His view of the
hold spun horizontally, and through dizziness he glimpsed
customs seals and the opened hatch of the cargo capsule.
Then MacKenzie James brutally started cramming his
body inside. Jensen exploded in panic.

He struggled, and got a bang on the head for his
effort. Mac James shoved his shoulders down. Scarred fingers reached for the latch.

Jensen twisted frantically and managed to tear the gag
loose. "Wait!" he said breathlessly. Desperate now, his
ambition reduced to a fool's dream, he begged. "I could
take Evans's place for you!" Except for the piloting, he was
qualified; and he wouldn't defect, not really. Once he
gained MacKenzie's confidence he could alert Fleet
authorities.

But his proposal met with silence. Shoved protesting
into the cargo capsule, and panicked by the prospect of
confinement, Jensen abandoned his pride. "Damn you, I'm

of an Alliance Councilman! That should be worth
ough to hold me for ransom."

No spark of greed warmed the eyes of MacKenzie
James. Single-mindedly efficient, he banged the hatch
closed over his captive's head. Jensen kicked out in disbelief and managed to skin both his knees. The slipped gag
constricted his wind. Over his ragged, frantic breaths came
the unmistakable click of latches, the inexorable deadening
of sound as the seals of the container clamped closed. He
banged again, uselessly. He might suffocate, or die of
hypothermia in *Marity*'s unheated cargo hold; surely Mac
James would see reason, contact his father and arrange an
exchange of money.

Jensen felt the capsule bump and rise; through its shell
he heard the unmistakable hiss of a lock. He screamed in
uninhibited terror, then; but nothing prevented the sicken-
ing, tumbling fall into weightlessness and cold which followed. He curled up, shivering in the bitter end of hope.
MacKenzie James had jettisoned him, living, into deep
space.

The cargo capsule's seals preserved atmosphere. For
awhile its honeycomb panels would conserve body heat,
but with no air supply it was an even draw whether Jensen
would die of asphyxiation, or tumble back to fry in the fury
of Castleton's star. At best, he might be salvaged alive by a
Khalian scout ship. Worst and most galling was the fact
that MacKenzie James went free.

Jensen shouted in frustration. Unable to forget those
coil-scarred fingers flexing and curling, tirelessly beating
the odds, he longed for one chance to shoot his antagonist,
even as he had Evans: from behind, with no chance for
recriminations, just death—fast and messy and final. But
anger only caused the nooses to rip painfully into his
wrists. In time, all passion, all hatred, unravelled into
despair. Jensen's tears soaked the hood of the Freer robe
and curled the dark hair at his temples. After Mac James,
he reviled his disciplinarian father, for stifling his career
with the stipulation that under no circumstances was
undue favor to be granted him. Competence became a

sham. Such was the influence of fame and politics, no board of officers dared to grant promotion without performance of outstanding merit. One by one, Jensen had seen his peers advance ahead of him. Balked pride and rebellion had landed him here, trussed and sealed like flotsam in a cargo capsule. Too late, and in bitterness, he questioned why the promise of money had failed to motivate MacKenzie James.

The air in the capsule quickly became stale. Jensen's thoughts spiraled downward into a tide of black dizziness. His limbs cramped, then grew numb; the transmitter in the Freer sash dug relentlessly into his neck, but he was powerless to ease even this smallest discomfort. Presently, none of that mattered. Resigned, Jensen directed his last awareness to cursing MacKenzie James; as consciousness began to dim, sometimes the name of his father slipped in . . .

Something banged the cargo capsule. Jostled against the side panels, Jensen heard the whine of grappling hooks. Fear roused him from lethargy as they clamped and secured his prison. Suffocation seemed a kindness next to threat of Khalian cruelty; but the young officer lacked strength to do more than shut his eyes as whatever being had salvaged him popped the capsule's release catches. Clean air rushed in around the seals, and light fell blindingly across Jensen's face.

"I'm surprised he left you alive," said an acerbic voice he recognized.

Jensen started, drew a shuddering breath, and ducked sharply to hide cheeks still wet from crying. "My god, how did you know where to find me?"

Perfectly groomed, and correct to the last insignia on her uniform, Ensign Shields regarded him with that whetted edge of antagonism she had affected since the morning he had compelled her collaboration in his scheme to capture MacKenzie James. "*Marity*'s instruments weren't shielded," she said at last. "You're living lucky for that."

Jensen tried to scrub his damp cheeks against his

shoulder, and awkwardly found he couldn't, not with his hands still bound. His embarrassment changed poisonously to resentment. He faulted himself bitterly for lacking the presence of mind to note the implications of *Marity*'s opened instrument panels. Evans had programmed the autopilot for the FTL jump with the keyboard circuitry wide open to surveillance; if the scout ship assigned to Shields was not one of the fancy, new brain models, she still carried a full complement of electronics. "You read our destination coordinates from our tempest signal," Jensen murmured, shamed by memory of Mac James's amusement as he allowed the transmitter to remain twisted into the Freer sash. The captain had known then that his victim would be rescued. He must have considered Jensen a fool, harmless or incompetent enough to be no risk if he were set free.

"Maybe not so lucky after all." Shields shoved the cargo capsule over, interrupting Jensen's thoughts and spilling him ignominiously onto the courier ship's lock platform. "You'll wish you'd died in deep space when our dispatches come in late. Serve you right if the old man himself calls you onto the carpet."

Stung by more than humility, Jensen twisted until he gained a view of his shipmate's eyes. "Play things right, and we'll get a commendation."

Shields stepped back. Rare anger pinched her face; Jensen had never thought her pretty, but she had slenderness, and a certain grace of movement that had half the guys back at base off their feed. "You're obsessed, Jensen. *Commendation for what?* You've been an overambitious jackass and now, finally, the brass in Fleet command will know it, too."

Jensen made a vicious effort to sit up; but the nooses cut into his wrists, and he gave up with a curse at the pain. "You'll go down with me," he threatened. "As my senior officer, piloting a Fleet dispatch courier off course calls for court-martial, not a dressing down."

He heard Shields's sharp intake of breath, and could not look at her. Once he might have veiled his threats in gentler language; but now, the cruelly injured dignity inspired by MacKenzie James impelled him to roughness. "Don't be a stupid bitch." But he couldn't quite bring himself to finish; by the whitely locked knuckles of Shields's hands he saw he did not have to mention her brother, who was ill and under treatment in an Alliance medical facility, a benefit of her enrollment in the Fleet. Should she be discharged now, he would lose his benefits. But pity came second to necessity. Ambition and his driving desire to command a vessel that carried weapons instead of dispatches cut with a need like agony. Coldly Jensen outlined his alternative.

The dome at Port was packed to capacity on the day the citations were read. Banners overhung the stage where the Fleet high command were seated. At attention alongside Ensign Shields, Jensen surreptitiously checked his uniform for creases. Finding none, he stood very still, savoring the moment as the speaker at the podium recited his list of achievements.

". . . commendation for bravery; for innovative escape tactics, when asked at gunpoint to surrender to three Khalian warships, which imagination and daring in the face of danger has resulted in the furtherance of Fleet knowledge of enemy behavior; for performance above and beyond the call of duty, these two young officers will be promoted in rank, and be decorated with the Galactic Cross . . ."

Shields went very white when the Admiral laid the ribbon with the medal over her shoulders. She shook his hand stiffly, and looked away from the cameras when the press popped flashes to record the event.

Jensen also stood stiffly, but for very different reasons. Warmed by his father's proud smile, he reflected that the story they had presented to Fleet command had held as many half-truths as lies; the tactics which had brought word of the takeover at Castleton's had been real enough, though only Shields and he knew they had originated with the wiliest skip-runner in Alliance space. The weight of the Galactic Cross which hung from his neck carried no implications of guilt; at last granted the command of a scout ship with armament, Jensen swore he would redeem his honor. One day MacKenzie James was going to regret the humiliation he had inflicted upon a young officer of the Fleet. Jensen intended to rise fast and far. In time he would retaliate, find means to bring down the antagonist who had bested him. The honors he took credit for now were only a part of that plan.

Tale of the
Snowbeast

That year, the season of white cold was worse than any elf in the holt could remember. The storage nooks were empty of the last nuts and dried fruit; and still the wind blew screaming through bare branches while snow winnowed deep into drifts in the brush and the hollows between trees. Huddled beneath the weight of a fur-lined tunic, Huntress Skyfire paused and leaned on her bow.

"Hurry up! It's well after daylight, past time we were back to the holt."

A soft whine answered her.

Chilled, famished, and tired of foraging on game trails that showed no tracks, Skyfire turned and looked back. Her companion wolf, Woodbiter, hunched with his tail to the wind, gnawing at the ice which crusted the fur between his pads.

"Oh, owl pellets, again?" But Skyfire's tone reflected chagrin rather than annoyance. She laid aside her bow, stripped off her gloves, and knelt to help the wolf. "You're an unbelievable nuisance, you know that?"

Woodbiter sneezed, snow flying from his muzzle.

"This is the second night we come back empty-handed." Skyfire blew on reddened hands, then worked her fingers back into chilled gloves. Woodbiter whined again as she rose, but did not bound ahead. Neither did he hunt up a stick to play games; instead he trotted down the trail, his bushy tail hung low behind. Hunger was wearing even his high spirits down. Skyfire retrieved her bow in frustration. The tribe needed game, desperately; the Wolfriders were all too thin, and though the cubs were spared the largest portions, lately the youngest had grown sickly. Tonight, Skyfire decided, she would range farther afield, for plainly the forest surrounding the holt was hunted out.

A gust raked the branches, tossing snow like powder over Skyfire's head. She tugged her leather cap over her ears, then froze, for something had moved in the brush. Woodbiter stopped with his tail lifted and his nose held low to the ground; by his stance Skyfire knew he scented game, probably a predator which had left its warm den to forage for mice in a stand of saplings. Skyfire slipped an arrow by slow inches from her quiver. She nocked it to her bowstring and waited, still as only an elf could be.

The shadow moved, a forest cat half-glimpsed through blown snow. Skyfire released a shot so sure that even another elf might envy her skill; and by Woodbiter's eager whine knew that he scented blood. Her arrow had flown true.

But unlike the usual kill, her companion wolf did not rush joyfully to share the fruits of their hunting. Woodbiter obediently held back, for in times of intense hardship, game must be returned to the holt for all of the tribe to share. Skyfire elbowed her way through the saplings, grumbling a little as snow showered off the branches and spilled down her neck. She picked up the carcass and felt the bones press sharply through the thick fur of its coat. Half-starved itself, the cat was a pathetic bundle of sinew; it would scarcely fill the belly of the youngest of the cubs. Skyfire sighed and worked her arrow free. She permitted Woodbiter to lick the blood from the shaft. Then, as wind chased the snow into patterns under her boots, she pushed her catch into her game bag and resumed her trek to the holt.

She arrived exhausted from pushing through the heavy drifts. Breathless, chilled, and wanting nothing more than to curl up in her hollow and sleep, she unslung her game bag. Shadows speared across the packed snow beneath the trees that sheltered the holt; but the tribe did not sleep, as Skyfire expected. Elves and wolves clustered around the blond-haired form of Two-Spear, who was chief. Closest to him were his tight cadre of friends, including Graywolf, Willowgreen, and sour-tempered Stonethrower.

Skyfire frowned. Why should Two-Spear call council at this hour, if not to take advantage of her absence? The chief might be her sibling, but to a sister who liked her hunts direct and her kills clean, Two-Spear's motives sometimes seemed dark and murky, as a pool that had stood too long in shadow. And his policies were dangerous. Elves had died for his hot-headed raids upon the humans in the past, and the chance he might even now be hatching another such reckless solution for the hunger which currently beset the tribe made Skyfire forget her weariness. Woodbiter sensed the mood of his companion. He pressed against her hip, whining softly as she pitched her game bag into the snow.

A younger elf on the fringes turned at the sound. Called Sapling for her slim build, her face lit up in welcome. "You're late," she said, cheerful despite the fact that hunger had transformed her slender grace to gauntness.

It was unfair, thought Skyfire, that lean times should fall hardest upon the young. She pushed the game bag with her toe, trying to lighten her own mood. "I'm late because of this." Then, as Sapling's thin face showed more hope than a single, underfed forest cat warranted, she forced herself to add, "Which was hardly worth the risk."

Sapling paused, her hand on the strap of the game bag, and a wordless interval passed. Dangerous though it was for an elf to fare alone during daylight, when men were abroad and chances of capture increased, the game in the bag was too sorely needed to be spurned. "The other hunters made no kills at all," Sapling pointed out.

The admiration in her tone embarrassed; brusquely, Skyfire said, "Is that why Two-Spear called council?"

Sapling hefted the game bag. "He plans to send a hunting party deeper into the forest than elves have ever gone, to look for stag."

Which was wise, Skyfire reflected; except that all too frequently Two-Spear's intentions resulted in discord and chaos. Frowning, she pulled off her cap, freeing the red-gold hair which had earned her name. "I think I had better go along," she said softly. And leaving the game with Woodbiter and Sapling, she stepped boldly toward the clustered members of the tribe.

Her approach was obscured by the taller forms of the few high ones whose blood had not mixed with the wolves, yet Two-Spear saw her. He stopped speaking, and other heads turned to follow his glance. "Skyfire!" said her brother. "We were just wondering where you were."

Skyfire endured the bite of sarcasm in his tone. She looked to Willowgreen, and received a faint shake of the head in reply; no. Two-Spear was not in one of his rages. But at his side, the half-wild eyes of Graywolf warned her to speak with care. "I wish to go with the hunting party, brother."

"You went with the hunting party last night," Two-Spear said acidly. He tossed back fair hair and shrugged. "Yet again, you returned alone. In strange territory, that habit could endanger us."

Skyfire bridled, but returned no malice; the carcass in her game bag was too scrawny as a boast to prove her success on the trail. Instead she sought a reply that might ease the rivalry that seemed almost daily to widen the breach between herself and this brother who was chief; above anything she did not want to provoke a challenge. The white cold made difficulties enough without elf contending against elf within the tribe. Still her thoughts did not move fast enough.

Sapling came hotly to her defense, calling from the edge of the council. "The Huntress brought us game! She was the only Wolfrider to return with any meat."

Skyfire gritted her teeth, embarrassed afresh as hungry, eager pairs of eyes all focused past her. Jostled as tribemates pushed by to crowd around Sapling and the pathetic bundle in the game bag, she hid her discomfort by pressing her hair back into her cap. Aware only of Two-Spear's sharp laugh, she missed seeing Graywolf part the drawstrings. The bloody, bone-skinny cat was held aloft, a trophy of her prowess for all the tribe to see.

Yet hunger robbed the mockery of insult; and even the tribe elder who had taught her dared not mock her affinity for the hunt. When the vote was cast, Skyfire found her name included in the party of seven that would seek new territory to forage. That satisfied her, though the choice of Two-Spear's henchman, Stonethrower, as leader of the foray pleased her not at all.

The kill was skinned, then divided among the youngest cubs. Emulating Skyfire, Sapling tried to refuse her portion, until the focus of her admiration sternly instructed her to eat. At last, bone-weary, the finest huntress in the tribe since Prey-Pacer retired to her hollow and curled deep in her furs. The only things she noticed before she fell asleep were the dizzy lassitude of extreme hunger, and the snarls of the wolf-pack as they fought over the forest cat's entrails. The sound gave rise to discordant dreams, in which she faced her brother over the honed points of the twin spears he carried always at his side . . .

"Get up, sister."

Skyfire opened her eyes as the fair head of her brother tilted through the entrance to her hollow beneath the upper fork of the central tree. His eyes were blue, and too bright, like sky reflected in ice. "You promised to hunt down the grandfather of all stags, remember? Stonethrower is waiting for you."

Stung by the fact that this was the first time since she had been a cub that her brother had succeeded in catching her asleep, Skyfire peeled aside her sleeping furs. She reached for laces and stag fleece to bind her legs against the cold. "Tell Stonethrower to sharpen that old flint knife he carries. I'll be ready before he's finished." But her retort fell uselessly upon emptiness; Two-Spear had already departed.

The worse ignominy struck when she emerged, arrows and quiver hooked awkwardly over one arm while she struggled to lace her jerkin. Her other hand strove and failed to contain the brindled fur of her storm cape. She hooked a toe in the trailing hem and nearly fell out of the great tree before she realized that sunset still stained a sky framed by buttresses of black branches; the cleared ground beneath was empty of all but the presence of her brother. In all likelihood, Stonethrower was still in the arms of his lifemate.

Hunger made it difficult for Skyfire to control her annoyance. With forced deliberation, she sat on the nearest tree limb and began to retie the bindings that haste had caused her to lace too tightly. She pulled the chilly weight of the cloak over her shoulders and hung her quiver and bow. Then, hearing Stonethrower shout from below, she rose and grimly climbed down. By the time her feet sank into the snowdrifts beneath, her temper had entirely dissolved. Woodbiter had bounded up to nose at her hand, and her thoughts turned toward game, and thrill of the coming hunt.

The hunters gathered quickly after that. But unlike more prosperous times, as the afterglow faded and twilight deepened over the forest, they did not laugh or chatter. Their wolves did not whine with eagerness, but stood steady as riders mounted. Then, Graywolf with his unnaturally silent tread breaking the trail, seven elves departed with hopes of finding meat for a starving tribe.

Night deepened, and the cold bit fiercely through gloves and furs. Fingers ached and toes grew slowly numb. Yet the elves made no complaint. Generations of survival in the wilds had made them hardy and resilient as the wolf-pack that shared their existence. Beasts and riders traveled silently through the dark while the wind hissed and slashed snow against their legs. The weather was changing.

Though stars gleamed like pinpricks through velvet, the air had a bite that warned of storm.

Skyfire did not travel at the fore, as was her wont; on foot, to spare Woodbiter the stress of carrying her when his ribs pressed through his coat, she hung back toward the rear of the line. These woods were barren of game, and she preferred to contain her eagerness until the holt lay well behind.

Yet even starvation could not entirely curb Woodbiter's high spirits. He cavorted like a cub through the snow drifts, snapping at twigs to show off his strong jaws. Skyfire smiled at his antics, but did not join his play. She dreamed instead of green leaves, and the fat, juicy haunch of a freshly killed stag.

Clouds rolled in before dawn, flat and leaden with the threat of snow. In the hush that preceded the storm, Skyfire sensed movement behind her on the trail. She paused, a shadow among the snow-draped boles of the trees. The other elves passed on out of sight ahead. Skyfire held her ground, and again the faintest scrape of leather on bark reached her ears; someone followed. Not a human; the tracker moved too skillfully to be anything but an elf. Tense, and troubled, and wondering whether Two-Spear's madness had progressed to the point of setting spies after his own hunting parties, Skyfire bided her time.

After a short wait, an elf emerged between the trees, thickly muffled in furs, and moving with the stealth of a stalker. Huntress Skyfire did not wait to identify, but sprang at once on the unsuspecting follower. Her victim squealed sharply in surprise. Then momentum bore both of them down into a snowdrift. The tussle which followed was savage and sharp, brought to an end when Skyfire pinned the other elf's neck firmly beneath the shaft of her bow. Her cap was knocked askew; enough snow had fallen down her collar to put fire in her temper as she shook the hair free of her eyes to view her catch.

A merry face with tousled dark curls grinned up from a pillow of snow.

"Sapling!" Skyfire raised her bow, angry now for a

different reason. Two-Spear's recklessness had provoked the humans to boldness; often now they set snares for unwary Wolfriders. And Sapling was still almost a cub, having yet to shed her child-name for the one she would earn as an adult. "What are you doing following the hunters?"

Sapling sat up, the hollows carved by famine accentuated in the growing light. "I wanted to be with you."

Skyfire turned her back, arms folded, and her cap still crooked upon her head. "You're lucky the humans didn't catch you instead." She spun then, and glared at her young admirer. "You know they caught Thornbranch. They burned him. You're not too young to remember."

Sapling scuffed at snow with her toes. She seemed more embarrassed than cowed by the reprimand. Tall, now, as her mentor, Skyfire was forced to realize that little remained of the cub who had once tugged at her tunic. Sapling had nearly grown up. If she had tracked this far without drawing notice, she would not disturb the game, and she would be safer with the hunters than on a return trek to the holt.

"All right." Skyfire set her cap straight with a hard look at her junior. "If you dare to track your elders, then you can act like one."

Sapling's face lighted up. "I can stay?"

"That's for Stonethrower to decide." Skyfire hooked her bow over her shoulder. "Now, come on."

Dawn brightened steadily as the two elves followed the trail of the others. Clouds lowered over the blown tops of the trees, and the air smelled of storm. Wisely, the Wolfriders had chosen to sleep out the day in a hollow by a frozen waterfall. By the time Skyfire and her companion found them, an enterprising elder had broken the ice to hunt for fish. The others had rolled in their furs, pressed close to the wolves for warmth, except for Stonethrower.

"You dallied, but not to hunt game this time," he commented as Skyfire appeared with Sapling in tow.

Yet his sarcasm was wasted on Huntress Skyfire. Woodbiter had not answered her call, and a swift review of the pack revealed the fact that he was not present. Owl pellets, she thought; with Sapling now under her care, the last thing she needed was that wolf getting into another scrape. Feeling the cold, the hunger, and all the weariness of the night's march, she met Stonethrower's dark glance. "Woodbiter's not with the pack."

The older elf shrugged. "He ran off ahead of the others. Like you so often will."

Skyfire bit back a retort. Instead, she closed her eyes and sent, seeking that pattern of awareness that was uniquely Woodbiter's. She found nothing. Alarmed, she put urgency into her call; and the wolf-consciousness that answered showed a thicket of briar and hazel, shot through with fear and the terrible, burning pain of a pinched leg.

"Woodbiter's in trouble!" Skyfire freed her bow. She tensed like a wild thing, ready to run and aid her wolf.

But Stonethrower stepped squarely in her path. "There's a storm coming. You gave Two-Spear your word that you wouldn't be going off alone."

At this, Skyfire felt a soft nudge from Sapling. Warmed suddenly by the presence of a friend, she smiled. "But I won't be alone. Sapling will come with me."

Stonethrower narrowed his eyes, and sent, "She doesn't belong here."

"I know," Skyfire returned. "What are you going to do about it?"

Stonethrower considered the young elf at the Huntress's side; he also thought upon other instructions that Two-Spear had given concerning the sister who always found ways to evade the will of her chief. "I'll go with you," he said at last.

In other circumstances, Skyfire would surely have argued against taking her brother's henchman along. But Woodbiter was in pain; for that she would brook no delay. She sprang into the forest, Sapling a shadow at her heels, even as Stonethrower moved to gather his weapons. He had to run to catch up. Though day was fully come, the wood seemed dim, gray with the threat of a gathering storm.

Gusts rattled the branches like bones overhead, and the first flakes whirled and stung the faces of the elves who hastened to Woodbiter's aid. Soon the snow fell more thickly, the surrounding trees veiled in white; even Stonethrower appreciated the forest instincts for which Huntress Skyfire was renowned. She led her companions without error through a tortuous maze of ravines. Once her keen ears caught the chuckle of current beneath an ice-covered stream; and only swift reflex saved Sapling from a dunking. Although Stonethrower questioned the wisdom of continuing with the weather against them, a glance at Skyfire's face forestalled any comment. The green of her eyes shone with a clear, fierce anger that elves who hunted with her had seen only once before, and that the time Woodbiter's mate had been killed by a human hunter.

For by now they had come far enough that the wolf's sending became clear enough to interpret. Skyfire gripped her bow until her knuckles whitened and said, "He is caught in a trap, the sort that humans set to break the legs of foxes." She paused, and as an afterthought added, "We have not far to go."

Skyfire drew ahead, then, despite the efforts of Sapling and Stonethrower to keep up. They followed breathlessly, twisting past trees gray and scabbed with ice, through hollows where the wind howled like a mad thing, and over snowdrifts spread like snares for unwary feet. Sooner than either elf thought possible, they came upon the Huntress, bent upon one knee in a depression between a steep bank and the roots of a twisted tree.

"Look," she said without turning.

Stonethrower and Sapling crowded closer, and saw the track of a huge beast, oval-shaped, with evidence of a pointy claw at one end. The snow fell less thickly in the shelter of the draw; the track, though not fresh, was plainly discernible as something not made by chance.

"What is it?" asked Sapling, more than a little scared. The track was wider than four handspans, and half as long as her spear.

Skyfire frowned, and Stonethrower knuckled his

beard, a habit he had when something distressed him. No Wolfrider had ever seen anything like such tracks, and quick sending among them established understanding they were troubled. A beast that size was bound to be dangerous.

Stonethrower quietly suggested they turn back.

Frightened herself, but driven by loyalty to Woodbiter, Skyfire regarded him with the contempt she usually reserved for humans. "Why should we? Are you afraid to go on?"

Swirling snow and the wail of wind through the draw filled a tense interval. Then, without speaking, Skyfire whirled and continued on. Sapling accompanied her. Left an untenable implication, Stonethrower followed after; but under his breath he muttered that Skyfire's belief that Two-Spear's reckless ways would eventually lead the tribe to ruin was an unbalanced accusation at best. In the opinion of the older elf, the sister was as stubborn as the brother, which was precisely why the two were continually at odds.

The draw deepened, narrowing into a defile where snow fell thinly, and then only when driven by odd eddies of wind. The prints of the strange beast showed plainly upon the faces of the drifts. Skyfire followed, nervous, but insistent the place of Woodbiter's captivity lay very near at hand. The elves labored through deeper and deeper drifts, sometimes sinking to their waists. The terrible tracks kept pace with them, even when the cleft of the gully widened and they found the wolf, crouched in the open and chewing at his bloody right hind pad.

No one rushed forward with joy. The tracks here were many, and thickest, and plainly associated with the snare. Perhaps they were made by monstrous, splayfooted humans, or bears with terrible cunning. But Skyfire refused to be cowed. She scouted the area with a thoroughness even Stonethrower respected. Then, borrowing Sapling's spear, she advanced into the clearing and bent at the side of the injured wolf.

"Steady," she sent. Woodbiter whined, but he stopped struggling as his companion knelt at his side. Gently she scraped away the snow, felt through wet and matted hair to assess the injuries to her friend. The trap which held him was primitive. Green, springy sticks of sharpened wood had clamped his leg just above the first joint, strong enough to tear the skin and confine, but not to break bones. Angry enough to kill, Skyfire steadied Woodbiter's leg in one strong hand. Then, using Sapling's spear as a lever, she forced the sticks apart.

Woodbiter jerked free with a yelp. Trembling from his ordeal, he leaned against Skyfire, nosing her hair and ears in appreciation. Yet his friend did not respond with scolding for his carelessness, as she might have done another time. Instead, leaning on Sapling's spear, she stared at the perfect, reddened paw prints pressed into new snow by Woodbiter's limping steps. She ran her tongue over her teeth. With her wolf safe, now was the prudent time to start back to the stream where the other hunters had camped. But something too deep to deny rejected the safety of retreat.

Stonethrower arrived at her shoulder. Though impatient to be off, he did not intrude upon Skyfire's mood; instead he knelt beside her and with the flint knife he had once stolen from a camp of humans, began methodically to hack the water-hardened thongs which bound a collection of green branches into a deadly snare for the forest-born.

Skyfire spoke as the last bent bough whipped straight, then snapped between Stonethrower's thick fists. Her tone was cold as the wind that hammered snow through the branches beyond the shelter of the draw where they stood. "I'm going after them."

Stonethrower cast away a snarl of severed thongs. "That's folly. You saw the tracks. Whatever creature set this snare is large, and clever, too much for an elf."

Skyfire curled her lip. "Larger, yes, but not so fierce, I think. Only cowardly beings like humans ever set traps for animals."

"But Two-Spear said—" began Stonethrower, only to be cut off.

"Two-Spear isn't here. *His* wolf did not lie bloody in a

trap for half a night." Skyfire jabbed the spear into the ground hard enough that ice scattered from the butt. "Are you stopping me?"

Stonethrower met her angry eyes, his hand tightened on the haft of his flint knife. "I should." But he made no move to do so as Skyfire spun away and continued down the gully. Woodbiter whined and followed, and Sapling did likewise, too young to know any better.

Stonethrower went along as well, out of duty to his chief, but he regretted that decision almost immediately. The wind bit like the hatred of the humans, and the tracks, half-obscured by blown snow, were soon joined by a second set, and then a third; the new prints were twice the size of the first ones.

Skyfire stopped to test the tension of her bowstring, and Sapling wordlessly took back her spear. Stonethrower tried to resume his argument, then waited, as he realized that the Huntress herself was deaf to any spoken word. Deep in communion with her wolf, she waited while Woodbiter applied his keen nose to the frightening tracks in the snow.

The effort was a vain one; freezing wind had long since scoured any scent from the trail. On nearby twigs the wolf detected faint traces of resin, but the smell was unfamiliar to his experience, and to the elves as well. Unable to imagine this beast as anything but huge and dangerous, even the boldest of the four companions hesitated while the snow whirled and stung their exposed faces.

"We should go back," Stonethrower repeated. "The others should be warned that this part of the forest is unsafe for elves."

Skyfire stood poised, her hand less than steady on her bow. Then, suddenly resolved, she said, "No. Danger to us is danger to the holt. And the snow makes good cover. I say we follow these tracks and find out what sort of beast sets traps that snare wolves."

Her tone would brook no compromise. And unlike her brother, who was chief, Skyfire was not susceptible to counter-argument, or cajoling, or flattery. Once she made

up her mind, she stuck to her purpose like flint. Stonethrower had a scar to remind him, for when she had been
a cub, he had once scooped her off some sharp rocks in a
streambed when the current had swept her young legs out
from beneath her. He remembered how she had sulked
because he had refused to let her attempt another crossing
at the same site. If anything, her determination had grown
with her years, and Woodbiter's limp made her angry and
dangerous to cross. Quite likely Huntress Skyfire herself
was fiercer than the great beast she tracked, the older elf
concluded as the others set off once more. But his attempt
at humor failed as snow chased itself in eddies down his
collar, and his fingers numbed on the flint haft of his
knife.

The gully narrowed and widened, then opened into a
frozen expanse of marsh. Wind rattled through ranks of
frost-killed reeds, the tracks now showing through a swath
of crushed stalks. Here and there a softened patch of bog
had frozen the imprints intact. Woodbiter sniffed and
snarled, and favored his hurt leg. Only Skyfire and Sapling
seemed unaffected by the bleakness of the landscape, the
former warmed by her desire for redress, and the latter, by
the thrill of being away from the holt on her very first
adventure. Stonethrower endured in dour silence, and
almost rammed into the thong-laced tip of Skyfire's bow as
she stopped without warning and pointed.

"Do you see that?"

Stonethrower looked where she indicated and felt his
heart miss a beat. The snow had slowed, almost stopped,
and rising above the ridge he saw blown smudges of
smoke; *where there are fires*, the old adage ran, *there are
always humans*. Worse, the fearsome tracks led off in the
same direction.

Sapling jabbed her spear-butt ringingly into the
ground. Skyfire tested the points on her darts, each one with
singular care. This once Stonethrower did not argue when
the sister of the chief suggested they scout out the size of the
camp on the ridge. Though the site lay outside the
Wolfriders' usual hunting ground, no humans had inhabited

this portion in past memory. The fact that giant, splayfooted ones did now might threaten the entire holt.

Grimly, three elves and one companion wolf started forward. The bare ice of the marsh offered little conceal-ment, which obliged them to go carefully. Only the wolf spoke, soft, high whines of uneasiness at the scent of the humans on the wind. The elves moved in silence, absorbed in their own thoughts. Skyfire squinted often at the fire-smoke and wondered what game the humans might have caught in their traps besides the unfortunate Woodbiter. Sapling tagged at her heels, excited to be included, but wary and nervous. Over and over she tried to imagine what sort of creature had walked over the snow to lead them here. The tracks were fearsomely large, yet they crossed the deepest drifts seemingly without miring; that humans might use strange beasts to tend their traplines seemed dangerous and cruel to an elf brought up to love the thrill of the live hunt.

Stonethrower did not think of men or fearsome beasts. Instead he considered Two-Spear, whose dark, fierce tem-per did not run to temperance. He believed all humans existed to be battled, and likely this camp would merit no exception. A message must be sent back to the holt, and at the soonest opportunity, the older elf decided. Yet he men-tioned nothing of this as he set foot in Skyfire's boot tracks and began his ascent of the ridge.

The elves climbed, buffeted by gusts that were barbed with ice driven off the flatlands below. Even the least expe-rienced, Sapling, blended invisibly with rocks, hummocks, and tree boles. Soon the three lay flat on their bellies at the crest of the rise, the white puffs of their breaths mingling with the last, thinning veils of snow.

The air smelled of smoke. Woodbiter growled low, almost soundlessly, while the others gazed upon tents of laced hides, and fires beyond counting. Noisy packs of humans trod the snow to mire in between, more humans than the elves of Two-Spear's holt could have imagined existed in the whole of the world of two moons. The men carried weapons, spears, and flint axes and shields of hide-covered wood. Their cloaks were shiny with grease, and their cheeks dark hollows of starvation. No game roasted over the fires, but small children huddled close to them for warmth, too starved and dispirited to cry.

Huntress Skyfire pushed herself back from the crest and rolled on her back. Her green eyes stared sightlessly at sky. "They, too, lack game. No doubt that's why they're on the move."

Stonethrower offered no comment.

But Sapling said, "I saw no beasts among them, not one in the entire camp."

Skyfire rolled onto one elbow and eyed her keenly. "That's true." She smiled, more with relief than humor. "I don't think beasts made such tracks. Come look."

The two of them wormed back toward the crest, noses all but buried in the snow. Silently, Skyfire pointed, and Sapling saw large, wooden frames with sinew laces interwoven between. The middles had lacings; and a moment later, when a band of human scouts entered the camp from the east, they wore the same devices strapped to their feet. Sapling stifled a giggle. Obviously, the heavier humans needed such clumsy things to keep from miring in the snowdrifts, inconvenient though they would be for walking or running with any speed or stealth.

"No wonder they catch no game," she whispered to Skyfire, then turned, only to discover the Huntress had retreated back down the slope and was engaged in a subdued, but heated argument with Stonethrower.

"Two-Spear must not be told!" she whispered emphatically. "I agree the humans offer threat, but we cannot fight so many and hope to survive. Better the entire holt moves to another part of the forest than have everyone killed in a war."

"Now look who's talking of running!" Stonethrower glared at the redheaded sister who was so like, and yet so different from the brother who held his loyalty.

Uneasy to be holding a confrontation so near an encampment of humans, Skyfire tilted her head to one side in a way that never failed to endear. "At least wait until nightfall before starting back to inform the other hunters," she pleaded. "Woodbiter's lame, and all of us could use a few hours of rest."

Stonethrower grunted through clenched teeth, but offered no further argument as the three descended the slope. The snowfall thickened again as the Wolfriders crossed the marsh, icy flakes rattling among the dead stalks of the reeds and whispering across bare ice. Finding a sheltered place to spread sleeping furs took longer than any of them anticipated. Weary, and weakened still more from hunger, Skyfire and Sapling fell immediately asleep. Neither was aware that Stonethrower sat brooding and awake. By the time he rose and slipped soundlessly into the storm, not even Woodbiter noticed, dreaming as he was of game, with his nose tucked under his brush, and his injured paw curled carefully beneath.

Sundown came with snow still falling, and the light failed swiftly, turning the forest the gray on gray of winter twilight. Skyfire dreamed the dry crack of snapping bones as humans decimated the holt of the Wolfriders. She jerked awake. Snow flurried from her furs, and she took a moment to orient. Sapling still slept, but the snap of the bones was real enough; not handspans past her still form stretched Woodbiter, the rich scent of blood on his muzzle.

"Where did you get that?" demanded Skyfire, eyeing the meat between his paws with an envy impossible to hide.

Woodbiter blinked, a flash of triumph in his light eyes. He sent a confused flurry of images, and through them Skyfire gathered that he had learned the secret of the humans' traps; this kill, or at least this portion, had been stolen from one of them.

"You rogue!" Skyfire's merry laugh caused Sapling to stir from her furs. "If that's a haunch of stag, the least you can do is share."

Woodbiter rose with the grace of a sated predator, a grace that bordered upon disdain for the rag of meat he had spared for his companions. Still smiling, Skyfire shook Sapling's shoulder and said, "Look, we have something to eat before we must go into the cold and dodge humans."

Sapling sat up and stretched. "Where's Stone-thrower?" she said, and came swiftly alert as Skyfire's green eyes narrowed to slits. The hollow where they camped was empty, but for the two of them and the one wolf. Stonethrower was gone.

"He'll be running to fetch Two-Spear, like an owl after mice." Skyfire slung on her bow and quiver, anger infused in her very motions. "That means you and I have to think very fast, and find a way to send these humans packing out of this section of forest!"

"What about Woodbiter's catch?" demanded Sapling.

The reply came brisk as Skyfire shook snow from her cap and jammed it over her hair. "We'll eat on the move. Come on!"

The elves slipped out into the bracing twilight chill, the wolf a shadow at their heels. They stole from tree trunk to thicket to thornbrake, wary of leaving tracks for humans to find. Once they had to duck into cover as a party of hunters passed by, returning to camp after checking their traps. The humans walked unaware they were watched from cover, or that the devices they wore strapped to their feet to make going in snow less clumsy were a marvel to beings more nimble than they.

Skyfire chewed thoughtfully on a strip of stag meat for a long while after the hunters had gone. Wary of her mood, and striving not to fidget for the first time in her young life, Sapling waited while the woodland slowly darkened. The clouds thinned and parted, leaving the night all velvet and silver with moonlight.

At last Skyfire stirred. "We have no choice. We'll have to investigate the humans' camp by ourselves."

At once Sapling feared the Huntress would forbid her to go forward into danger; but Skyfire only tested the tautness of her bowstring and looked levelly at her young companion. "Can you move as quietly as a wolf?"

Sapling nodded. At Woodbiter's eager whine, she and

Skyfire crept from the thicket and tracked the humans' strange footsteps. Moving swiftly, and in silence, the elves overtook the trappers before long; careful to remain out of sight, they followed closely as they dared.

Apparently the hunting had been poor, for the humans grumbled constantly as they shuffled over the drifts on their strange footgear. Skyfire and Sapling caught snatches of cursing between descriptions of traps raided by fierce wolves. In time, the first group of hunters was joined by a second party, which reported another snare tripped and tampered with by some woodland demon with three fingers. Wolf-signs had been seen at that site also, and when the first band of humans heard this, they made signs to Gotara, and looked often over their shoulders. Without comfort, the elves noted that curses shifted to threats. They ducked unobtrusively behind a fallen log while their enemies drew ahead, a huddle of knotty silhouettes against the moonlit ice of the swamp.

"What do you think they'll do?" whispered Sapling.

Skyfire silenced her with a gesture, listening intently as the loud-voiced leader of the humans shouted querulously to the others. "And I say this camp is ill-favored! We must continue south at daybreak, and seek the lands that our prophet has promised."

Skyfire and Sapling shared a glance of alarm. The threat presented by the humans now went from dangerous to sure disaster; for if they moved their camp as planned, no saving grace could prevent an encounter with Two-Spear and his war-minded comrades. Even sending was inadequate to describe the grief which would inevitably result if human and Wolfrider met openly in conflict.

"We have to find a way to stop them," Sapling whispered.

Skyfire said nothing, but grimly started for the swamp. Thwart the humans' migration they must, but no strategy could be plotted until elves had thoroughly scouted the enemy encampment.

The task took longer than expected, for the tents of the humans numbered beyond counting. "Thick as toads in a bog," griped Sapling. Tired, chilled, and scraped raw from crawling through briars and brush, she shook snow from her collar, packed there in a miserable wad since her dive into a drift to avoid a sentry. Her normally sunny nature had soured to despair. What could a skilled Huntress and a barely grown cub do against a band of humans big enough to overwhelm the forest? Skyfire could not offer a single idea; even Woodbiter walked with his tail down. In the valley below, between alleys of dirtied, trampled snow, the fires of the humans glittered like a multitude of fireflies during the green season.

Skyfire leaned on her bow, her frown plain in the moonlight. "I'm going down there," she said finally. "You must wait here until I get back."

Sapling offered no argument. What had begun as a merry prank, an adventure to make her young heart thrill with excitement, had now turned to nightmare. There seemed no end to danger and hardship imposed by the terrible cold, that untold numbers of humans should travel in search of new hunting grounds. Sapling huddled into her furs, uneasy and afraid, as the Huntress she admired above all else checked her weapons one last time, then vanished swiftly down the slope.

Accustomed to the clean scents of the forest, Skyfire found the human camp rank with the smells of burnt embers, rancid fat, and sweat mixed with poorly cured furs. She wrinkled her nose in distaste as she passed the first of the tents, but forced herself to continue. Moonlight transformed the terrain to a tapestry in black and silver, the tents like ink and shadow against snow. Embers glowed orange from the dark, where the occasional fire still smoldered. Skyfire crept forward, past the tenantless frames of snow-feet which lay stacked in pairs by the tent flaps. She ducked through racks of sticks bound with thongs that supported the long, flint-tipped spears of the humans. The design of the weapons proved that this tribe did more than hunt; they were warriors prepared for battle as well.

Briefly, Skyfire entertained the idea of stealing the spears; even cutting the lashings and stealing away all the points. But the racks were too numerous to tackle by herself, and too likely, the humans stored other weapons inside their tents. Lightly as a Wolfrider could move, she could not raid on that scale without one enemy waking in alarm.

Dispirited, Skyfire ducked into the shadow of a tent. Never in her life had the tribe confronted such a threat; and her excursion into the camp yielded no inspiration. With little alternative left but to go back and attempt against hope to reason with Two-Spear, the Huntress faced the forest once more. Bitterly disappointed, she started off and failed to notice that her storm cloak had snagged upon a pile of kindling. A stick pulled loose, and the whole stack collapsed with a clatter.

In the tent, an infant human began to cry.

Skyfire froze. Barely daring to breathe, she hunkered down in the shadows. How Two-Spear would laugh if carelessness got her roasted by humans! Wishing the human cub would choke on its tongue, she waited, and heard a stirring of furs behind hide walls barely a scant finger's width from her elbow; at least one parent had wakened to the cries of the child. If the Huntress so much as twitched an eyelash, she could expect a pack of furious enemies on her trail. She forced herself to stillness while a man's irritable voice threaded through the young one's wailing. His curse was followed by a placating murmur from his wife.

Skyfire fingered her bow as something clumsy jostled the tent. Then she heard footsteps, and light bloomed inside. Described grotesquely in shadows upon hide walls, she saw the human mother bend to cradle her wailing cub. The woman crooned and rocked it, to no avail, while Skyfire weighed the risk of bolting for the forest under cover of the noise.

Angry shouts from the neighboring tents spoiled that idea. Galled by the need to stay motionless while the entire human camp came awake, Skyfire shivered with impatience. If she was caught, she hoped Sapling had the sense to stay hidden on the ridge.

• • •

The infant continued to wail. Even the mother grew irked by its screams, and her voice rose in reprimand. "Foolish child, be still! Or your noise will waken snowbeasts from the forest, and they will come and make a meal of your bones with long, sharp teeth."

The cub gasped, and sniffled, and quieted. In a frightened lisp it said, "Mama, no!"

"Don't count on that, boy." The light in the tent flickered, died into darkness, as the woman slipped back into her furs. "If I wake tomorrow and find nothing left of you but blood on your blankets, I'll know you didn't heed my warning."

Her threat mollified the cub to silence, and the woman's breathing evened out as she returned to sleep.

Outside, in the shadow, Huntress Skyfire lingered, still as a ravvit in grass. She waited, listening to the sniffles of a terrified human cub; her mind churned with thoughts of the fear inspired by the tracks of the humans' strange snow-feet, and the terror she sensed in the mother's voice.

Skyfire began to formulate an idea. By the time the little human had snuffled himself back to sleep, that idea became a plan to save the holt.

Cautious this time to stay clear of the kindling, the Huntress darted for the forest.

She arrived breathless on the ridge, and found Sapling and Woodbiter curled warmly in a hollow, asleep. "So much for undying admiration," she murmured, and laughed as Sapling awakened, sneezing as she inhaled a nose full of Woodbiter's tail fur.

"Up," said Skyfire briskly. "We have work enough for ten, and not much of the night left to finish it."

Sapling sat up with a grin. "You have a plan!"

The Huntress tilted her head, more rueful than serious. "I have a ruse," she confided. "Now waken your imagination, for before the humans awaken, we have to invent a nightmare."

So began the hardest task Sapling had known in all her young life. All night long they carved wood and trimmed the skins of their storm furs and sewed them into the shape of a great beast, which they padded with cut branches. Woodbiter raided another trap, gaining a set of stag horns which they set in the jaws for teeth. Skyfire fashioned eight monster-sized imitations of a beast's clawed pads and, in the hour before dawn, announced that her "snowbeast" was ready for action.

"Strap these paws to your feet," she instructed Sapling. Then, saving two of the clawed appendages for her hands, she called Woodbiter to her side and tied the last four on him, while Sapling experimented by making fearsome trails of beast-prints in the surrounding drifts.

"That looks horrifying," Skyfire observed when she finished, and allowed one very disgruntled wolf to clamber upright. "But now I need you to help with the final touches."

The Huntress mounted the back of the wolf and placed the jaws of the snowbeast over her head. Muffled instructions emerged between the teeth, explaining that Sapling should place herself at Woodbiter's tail and lace the furs around them both, to flesh out the "body" of the beast. After an interval of laughter, and much tangling of elbows, the task was complete. A fearsome apparition snorted and pawed at the snow in the hollow.

"Now we make mischief on humans," the voice of Skyfire proposed from the gullet; and the snowbeast shambled off, with a wolfish whine from its second head, to do just that.

Once the two elves and the wolf coordinated with each other, they found they could run fairly fast; but the clumsy contraptions on their feet made silence impossible. Wherever the snowbeast passed, it made a fearful rattle, and the snapping of sticks and branches, added with the creak of its framework, carried clearly in the frosty air.

"If there was any game in this forest, it's on the run

now," muttered Sapling. A giggle followed, half muffled by furs.

"Quiet, now," sent Skyfire. "We've arrived at the first of the humans' traps." Now began the dangerous portion of their night's work; for dawn was nigh, and the results of the snowbeast's frolic must not be discovered too soon.

Quiet reigned in the forest until shortly past daybreak, when the humans stirred blearily in their tents. The earliest risers crept out to light fires, and soon thereafter an outcry arose. Two supply tents on the camp perimeter were found ripped to shreds, and the culprit, whose tracks were pressed deeply in the snow, seemed to be a monstrous beast. No one had ever seen the like of such paw prints, but old tales told of a snowbeast which haunted the winter forests during seasons of extreme famine.

Fathers took no chances, but ordered their wives and children and grandfathers not to stray from the protection of the central fires. And the hunters sent to check the traps carried war spears, as well as knives and torches. They moved in bands of ten, for safety; but everywhere they encountered evidence of violence. The snowbeast had ravaged the traps, torn them to slivers, then trampled and clawed the surrounding snow to bare earth. Trees bore deep gashes, and near one trap the skull of a stag lay gnawed by powerful teeth, amid snow stained scarlet with gore. The band of hunters who found that trembled in their boots as they resumed their rounds of the trapline. The rattle of wind in the branches made them start, hands clenched and sweating upon the hafts of their weapons.

For all that, none were prepared for the apparition which lurked in the brush. Crouched like some nightmare forest cat, it fed in the shadows of a thicket, crunching the carcass of the stag with jaws that might have snapped a human in half at one bite.

"Gotara!" breathed the man in the lead. His snowshoe snagged on a twig, which cracked loudly, making him jump.

The snowbeast raised its head, spied the intruders, and raised an ear-splitting scream of rage. The humans saw then that the creature had two heads, the larger one eyeless and crammed with bloody fangs, and emitting a frightful, ululating wail. Below this, between clawed forelimbs, a second, wolflike head snarled and slavered and snapped. Six legs thrust powerfully beneath masses of brindled fur, gathered to bound to the attack.

The human in the lead screamed and cast his war spear. It struck the beast's flank and rebounded; and the beast leapt, plowing a shower of eddying snow.

The hunting party screamed and ran in stark terror. Tree branches whipped their faces. They dared not look back; the ravening snarls of the snowbeast sounded almost upon their heels. The breath burned in their chests, yet they did not slow until they reached the border of their camp. The snarls of the snowbeast sounded ominously through the wood as the men excitedly jabbered their tale. Howls echoed across the marshes, hastening the women who ran to wrap children in blankets and bundle up belongings and tents. Fear gripped the hearts of the humans like cold fingers as they banded together and departed, northward, where the lands were known, and safe.

By sunrise, no intruders remained to watch an elf back butt first from the bowels of the dreaded snowbeast. Tired, trembly, but able to contain herself no longer, she collapsed in a snowdrift, laughing.

Peering through the fangs of the snowbeast mask, Huntress Skyfire regarded her young companion with reproof. "Is that how you're going to greet Two-Spear, when he arrives here with his war party?"

Sapling sat up, snow dusting her eyebrows and her merry, upturned nose. "At least I look like an elf. If you keep standing there in that silly-looking mask, Graywolf will likely spear you for dinner."

At which point the jaws of the snowbeast clicked shut, and a tangle of wolf, and elf, and a mess of jury-rigged storm furs swooped and jumped Sapling in the snowdrift.

The Crash

We saw it up in the sky. Then it was gone. At least Jamsey agrees with me. He saw it, too. Ask him, he's eight, and he lives on my street. I'm only six, but soon I'll be seven and eight comes after that.

Anyway, it was night, and we were sitting on the railing looking up at the stars. The railing goes around the porch, and Mom says it keeps people from falling off, and I told her that somebody would have to be stupid to fall off. The porch, I mean.

I wasn't supposed to be outside. Janice was babysitting. She's fifteen, and she always watches TV and forgets to call me in. I was sitting with Jamsey when Tommy began to cry. He's my brother. He's only two.

I said, "Shut up." I know that's not nice, but I was mad, so I said it anyway. Tommy always cries, and then Janice remembers that we aren't in bed yet.

That was when we saw it. The thing, I mean. I saw it first, and then Jamsey saw it, too. Then it was gone, and it looked sort of like a shooting star, but it was green.

"Annie, did you see that?" Jamsey whispered.

I nodded, and we saw it again. It was bright green and blue, and it was getting closer. There were lights on it.

Jamsey was so excited he was wiggling, and he never wiggles. Not even at the circus.

The thing got really near, and we could see that it was burning. Tommy was howling, and Janice was shouting at him to be quiet.

The thing kept falling, and it got greener and greener, and I said maybe it was a fairy that ran out of fairy dust and couldn't fly, but Jamsey says there's no such thing as fairies, and he knows cause he's eight.

The green thing was so close we could hear it crackle like fire, and it was bright as a sky rocket on fourth of July. Then, smash, it hit the ground near the back fence, and it sizzled like when Mommy puts hot pans in the sink.

Tommy had stopped crying, and Janice stuck her head out the door, and she was madder 'n Dad when a dog stole his glove once.

"What are you doing out there?" she said. I stuck out my tongue and pretended she wasn't there.

She yelled at me some more, so I said, "Wait, there's a green thing that fell in the yard, and it's near the fence, and Jamsey and I want to see what it is."

"Annie! Get in here this minute. Tell Jamsey to go home."

"I'm not going, stupid, until I can look at the green thing."

Jamsey and I jumped off the porch and ran so Janice couldn't catch me and make me go to bed. She always makes me go to bed.

Where the green thing had smashed up, there was a pile of shiny stuff and something was moving near it. It was hard to see in the dark. It looked like the weasel I saw in the zoo, kind of, but it had big, big eyes. Bigger than my silver dollar and its skin was smooth like the cloth the sofa is made of.

And it was hurting. I knew it was hurting and I asked Jamsey and he said he knew it too, and we both felt it was hurting, but we didn't know why. We wanted to help it very much, but it felt to us that we couldn't, but we wanted to anyway.

Then Janice came up. She was mad because I had disobeyed her by not going to bed. When she saw the weasel-thing that was hurting, she got real scared. She told me and Jamsey to take a stick and hit it.

We didn't want to, because it wasn't bad, and besides, it felt to us that we had better not. Janice said that she would make me go to bed without a drink of water if I didn't hit the thing with a stick, and I told her I didn't care.

Then Janice came closer, and she said she would step on it herself. I told her that the thing didn't like her. She was making it mad. It felt that to me, and I told her but she said I was fibbing.

The thing felt to me to tell her to stop, and I did, but she wouldn't. She went to step on it, and suddenly she was gone. Honest.

Jamsey and I were scared. We started to run, but the weasel-thing felt to us to stop. It wasn't mean. It wasn't feeling to us very strong anymore, and we thought maybe it would die.

It felt to us that it was dying because it couldn't breathe air, and I didn't understand, but it felt to me that that was all right.

Soon it was dead. We buried it somewhere like it wanted us to. I can't tell where, because I promised I wouldn't. It's a secret, and I don't want to disappear like Janice.

The Firefall

The gauges on the instrument console lit Ataine's hand like stagelights as she reached for the switch which locked the *Quest III* probe on autopilot.

"I'm not going to be manipulated," she said through clenched teeth, though the spacecraft was a single-hander, now irrevocably severed from outside contact. The transmitter was a tangled ruin. Ataine had sabotaged the unit herself when an angry superior had beam-arced a recall command: the *Quest*'s launch from Station was unauthorized.

"That's right, you sonuvabitch." Ataine shoved a fist full of uprooted circuitry at the astonished face on the screen, thereby sparing herself the fury of the man's response. Since the visual monitor still functioned, his balding, purpled image mimed anger by her left elbow, but she gave it scant notice, the toggle a small point of cold at her fingertip.

"And I'm a damned good astrogator, thanks to your turkey of a second lieutenant." She tripped the switch from "autopilot" to "manual."

As though on cue, red lights crowded the screens, and a buzzer shrilled. Ataine wished she could silence it. She certainly didn't need fail-safe sensors to recognize threat to the

Quest's frail shell. The planet engulfed the portside screens like a hideous bruise, and its gravity field dragged against the probe's thrust insatiably as a nightmare lover. The smallest mistake would hurl the *Quest* to a meteor's incandescent death. Ataine grinned. The electronics didn't trust her.

"You shouldn't either," she said to the small, white dash which was the aft screen's rendition of her pursuit; a late-model Sabre, Ataine guessed, with a very determined man at the controls. He had used weapons, tried repeatedly to cripple her. The *Quest*'s shell carried scorchmarks from a leak in the deflection shields. But Ataine made a difficult target, and the drive engines still functioned to designer specifications.

With damp fingers, she pressed the basket-weave frame of the headset over her ears. Electrodes prickled her scalp, and signals merged with neurological impulses, uniting her mind with her spacecraft. Though direct-link control systems were still highly experimental, Ataine absorbed the influx of electronically induced sensations with no side effects. Other astrogators became paralyzed with vertigo, nausea, and headaches without drugs to balance the artificial impulses generated by the ship's system. Yet Ataine used no drugs.

"Anomaly," the Station physician had said with a shrug, when he learned how many hours Ataine had logged under manual control in the *Quest* without a single request at the dispensary. Tired of an infirmary filled with puking test pilots, he'd dismissed the subject out of laziness.

Ataine never corrected him, never explained that she had used the vertigo, nausea, and headache like a drug to shadow a different kind of pain; and when her body's natural resistance had finally, reluctantly, acclimated to the *Quest*'s sensory hardware, she went on using the ship's electronics to bury her own humanity. Her passion was obsessively simple: when she flew, she was spared the emotion which prisoned her thoughts like a shroud.

Now, impulses from the *Quest*'s sensors ruled her thoughts, blanketing awareness of her woman's body and the tormented memories it contained. Her existence became that of the ship, hurtling through space at speeds impossible for flesh alone to achieve. But this time the joy of release was marred. Attuned to the ship itself, she felt the drag of the orange gas-giant like a fish hook in her guts, tearing. Pictured by electronic circuits, the planet's monstrous mass eclipsed her left-hand vision, perilously close. Never intended for such stresses, the *Quest*'s light, high-impact shell came equipped for reconnaissance of asteroids. Government mining operations had no interest in gas-giants. The craft resonated under abuse enough to make her designers weep to a man.

Ataine's mouth twitched in amusement. She'd made off with an exceptionally sophisticated chunk of technology. The brass at Station would roast in hell sooner than pardon her. But she had no intention of returning, which meant shedding the man in the Sabre as soon as possible. And for that, the bloated orange planet would become her ally.

Ataine tightened her grip on the control yoke, bent the *Quest*'s course closer to the planet. Alarm bells screamed. But linked as she was to the anguished increase in resonance in the *Quest*'s shell, she needed no warning.

"Come on, *baby*." Her voice shook, though she'd spent hours of computer time over the equations. Delicately, she inched the lever forward, increased thrust. The hull shivered in protest. Her tiny cockpit glittered with lights like an arcade. Ataine licked sweat from her lips as her spacecraft plunged toward the gas-giant's surface. Though impulsive by nature, she had rehearsed her escape through seven weeks of misery. She hadn't miscalculated. She couldn't have. Too much lay at stake.

Ataine steepened the pitch of the *Quest*'s trajectory once more. The hull shuddered, trembled under her like an overextended race horse. She nudged the lever again, fractionally, and checked the aft sensor. Everything, wholly *everything* depended upon the man who chased being reckless enough to follow. He would know she had reached the absolute limit of the *Quest*'s capabilities. Certain of his

victory, he might follow and descend inside her arc, awaiting the moment when hull failure would leave her at the
mercy of gravity. She looked back.

A fleck of light hovered off her tail vane, solitary as a
star. The Sabre still pursued.

"Foolish," said Ataine, and laughed aloud. She had
him. Though he didn't know it yet, rescue was not part of
her plan. She took a bearing on his position. The computer
matched vectors, and the results made her laugh again, tri-
umphantly. Trusting the higher tolerances of the Sabre's
hull, he too had steepened his dive, and used the pull of the
giant planet to increase speed. His thrusters flamed as he
corrected course.

"Clockwork," said Ataine, and her hand quivered
feverishly on the controls. *Why did you have to behave so
damned predictably?*

Anxiously, she waited. At length, the Sabre dropped
below, flashy as a child's model against the muddled surface of the planet. The moment had arrived. Ataine
whipped the *Quest* into a banking curve, increased thrust,
and kicked in the repulsion field designed to protect the
spacecraft from collision with rogue asteroids. Like a small,
flat rock pitched spinning across the calm water, the *Quest*
would skip free of the gas-giant's field. But the heavier
Sabre, belted by the force of her field, would sink like a
stone.

Ataine ripped off the headset, punched the craft into
autopilot, and ground the heels of her hands into her eyes.
She had murdered a man. She'd planned to. A voice inside
her head calmly affirmed her action as right; the man must
die, for justice, that others might survive. She sat, and
shook, and after a long minute, realized that someone was
speaking, outside, and it was the man she had sent to his
death. Separate from the main transmitter, the emergency
distress monitors could never be shut off.

"I won't listen," she whispered.

But the voice called her name, and the inflection was
wrenchingly, horribly familiar.

"No!" Ataine banged her palms against the console. A

new glow from the screen tinged her knuckles blue, and with an ugly shock, she saw the emergency code signal had also invaded the video portion of the transmitter. She wished, desperately, she'd smashed it with the rest. Dorren's face confronted her.

"Ataine, you were wrong about me." He spoke calmly, as though he sat safe in Station's lounge. But the look on his pale, tense features cut her like steel.

Anger claimed Ataine, vengeful and hot as desert wind. Naturally, the Commander would have sent Dorren after her. Who better? All of Station believed she had a weakness for him.

As though he'd read her mind, Dorren gestured impatiently. "I came myself. The Commander had nothing to do with this."

Grimly, Ataine wrenched off the access panel. So he'd volunteered. Not even Second Lieutenant Dorren Carlton would get her to return to Station.

"Ataine, will you listen?"

But the desperate, imploring note in his voice rang dissonant in her ears. She found the wire she sought, and pinched it viciously from its contact. The screen went blank. And bitter tears flooded her eyes. Hunched in the *Quest*'s cockpit, with her elbows crammed miserably against the arms of the pilot's seat, Ataine found that she couldn't let him die. Anyone but Dorren . . . anyone . . . her luck was rotten. Hours of emotional anesthesia in the *Quest*'s fancy astrogational systems had enabled her to live without him. But no escape existed which could negate responsibility for his death.

"Coward," she sobbed, and jammed herself back into the headset. Tears dripped off her chin as she banked the *Quest* around, this time without equations, calculations; this time with nothing but her wits and the knowledge that if she saved him, others less deserving would die.

"I hate you," she said, as she once had to his face, but the words changed nothing.

The controls shuddered under her fingers, as though protesting betrayal. And the gas-giant swelled in the starboard screens mocking the futility of every month spent in preparation, wasted effort, now, because of Dorren. Wracked by self-loathing she fought to steady the *Quest* against the planet's cruel pull, tried not to think, and lost, as she always did, to memory . . .

"Don't frown so hard," said a quiet male voice at her elbow. "Didn't you play Jacks and Aces as a child?"

Startled, Ataine glanced up from the instrument simulator's console to discover a young man of medium height leaning on the armrest beside her. A grin softened the lines of decisively set features, and the wheeze of the overhead ventilator ruffled perfectly trimmed brown hair. The eyes were direct, and very blue.

"Were you deprived?" His grin faded into puzzled inquiry. "I thought every kid played Jacks and Aces. I'm Dorren, assigned to coach you, and if you hated cards, you're going to make a difficult job for me."

"I played," said Ataine. As he crouched beside her seat, she buried a moment of vulnerability by staring stonily at the screen. *He's nobody special*, she told herself firmly. But the instinctive platitude was useless. Theirs was a rapport so perfectly balanced that nothing she had experienced since was the same.

Using whimsical analogies drawn from card games, Second Lieutenant Carlton taught her to handle the sensitive instrumentation of Station's ore probes faster than any trainee had done in the past. Long after the others had shut down their systems for lunch, she and Dorren had lingered in the trainer, mixing instruction, anecdotes, and tasteless jokes with unparalleled enthusiasm. Time stopped. Neither of them noticed. Finally, the disgruntled technician in charge asked them, please, to leave. He had a date.

Ataine slapped the power switch off, smiled at Dorren. "Are you busy? We could have a date, too."

Instantly, his expression lost its vitality. She swallowed. It never occurred to her he might already be mated.

"Not today." He sounded stricken. "Another time."

Ataine shrugged. She guessed he was avoiding her. Yet as he left, she experienced a distinct uneasiness, as though something unnatural had occurred. Her disappointment must have leaked into her expression, because the technician paused in his haste to see the doors locked.

"Dorren's not mated," he said, his face sympathetic. "He simply prefers to be alone."

Ataine blinked, icily sobered. "Then keep him away from me," she said, because too often in the past she had been attracted to the independent sort of man who "simply needed no one." Another was a heartache she'd avoid.

But Station was as small as a closet; inevitably Dorren's superior heard about their supreme compatibility as a team. They were assigned together.

The morning of her first survey mission, Ataine stood under the ribbed belly of the Prospector she and Dorren were to fly. Landing beacons beyond the airlock ports spilled hellish reflections through the launch tube, increasing her uneasiness. Dorren was late. Ataine waited, buffeted by drafts as the escort teams who would accompany them sealed hatches and fired up systems prior to ignition.

Dorren appeared, finally, in the service passage, still fastening his gloves. His face bore a deep scowl, and as he approached, Ataine saw his chest heave in short, hard jerks. His evident temper smothered her greeting unspoken.

Dorren seemed oblivious. He glanced at the helmet which dangled stupidly from her fingers. "Put that on. I don't want to look at you."

Stung past restraint, Ataine looked squarely into his face. "I didn't ask for this. Why take your frustrations out on me?"

The hurt she tried uselessly to hide made him check abruptly. He paused and studied her, and the unguarded feelings she discovered in return took her breath away. The scowl softened.

"I'm sorry." He sighed, knuckles locked and white

over the seal ring of his own helmet. "We're stuck for today. I'll speak to the Commander when we get back."

Prompted by intuition, Ataine said, "You already did. He refused to change the roster, didn't he?"

Dorren's eyes narrowed. His expression became harried, as though he fully acknowledged her presence only that moment. "He'll change his mind. Now, *get in*."

Disgusted by his unpleasantness, Ataine obeyed. Without protest, she found her way into the co-pilot's seat, and scooped her auburn hair into the helmet. She left the face-plate down. Secure within its shelter, she assumed control over her half of the cockpit, and promptly forgot the man who readied systems for launch at her side. The demands of flying brooked no distraction. Ataine settled into routine, absorbed by the gauges on the console before her.

The mike in her helmet crackled. "All set?" Dorren's voice was neutral.

Ataine signaled affirmatively and released the magnetic field which anchored the craft to Station's flight deck. Dorren snapped a switch, and the air lock irised open.

"Lift," he said softly.

As one, their hands closed over the controls. The Prospector shuddered. Thrusters flamed, and the launch tube shot past, replaced by darkness pinpricked with stars.

"Bank left."

Ataine responded, startled by an unexpected thrill. She'd flown most of her life, but even the sportiest dual-handers had never responded as cleanly as the common, work-battered Prospector did that day. As the Sabre escort launched from Station to trail like beads behind, she found she barely had to adjust for trim; they flew without need to compensate. Dorren's touch on the controls complemented her own with a perfection akin to ecstasy.

Her helmet mike clicked. "Enchantress," said Dorren. He laughed, exuberantly. "My stomach just sank into my boots. Too much peaches and cream. *Who taught you to fly?*"

"Chromosomes. And a father who named his children

after spacecraft." Ataine grinned, enthralled by his fussy, precise sense of timing. Transformed by laughter, her bad temper vanished as though his rudeness had never existed. And the Prospector flamed through space like a star-class yacht.

This can't last, Ataine thought. An indicator flared yellow, warning the approach to the asteroid field they were assigned to survey. Dorren would certainly brake to quarter speed, fresh as she was from orientation training. Skilled astrogator she might be, but at ore prospecting she was a novice. The first obstacle loomed on the screens, dead ahead. Instinctively, Ataine reached for the portside throttle, to cut back for the turn, just as Dorren began a bank to the left. He toyed with the trim, unnecessarily, and said, "You knew which direction I would go."

"Yes." Ataine paused to wonder how she'd known, and gave up. The move seemed natural at the time.

"Don't reduce speed." Dorren leaned over the controls, suddenly impulsive. "I don't know why, either, but there's something between us I can't leave unexplored. Do you mind if we simply let rip . . . ?"

Ataine returned a pleased smile. "The Commander will scorch our shorts off, when we get back to Station."

"*If* we get back to Station." Dorren fingered the lieutenant's stripes on his cuff. "Those rocks out there won't be half so forgiving if I'm wrong."

Ataine laughed. "We'll get back to Station, and maybe wish we hadn't." She kicked in the thrusters, her movement precisely co-ordinated with his.

The Prospector leapt ahead, cut a tortuous, blistering course through the tumble of debris. Very quickly they discovered they shared something preciously rare. As a team, they were subconsciously, if not telepathically, attuned.

Glued to her controls, Ataine knew a companionship untainted by any human doubt. She and Dorren Carlton thought alike, acted alike, and the mixture was addictively heady. An asteroid skated onto the screens. She banked right, certain Dorren would balance for the slop in the vanes. *Between us there are no limits*, she realized, *none at all.*

The communicator buzzed. Dorren sighed, throttled back, and punched the "receive" toggle.

The speaker shrilled to life. "Are you two nuts? Hotshot any more, and you'll make hamburg of your escort. You've outdistanced us, to understate, and if you get sighted by anti-nationals, serve you both right."

Dorren shrugged. "Flame the anti-nationals. We haven't seen any in months, and they'd have to catch us, first."

The Sabre captain sighed into his mike. "Right. Wait up, will you?"

They passed the remainder of the assignment with more decorum. But upon their return to Station, even their disgruntled escort boasted over the territory they had covered.

"Two claims, and a twelve beacon mark-off," said the Sabre's captain in admiration as Dorren stepped through the Prospector's chipped hatch. "You and that greenie did a helluva day's work."

Ataine followed the second lieutenant out, tired but content. She slipped off her helmet, and smiled, freed hair tumbling in slow motion over her shoulders in the flight deck's low gravity. Yet as she met Dorren's eyes, she watched his pleasure die, pinched deliberately from a face still flushed from happiness.

She felt as though he'd struck her. Warily interpreting his mood, she said, "You're going to insist on reassignment."

Dorren frowned. "Especially after this."

"Why?" Her outburst escaped before she thought to quell it.

But Dorren strode off without reply, leaving her desolate with uncertainty.

"What's with him?" said the puzzled captain at her shoulder.

Ataine shook her head angrily. "Blast if I know." She left abruptly for her quarters and hoped for a better partner next shift.

• • •

But three weeks brought no change in the roster. Inured to Dorren's uncertain temperament, Ataine avoided conversation. By barring her heart against feeling, she learned to anticipate his mercurial shifts of mood, and respond only during those moments when the rigors of their profession drove him to reciprocate the gift they possessed between them.

When things went well, his supply of banter seemed endless. "Don't bring home any strays," he said as she hauled out the tools to take a core sample. Dorren usually handled the task. But lately Ataine had grown restless waiting for him in the cockpit.

"You're kidding. No anti-national hardware has turned up for months." Ataine clipped the tool satchel to her shoulder harness and looked up, startled to find him watching with the same concern she'd shown each time he "walked" an asteroid. "I'll be fine. Safe as sugarcake."

"But clumsy." Dorren grinned as she stumbled into the air lock, unaccustomed to the awkward bulk of the tools. "Be careful. And watch that outside hatch. It's defective."

"Grandmother." Ataine dogged the inside seals and kicked the depressurization switch. The lock slid open, and she rolled clear, weightless as a swimmer, the asteroid a convoluted coral head in the beam of the Prospector's floodlamps. Air-hose and tether unreeled behind as she drifted downward. The magnetic soles of her boots touched first, and clung.

"Iron here," she reported. "Are we out of claim buoys?"

Dorren's reply crackled over her suit mike, strangely distant. "Set your charge. I'll check."

She collected her sample without incident. Odd, she thought; the anti-national fanatics seemed to have given up sabotage. So far, the risk pay she collected each week had proved a waste of government funds. Not that she was sorry. Presently, Dorren's voice answered her request for a buoy.

"Cupboard's bare," he said lightly. "I've sent a Sabre back to Station for more. Why not wait inside until it arrives?"

"Fine. I'm on my way up." Ataine kicked off for the Prospector's hatch. She caught the boarding rail without difficulty. But as she swung herself through, the tool satchel bumped the seal ring of the air lock. Vibration under her fingers warned her; by freak mischance the mechanism had engaged and started to shut.

Instinctively, Ataine pushed clear. Halfway through, she noticed her air-hose and tether had hooked on the boarding rail outside. The lines jerked taut before she could react. Caught in zero g without a handhold, recoil spun her back between the seals. The lock trundled inexorably closed. Gear teeth ingested air-hose and tether, trapping her with the disengage switch beyond reach. In panic, Ataine saw she was going to be crushed.

That moment, the lights went out. Ataine yelled, overcome by terror. Unwilling to watch, she stared past the black shoulder of the asteroid, as though fixed and changeless stars beyond could negate the certainty of death. *But the hatch had stopped.*

Quivering and sweating inside her suit, Ataine realized Dorren must have acted. He'd hit the breakers, killing all power on the ship to prevent the hatch from closing. But with her tether jammed in the gears, and her air supply cut off, she was not out of danger. She tried to stay calm.

"Dorren, suit up." A yank on the lines confirmed the gravity of her predicament. "I need . . . oh, *damn . . .*" Because with the ship's systems down, *he couldn't hear her.* At any moment, believing her clear, he might restore power. *Don't close the switch,* she thought desperately. *Dorren, don't.*

She dragged herself around, clawed at the tether. Stuck. Dizziness hauled at her balance. She groped in the tool satchel for something sharp to cut the lines. Her lungs burned. She couldn't hold her breath much longer. Her frantic fingers closed over the steel casing of a core bit.

Condensation blurred her face-plate as she began to

hack at the tether line. A vast, sucking roar filled her ears. *I'm not going to make it*, she thought, and chopped harder. Light swam across her vision, which seemed ludicrous, wrong. Suffocation went with darkness. The bit drifted out of her grasp. She reached for it, drunkenly, and someone's fingers closed over her wrist.

Dorren's helmet bumped against hers. "Hang on." A knife flashed in the search beam clipped to his belt, and she floated free. "Don't quit now, d'you hear? I'm going to push you through the supply lock."

Cramps in her chest prevented answer. She felt his arms enfold her, as her vision swam out of focus. Her next clear sensation was the click of her helmet seal breaking, and new air rushing into wracked lungs. Dorren knelt on the loading stage with her cradled against his shoulder.

"You knew," Ataine said thickly, between gasps, and almost passed out again as his lips covered hers in a kiss which bared his soul. She abandoned restraint, trusting the intuitive rapport which had miraculously saved her life. Peace overwhelmed her, as though she'd lived in the cold since birth, and only that instant learned warmth.

"Dorren, I love you," she said when he set her free.

He disengaged his embrace. Silently, and with an expression of naked regret, he left abruptly for the bridge. The retreat went against his nature. She'd been too close not to see. Yet whatever compulsion drove him to destroy what was good between them stung her into raw fury. She shouted, "Why can't you just let the inevitable happen?"

The companionway slammed and loosed a flurry of echoes in the chamber's barren confines. Ataine scraped damp hair off her forehead and rolled to her feet. She felt wretched. But physical discomfort became trivial beside the crushing ache of loss brought on by Dorren's withdrawal. Disconsolate, she followed him to the cockpit.

He sat hunched over the controls, helmet off, and chin rested on closed fists. The glow from the screens outlined features set rigidly as a mask.

"Does my presence sicken you? Or threaten your

damned male pride?" Ataine was unable to hide the bitterness in her voice.

He responded without moving. "You're a wonderful person, Ataine. Sensible, intelligent, and gifted beyond belief, not to mention attractive." The dismissal sounded rehearsed. "But I don't want a woman in my life." He shrugged irritably. "Even you. I'm sorry. One day perhaps you'll understand."

Before she could reply, he punched the transmitter into "send" and spoke crisply into the mike. "*Prospector IV* to Sabre escort, has Captain Jern left Station with the claim buoys?"

The speaker crackled overhead. "He's on his way. Did you just have a power outage?"

"Trouble with the lock," Dorren glanced back to Ataine. "Get your helmet on. I'll have to clear those messed gears and then set that buoy. Jern can help me. You can easily be spared, and no doubt you'd be more comfortable after a rest back at Station."

Ataine pitched herself into her chair, fighting tears. "I'm staying. I don't trust that glitched lock, and Jern can't help you like I can if it malfunctions again."

Which was all true, but Dorren's lack of argument made the remainder of the shift pass like arctic winter, unbearably lonely and bleak. By the time the Prospector docked at Station, Ataine's nerves were drawn to snapping point.

Her quarters seemed a prison. And the company of others only emphasized her matchless compatibility with Dorren. Isolated by her loss, she sought refuge in the cockpit of the Prospector, and with every shred of compassion she possessed, tried to understand what might motivate Dorren to reject her.

He found her there still, an hour before the next day's shift. She didn't ask how he'd known where to look, didn't need to see to know whose hands rested gently on her shoulders. She stared stonily at the shadowed banks of controls, unwilling to meet his eyes.

"It's hopeless." Unwanted moisture prickled her eyelids. "The whole flaming situation is utterly, wretchedly *hopeless*."

Dorren reached over and caught the tear which escaped down her cheek. "I know," he said simply. And he did. But nothing changed between them. "I asked for another team mate. This time the Commander granted my request."

The statement ruined Ataine's composure. Blistered to outrage by his coolness, she slammed her fists into the console. "Are you heartless?" Her voice rose to a shout. "Do you think that changes anything?" She spun to face him, and flinched from a mirror reflection of her own distress.

Angry words died unspoken. Ataine rose and left the cockpit, ravaged by emotions too deep for expression. Oblivious to the stares of the teams who reported for shift, she fled down the service passage, into the lift, and burst headlong through Station's most unapproachable door without even a knock.

She ignored the secretary who tried to block her path to the desk. "I want to sign for test flight duty in the *Quest*."

Caught with his mouth full of coffee, the Commander swallowed hastily. He excused the secretary with a gesture and frowned. "Didn't you know? The prototype gave her crewmen a debilitating case of the dizzies. Though the medics have an antidote in mind, they said yesterday they'd need a week."

"That doesn't matter." Ataine stood, and blinked. After the gloom of the flight deck, the office lighting ached her eyes. "I want to fly alone."

The Commander didn't ask why. Instead he regarded her with a mixture of sympathy and distaste. "Very well. If you last, the design boys will be delighted."

Revolted by his patronizing tone of voice, Ataine smiled with outright malice. "Then they can buy me roses."

Flight became her release.

When she reported for shift after the third straight month, Station's chief engineer met her with startled admiration. "You got guts, I'll grant you that."

Ataine fussed with the seal of her suit. "Why?"

The engineer gestured toward the spidery framework of the *Quest*'s launch cradle. "No weaponry. Last shift, we lost an entire drilling team to a mine."

"What? Another?" Ataine paused, stunned, and thoughtfully snapped her collar stud. "But no one's seen any anti-national hardware for months!"

The engineer shrugged. "Want out?"

"No." Ataine quickened her step. She swung herself over the *Quest*'s sleek vanes, into the cockpit, while the engineer launched into a companionable description of the Challenger series, which extended the *Quest*'s capabilities to a crew of two, and a gun station.

Ataine nodded vaguely. Anxious to get away, she dogged the hatch closed. Once under the headset, love, death, and emotional tumult would all cease to trouble her . . .

Shortly, conjoined with electronic circuitry, she piloted the *Quest* through the asteroid field she had surveyed last shift. The area had been clean then, and anti-nationals would hardly trouble an unmanned claim.

Sensors granted her vision in all directions. Entranced by the random dance of rocks whose motions would outlast the ages, Ataine killed the engines and switched off her running lights. Hours, she drifted, aimless as flotsam amid the dusty tumble of debris. Second Lieutenant Dorren Carlton ceased to matter. Attuned to radio frequencies through the *Quest*'s systems, the soft, repetitive beep of a nearby claim buoy remained the only human intrusion upon her solitude, until the moment her sensors picked up a metallic flash of reflection.

Anti-nationals, Ataine guessed. She was unafraid. Without lights, she was too small to be noticed. Ruled by the nerveless logic of the *Quest*'s electronics, Ataine settled back in her darkened cockpit and stepped up magnification.

The red-and-white-checked sphere of the claim buoy jumped out of the darkness, spotlighted by a Prospector's search lamps. Odd, Ataine thought. Why would a team resurvey an area already covered? She frowned, and looked closer. Registration numbers marked the craft as one of Station's own, but the crewman who "walked" the claim carried no core charges. Clipped to his harness, like a hideous, tentacled parasite, was a string of contact mines.

Small wonder no one had seen any anti-national activity. Ataine's hands tightened against the control panel. Somebody had sold out. *The traps were being set by Station personnel.*

"Dorren." Sickened by her discovery, Ataine cornered the second lieutenant alone in the access lift. "Dorren, they're killing people out there." And she told him what she'd seen, because he was the only one on Station whose integrity she trusted.

He whirled so abruptly she bruised her spine against the handrail. The concern in his eyes caught her totally unprepared. "I didn't hear that," he said curtly.

The shock of her surprise set distance between them, shattered the instinctive rapport. He laughed, deliberately widening the breach, and the lamp overhead lit a face she barely recognized.

Ataine gestured in disbelief. "You're in league with them." Her heart turned sick at the thought, yet it fit. No doubt he'd pushed her away out of fear of discovery.

"I'm not," said Dorren. The lift slowed. He stabbed a button, kept it moving. "But I'm smart enough to keep quiet. Stir up trouble, and the survey teams will be next. We'll all be dead, not just the drillers."

Her expression must have betrayed rebellious thoughts, because the lines around his mouth deepened. "Don't be a fool. Let it be. Or I'll tell the Commander about you myself."

"Son of a bitch!" said Ataine, scarred by his betrayal. "I hate you." But she knew, even then, how shallowly she lied. The vehemence of his reaction told its own story: deny her though he would, he could not endure having her life endangered.

Shaken, Ataine caught the rail as the lift bumped to a stop. She watched Dorren step out, numbed by upwelling fear. Already it was too late to heed his warning. Because the one thing she had kept quiet was the fact she had recorded the activities of the Prospector's treasonous crew on the *Quest*'s emergency log tapes. With deadened fingers, she punched the button for the next level. The log was a security system, accessible only to higher authorities; if the corruption at Station extended even to the Commander, she was in trouble.

Ataine shut her eyes, clammily sweating inside her suit. She had no option. She'd have to steal the spacecraft . . .

The gas-giant's equatorial band swelled, a livid smear across the forward sensors. Tensely, Ataine nursed the controls. Stresses multiplied in the *Quest*'s tiny hull, translated across the electronic linkage as pressure against her body. The sensation increased continually, until even her bones seemed to ache. Ahead, a streamer of flame marked where the Sabre's thrusters battered uselessly against gravity. Ataine adjusted course to intercept. Sweat dripped with the tears on her cheeks as the *Quest*'s nose tipped into a deeper arc. The screens pulsed with an unbroken row of danger lights.

Suddenly something snapped. Half her vision dissolved into an electrical crackle. Ataine gasped, choked by fear, until she realized she'd sustained no injury. Only the *Quest*'s starboard sensors had failed. Concerned she might lose the remainder and tumble blindly, she re-oriented the craft's docking gyros to track the Sabre's position. A siren wailed, confirming how little margin for error remained.

Ataine teased more speed from the thrusters. An alarming vibration rattled the deck under her feet. She tried to ignore it. Intent upon her goal, she located the Sabre, now grown to a speck against the planet's bloated mass. A bank of screens flickered under her elbow. The headset recorded the event with a crisp snap. Ataine flinched, swore, and faced the facts; the systems might soon pack up entirely. With closed eyes, she focused total concentration into faltering circuitry and drove the *Quest* into the final plunge which would match her course with the Sabre.

Immediately she wished she hadn't. Resonance collapsed the aft vane like foil. Ataine cried out, punched through the link by physical pain. The *Quest* bucked under her, threatening to spin. Ataine wrestled with the controls. Through the electrostatic snow which laced the image from her functional sensor, she noticed something odd about the Sabre's structure . . . but the image quickly became unreliably fuzzy. Ataine dismissed the distraction. Dorren's survival, as well as her own, depended upon critical timing.

Ataine adjusted the headset, every reflex pitched for the instant when her fall would carry her abreast of the Sabre. She touched the drive system, relieved to find it still responded normally. As the Sabre's bulk grew larger, she ducked the *Quest* into a roll and presented her aft thrusters toward her former adversary. Then her vision darkened, eclipsed by the Sabre's greater mass. *Now!*

Ataine slammed the drive systems wide open and a rush like surf battered her ears. Her stomach turned, pulled horribly by the force of defied gravity as the *Quest* swept into a wide hyperbolic curve. The deck quaked. Something metallic rattled loose and clattered across the cockpit. Ataine squeezed her eyes closed and maintained full power.

Let that be enough, she thought fervently. And somehow, against all logic, she *knew*; the kick from her thrusters had loaned the Sabre angular momentum enough to tear free of the planet's killer hold. Dorren steered a course similar to her own, but in the opposite direction.

"Let that be enough," Ataine repeated aloud. Her voice shook. The *Quest*'s direct-link systems had been punished to the edge of failure. If Dorren gave chase, she'd be finished.

Suddenly a buzzer shrilled. Ataine opened her eyes to a star burst of alarm lights. Then sharp pains in her chest bent her double. Aware that malfunction of the *Quest* must be the cause, she blinked back tears of agony and studied the indicators. The *Quest*'s main fuel line had ruptured.

Ataine yanked the headset off. The pain faded instantly. Stressed and tired, she leaned on the console, swore, and killed all power in the drive systems. The move was necessary to prevent explosion, but afterwards she felt as though she'd cut her own throat. She was helpless. Her instruments showed she still had enough momentum to escape the gas-giant's gravity field. Yet without thrust, she had no control over drift. *Helpless.*

Despair enveloped her. She cursed her early, impetuous destruction of the transmitter. The distress beam-arc still functioned, if she reconnected the hotwire, yet emergency codes were unselectively monitored. Ataine buried her face in her hands. Rescue would come, but *from* Station, and subsequent examination of the *Quest*'s logs would expose her intentions to the anti-national faction she had left base to destroy.

I can drift, Ataine thought; drift until the *Quest*'s oxygen canisters could no longer recycle air. She reviewed the gauges. Her speed was considerable. If she could last forty-eight hours before hooking up the distress "arc," her signal might be received by an outbound transport. Law would compel pick-up, and if the crew was loyal to government, she might yet escape with the *Quest*'s log intact.

Shaking, Ataine straightened in her seat. The odds were like light years, inconceivably long. But no other alternative remained. Resigned to her fate, she dredged her memory for the timetable, and hoped bad luck would roost elsewhere.

Her wish proved futile. She'd barely converted the chronometer reading back to Station time before an uncanny sensation of company invaded her cockpit. The presence was familiar.

"Dorren!" Never had his mental touch been clearer. Ataine banged her fist against the console and shouted angrily, as though he could hear. "Don't pick me up. Please, Dorren, grant me that much."

But his contact only intensified. "I'm coming for you."

"No!" Ataine felt her throat constrict. "You owe me, remember?" If she hadn't spared him, the *Quest* would not be crippled.

I'm coming. Unarguably final, the response seemed graven in stone.

Outraged by his ruthlessness, Ataine laced stiff fingers through her hair and tried desperately not to weep. *Tell them I'm dead!* But she knew he was beyond listening to her pleas. He would come for her, and short of suicide, she had nothing left to prevent him . . .

The bump as the Sabre's docking collar made contact jostled Ataine where she sat hunched over dead banks of controls. She reached listlessly for her helmet. Anger had ebbed, leaving resentment no sentiment could thaw, and numbed by the immediacy of defeat, she sought nothing but the chance to hurt the man who had stolen her inner trust, and betrayed her.

She sat, helmet clutched in cold fingers, as seals meshed with the *Quest's* hatch and locked her craft in tow. A signal from Dorren's console opened the lock. Pressure equalized, rippling the hair against her neck.

"Damn you," she said succinctly, aware her suit mike would now transmit to Dorren's cockpit. A wave of consciousness probed her barriers in response. Passionless as ice, she rejected him.

A soft, shuddering sigh arose from her helmet, followed by Dorren's voice, thinly and inadequately amplified. "My dear lady, this time we're in the same boat. Will you let me explain?"

Driven to viciousness, Ataine said, "Don't try. Just take me back and collect your commendation from the Commander."

"Ataine." His breath caught. "Ataine." And the quaver in his tone spilled chills down her back. *Something was wrong.*

Ataine rose and pushed off for the hatch, unable to

stop her reaction. Hatred withered as, incapable of denying the link, she stopped fighting. *Dorren was ill, and in trouble, and afraid for her life.*

Too bewildered to analyze, she caught the seal ring and passed through into an air lock no Sabre ever built could possess.

Ataine paused, arrested by shock. "They sent you after me in the *Challenger*!"

"No." Dorren's voice sounded queerly strangled. "I stole it."

He was wrestling nausea, Ataine realized, because he'd forgotten, or had no time to take drugs against the effects of the direct-link system. He hadn't lied. Puzzled, she left her helmet weightlessly adrift and headed for the cockpit.

The companionway door opened into gloom punctured by the glow of instruments. Dorren shivered in the pilot's seat, drenched in sweat. Ataine fought off an overpowering urge to go to his side.

"Why?" she said quietly. The word carried multiple meanings.

Dorren shuddered, faintly amused even through his discomfort. "Because if I'd let you close to me, I'd have lost my cover. Government sent me to Station to acquire proof of an anti-national defection *higher up*. They suspect the man responsible for security screening of officers. But you bolted before I had finished, and the Challenger was the only craft left unguarded at Station." He pressed wet hands against his forehead. His final lines emerged muffled. "There's an armed squadron of Sabres on my tail. Had I not stood between you, they'd have scorched the *Quest* out of space. Now, *fly us out of here.* I'm going to be sick."

Ataine left the companionway. Bruised by the details left unsaid, she swung herself into the co-pilot's seat. Dorren had wrecked another trust to save her, left anti-nationals free to murder back at Station. She reached stiffly for the headset, wounded by the integrity he had sacrificed because he could not tolerate her death. His self-disgust left her hollow.

At her side, Dorren stumbled to his feet. His hand

touched her shoulder, but the contact was dead. "I'll jettison the *Quest*." He moved to leave.

But Ataine caught his wrist and looked up into drawn features. "Salvage the log canister, first." And she told him why.

"You filmed them?" Dorren stared incredulously. "Blazes, woman, I should have guessed." And slowly, his expression changed to chagrin. "Could you forgive me? I think my superiors are going to want you in the co-pilot's seat. This time, I think I won't argue."

Silverdown's Gold

Trionn the scullion could never pause anywhere for
more than a minute without attracting a heap of
cats. It did not matter whether his clothes reeked
of the midden on those days when he raked out the
garbage, or if he was simply sitting, huddled against the
wind, awaiting his turn at the privy. The cats always found
him. They settled, arranged comfortably in his lap, or
stretched across his feet in sprawls like dropped knitting.
All too often they betrayed him by leading those very people to him that he fervently wished to avoid.

That was how he came to be lying prone in high grass
on an afternoon when he should have been helping to
butcher a pig.

The blood and the smell of the slaughter pen made
him sick; the cook knew as much, and cursed him for a
puling ninny. There had been too many pigs killed for the
table since the new Lord had inherited the rule of
Silverdown; as if a feast must grace the tables each night
until every pasture was emptied. The squalling as helpless
animals were dragged out for the knife made Trionn sweat
and turn pale. The heave of his stomach always followed,
until lately, no meat sat well in his gut. Discomfort held
him prone, though he knew today's victim was by now far

beyond feeling; the tripes would be boiled and the last ham set up in the smokehouse. Pots left over from the rendering waited in the scullery for washing, stuck with grease, and crusty with charred rings of gravy. He would earn another beating for his shirking.

Trionn did not care. With one cat curled between his shoulderblades, two more nestled against his flank, and the white female who was heavy with kittens flopped over the backs of his knees, he sucked at a grass stem and stroked the ears of the tom who gnawed at his thumb. He was safe enough here, where the cook would never venture, in the neglected field that was the demesne of the blue dun stud.

The stallion that was a killer, that hated everything alive.

Mad creature that he was, the horse disdained to step on cats. Trionn basked, protected, under a warmth of beasts and autumn sunlight. No one would look for anyone here, far less the most tongue-tied of Silverdown's kitchen staff.

"There he is!" someone shouted.

Trionn started in alarm. The cat on his back was dislodged onto the turf where, with arched spine and crooked tail, it glared at him in feline displeasure. Had apprehension not held Trionn rooted, he might have laughed at its injured dignity. But the voice that had raised the outcry was the new Lord's own, and for any man of highborn stature to go beating the fields for a scullion bespoke worse than a cook's irritation.

Trionn levered himself up on one elbow and peered over the grass tips. He dared not spring to his feet, whatever the Lord's displeasure; did he rise, the cats might leave, and the vicious dun would take note that a man had invaded his turf. His ears would flatten, and his nostrils flare warning, just before he thundered into a charge.

Fear of the stud saved Trionn an embarrassment, since the Lord intended a different errand altogether. He was leaning on the fence in his velvets. Combed blond hair tousled in the wind as he conferred with a balding companion, less finely dressed, a leathery appearance to him that bespoke hard living. Both men watched the horse, which spied them and bowed up his neck. He blew a snort in challenge, his nostrils a flash of scarlet linings against the seal black of his muzzle. Then he flagged his tangled tail, struck once at the air, and galloped.

Trionn flattened himself against ground that shook to the impact of hooves. His peril promptly compounded as the stud's rampage upset the cats, who bounded away through the grass. Caught in the open, he risked getting trampled to a pulp. The sick fear inside him no longer for the pig, he crawled on his belly toward the fence. He escaped under the bottom rail, just barely, but his troubles did not end outside the pasture. Silverdown had never been kept like a manor, until now, when even the weeds that flowered in the hedgerows were unwelcome. The new Lord had ranted and waved his whip and found fault until servants set to with sickle and scythe. Trionn cowered down in the razed-back scrub that edged the meadow, and prayed the two men were given no cause to glance aside. Did they so much as turn his way, they could not help but catch him skulking.

Escape was impossible. Trionn dared not risk the noise of movement, even to cover his ears. Despite the spirited charge of the stud, neither could he help but overhear every word that passed between Lord and crony.

"Will you look at his stride!" the bald man exclaimed in boyish excitement. "He can cover ground, for a marvel."

The stud reached the fence, dropped his hind-quarters underneath himself with a grace that could stop the breath, and whirled in pirouette. Trotting now in taut-muscled extension, he resumed his patrol against invaders. His neck was high set, and curved like a bow, capped with a mane whipped to elflocks that no groom dared to unravel. The last one to try had suffered a broken wrist. Trionn had been assigned the clearing of the supper boards at the time the late Lord, who had been young and a cripple, had gently made disposition.

"Cordiar was never bred to be gentled, but to ride to the fields of war." The Lord raised shaky hands and worried at the shawl that covered frail shoulders. His flesh was pale with ill health, the skin nearly transparent against the blankets piled in layers over his lap; his smile seemed the grimace of a death's head. "My father might have mastered him, had the fighting not sent him to the grave. Leave the horse to his field. Nail the gate closed and let him live as his nature allows. He is wild and filled with hate, but beautiful. He will run free, as I cannot, and give me simple pleasure by watching him."

And so the dun stallion had matured, handled by no man, left to gallop and kick up his heels as he pleased for the two years before Silverdown's master had succumbed to his wasting disease. Unmarried at the hour of his death, leaving not one bastard as issue, his inheritance had fallen to a cousin who was also young, but thick-set and muscled, and vigorous.

"You were right to have me come," the bald man was saying to the new master. "Everyone brags on the virtues of their horses, but this one—he's more than magnificent."

"A treasure," the Lord allowed with an offhand cuff at his cloak. Grass chaff ripped up by the stud had clung and sullied his velvet, and he fussed until the last damp stems had whirled away on the wind. Eyes narrowed against lowering sunlight, he watched the stallion reach the corner and whirl. "A good thing, too. Silverdown's treasury is empty."

Surrounded by a wealth of bearing fields, the bald man raised eyebrows in disbelief.

"Oh, yes," the Lord affirmed with a bitten-off snap of contempt. "Spent out to pay the King's levies, until war took the old man's life. The cripple who survived him had too soft a heart. Left the tenants their harvests, and ran the household on profits from the orchards. Apples and pears!" The Lord gave a laugh not meant to be pleasant. "What a fool's game! The manor house might not leak, through a miracle, but the tenants are sullen and spoiled. They'll have to be taught better manners, if I'm to win Tanemar's daughter. This stallion is all of Silverdown's gold, can we break him. If his bloodline is any judge, his get should look as fine. As a gift he will be unmatched. Duke Tanemar will take notice of my suit, and the hand of his daughter will be mine."

The bald man stroked his chin, while Trionn cowered. "Large plans," he mused, the direction of his gaze never shifting. In the pasture, unaware his wildness was at risk, or that he was being discussed as an item for barter, the stallion kicked up his heels. Hooves sliced across wind with a force that whistled the air. "He's fast enough for a fact, and made well as any man must envy. I'll start on his breaking tomorrow, right enough, but tonight, we'll settle on a fee."

The Lord banged the fence with such force that the planking rebounded with a rattle. The stallion flung up in a rear at the noise, his shadow scything across his admirers. Hooves struck out in a dancer's grace that masked blows as murderous as assassin's cudgels. "No fee," came back the clipped answer. "As I told you, the treasury's empty. Break the great brute so he can be caught and stabled. Then send in three of your broodmares. There's fee enough. While my war captain rides the beast fit so he can be shown off under saddle, the foals will be yours to increase the dun's reputation."

The horsebreaker slapped thighs clad in worn and dusty leather. "I break other people's stock," he declaimed. "I don't keep any for myself." As the Lord beside him left the fence, the horsebreaker remained riveted by the stud, who pranced and stamped in tight circles. The longing on even that man's jaded face was fresh and bright and transparent as at last he turned to catch up. "Still, we'll see. Would you consider a split? Payment in silver, and one foal?"

The Lord snatched his cuff from the clutch of a briar the mowers had missed. His mouth turned down. "Certainly not. Duke Tanemar's enough man to please, for setting such store by a daughter who's nobody's beauty. It's the foals or nothing, for you. Press too hard, and I'll send for a gypsy."

"What, and see your treasure stolen the moment it's tamed enough to halter?" The voices of the two men dwindled, amiably contentious as they hammered out terms for their bargain. Trionn sat up in the brush, feeling whitely shaken. He wished all the cats had not left. In balled up, tongue-tied frustration, he watched the stallion storm out one last gust of air, then settle his head down to graze.

A sadness near to pain ached in his chest at the thought that such a beast should ever be trapped or taken.

Distressed beyond concern for the slaughtered pig, Trionn saw the sun gone, and the sky turned silver at twilight before he trudged back to resume his neglected chores. The first thing he noticed as he approached the haphazard cluster of frame buildings that made up Silverdown's manor was that lights burned in nearly every window. Reflections of a hundred flames danced in the boggy, sediment-choked ditch that fronted the tumbledown breastworks. Trionn might have a clumsy tongue, but he was exceptionally quick at balancing. He crossed the ditch by footing across a slime-caked log, last remains of the decrepit palisade. He reached what the servants called the yard, a narrow, irregular court whose cobbles were furred in moss; or had been. A fresh, dirt-colored scar sliced one corner, where a drudge labored by torchlight to scrape the paving bare.

More of the new Lord's fussiness, Trionn concluded. Stones could not grow clothes of moss, and wax lights and tallow dips could be burned without care, as the animals were slaughtered for the table; as a great dun stallion could be torn from his freedom and used as a bribe to court a girl. Wrapped in unhappiness, Trionn failed to notice the cat that had found him already. It trotted up and shouldered between his shins, joined at a run by two more.

The alley past the stables bustled with activity. Horseboys jogged between stalls with buckets and grain to tend a half dozen strange mounts. Notes spilled in haphazard arpeggios from the gallery window as a minstrel tuned up to entertain. A woman laughed and a hound howled, while guards who normally would have argued over dice stood up straight and silent at their posts. Their weapons had never been less than sharp, and they had stayed alert enough to challenge intruders; yet their past rows had enlivened their duty watch, ending always in companionable laughter. The change in Silverdown's rule had seen new uniforms with badges at the shoulder. Trailing streamers adorned each man's polearm, as if they were bedecked for a tournament.

But the occasion was no holiday. The servants had little cause to celebrate. All of Silverdown had been swept into change, until Trionn no longer felt at home. He hurried between a drudge with a basket of soiled linens, and the fowler, who carried the cranky old goshawk hooded, and muttered that his dearie should be mewed up and asleep to keep her health.

Trionn threaded a practiced path through the turmoil, until the orange tabby streaked across a patch of torchlight to join his impromptu escort. The cat's arrival drew the eye of the cook, en route from root cellar to bakehouse to chastise the Lord's page for dawdling.

"You! Trionn! Where've you been all afternoon, and the pots all stacked up for washing? You're a wastrel, boy, and due for whipping. Get inside and back to work, or it's the Lord's own war captain'll be the one who stripes your back."

Trionn ducked his towhead between his shoulders and ran. The cats obligingly followed. Clumsy all of a sudden, he tripped over the door stoop and crashed into a servant with a basket.

"Boy! There's good bread you've close to spilled and wasted, and the new Lord with a hall full of guests to feed! Say you're sorry now!"

Trionn bobbed his head. He did not answer, though he was capable; speech did not always tie his tongue up in knots. His silence had long since branded him half-wit, and shy to the point of cold sweats, Trionn did not argue the misconception. Let Silverdown's staff think him stupid. The sting of their scorn was less than his dread of using words to correct them. He talked to the cats well enough when he wished, and had held very halting conversations with the old Lord, before his illness had brought physicians who would bar the master's door rather than admit a scullion presumed to be a simpleton.

With the cats, now four, trailing on his heels, Trionn left the bread girl to her curses. He zigzagged past the spits into the pantry to avoid the butcher's notice, lest his absence at the slaughter pen cause contention.

For all his care, he was spotted.

"The pigs take the knife better when you're there, Trionn," the butcher reproached gruffly. "You want them not to suffer. Well, if they're held still, the cut is fast and clean."

But it was not at all the matter of the pig's dying; had Trionn been asked his own wish, he would have let the animals stay alive. His oversensitivity was no simple affectation. Where others in Silverdown's service might lament upon the waste, and curse the Lord's lavish feasting that saw a surfeit of scraps thrown to the hounds, Trionn woke up each night in cold sweats, apologizing in half-smothered whispers to the dead beasts needlessly sacrificed.

Today's pig would haunt his dreams no less for the fact he had not bloodied his own hands.

Left at last to his duties, Trionn hauled water to the washtub and started to work the dirtied pots. Cats curled around his feet, knotted together in contentment, while the speculative gossip of the servants came and went through the rattle of plates and crockery.

Enith, as always, was most outspoken. She did not sigh over her new romance with the war captain, but turned sharp-tongued invective against the master. "Chased the linen maid as if she wasn't married, and never mind the tart he worships in his next breath is this highborn daughter of a duke."

"She may well be Silverdown's next Lady," interrupted the page. "You should be careful what you say of her."

His comment was ignored.

"She's small, and no beauty, it's said. All dark hair and wide eyes, and hips too narrow to bear a child." This from the cook, who had a brood of eight, and his wife once again near term.

"Never mind looks," the butcher ventured his opinion. "It's the lass's dowry that's at issue. She'll bring three chests of gold to her bridegroom, and if we're to have candles for the dark nights this winter, better all of us pray Silverdown wins her."

Trionn reached for another pot, and a gob of wet sand for scouring. Behind him, watched by the lazy eyes of his cats, the Lord's steward hurried in, looking harried. "Another five bottles of the red wine, and quickly, before there's trouble."

"Man's brought his horsebreaker to table," the cook grumbled. "Those kind always drink." He wiped greasy hands on his sleeves. "Enith, take down the lantern and go for more red!"

"Been to the cellar twice already tonight," she howled back. "More big spiders than bottles left, that's certain."

"No help for that." Still mournful, the cook added, "Do you suppose the horsebreaker's here to handle that murdering dun stud? If so, he'll want the wine. It's the last drink he'll have before he's dead."

The pageboy took umbrage at this. "Khaim's better than that. I once saw him break the neck of a colt who tossed him. Hit it a blow that knocked it sideways, and it couldn't stand up afterward."

"No man's that strong," the cook objected over the creak of the hearth chain as he dragged a kettle off the fire.

"Horse had to be a weak, spindly thing, maybe," ventured the butcher.

The page insisted not.

Trionn let his scouring sand sink to the bottom of the wash water, sickened all over again. Though he strove over the noise and the chat to picture the stallion at his flat, free run across the meadow, instead he was poisoned by visions: of blood in the grass and the air split by a scream that might have been a woman's. Except that a horse in agony will make the same shrill sound. Trionn doubled over and shivered.

A hard hand cuffed him back upright. "Get back to washing, boy," snapped the cook. "There's barely a clean pot in the rack yet."

Half dizzied, Trionn groped for a ladle. His hand

stopped still in midair. He could not touch the gravy that seemed suddenly the same color and sheen as congealed blood, nor could he look at the wash water clinging to his skin, so much did it shine like salt tears. The cook saw his stupefied pallor, and cuffed him all the harder.

"Oh, no, lazy boy. Though you're sick clean down to your boottops, you'll stay and scour, until all this stack of washing is done and dry."

Trionn nodded dully. Midnight came. The lanterns and candles all burned down, leaving darkness cut only by the struggling wick of a tallow dip. Alone in the cavernous kitchen, he finished his appointed chores. When he stumbled out at last to find his cot, the mists had hidden even the moon.

Banners snapped, and dust blew. The new Lord had invited two friends and all of his companions at arms to watch the dun stallion's breaking. Once again Trionn had shirked his part in the slaughter pen, since a calf roast was to finish the occasion. Hidden in the crowd of Silverdown's servants, he stood in cap and apron, only one cat by his shins; the commotion had driven all but the boldest and most determined tom away.

The stallion on whom all this interest centered galloped the far fence line, ears tripping backward and forward, and nostrils distended in deep-chested snorts of alarm. Trionn could not watch him. He could not be as the others, and admire the glossy silver coat, nor the high, black tail that cracked like a flag in the wake of his thundering run. Trionn could not bear the sight of the creature's eye, rolling white, nor could he forget the dreams that had repeatedly broken his sleep: of blood in the grass, and the stallion's ringing neigh of distress.

And yet, unlike the dragging of animals to the butcher's knife, here, he could not be absent. Tormented by a sickness of fear that ate at his spirit from within, he could not run, but only stare down at the worn-through leather of his boot toes, his shoulders as hunched as though he expected a beating; as if he carried upon them a burden that could bend and break, as finally and carelessly as grass stems were trampled under the feet of today's thrill seekers.

The scullion knew when the horsebreaker climbed the fence by the scream of the dun stallion's challenge; second and without importance came realization that the onlookers had ceased conversation, even the cordwainer's apprentice, who was said to jabber in his sleep. The slap of a rope shaken out of its coil reached Trionn's ears, eerily and evilly distinct over the drumroll of the stallion's charge. The scullion bit his lip. He felt through his feet the shake of the ground, and his sensitized nerves seemed to shudder at the step of the man who paced the greensward, eyes narrowed and line poised to toss.

The stallion came on like thunder, like storm. The crowd sucked in a taut breath. The horsebreaker poised with slightly bent knees, admiring, though his life stood endangered. He was confident when the dun snapped up short from his run and towered into a rear. The man's hand on the rope did not tremble as black forelegs raked out to strike. He tossed his loop then, supremely, recklessly sure that his lifetime of skill would not fail him.

The throw missed.

Too fast for the eye to follow, the loop collapsed in a whipping slide off the stallion's knee as his head snaked down, and he whirled.

Not off his guard, nor yet shaken, the horsebreaker shouted and snapped the rope. This horse, like a thousand others, would be bound to shy from any movement, half-seen where equine vision was obscured by the length of his muzzle. Stallions could be predicted. Their forehooves came down, then their head, with ears pricked to assess the threat to their footing; the shy ones would often whirl and run.

The dun stud twisted instead. He landed, still spinning, his ears pinned flat. The horsebreaker shouted to drive him back to a gallop, his hands swiftly reeling in rope. But the stud had done with running. His silver-blue quarters bunched, and one hoof flashed back in deadly perfect accuracy to hammer the man where he stood.

Bright blood flecked the green grass. The horse-breaker lay unmoving, while a woman screamed, and men on all sides started shouting, most jostling back from the fence, but others pressing forward. The stud danced a half pirouette, some swore, in celebration of his unholy victory. The grooms and the stable hands disagreed; the horse was a killer, but not so driven by rage that he ever once stopped thinking. The blue dun was far too crafty to mire his pasterns in a corpse or a tangle of rope.

Solitary, unmoved to any human commiseration, Trionn crouched with his hands laced over his face. He alone had not exclaimed in shocked sympathy as the Lord's men reached beneath the lower rails, and dragged the horsebreaker's body beyond reach of further mauling. The victim was wounded beyond solace, if not immediately dead, and the tears of Silverdown's scullion were shed only and completely for the horse.

His terror-inspired visions did not leave him. There was blood on the grass, but a man's, and the beast's, for a surety, must follow.

The talk in the kitchens after sundown encompassed nothing else. Trionn scrubbed his pots in his corner, and took no solace from the cats, who were thicker than usual about his feet. They might not have speech, but as he did, they could sense when trouble was afoot.

Enith was shrill in her complaints, as she tapped chilled butter from the molds. "What if the Lord sends his captain to do the killing? Waste of a fine piece of man-hood, did that happen, and our champion took a kick like that horsebreaker."

"Won't," grunted the butcher, who recalled just short of a mistake that the cook would run him out for spitting in contempt on the floorboards. "The captain's a bastard for pride. He'd scarce soil his sword on a job better suited for my flensing knife. Though, mark, if I'm asked to cut that devil creature's throat, I won't, unless he's tied down."

"Who's to tie him," Enith snipped back. "No man but my captain has the courage."

"Your captain?" muttered a stable hand, in to grab dinner between seeing the guests' horses harnessed. "Man's owned by nobody, least of all any one lass. He tumbles anything in skirts, every chance he gets."

His muttering tangled with the voice of the cook, who offered, "T'were mine to say, I'd use poison. Why take chances, when a bit of tainted feed dumped over the fence could do the job just as well?"

The Lord's page overheard, as he entered with an emptied platter. "The horse won't be killed," he called clearly. "He's much too valuable for that." Heads turned, all wearing hostile expressions, except Trionn's; he stared fixedly at his hands, immersed to the wrists in grease-scummed water, while the cats butted heads against his ankles.

"The Lord has already decided," announced the page in crisp arrogance. "He's sent for a gypsy horse-caller. It's broken for saddle he wants that stud, not dead."

The cook slammed his cleaver upon the cutting board. "Magic," he said in contempt. "Where's the coin to pay for such? Gypsies with the caller's gift come dear." His thick, sure hands did their task slowly as he heaped steaming meat on the platter the Lord's page held ready.

"It's the girl he wants to impress." Enith sniffed. "Silverdown will be beggared ere his Lordship wins her."

"That's not your trouble," the Lord's page sniped back, out of sorts because he was no longer entrusted to wait upon his master's table. With Duke Tanemar's daughter expected to accompany her father when the stallion was presented as a gift, the Lord had borrowed a page of higher station, and presumably more refined manners, from his brother's household in Tanley. Appointed to serve the lower hall until a gypsy could be found to tame the stud, the displaced page made his resentment felt at every opportunity. Only Enith was exempt, since the boy yet held out hope he might win her favors from the captain; to any who would listen, he bragged that soon it might be he who tumbled her in the hayloft over the barn.

Crouched over the washtub until his hands shriveled and his cuticles chapped and split from the unending mess of dirtied kettles, Trionn reflected sourly that he lost nothing from his disinclination to speak. What were words after all, but winds that blew here and there to no purpose? The cats had better sense, to express their contentment through purring. They yowled only for misery, and met daily disaffection in dignified, unblinking silence.

The slaughtering continued the next afternoon, yet Trionn was excused. The master commanded, and for fear of his Lordly displeasure, every servant not required for other duties set to work in the sun, pulling out briars by hand. Trionn was given the noisome task of raking dirty rushes from the hall. The wooden boards underneath were to be sanded and cleaned. Enith, between frequent sniffs, claimed carpets were sure to follow. When the last wheelbarrow filled with beetle-infested straw was carted out, Trionn set to with sand bucket and rags. As cats scattered back from the spatter of his scrubbing, he reflected that Enith was spiteful. The rushes had been spread at the behest of a lazy house servant, and only after sickness had confined Silverdown's doomed cripple to his bedchamber. The floors before then, back to the old Lord's rule, had been shiningly kept oiled.

Trionn was still at his work, mopping up sand in the shadows of a back corner, when the gypsy horse-caller arrived. She proved to be a woman, to the surprise of all; tiny, raven-haired, and wearing a patched mantle of greens and browns that might have been pilfered from a minstrel. The tassels at the hem were worn to a ragged motley of threads, and though her hair was braided and clean, her skin was the ocher of mud baked dry in the sun.

Trionn recognized her gift when the cats at his heels fled her presence. Silent as shadow, they stalked off in stiff-backed irritation. The scullion watched their retreat. A chill brushed his skin; as if he, too, sensed the power over beasts that this gypsy sorceress could command, and his spirit raised hackles in protest. The hounds did not run. Fickle creatures that they were, bred over generations to subservience, they converged in a pack of wagging tails, tongues lolling in canine enthusiasm. They reacted as if the strange woman in her dusty, faded finery had been the mistress they had obeyed since their whelping; as indeed she could be, if she chose. No dumb beasts, and few men, were proof against a gypsy caller's craft. But unlike humans and cats, dogs set small value on independence. Like whores, they flocked in unabashed eagerness around the woman's boots, begging and whining to be dominated.

Trionn threw down his rags, oblivious to the fuss as servants and guests, and at last the Lord himself took loud-voiced notice of the intruder. The scullion unseen in his corner did not follow the woman's words as she announced herself, but heard only the silvery timbre of her voice. The pitch set up echoes inside him that no amount of clamor could still. He saw courtiers eagerly joining the circle of dogs, who were now belly down and begging. Yet Trionn's senses gave back false sight. In place of hounds and gentle-folk, his mind could not throw off the vision of the silver-dun stud with his grand neck bowed in submission.

Sudden tears stung Trionn's eyes. His stomach heaved. The blood on the grass had not been the horse's; better by far that it had been. The Lord who had died a cripple had insisted many times that death held the keys to final freedom.

Moonlight washed over the meadow. It limned soft silver over the stallion who grazed content in tall grass. Trionn sat outside the fence, his lap encumbered by sleeping cats. His hand caressed the bone handle of the butcher's flensing knife, stolen after dark from the closet. Over and over, Trionn stroked the blade's edge, checking its razor keenness. He turned the weighty steel in his hands, and remembered the kick of a pig held pinned in his arms as it died. He licked dry lips, and sighed as he tested the resolve he had made in desperation, and found himself wanting. He lacked any kind of brash courage. The fate of the horse-breaker did not haunt him, nor fear for his own life and limbs. He simply knew. When the dun stallion bent his knees and laid down to rest, Trionn had no will to creep through the fence and cut the creature's throat to forestall its misery. Whatever freedom death might offer could not compensate for the pound of wild hooves, or the ripple and play of muscles burnished like shining silk under sunlight. The stallion would live to be broken, for Trionn did not have in him the requisite hardness for murder.

He sat in the calm of the night, surrounded by cats and the chirp of crickets, and miserably wished he were bold enough to run away. Yet far as a lifetime of travel, though he crossed the rocks of the mountains beyond the sands, the memories and the visions would follow him, locked inescapably in his mind. The gypsy caller's powers would sting him, no matter where, and he would ache for the stallion's lost spirit. Like the cling of the cats, the persistence of his dreams could not be shed.

The deepest and worst of his misery was that he could not even turn the steel upon himself. The pain did not deter him, nor the dying, but the strange, insistent surety that the cats would be left bereft. Wise as the creatures could be, they would not understand why he should desert them for the sake of one horse's lost liberty.

The butcher recovered the purloined knife after Enith, returning from her nightly tryst in the hayloft, caught Trionn in the yard by the kitchens. Particular to a fault when it came to his cutlery, the butcher's shouted obscenities progressed to extra work as punishment. Trionn was assigned the task of sharpening every tool left dull in the course of shearing Silverdown's weeds and grass.

Left wary after the slaughtering that Trionn was practiced at haring off, the butcher took no chances. He locked the scullion in the tool shed with a half-filled bucket and a whetstone. The cats could find no way in, however hopefully they sniffed and circled. In time they were compelled to settle in disgruntled bundles on the door stoop.

Inside, the shed was suffocatingly hot. Hedged by darkness inadequately beaten back by a bark spill soaked in resin, Trionn set to with the whetstone. He braced the bucket between his knees, and worked the marred edge of a sickle, his mind consumed by awareness of the cats' balked desires. He was powerless to ease their unhappiness.

The butcher jammed a wedge under the sill outside. Until he chose to return, or someone else happened by to fetch a tool, Trionn's imprisonment was complete. The likelihood nobody would visit the shed before the spill burned out did not matter. Silverdown's servants had left for the meadow, the reason for their gathering a distress that already fretted the scullion raw. He dipped the stone and resumed honing, relentless in his determination. He would not think upon what must inevitably happen when the gypsy raised her powers to subdue the stud.

And yet the moment touched him, all the same.

The tones of the gypsy witch's call clamored through him like the struck chime of a bell. The whetstone slipped from Trionn's fingers and splashed into the bucket. Droplets warm as blood trickled down his shins. He did not feel their wetness. Nor did he notice as the spill flickered out, leaving him kneeling in darkness. His eyes were vision-bound to a sunlit meadow, and the form of the slate dun stud shaking back his mane, his ears snapped forward to listen.

The gypsy sorceress repeated her call, lower now, almost wheedling.

Trionn felt the resonance of her tone play through the marrow of his bones. He remained oblivious to the ribbon of true blood that laced his wrist, from the knuckle laid open on the sickle.

His eyesight remained locked as his mind: on the horse, who twitched glossy skin, as if to drive off flies. But it was no insect that stung him. From her perch half on, half over the fence, the gypsy crooned out a binding. The stud's ears flattened and he stamped, where once he would have thundered into a run with his teeth bared in fury.

The call came again, compelling. As if whipped, the stallion started. He edged one step forward, then two, while in the soundless isolation of the shed, Trionn winced. Sweat rinsed his cheeks and his nails gouged his palms as his fingers clenched to fists in the throes of unasked for empathy.

Now the gypsy began a sing-song rhythm that raised the hair at Trionn's neck. He shivered and jerked in concert with the stud as need swelled into compulsion. The horse lowered his proud crest. His hooves raised no dust as he advanced. To Trionn, the gypsy's magic squeezed and confined, as if the leaping flame of a bonfire were compressed down into one spark. His breath jerked in gasps from his chest.

"No," he whispered. "No." He closed eyes that had long since stopped seeing. "No!"

Yet his physical cry could not alter the spell. The stallion moved inexorably onward. He had crossed half the distance to the fence, and the woman, tasting victory, climbed down with her hand outstretched.

The murmurs of the servants, and the Lord's triumphant laugh rang brittle as breaking ice against the deeper vibration of the summoning that continued to draw its victim in.

One touch from the witch would seal the stallion's submission. Trionn understood this in a gut ache of intuition, and something inside of him snapped.

He bit his lip, knees clasped, as his body spasmed with the same wrenching sickness he felt at the slaughtering of the pigs. Only this time, the cramping and the agony were a thousand times more severe. He fought to breathe, fought to think, while the sweat mingled unnoticed with his blood and pattered on the dusty floor.

The stallion was a half-stride away from defeat. His lowered muzzle brushed the grass tips. His eyes were dull, unfocused, and his tail, as lackluster as any gelding's.

Trionn knew a spearing agony that threatened to rip

away his reason. He clamped his hands over his sweat-slicked face and forced a half-strangled breath. "No."

Before his heart could burst, before the great dun could nuzzle the woman's outstretched brown fingers, he imagined the horse as he had been, a creature of terrible beauty that no man in his right mind dared touch.

Trionn pictured the stallion with his head upflung, and his eyes rolling white rings in hatred.

There followed a moment of torment, as if the inner fiber of his being was seared by a whirlwind and torn apart. He had no voice to cry out, and no thought beyond a pin-point awareness that centered on the slate-blue stud.

For a second he seemed to be that horse, his senses overwhelmed by the scent of summer grass, and a second, sourer odor left by a trespassing human. Trionn saw through the stallion's eyes the vista of the fence, and the crowd that lined the rails in maddening noise. He felt the unleashed tension that whipped through the horse as the gypsy's near-finished binding snapped like so much spun thread.

Ever mindful of the horse's speed and power, the woman was faster than her predecessor. She dropped and rolled, even as the stallion screamed in rage. He reared. His shadow raked over the onlookers, driving them back in a panic as his forehooves slashed through air. The woman was no longer there, but already through the fence in a whirl of motley robes. The stallion spun, and from his hind legs launched himself into a gallop. A bolt of silver fury, he ran. His mane flew, and his tail whipped behind like the curl and twist of a war banner.

The shouts of the irate Lord of Silverdown seemed insignificant before the racing tattoo of hooves.

In the tool shed, Trionn woke to himself, sobbing beyond all control. The finger unwittingly sliced on the sickle was stinging in the salt of his sweat. He splashed water from the bucket over the cut, and found his limbs heavy with weariness. His lungs hurt, as if he had been rac-ing on foot alongside the galloping horse. The fact he had not been seemed unreal. Still weeping, he lay back against the rolled burlap used to save seedlings from the last blighting touch of spring frost. His soaked hair plastered to his forehead, he fell into a dreamless oblivion nearer to unconsciousness than sleep.

The day waned. Trionn wakened to a slap. He gasped, started upright, and, dazzled by the glare of low sunlight, saw the butcher standing over him.

"Lazy lout!" the man was shouting. "All day you were in here, and nothing to show for your time. I should have guessed you'd pass the hours sleeping if you could!"

Trionn propped himself up on one arm. He blinked, rubbed his aching cheek, and glanced around to locate the cats, who should have stolen their chance to bolt inside the instant the door was cracked open.

No cats were in evidence.

For the first time in his life that he could think of, his feline friends were not there. The stone stoop was empty of their presence, and the butcher was still howling nonsense.

If Trionn was grudging with his speech, he was equally adept at not listening. He rubbed his arms to ease the chill that swept his skin. If the cats had left due to the butcher's ranting, the troubling fact remained: none of them lurked in the shadows behind the seed sacks, or crouched with flattened ears beneath the shovels.

Above anything else, Trionn dreaded to know what awaited when he ventured out of the shed.

"I should be throwing cold water at your head, boy, to snap you out of your stupor!" The butcher raised the handle of the bucket, prepared to act on his threat, when a second voice cut him off.

"There you are, Trionn!" hollered the cook, his fat bulk damming the small band of light that made its way through the doorway. "Been following cats into crannies all afternoon, and it's here you've been skulking all along!" Oblivious to the butcher's prior grievance, the cook barged past and grabbed his errant scullion by the wrist. "Get moving, you lunk. There's a stack of pots need scrubbing, and his Lordship in a temper since that cheating snip of a gypsy disappeared and can't be found."

Distracted from his ire over scythe blades, the butcher thumped down his bucket. "It's true, then? The woman was a charlatan?"

"The fact she ran off makes you think so." The cook jerked Trionn after as he plowed a path toward the door. "The Lord's set his riders to find her. When she's caught, I'd guess there'll be a hanging."

"And the horse?" Turned thoughtful, the butcher fished his whetstone from the water, and reached for an unsharpened sickle. "What's to become of the stallion?"

"Dogmeat," the cook affirmed, his head cocked over Trionn's shoulders. "The captain at arms was told to down the rogue with an arrow, next time the kennelman needs a carcass." Then, bothered back to priorities by his scullion's dragging feet, the cook turned his invective upon Trionn. "You heat sick, boy? Pick yourself up and walk, else I'll pack your bones for the knackerman along with that devil of a stallion's."

Engrossed in miseries far removed from the cook's irritation, Trionn stumbled through the wicket gate into the courtyard. No cats came flying to greet him. Not even the mackerel-striped tabby sunning herself on the wall. Dread left him the appearance of listlessness. He responded mechanically to the cook's yanks and prods, not wanting to test what change might have touched him while he had been locked in a tool shed, and a gypsy had signally failed in the taming of a man-killing stallion.

The entry to the scullery loomed ahead. On the stoop lolled two white-muzzled hounds, skinny and scarred, but not too old or too proud to disdain begging for scraps. Enith leaned against the doorlintel, sampling a slice of sausage, while the hounds tipped their heads at her and rolled their moist brown eyes.

Trionn stiffened, half-wild with trepidation.

"Are you daft, boy?" exploded the cook. He gave an

abusive yank. The scullion gripped in his meaty fist stumbled forward with a breathless cry.

The dogs immediately stiffened and turned their heads. They saw Trionn. Enith and her sausage were forgotten as they shuffled into a lope, tails wagging, and eagerness in their cloudy old eyes.

Trionn flung back from their rush, appalled to a burst of speech. "No," he croaked, "not this," as the dogs rushed to him and leapt for joy around his knees. They whined and nosed at his fingers, as if greeting a long-sought friend.

"What's happening?" yelped the cook, put out afresh by confusion. He threw off the scullion and the dogs, hands raised in nervous trepidation. "Always before it was cats." His tone held a bite of accusation as he added, "Or have the Lord's bitches gone crazy?"

Enith shifted a lump of sausage into the back of her cheek. Around chewing, she said, "Looks uncanny to me, as if that gypsy witched the dogs instead of the stallion." Then she fixed hard eyes on Trionn. "You never said you could talk."

"Oh, he can," supplied the cook. "He just hates to. When he was little, his parents beat him for stubbornness. Didn't do any living good." He raised a booted foot and kicked the nearest dog, which yelped and bounded back, to shelter behind Trionn's knees. The scullion flinched from its touch, hunched and unaware as the discussion continued around him.

"Enough foolishness now, Trionn," berated the cook. "The pots aren't getting any cleaner while you stand out here acting foolish."

"If he fakes being dumb, maybe he's not so stupid," Enith suggested, while the cook pushed the scullion reluctantly toward the kitchen doorway. She stepped disdainfully aside to let them past, adding, "Are you stupid?"

He gave no answer.

When the dogs sought to barge through on Trionn's heels, both she and the cook howled in chorus. Ousting the dogs required all their attention, and until the door to the kitchen was secured, neither one noticed that Trionn had not retired to his corner to silently, doggedly, scrub pots.

"He slipped out the side way," snitched the Lord's page, idle at the table chewing sausage. He gave a hopeful smile toward Enith, who responded with a flounce, cut short as the cook had a fit.

"I'll have the both of you washing pots!" he roared in fist-waving fury.

The page snickered, as if the threat was a joke. An instant later, he found himself installed at Trionn's wash-tub, cursing the stink of tankards and plates left awash in skins of rancid grease.

Well beyond earshot of the fracas in the kitchen, Trionn ran as a man might when driven by whips. Wherever he went, the cats in their turn fled his presence. Uncannily choosy by habit, they recognized precisely what the gypsy caller's gift had wakened in him. A horse had been wrested from her spell by his bidding, and of humans with such powers they were chary. Trionn knew pain beyond words. The dependable warmth of the cats' companionship was lost to him, reft away by an afternoon's longing that in ignorance, he had never known to fear.

In his passionate wish to keep the stallion wild, he had never guessed that desire by itself could afflict him. He raged to admit what the cats knew, and the dogs by their mindless fawning: that the caller's talents had been somehow thrown awry by his meddling. The taint of her mystery had touched him. He did not know if the fluke could be reversed. Though his lungs ached and his muscles burned, he pressed on in useless exertion. For the inevitable outcome had not altered. The kennelman was promised a carcass, and the huntsman's arrow must fly. However far Silverdown's scullion drove his body, the vision pursued and harrowed him. Still, he saw blood in the grass, the scream of the stallion's dying an echo that resounded through his mind.

Dusk found him crouched on the rise above the meadow, his forehead cradled on crossed wrists. He had decided to break down the gate, a desperate act that would ultimately not solve anything. Loose, the dun stallion was a liability. He would steal mares from all but the sturdiest paddocks, and kill any fool who interfered. In the end, he would be chased down. The archer's shot would take him, but in the open, as he ran in all his pride and splendor.

If Silverdown's scullion escaped the fury of the horse he resolved to set loose, what should befall him at the Lord's hand for presuming such interference defied imagination. In his misery over the desertion of the cats, Trionn did not care. His fretting over the stallion's fate had long since destroyed his peace; the pain of spirit he already suffered could hardly be made any worse. All that remained was to endure until the darkest hour before moonrise.

The birds quieted, and the crickets began their chorus. Above the small sounds of the night, Trionn heard the bell that summoned the field hands to supper. Past the bog he saw the glimmer of candles wastefully alight in the Lord's hall. The feast went on regardless, the gypsy's failure with the stallion no impediment to the pleasure of those highborn guests still in residence. Yet the thriftlessness of Silverdown's Lord was of little concern to Trionn. Now that he had firmed his course of action, the stillness as the stars brightened lent him a measure of peace. The Lord's riders were fanned out across the countryside in search of the vanished gypsy; patrols on the estate would be light, and widely spaced.

The gloom deepened. The breeze carried snatches of Enith's laughter. The Lord's page could be heard shouting curses at the cook, while in the gatehouse, the captain berated a dozing sentry. The cobbled yard between lay empty, most of the household settled inside at their supper. Trionn chose his moment. Sweat chilled on his body as he rose and crept downhill through mown grass toward the stallion's pasture. From a pile of cut brush left by the laborers who cleared the fields, he selected a stout branch of oak. He stripped off the bark and twigs, then hastened on toward the gate, nailed shut ever since the forgotten proclamation that the stallion might live undisturbed.

No one stopped him; no rider emerged to cry challenge.

Trionn moved in fixed purpose, too numb to acknowledge his trepidation. The gate loomed ahead, a barred silhouette against a starlit expanse of open grass. He shot his branch home between the heavy planks and the post, snatched a quick breath, and threw his shoulder into prying.

The nails were well rusted. The ones nearest the oak branch groaned and loosened, while the others stubbornly stuck fast. Dry, weathered wood resisted the strain with a crack. The stallion could not help but be drawn by the noise. Horses were curious by nature, Trionn knew; he desperately shoved all the harder, digging his toes into dew-drenched grass to keep his stance from slipping. At best he had a space of seconds before the stud cried challenge. His neigh would draw the Lord's riders. Did they catch the scullion at his meddling, they would kill him, cut him down without trial as a horse thief.

Never mind that the stud was a rogue, and the only one wronged might be the kennelman. Luck might sour for him, since as a runaway, the dun was as likely to be slain on some other noble's demesne, with the carcass claimed as spoils in compensation. The kennelman would beat any scullion till he bled, when he learned who had cheated him of fare for his hounds.

Trionn jammed his hip into the prybar until sweat stung his eyes like tears. "Go," he grunted to the groaning, giving nails. "Go!"

The rusted steel proved oblivious to pleading; heavy oak might split, but resisted breakage. Trionn thumped his fist on the gate in frustration, then set his branch to the base of the panel and hurled himself into fresh effort.

He shoved, his sinews straining in agony. The lower boards gave way in a shower of jagged splinters. Trionn shifted his prybar, any moment anticipating the rapid-fire pounding of hooves, followed up by the bone-cracking punishment of an angry stallion's teeth. He was taking far too long. Every second his struggle lasted wound his nerves to the edge of snapping. Dizzy before he realized he was inadvertently holding his breath, Trionn jerked, dragging the next nails from the post with a force fueled by terror. He needed a rest but dared not pause as he confronted the final plank.

Something bumped his shoulder. Startled, Trionn emitted a yelp that silenced the crickets. His pry branch dropped, thudding into the ground. The stud shied back on his haunches with a snort.

Horse and boy regarded one another, each one poised to run.

Trionn licked his lips. Panic held him rooted before the gapped boards of the gate. His thoughts raced with his heartbeat. Should he bend to retrieve his branch, the stud would strike and kill him; turn and flee, and he risked a ripping bite that would cripple him for life. Should he escape with the gate just half broken, his resolve would end in bleak failure.

The dun stud stamped in the starlight. His ears flicked and he shook his neck, his mane spattered like ink down his crest. He snorted again and took a tentative, interested step forward.

Trionn watched, paralyzed, as the horse shoved the loose boards with his head.

"Dear God," the scullion mouthed, astonished. Then his startlement faded as he noticed the horse's manner held no fury. A charged, unnatural shudder left him trembling to the soles of his feet.

The stallion shouldered his neck between the gap and snuffled the sleeve of Trionn's shirt. He lipped the cloth, and snorted again, messily wet in his inquisitiveness.

"Dear God," Trionn repeated, this time in a choked off whisper. His every assumption had been wrong. After all, he had not bidden the stud to assert his own savage nature; not a bit. In his colossal, scullion's ignorance, he had done worse, in fact overturned the gypsy woman's spell with a binding entirely his own.

The dun stallion that had been a killer now answered only to him.

Blindly Trionn bent, groping through dew-drenched grass for the branch he had dropped in his terror. Shaken to cold sweats, he loosened the final boards of the gate, while the stallion lipped at his hair, and blew gusty breaths in his ear. The huge creature eyed him through tangled strands of forelock as the last few nails gave way. Trionn yanked down the battered boards. "Go!" he urged, his face averted, that he need not be tormented by the absolute trust the powerful stallion placed in him. "Get out of here!"

The stud obliged by standing still.

"They'll kill you!" He waved his hands. "Run!"

A bony head banged his elbow.

"Oh, be off," Trionn cried. He stumbled back in a flummoxed fit of frustration. Never in his ugliest nightmare had he thought to guard against an assault by the mad stallion's friendliness.

Unfazed by human foibles, the horse followed, his nostrils widened in a companionable snuffle that stopped just short of a nicker. As briskly as the boy whose unwitting call had touched him could back away, the stallion strode after, unhurried, but unshakable in equine determination. Trionn belatedly understood that short of outright shouting, or a blow to the nose with a stick, nothing would drive the stud from him. The noise of his outcry would certainly bring investigation from the riders; and any blow he might strike would now be an unthinkable betrayal. The horse was no longer wild, nor tamed to any touch but Trionn's own. His dilemma over the stallion was compounded.

Bonded as he was to the horse, it was inconceivable to leave him loose to be hunted and butchered for dogmeat.

Trionn sat in the meadowgrass, glaring morosely at his boots. They were worn at the toes, unsuited for the miles of wear he was now going to have to require of them. The already tired leather would rot off his feet by wintertime, and where could he steal or beg enough coin to pay for the stallion's upkeep? Such worries were moot if he failed to hide such a distinctive and costly animal from discovery by the Lord's patrols.

The rising moon already glimmered through the trees. No time remained to restore the gate and formulate a reasonable escape. Shoved again by a warm nose, then tickled about the ears by the inquisitive stallion's lips, Trionn cursed. The horse raised his head as if puzzled.

"Well, I don't know what to do," Trionn said aloud, more words than he had used in one breath for the better part of a month.

In the end, he settled for walking. The great dun paced at his heels with no more shame than a dog might show, adoring a master who had kicked him.

"You were wild," Trionn accused bitterly. "You liked it that way, remember?"

The horse only snorted, wetting the back of his neck.

The path beyond Silverdown's back thickets stretched away through an expanse of tenant farmland. It was dusty, left rutted from the passage of the costermonger's carts that would rattle to the market before dawn. Now, when the field-hands were sleeping, and most nobles sipped wine in the comfort of candlelit halls, the way was empty, a silvered ribbon twisting away toward lands that Trionn had never dreamed of seeing. He was hungry, tired, and lost outside his corner in the kitchen where the pots and the washtub waited. He brooded as he walked, while the stallion grazed the verges, then trotted between mouthfuls of snatched grass to keep up.

At intervals he would nudge Trionn, or playfully nip at the boy's sleeves. To turn around, even once, was to acknowledge the creature's magnificence. The full impact of what had gone wrong at the moment of the gypsy witch's call left an ache of inconsolable frustration.

"I'm the last person you should trust to look after your fate," Trionn cried, exasperated.

He crossed a plank bridge, the boom of the stallion's hooves at his back a disturbance that shattered the stillness.

A rustle from behind the span, and a half-seen, fitful movement, caused the stallion to shy back. He arched his neck, ears flattened, then feinted with bared teeth toward what he saw as a threat. Startled silly, Trionn gaped as what looked like a bundle of rags extricated itself from the undergrowth.

The moonlight revealed a small woman, her manner

decidedly vexed. "By my mother's blood! It was you who turned my call!" The fury on her oval face was justified. "Why in hell's name did you do it, boy? My reputation's thoroughly ruined."

The stallion screamed and struck. Quicker than he by a hairsbreadth, the gypsy hopped the rails of the bridge, still carping. "Call him off, idiot. Before we're noticed, and find ourselves cut down for stealing."

Mistrustful of words, Trionn gave a shrug, palms up.

The woman snapped back an obscenity in the gypsy language of the hills. "You've got uncommonly strong talent, for a boy who doesn't have the faintest idea what he's doing." Her acid commentary cut off as she ducked beneath the bridge to avoid the enraged stallion's strike. As teeth lunged for her wrist, she dropped out of reach and landed mid-stream with a splash.

"Lay your hand on him," she instructed, annoyed as if she had just turned her ankle on a stone. "The horse will feel your touch, and sense through you that I mean no harm."

Trionn feared to approach the whirling mass of equine nerve and muscle that could, and had, killed men outright. But the clatter as the horse rampaged across the bridge span demanded immediate reaction. He steeled his nerve, reached out, and was startled yet again as the stallion anticipated his movement, and seemed at one with his intent. The creature settled back on all fours, curved his neck, and lipped at Trionn's fingers.

From the far side of the bridge, bedraggled and wringing wet, the gypsy woman shouldered out of the briars on the river bank. She regarded the mismatched tableau presented by the awkward, diffident boy and a stallion bred to carry princes. Her eyes turned absorbed and thoughtful, while the moonlight glinted off the water that dripped from her rags like a fall of thrown diamonds.

"You're exceptionally gifted with animals," she mused. "I expect you also know how to ride?"

Trionn cast her a look of mortified affront, and the stallion snorted warning in concert.

The gypsy witch shook her head, and busied herself wringing muddy water from her skirts. She sighed at last and straightened. Trionn received a long look that chilled his flesh, and set his knees to trembling.

A gypsy horse-caller's spells could be used on more than a beast; her voice when she finally spoke held a whetted edge of threat. "If you never dreamed of owning this horse, of riding him, why in the name of the mysteries did you wrest him from my control?"

Trionn swallowed. There would be no running away from her; he must force his throat to loosen, and his tongue to shape coherent speech. "I didn't," he blurted clumsily. "I wanted the stallion to stay wild." And unbidden, the tears started, born of shame, that he, and the last person living to crave dominion, had been the one to spoil the stallion's fiery independence.

"My mother's blood!" the gypsy swore in a voice that cracked into laughter. "You've a gift to outmatch mine, and you thought to stay a simple scullion? I suppose the cats jumped into your cradle since the moment of your birth, and nobody knew what that meant?"

Trionn nodded. He swallowed again, painfully. "I hate myself. For breaking the stallion's spirit."

The gypsy gave another breathless laugh. "You didn't. Not at all." Her brusqueness was intended to reassure, but caused Trionn a start of alarm. Dropping handfuls of wet hems, she sat down in the dust by the roadside, and rested her pointed chin in delicate, almost elfin hands. "Boy, listen to me carefully. You did not harm that horse. What you did was bond with him. He is now your best friend, and more. He is twinned to your thoughts. I will teach you what that means, but for now you must understand. You called, and he answered entirely of his own will. His wildness was won over by your depth of compassion, and that was no mean feat. Believe me in this, for I know. I also touched that horse, and the distrust in his heart was buried deep. You bested my skills through no mistake. That stud was listening for your voice to command him from the moment he was first foaled."

"But I don't understand how that happened!" Trionn cried in rising unhappiness. "And I felt your call! It was painful!"

The gypsy shouted back, "Hurtful to you, boy, because it was not pitched for your spirit!" Her manner suddenly gentled. "I know you're confused. But what counts this minute, is that the Lord of Silverdown will not pardon either of us if we're caught. He will find his rogue stallion gone, and believe that I accomplished the task I was bidden to. The dun's attack upon me in the meadow will be taken for a witch's trick, arranged to cover my escape. You must understand what you've caused, boy. I'll be blamed for the stud you called, and be hunted and hanged as a horse thief."

She did not exaggerate. Too well Trionn recalled the horsebreaker's warning to Silverdown's Lord, that were he to summon a gypsy, the stallion he desired to break would be stolen the first night after gentling. Awkwardly the scullion locked his fingers in the warmth of the horse's mane. "What's to be done? I know nothing at all beyond pot washing."

The gypsy caller sighed. "I'll become accomplice to a horse thief, after all." She shrugged, rose, and gave another of her silvery laughs. "The hangman might as well find me guilty. Still, my skills should be enough to turn the Lord's riders awry. With luck, I can hide all three of us. But I have a condition to set." She regarded the scullion and his unlikely companion, a horse so nobly proportioned, that men might try murder to possess him.

Trionn looked warily back, never before conscious of how tiny she was, and how determined. Even clad in drenched rags, she had the poised tension of a wild thing, or an owl in the moment before flight. For the first time he could recall, words came easily in the presence of another human being. "What do you ask?"

"That you learn to ride, because we're going to need to travel faster and farther than either of us can go on foot." At Trionn's scowl, she bore unmercifully on. "And you must swear to stay with me until such time as you can marshal the talent you were born to."

"That's two things," Trionn pointed out.

At his shoulder the stallion stamped.

The gypsy woman caught his eyes and compelled him to hold her gaze. "Is it yes?"

And the boy who was destined to be other than Silverdown's scullion bit his lip. Haltingly he gave his oath. When he finished, he added vehemently, "I am not a horse thief!"

To which the gypsy witch laughed as she hurried him on down the road. "As you wish, boy, but face fact. That's what your gifts make you best at."

The stallion's disappearance was years in the past, and forgotten by all but a few when the stranger arrived at Silverdown. He came to the gates just past dusk, clad in a dark dusty cloak. To the watchman who called him challenge, he gave no name. He insisted, quietly firm, that he had business with Silverdown's Lord.

"Lady," corrected the guardsman, his chin out-thrust over the pole of his halberd. "Have you no news of the folk you've traveled to visit? The Lord's been dead these five years, and his wife and one son survive him."

The stranger bowed in apology. He did not appear to be a brigand. Nor could he be mistaken for a beggar out to win a meal. He waited in the twilight with his head cocked, as if the palisade and stone gate keep were a surprise he had not expected. The buttons on his cloak were silver. He journeyed on foot by choice: at his shoulder stood a magnificent silver-dun stallion, bridleless, halterless, saddleless. Muscled and shining like high-gloss silver, the creature had the fire of a warhorse, but with significant difference. He followed the man without restraint, apparently of his own free will. Dark, equine eyes regarded the gatekeeper, who studied the horse-master in turn with searching distrust. Yet the man carried no war gear. He was, in point of fact, unarmed.

"Let me speak with the Lady, then," the stranger insisted. The timbre of his voice was persuasive, if not impossible to deny. "I will take but a minute of her time, and need not ask lodging for the night."

Much against his orders and inclination, the guard grudgingly opened the gate. The stranger strode inside. Without any visible signal, the horse flanked him stride for stride.

The pair reached the courtyard, where a tabby cat leapt up from cleaning itself. One glance at the stranger, and it fled with flattened ears and streaming tail. The stable boy who came to tend the horse was waved back.

"He will stand," insisted the man in the same voice that had placated the gate guard.

The stallion remained at liberty in the courtyard, obedient to the letter of command while his master pursued his business inside the keep. Beyond the occasional switch of his black tail, the creature might have been a statue. He raised no hoof, but laid back warning ears at the stable boys who ventured too close in admiration, and the old, half-blind master at arms whispered behind his scarred hand that despite the silver buttons on his cloak, the visitor must have a taint of gypsy blood. "At least, that stallion shows a witch's touch for a surety."

"But he had light hair," objected Enith, grown blowsy through the years since she had claimed distinction as the captain's latest conquest. "The man didn't look to me like any gypsy!"

Still regarding the horse, as if he were pricked by a memory just beyond grasp of his awareness, the armsmaster gestured in contempt. "You would see as much or as little as that man allowed, for such is the nature of his sorcery."

The discussion heated into argument, as darkness deepened over a yard left sadly gloomy by the utter absence of torchlight.

Upstairs in the hall, before trestles more scarred than he remembered, the stranger paused in the flickering firelight that spilled across the floor before the hearth. On boards scraped bare of wax or polish, he bowed in respect to the Lady. The dimness, or maybe his economy of movement made him seem at one with the shadows as he lifted a pouch from the crook of his elbow. This he placed with a clink on the table beside the embroidery she had abandoned since the last daylight had fled. He did not comment on the dearth of candles as he said, "This belongs to you."

The Lady's silk-dark eyebrows arched up. "I beg your pardon, sir? My Lord left debts, not debtors, or none that he mentioned at his death."

"This one he must have forgotten," the strange man corrected most gently. "Let me offer my condolences on your husband's passing, though we were never friends. His heir is the proper recipient. The coin in that purse is Silverdown's gold."

"Might I know what service was rendered to require such generous payment?" Piqued to curiosity, the Lady leaned forward enough that the firelight touched her. She locked trembling hands in her lap, though the gesture failed to conceal the callouses that marred her fine skin. Silverdown had fallen on hard times and yet, even as her straits were exposed to the eyes of her visitor, she did not snatch up the pouch. As if need did not demand that she count the money inside, though the fringes of her shawl were dark with tarnish, and her dress had been embroidered at the bodice to hide its past history as a cast off. Poor as Silverdown's Lady might be, her bearing never deserted her.

She carried herself regally as a queen.

Her presence was forceful enough that the stranger stood as if tongue-tied, betraying awkwardness before highborn grace. Or perhaps his diffidence stemmed from reluctance to reveal an unpleasantness between himself and the late Lord, whom very few folk had cause to love. In a musical softness that somehow did not convey the impression of grudging character, he said, "Mark the entry in your ledger as stud fees, and back payment for the purchase of a horse."

"I don't understand," said the Lady. "My Lord never stood any stallions."

Something about her smallness stirred recognition, or

maybe her careworn, homely face made him ask, "Are you the Earl of Tanemar's daughter?"

Startled to an intake of breath, she admitted, "I am." Since her father had fallen out of favor with the King, not many cared to mention his name with kindness.

"Then," said the stranger in sweet courtesy, "ask his grace the Duke of the blue-dun stud he was promised as a gift when your late Lord aspired to become your bridegroom."

The Lady glanced aside too quickly. "I can't," she admitted after a difficult pause. "My father has been imprisoned. The fine to secure his freedom is more than my brother or I have in our powers to pay."

But politics and the feuding of the highborn lay outside this stranger's concern. His silence grew prolonged. When the Lady at last sought to prompt him, she discovered the chamber left empty. Her elusive visitor had departed. Only the pouch on the table remained as proof of his presence.

The coins inside were heavy gold, and the full count of them, a miracle. When the Silverdown's ancient steward checked on his mistress hours later, he found the Lady silently weeping. A shining spill of coins lay in her lap, and in sparkling piles around her feet.

Months later, Silverdown's Lady did the stranger's bidding for more reason than to ease her curiosity. She did not inquire of her father, for the Duke became irritable at reminder that Silverdown's gold had bought his reprieve from the King. The tale was recounted by the butcher, of a man-killing stallion that had been stolen on the same night as a scullion, mistakenly called dumb, and a half-wit, had disappeared without trace from the estate.

"He was a shirker, a sneak, and a liar, too," the butcher vehemently summed up.

The Lady frowned. "I thought you said he could not speak?"

"Well, not entirely," the butcher allowed. He stroked his unshaven chin. "Trionn never talked to anybody, a queer enough habit to have. He wasn't the sort to care about repayment of a debt. He stole my best blade, you know, the same day he took off with the stallion."

The Lady tucked a fallen strand of hair underneath the edge of her hood. "You got the knife back?" she asked outright.

The butcher shrugged, then nodded. "One of the servants caught him crossing the open yard. He never said what he'd intended to do with it," this last, on a note of self-defense.

Silverdown's Lady gave back no reproach beyond a sigh. "From the look on your face, I'd expect that nobody ever asked him." She reflected a moment on the gold, the value of which added up to a surprising fortune. The man who had repaid the coin, and then gone his way after scarcely a dozen words, had left wealth enough to buy out the estate and its lands, twice over; the irony of that raised a mystery. As if the fortune itself had been the pittance, and the principle behind, the tie to conscience. "If I were to guess," the Lady ventured, "I should say that none of you knew the boy."

The butcher's only answer was a mutter that may have masked contempt.

Alone in the cut of the wind through the yard, the Lady huddled into her cloak. Fiercely, and for the rest of her days, she regretted her well-bred restraint. Too late she wished she had asked the strange visitor to stay, or at least to take a light supper. He may not have been comfortable telling about himself, but perhaps she might have learned more about the horse that had restored her to fortune and future.

Double Blind

The encounter happened entirely without warning, in the thick of battle at Dead Star 31. As if by design, the Fleet's most junior lieutenant sat drumming his fingers at the controls of a state-of-the-art Fleet scoutship. Light from the monitors silvered his aristocratic profile, which expressed bitterness, frustration, and longing. The scout craft *Shearborn* was commissioned as a chaser, handily styled for concealment. She carried just two plasma cannon. Hit and run, or follow and hide, had been her designer's intentions; "mop-up following engagement" read the bottom line in her battle orders. Last month, even yesterday, Commander Jensen had burned for a small part in the Alliance offensive at Dead Star 31. Today, while others were earning advancement and citations of valor for crippling the new Khalian dreadnoughts, he ached for action.

The firing studs so near his tapping fingers were dandy, except there were never going to be enough of them to satisfy the ambition that smoldered beneath the lieutenant's faultlessly correct Fleet bearing.

Across the cockpit, Harris slouched in the untidy gray of his pilot's coveralls. The wing patch at his shoulder crumpled under his fingers as he scratched himself, paused, then whistled as if at a woman. "What the hell?" His eyes widened, bright with the reflected flashes of battle off the analog screens.

Jensen spoke frostily from his crew chair. "Have you something to report?"

The pilot raised his eyebrows at the reprimand. His most insolent grin followed, as he banged a key for redefinition, then added in lilting admiration, "What the blazes is a tub-engined private hauler doing blasting ass across a battle?"

Narrow-eyed and intense, Jensen regarded the offending speck on the screens, hedged now by flashes of plasma fire as she sliced through warring factions of Khalian and Fleet dreadnoughts. Overhead, the monitor on citizen's frequency blared a curse and a startled challenge; the tone of the officer who hailed the offending merchanter matched that of Harris, exactly.

As the civilian vessel continued to hurtle across the lines, a prickle of intuition touched Jensen. His gut went cold and his fingers clenched. "That's nobody's merchanter."

He keyed his board for more data. At once the craft's configuration flashed in design graph on his screen, ugly and ungainly as a toy assembled by a kid from unassuming bits of junk. Recognition struck Jensen like a blow to the vitals. He knew that craft, would remember her anywhere, from any angle, even to his dying moment. What could the *Marity* be doing carving a line across a Fleet offensive? It meant nothing but the worst sort of trouble; her captain happened to be the craftiest skip-runner in the Alliance.

Harris stared, captivated at the analog screens. "Bugger, that pilot's got the gift. Will you look at that evasion?"

Jensen needed no proof of the *Marity*'s maneuverability. He had personally experienced MacKenzie James's corkscrew style at the helm. Recall left the young officer sweating, not out of nerves but in memory of the aftermath, and a degrading depth of humility a proud man would kill to erase. Jensen reacted this time without thought. "Follow him."

Harris looked up from the screens. Blank with incomprehension, he said, *"What? Are you brain-shocked?* That guy's Weasel steaks in the making, mate. He's ducked into the Khalian lines."

"I saw." Jensen turned his chair away. "I ordered a chase on that hauler. Section seven, bylaw four sixty two point zero, punishment for insubordination—"

"Court-martial, followed by death without appeal at conviction. I know." Harris flipped off his pilot's beret and scratched his red-thatched scalp. The hair sprang in snarls beneath his fingers. Challenge lit his eyes, which were blue, and about as innocent as a thief's. "Your faith in my ability is a compliment, mate. What I'd kiss fish to guess, is what excuse you've got ready for old by-the-book and his-grandpa's-an-admiral Meier. Because if your joyride doesn't get us slagged by Weasels, the commodore's surely going to sling your ass on a plate. Remember section seven, bylaw four sixty five point one, punishment for disregard of standing battle orders and leaving assigned position?"

Jensen said nothing. He sat straight in his chair, his hair was like combed ebony, and his fingernails trimmed short like a model's. Harris pressed switches and sequenced the *Shearborn*'s condenser coils into recharge for FTL. Then Jensen fussed with the adjustment of his chair belts, as Harris shrugged, punched up the gravity drive, and wrenched their little chaser out of Station.

Immediate protest issued from the ship-to-ship com speaker mounted above the controls.

"Commodore Meier, howling for both your balls," surmised Harris. His fingers hesitated ever so slightly above the flight board.

"Just carry on!" Jensen tripped a switch, and the angry voice of their superior became buried in background noise as the power banks gunned maximum thrust into the engines.

Harris grinned in that cocksure manner indigenous to

pilots. Skill of his caliber was too scarce to waste; when the boom came down, he could count on some measure of immunity.

Against the wrath of irate brass, Junior Grade Lieutenant Michael Christopher Jensen, Jr., had only the far-reaching influence of his politician father; if, that was, Jensen senior chose to bend his public stance of calling no favors for his son. Harris preferred to believe that paternal sentiment would prevail as he spun the chaser in a neat turn and opened throttle.

The lieutenant in command knew otherwise. Heart pounding, Jensen expected that hell would freeze before his family would bail him out of trouble. It had been his father's imperiousness about carving his fortune on his own that had tangled his fate with that of the skip-runner captain in the first place. The *Shearborn*'s pursuit simply resumed unfinished business.

Vigorous protest arose right on schedule. Commodore Abe Meier's voice barked angrily on emergency interrupt. "I'll have your officer's bars, boy, and a mark for desertion on your record that even God can't erase."

Slammed back into his crew chair by inertia, Jensen laced his fingers to stop their shaking. No threat could make him reconsider; by now, their course was committed. Harris's cocky grin was gone, dissolved into a frown of sweaty concentration.

"Snarking game of live pool," the pilot murmured, and intently slapped a control.

The *Shearborn* veered, narrowly missing the expanding nebulosity of a plasma burst vessel. Debris pattered against the hull, and something clanged against the port gun housing. Then they were past and screaming a tortuous course through the flank of the Fleet offensive.

Jensen barely noted the glittering bursts of fire on the analog screens. Harris's wizardry at the helm escaped him utterly. He saw only the white streak that was the *Marity*, twisting now with the immunity of a miracle through the thick of the Khalian fleet. Dead Star lay beyond, a disk sharp as a compass cut through a backdrop of scattered stars. As if that dark body were a magnet, MacKenzie James steered his craft for the core.

"Crazy," Harris muttered over the scream of the gravity drive. "Slag his coils for sure, if he doesn't slow down to shed heat."

Jensen sweated with his uniform fastened to the chin. The course Mac James had chosen was too predictable not to be deliberate. The lieutenant reaffirmed his intent to capture the space pirate. No price was too great to see the *Marity*'s captain brought to justice. "Don't lose him, Harris."

The pilot half spun from the controls. "I won't melt down an engine for anybody's pleasure, *sir*. Not to capture the devil himself."

Jensen knew *Marity*'s master was the devil incarnate. His shout for Harris to continue was cut off by the rising wail of the proximity alarm.

The pilot shrugged, stabbed the switch to raise the chaser's shields. The alarms went silent. Seated like a stone image and half-lighted by the angry yellow glitter of the monitors, he continued his silence, clearly challenging his superior to pull rank.

Jensen refused argument. Ruled by the need to evade the fire of Fleet and foe alike, Harris could not abandon their new course all at once; and a slight change on the analog screens offered a telling reason why the *Shearborn* should continue.

Absorbed with planning an evasive maneuver, Harris took longer to notice that the *Marity* appeared to be braking. If the skip-runner captain who flew her intended to slip pursuit, deceleration cost him the chance. Past Dead Star and the forefront of the battle lines, the Fleet chaser would be on him like a wasp.

Mac James never made stupid misjudgments.

Convinced that he witnessed the power lag as the *Marity* charged her coils for FTL, Jensen grinned with a candor normally kept hidden. The *Shearborn* was newly commissioned; fitted with gadgetry hot off the design boards, she was capable of following her targets through

FTL. "Harris, close in tight. We're going to trace the *Marity*'s ion trail."

"Just a snarking minute!" The pilot shot a glare at his superior. Giving a skip-runner chase across a battle line was a lark he could boast of to buddies, a daredevil affirmation of skills that might bring the customary slap on the wrist for high jinks that tradition accorded a gifted pilot. Deserting the scene of a battle was another thing, a speed-class ticket to court-martial and a firing squad. Left grouchy by the risks just taken, Harris ended with a gesture that brooked no argument. "Forget it, sonny."

Jensen's amusement vanished. His obsidian eyes never left the analog screen, where a tiny fleck of light winked into being. It blinked once, then steadied onto a vector that bent gently and matched course with the *Shearborn*. The lieutenant keyed for additional data and almost laughed outright in satisfaction. "We've picked up a stalker mine," he announced. Even his recalcitrant pilot must now bow to expediency; the only effective evasion was to transit to FTL before the missile closed.

Harris scanned the readout without alarm. "Stalker mine's a damned lousy reason to go AWOL, sir, when we carry the coded disarm frequency."

"For Fleet any offensive," Jensen responded. He sounded smug. "This one's manufactured by the Freeborn. Check your screen, pilot, only do it fast. If you hesitate, *Marity* escapes, and we get convicted posthumously."

Harris shot a withering glare, fingers flying over the controls. "What's Freeborn hardware doing crapping up this sector, anyway? It might just get us killed."

Jensen answered with a confidence born of ruthless networking. "Fleet intelligence scoped a Freeborn plot to slam the Khalian rear wave. But the codes for rebel stalkers weren't part of the package."

Harris cursed. Jensen's explanation made no sense whatever; since secession from the Alliance, the Freeborn were hostile to the Fleet. But dispute of the fine points made a fool's errand. The damnable fact remained: a

stalker mine of enemy manufacture had locked onto the
Shearborn as a target. Either Harris abetted Jensen's crazi-
ness and punched into FTL, or two million credits' worth
of chaser got cremated. The reasonable alternative was to
commit desertion in pursuit of a recognized criminal,
except that the pilot would need to fly a course like
macramé to make transit before the stalker took the
Shearborn out.

Harris tripped the controls with an attitude of reckless abandon. Spun hard against her limits, his spacecraft
flexed and groaned under the stresses of centrifugal force.
As a grade-one test pilot, Harris had survived a lot of mis-
takes; he had a sixth sense for gauging tolerances. The
chaser might protest, might develop a stress shear or two,
but her tail pins would stay tight as she twisted and spun
to gain distance from the less maneuverable mine. Harris
caressed the machinery, wooing the electronics as he
would a lady; the wail of the alarms and the digital display
showing the stalker's course of intercept made him itch, as
if the hot breath of the hardware fanned the back of his
neck.

Jensen followed only the skip-runner ship that drifted
like a lopsided jewel at the rim of Dead Star's disk.
Apparently nerveless, he cared for nothing beyond the
moment when *Marity*'s image flashed and vanished from
the analog screens.

By then *Shearborn* was barely inside the requisite
radius for an ion trail fix, with the stalker closing fast.

A green sequence of numbers flooded the navigational
screen. Harris waited a panicky moment for resolution of a
course readout. When the figure stabilized, he hammered
the lever down and blew a kiss in sheer relief. Never in life
had he been happier to suffer the queer hesitation in continuity that marked the transit to FTL. He blinked, elated
that no explosion had erased his existence. The next
instant, triumph died, quenched by the realities of the
moment. Harris unclipped his seat restraints and rounded
angrily on his superior.

"Snarking hell, Jensen. You damned near got us

roasted. You knew Freeborn stalkers were loose out there! For that I'd like to push your face in. I wonder if you understand how close we came to being ionized?"

Jensen swung his crew chair from the screens. His dark eyes showed not the slightest trace of regret. "Try to remember how close," he said. "If you lose *Marity* on me, that stalker mine will be the only excuse we have to offer at our defense briefing."

"And may you shrivel in front of the ladies for that," snapped Harris. He wanted a drink, and a chance to take a leak in real gravity. What began as a lark had turned seriously sour; until the sensors signaled *Marity*'s transit from FTL, nothing remained but to wait and brood, because certainly no sane man was going to fathom the intentions of Lieutenant Jensen.

The transit lasted days. Harris slept, or banged about in the chaser's tiny galley unearthing the beer he had stashed where he swore no Fleet inspector would check, never mind that access to his cache took most of his off-watch time. He needed his comforts. A man couldn't get booze in detention; to Harris's thinking that was precisely where *Shearborn*'s hare-brained officers would be headed.

"Autolog won't lie for us," he carped when the lieutenant in command crossed paths with him at meal time.

Jensen refused to debate.

Harris parked the heels of his boots on the table and cradled his mug, which untruthfully read coffee, between his knees. But even a barbarity of this magnitude provoked no reaction. Nettled by the lieutenant's secretive silence, the pilot added, "A leap this long could send us clear to Halpern's." Which was about as far from Khalian raid sites as a ship could go, and stay within charted Alliance space. "You better think up a very fancy alibi."

Jensen sat down opposite, drank his orange juice in chilly stillness. His uniform looked as if he had just stepped off parade. No stubble shadowed his chin. Just when had he taken time to groom? Harris wondered. Since the jump to FTL, the man had done little else but pace before the analog's blank screen, brooding over the unguessable motives of *Marity*'s skip-runner captain.

Despite such fanatical vigilance, the tracking alarm caught *Shearborn*'s crew of two napping. Harris shambled from his bunk, stretching like a bear and complaining of a hangover. As always, he slept in his uniform. Jensen had not. He bolted without ceremony from his berth, clad in fleur-de-lis pajamas that looked like they had been starched with his uniforms.

"You guessed right," he announced when Harris reached the bridge. "*Marity* broke light speed in Halpern's Sector." He flicked irritably at his uncombed hair and killed the FTL drives. The *Shearborn* abruptly ended transit, underwent that unnerving blurring of edges that heralded return to analog navigation.

Harris winced as his hangover flared in sympathy. Once reality stabilized, he laid his cheek against the cowling of the companionway and muttered something concerning martyrs and zealously sober commanders.

Jensen ignored the comment, fingers drumming impatience while the sensors assimilated data and the screens flashed to life.

Visual display revealed the dim red disk of a dwarf star, a strangling haze of interstellar dust, and no immediate reason for *Marity*'s choice of destination. Jensen chewed his lip. "Why should a planetless star in Halpern's interest MacKenzie James?"

Harris pitched himself into the pilot's chair, his coveralls halfway unfastened. He studied the readouts, then shot his companion a look of surprise. "That's Cassix's star." The lieutenant continued to look blank, which proved to a certainty that his source network had not included scientists. Harris explained. "Any test pilot knows. That's the site of Fleet's classified orbital R&D lab—the deep-space flight-and-weapons division, where the fancy new gadgetry gets prototyped. Security like a church vault, though. A skip-runner shouldn't be able to get close."

But along with gunrunning, MacKenzie James's specialty was trafficking military secrets; he'd stolen records from Fleet Base once and gotten away clean. Uncomfortably, Jensen considered implications. The skip-runner was a dangerously subtle man. If the *Shearborn*'s crew caught him attempting a raid upon the Cassix base, they would instantly become heroes.

Jensen thought quickly. "Where's *Marity*? Have we still got a fix on her?"

Harris raised his brows with dry sarcasm. "You haven't looked through the tail port?"

Jensen did so, and colored as if caught in a gaffe. The *Marity* drifted off the *Shearborn*'s stern, so close that the scuffs of every careless docking could be counted in her paint. To the last worn strut, the craft looked her part; that of a privately owned, hard-run cargo carrier that had suffered and survived a succession of mediocre pilots. Scratches to the contrary, the man at the *Marity*'s helm had to be Harris's equal or better to have achieved her present position with such delicacy. The chaser's most sensitive motion detectors had tripped no alarm.

"Serves you right for leaving FTL without taking precautions," muttered Harris. "That merchanter's inside our shield perimeter. If Mac James is inside, he's certainly laughing his tail off."

Yet Jensen surmised that the truth was very different. MacKenzie James had a smile like crystallized antifreeze; his eyes could be unnervingly direct, but no man in Fleet uniform had ever known the skip-runner captain to laugh.

When the *Shearborn*'s lieutenant offered neither comment nor orders, Harris's annoyance shifted to suspicion. "Why should a criminal of Mac James's reputation lure us out here in the first place? I say you've played right into this skip-runner's hands. Or did you maybe agree to collaborate with him beforehand?"

Jensen spun from the analog screen, furious. Whatever

rejoinder he intended never left his lips. That instant the communications speaker crackled crisply to life.

"Godfrey, but you boys like to bicker," drawled a voice. The accent was vague and untraceable, trademark of any operation engineered by MacKenzie James. Harris swore in astonishment, that any skip-runner alive should brazenly commandeer a monitored Fleet com band. Across the compartment, Lieutenant Jensen went threateningly still and cold.

Incisive as always, the skip-runner captain resumed. "If your pilot can fly covert, and if between you the initiative can be gathered to eavesdrop on local transmissions, you'll discover a terrorist action in progress. The director of research on Cassix is being coerced into breach of Alliance security. Now it happens that the *Shearborn* is the only armed vessel on patrol in this system. You'd better prepare to intervene, because your course log can't be erased, and your careers will both be stewed if you can't justify your precipitous withdrawal at Dead Star."

Harris slammed a fist into his crew chair and wished he could kick flesh. "Well, happy snarking holiday! Just who in hell does that arrogant sonuvabitch think to impress?"

But MacKenzie James returned no rejoinder. The *Marity* vanished, dissolved from continuum into FTL, leaving the *Shearborn* drifting unprepared. The instruments which flagged ion trails were not yet reset; neither Fleet officer had thought that a necessity, since every current theory assured them that the departure of the skip-runner's craft should not have happened solo. Within such close proximity, *Shearborn* should have been swept along as the coil fields collapsed. Yet *Marity* went FTL without a flicker of protest from the instruments.

"We've lost him." Harris lifted his opened hands, his light eyes bright with disbelief. "That rumor must be true, then. The bastard buys technology from outside."

"Maybe something an Indie found," Harris speculated.

But the whys and hows of *Marity*'s systems were suddenly the least of the issue. Hunched in the command chair with a frown of obsessed concentration, Lieutenant Jensen rose to the challenge. Cassix Station lay on the far side of the dwarf sun from their current position. If a raid were in progress, and if skip-running instigators had jammed communication by translink, they would be forced to coordinate their operation through local transmission. Temporarily they would be blind to more sophisticated sensory data, which meant everything scoped by deflection imagery. The *Shearborn* was shadowed by Cassix's star. She would not yet be noticed; but to stay that way and eavesdrop on the terrorists, she would have to launch a probe to relay signals from the dwarf's far side. Crisply, Jensen listed orders.

His pilot responded with indignant disbelief. "You aren't going to believe that criminal!"

"I never knew him to lie." Jensen gestured with extreme irritation. "Carry on."

Harris fastened the front of his uniform with uncharacteristic care, then entered the codes for navigation access. "Well, the society releases on the news bulletins don't cite that guy for humanitarian idealism. If I wore the stripes on your jacket, I'd be wondering what's in this for MacKenzie James."

But that was the uncomfortable question Jensen dared not ask. He had sworn to escape his father's shadow by outwitting and bringing to justice the most-wanted criminal ever to work Alliance space. For that he would have to beat the skip-runner at his own game, and the necessary first step was to play along. Jensen said, "I want surveillance on that station, and quickly. Secure trajectory data and sequence ignition for launch of a relay probe."

Harris could be strikingly inefficient when pressed against his will. But driven now by pique, and a morbid desire to humor Jensen until the young officer screwed himself through the folly of his own arrogance, the pilot donned his headset and applied himself to the navigation console.

The probe launched with a minimum of kick. No trail

showed on the monitors. Satisfied only momentarily, Jensen hastened off the bridge to don his uniform before his coveted data started to arrive.

Harris bided the interval by plucking loose threads from the cuff of his coveralls. Upon Jensen's return, he had fallen asleep in his headset, his large hands loose in his lap, and his mouth open with snoring.

The *Shearborn*'s officer in command spared no attention for annoyance. Tracking monitors showed the relay probe carving a wide parabola around Cassix's star. The moment the light flashed green on the signal board, Jensen reached without ceremony and stripped the headset from his pilot. Harris woke with his customary hair-trigger reflexes and banged his head on the bulkhead as he rocketed out of his chair.

"Damn you," he growled at Jensen.

Finding his fanatical commander absorbed by the new transmission, Harris stalked off to the galley.

He came back after an interval, munching a dessert bar. Jensen had already assembled details enough to confirm MacKenzie James's assessment. Harris stopped chewing as his senior recited the facts.

Trouble had found opening because the fleet which normally patrolled Cassix had been pared down to one ship, in support of the offensive at Dead Star. That cruiser had fallen to skip-runners who by long-range design had kidnapped the director of research's two infant daughters from an earlier raid on a passenger vessel.

"A straightforward case," Jensen reported, "except for their bent for terrorism. The bastards killed the director's wife to prove themselves capable. The two little girls they hold hostage will be spared, provided the staff at Cassix surrenders a working prototype of the new laser weapons system."

Harris stood for a moment, crumbs from his snack falling unnoticed down his chin. For once his blue eyes were direct. "Who hired the talent for this? Indies? Junk freighters equipped with that scale of armament could make for a very ugly mess."

"Indies, or rebels, or some independent faction who

buys through skip-runners, does it matter?" Jensen yanked off the headset, then reflexively smoothed his hair. "I want data on that station, as quickly as you can manage."

Harris sank mechanically in his crew chair. He shoved his last bite of cookie in his mouth by reflex, while the headset between his hands repeated in precise and ugly detail just what would happen to the director's little daughters if the terms of their kidnappers were not met. He swallowed with difficulty, for his mouth had gone dry. "I can't," he said finally. "The specs on Cassix Station are one hundred percent classified."

"But you flew test runs there," Jensen argued. Mac James had offered him a challenge he intended to win; and as a Fleet officer his duty was explicitly clear. "Reconstruct what you can from memory. The skip-runners intend to exchange the children for the weapons system by cargo cable at 2000 hours, which leaves us very little margin to prepare."

Harris looked up sharply. "Cargo cable? We have a chance, then. Security might be recovered, but only if we write off the lives of two kids."

"Just carry on!" Jensen added no promises. Ruthless as his choice seemed, in this case Harris knew the young officer was not playing for heroics. If the weapons system currently in development at Cassix fell into Indie hands, far more than two little girls would suffer.

The *Shearborn* prepared for intervention. Jensen activated the cloaking devices and ran checks on shields and weapons. Harris applied himself to navigation and mapped a course calculated to conceal their approach behind the mass of Cassix's star until the last possible moment. Neither man spoke. Harris held single-mindedly to duty for reasons of conscience; Jensen's penchant for advancement promised that his record in a crisis must be impeccable.

Presently, the *Shearborn* hurtled on a meticulously arranged course around Cassix's star. At the precise instant she crossed into scanner range, Harris kicked the attitude thrusters, killed her drives, and made a face as the snack in his stomach danced flip-flops to the pull of inertia. Tumbling with the random majesty of an uncaptured asteroid, the scout craft he piloted went dead to observation.

"Nice work," said Jensen. Awkwardly stiff in his command chair, he smiled. Their timing was perfect, a clean thirty minutes before the scheduled exchange between skiprunners and station. As the scopes resolved data, the lieutenant leaned anxiously forward. He expected the spider-armed sprawl of an orbital station, gravity powered, and glittering with the lights of habitation.

What he saw was deep-space darkness, scattered with distant stars.

His blank-faced dismay raised laughter from Harris. "Well, what do you want for a security installation? Billboard lights and a docking beacon?"

Jensen shut his eyes, opened them, and tried not to blush at his foolishness. Like the chaser he commanded, Cassix Station would be surfaced in camouflage. The complex would be dark except for lighted pinpricks that simulated stars. Her deep-space side would be painted in reflective, and unless a ship chanced to cross her orbital plane and catch her in occultation with her parent star, she would be invisible to passing traffic.

Jensen bridled rising annoyance. He dared not use the *Shearborn*'s fancy surveillance equipment. Without knowing how sophisticated his adversary's gear might be, he must assume that deflection beam interference would warn an already wary skip-runner that his activities had drawn Fleet notice. There were other ways to locate an orbiting body. The simplest involved time-sequence imaging, then a comparison of star fields to determine which objects were artificial by drift; except time was the one most glaring commodity this blitz operation lacked.

"There," Harris said suddenly, startlingly loud in the silence. "I've got a fix on the target."

His experienced eyes had spotted the skip-runner craft. A flat flash of reflection confirmed his sighting, as a shiny surface on her hull caught reflection from the dwarf

star. Jensen turned up the resolution enhancer on the analog screen. Though his pilot patiently informed him that
the hardware would not perform under *Shearborn*'s errati-
cally violent motion, the lieutenant continued searching
until his eyes burned.

Hope of coherent conversation seemed nonexistent;
Harris shrugged and made a show of initiating a star-field
comparison search. Lights flickered on the control panels as
computer circuitry normally reserved for navigation diverted
to speed his results. The pilot laced blunt hands in his lap.
Wearing the cynical expression he practiced for women who
pressed him for marriage, he stretched back in his crew
chair, adjusted his headset, and wished he could watch a
porn tape. Sex was a better sweat than listening to the terse
exchange between a desperate parent and an equally nervous
skip-runner who doubtlessly wondered whether any Indie
contract was worth taking risks of this magnitude.

Suddenly Harris shot upright, the mockery gone from
his face. "Sir, your plan won't work."

Jensen held his focus on the analog screens, where,
faint against the deep of space, a spider-filament of cable
arced out, then ever so gradually drew taut.

"They're sending the babies down, linked to a timed
explosive," Harris continued vehemently.

This time Jensen answered, very bleak. "Linked?
How? To the carrier capsule, or the cable itself?"

Harris listened. "Cable," he replied after a moment.
"The detonation code will be kept by the skip-runner.
Which means the scum will skip system, leaving station
personnel fifty-five seconds to reel that capsule in and cut
those kids free before the charge goes off."

Jensen became very still.

Harris showed a rare mix of deference and regret. "I'm
afraid we're shut down, sir. Best we can do is record data
that might help an undercover agent round them up."

"Which will be impossible to manage, not before the
Indies have replicated that laser design." All nerves and anger,
Jensen flexed the fingers of his right hand. "I'll shoot out the
cable link between the explosive and that capsule, first."

Harris grinned, sarcasm restored. "Boy, we're in problems up to our nuts already. Brass won't award a winning ticket for blowing two babies to bits. You'd have to be marksman elite to maybe hit that cable at all, far less the connecting link between a carry capsule and an explosive charge."

Jensen returned a nasty smile, then drew a chain from his collar. He dangled before his pilot's insolent gaze a medallion of skill that not one man in ten thousand held the privilege to wear.

"Shit," said Harris. "How was I to guess?"

"You couldn't," Jensen shot back. He was the youngest, by nearly a decade, ever to obtain the premier marksman's rating, but this once pride did not prompt his temper. The mission chronometer by his elbow advanced another fraction. A margin of minutes remained if the *Shearborn* was to foil the kidnappers.

The problems ahead were formidable, as Harris was quick to point out. "You can't hit that small a target without an attitude adjustment. *Shearborn*'s still tumbling, remember?" The pilot slashed a finger beneath his chin in graphic pantomime. "We break cover, and the little girls die. We're shot down the second we fire our gravity drives."

Jensen made contingency for that. "We wait," he said, an intensity about him that Harris had never seen. "After station personnel cable the plans up to the terrorists, the kids start down in the capsule. We stabilize our attitude then. Surprise will be in our favor. I shoot out the linkup. The kids and the charge are in freefall but recoiling away from the break in the line. Station personnel will reel the babies in, bet on that. And with an enabled charge drifting back toward its point of origin, the skip-runners will have their hands full cutting loose that trailing cable. That gives maybe ten seconds for us to blast their ugly presence out of space."

"Clever." Harris scratched his chest in that thoughtful manner his drinking cronies would have recognized for a warning. "But your range is extreme. You haven't allowed for drift, or for the proximity of Cassix's star. Gravity will pull your shot off target."

Jensen reached out, gently smoothed the wing insignia on his pilot's coveralls. "That's where your part comes. You'll plot my aiming point. If my shot were treated as an exercise in drive ballistics, you and that computer would have no trouble getting it right."

Harris felt sweat spring beneath his collar. The accuracy required would likely be past the limits of the technology. Though the more brilliant pilots did such things in the course of test-flight emergencies, this was another matter. A man had no business risking the lives of two little girls to instinct, the reflexive style of hunch which routinely carried a badly drawn design through without mishap. Harris had no grounds—but his wilder nature was piqued. Here was a daredevil stunt like no other; if he pulled it off, there would be accolades.

Harris set steady hands to the keyboard. "Give me the specs on your pellet rifle, and may the god of foolish ventures smile on us both."

Jensen grinned for the first time since the start of the operation. Whatever queer challenge MacKenzie James had handed the crew of the Fleet chaser *Shearborn*, one of his skip-running brethren was about to get hammered out of space.

The inner lining of the pressure suit wicked away the sweat from Jensen's skin. Doused alternately in shadow, then the burnished, bloody glare of Cassix's star, he belted himself into the service niche by the forward air lock. The state-of-the-art gauss rifle cradled on his arm hindered his movements very little. The *Shearborn* tumbled dizzily underneath him. Yet in null gravity, as long as Jensen did not fix on the scenery, the radical attitude of the hull did not disorient him. Any nerves and tension he suffered stemmed from the unrevealed motives of MacKenzie James. That point preoccupied the lieutenant to the exclusion of all else. The children and the laser prototypes

Jensen currently jeopardized his career to save had become prizes in a ritualized duel of wits.

Jensen checked the time. The suit chronometer read 2012. By now, the crate with the laser prototype lay in skip-runner hands. During the ascent, the speed of the cable's drive motor had been measured and recorded into Harris's flight computer. The lieutenant braced his rifle . . . and waited.

In the darkness beyond Cassix, the lift motor hummed and reversed. Cable turned through frictionless gears, and a capsule bearing two children and an attached packet of condensed explosive began the kilometer-long transit toward the waiting arms of the father. Harris finalized his calculations.

The chronometer read 2026. A buzzer trilled in Jensen's helmet, and the pilot's voice read off coordinates.

Precisely on signal, the *Shearborn*'s gravity drives kicked over. Centrifugal force slammed the lieutenant against his belt restraints; stars spun like a pinwheel around him as the *Shearborn*'s attitude corrected with vicious and vengeful precision, compliments of pilot Harris in sharpest form.

The scout craft stabilized.

The parting kick of inertia was punishingly severe. Jensen's helmet struck the hull with a clang that made his ears ring. His head spun sickeningly and he cursed. If his vertigo did not stabilize fast, he would be unable to orient and take aim. Obstinacy born of exhaustive practice allowed him to slot the rifle stock into the connector which linked to the suit's visual display. At a second signal, he switched on the targeting scope.

On the *Shearborn*'s bridge, the monitors would be screaming, one red alleyway of warning lights as the skip-runner ship trained weapons on the chaser which dared an intervention. Both ships had their screens down. On Cassix Station, speakers blared as personnel shouted in dismay . . . too late. The integrity of the exchange they had promised the skip-runner was disrupted now past mending. No last-minute plea would convince a ruthless band of criminals that this rescue had not been betrayal. A father wept while a skip-runner's mate with shaking hands stabbed the detonation codes into a keypad. All men waited—one of them grim and another in tearful anguish. In under sixty seconds the silvery capsule on the cargo cable would explode in a coruscation of light.

Jensen raised his gauss rifle in the absolute silence of vacuum. With a clear head he locked the targeting scope onto coordinates, then cool-handedly squeezed the trigger.

The rifle kicked. Very far off, tiny to insignificance, a pinpoint of light crawled along a fragile thread of cable. The pellet which raced to intercept sped unhindered through vacuum, its course bent gently by the pull of a red dwarf star.

Sweating freely now, Jensen counted seconds—five, six—the marking tone sounded a final time. The lieutenant gripped hard to the combing. The reflective markers on the cable glistened like dewdrops poised on spider silk. By now, the magnetized pellet should have cut through. Jensen felt an ache in his chest. Along with the possibility of defeat, he realized at some point that he had stopped breathing.

Then the cable parted. Jensen shouted in relief as the tiny fleck that was the children's capsule drifted in a graceful arc against the stars.

A flash answered almost immediately, as the skip-runner ship fired gravity engines. The technician in her hold abandoned his keypad. Cursing and furious, he wrestled into a pressure suit, desperate to free the locking clamp that secured the trailing cable that now rebounded treacherously under recoil. Jensen's marksmanship had brought havoc, for now the fully enabled plasma charge drifted straight for the kidnapper's cargo bay.

"Now, Harris, now," shouted Jensen.

His helmet went black. Reflex shielding protected his vision as Harris manned the weaponry, and both of the *Shearborn*'s cannons opened fire.

The helmet's shielding stayed opaque for a long and maddening interval. Jensen fidgeted like a child, cursed like a dock worker. His visor cleared finally to reveal a spreading, glowing curtain of debris that had once been a skip-runner ship. The moment warmed like vintage wine. Jensen smiled. He stroked his rifle like the thigh of a naked woman and said softly, very softly, "Up yours, MacKenzie James."

Jensen tugged the sleeve of his dress whites from the grasp of yet another congratulatory technician. The lieutenant had received a hero's welcome the moment the *Shearborn* touched the dock. Every member of Cassix Station personnel had come forward. They had shaken his hand, thanked him, and insisted upon an impromptu reception to meet the key administrators.

"Just coincidence we happened into this sector at all," Jensen said in answer to the technician's question, the same question he had repeatedly fielded over a three-hour supply of coffee and cakes. "The *Shearborn* was in pursuit of another suspect. Yes, that one got away, but his escape turned out to be fortunate. No Fleet scout would have entered this system if that chase hadn't gone sour. Yes, it was risky to shoot out that cable, but the children were unharmed. Now, if you'll excuse me? I've a promise to keep." He hefted the gilt-papered bottle he had cadged for his pilot. An unwilling victim of regulations, Harris had been forced to remain on duty aboard the scout.

The technician smiled and shook hands again. "You're a brave young man, sir, and a pride to the Fleet. You've saved the Alliance more than you know by keeping those weapon prototypes from the Indies."

Jensen smiled back, raised the bottle apologetically, then dodged another wave of admirers. Any other time the lieutenant would have reveled in public adulation; but not here, not now. A most telling question remained unanswered, one detail left loose to rasp his nerves. MacKenzie James was nobody's humanitarian. A criminal of his caliber was unlikely to act out of pity for a father's little girls. Jensen dared not consider the incident finished until he was back at his post on the *Shearborn* and out of the Cassix system altogether. The fact that Harris could not share the celebration became his only excuse to slip away.

The docking hangar was very dark. After the brightly lit access corridors, Jensen found it difficult to adjust. Strange, he thought, that the overhead floods should be switched off. On the heels of a major crisis, he would assume a conscientious staff would take extra precautions.

But when Jensen queried the guard on duty, negligence proved not to be at issue.

"Damned skip-runner blasted the communications turret." The security man gestured in resignation. "Lights in here run off the same solar banks, and we'll need more than one shift on deep-space maintenance for repairs."

Though the explanation seemed reasonable, Jensen's nervousness increased. He crossed the echoing expanse of hangar with swift steps and hurried up the *Shearborn*'s ramp.

Instinct caused him to hesitate just inside the entry. He sensed something amiss, perhaps from the conspicuous fact that Harris was not at his usual post in the galley with a row of empty beers for company. Jensen paused midstride, almost in the corridor to the bridge. That moment, a shadow moved just at the edge of vision.

Jensen ducked. The blow that should have felled him glanced instead off his ribs.

It knocked the breath from his lungs nonetheless. The bottle spun from his hand and smashed in a spray of glass and spirits. Jensen bent double, whooping for air that tasted sickly of whiskey. He snatched by reflex for his side arm. But the shadow moved ahead of him.

It proved to be a man, a large man who already dodged the shot he knew would follow. A Fleet officer accomplished enough to earn marksman elite could be expected to handle his gun as if it were an extension of his living flesh.

Jensen's shot crashed into the bridge-side bulkhead. Padding exploded into fluff where the intruder's head had been but a fraction of an instant before. Cursing, the lieutenant shoved another round into the breech. He hastened forward, skidding over the puddle of alcohol and glass. The cold portion of his mind wondered why the intruder had fled. A second blow, better placed, might have killed him in that instant before surprise kicked into adrenaline surge.

Jensen whipped around the innerlock, slammed shoulder first into a stowage locker. He trained his pistol squarely upon his quarry, only to flinch the shot wide. His curse of white hot anger blended with the clang as the pellet hammered harmlessly into high-impact plastic.

Over the heated end of his gun barrel, Jensen beheld the limp form of Harris, gripped like a shield in a pair of coil-scarred hands.

The name left his lips, unbidden. "Mac James!"

"Godfrey," came the muffled reply. "Tired of the party early, did you?"

The face, with its icy gray eyes, stayed hidden. Jensen was given no target for his murderous marksmanship, which was a feat. Mac James outweighed his unconscious hostage by a good sixty pounds. As to how the skip-runner had stowed away, Jensen recalled with sinking recrimination that the *Marity* had passed close enough to plant a boarder on the *Shearborn*'s hull. The stowaway's life-support of necessity would have been limited to the capacity of his suit pack, which meant that Mac James had gambled his life on the lieutenant's subsequent behavior. Had the *Shearborn*'s crew backed down, returned through FTL to Dead Star, the skip-runner would have been fried in the coil field. Instead, the heroics which had preserved the station's integrity and the lives of two children had earned the *Shearborn* a warm invitation, without security screening, into a classified research installation. With a dawning stab of outrage, Jensen understood. He had been nothing more than a pawn. His triumph over the terrorists had provided the linchpin of a plot for MacKenzie James.

"I could kill Harris to see you dead," Jensen said thickly. Certainly he was ruthless enough, MacKenzie James should recall.

But with insight that bordered the uncanny, the skip-runner sensed why the lieutenant dared not fire to kill. "First you'll want to know just what mischief I've set loose while you were celebrating, boy."

Jensen's fingers whitened on the grip of his pellet gun. His thoughts darted like a rat in a maze but found no opening to exploit. He had visited the control bridge on the *Marity*. Her captain's ability to manipulate hardware was real enough to frighten; and if Harris had slugged down drugs with his beer, the *Shearborn*'s systems had been open to sabotage for something close to three hours. Any havoc was possible.

Mac James's laconic observation interrupted the lieutenant's thoughts. "Now, I see you have two choices. Murder your pilot to get me, and you've got a Fleet investigation on your case. You can bet they won't send a lightweight to chew your ass. Not if you kill without witnesses and a suspect like me turns up dead on your chaser, smack in the middle of a classified installation."

"That won't save you," Jensen said quickly.

"Maybe not." Harris's head lolled to one side as Mac James shifted his grip. "But a review of *Shearborn*'s flight log will uncover a coded file, accessed through stolen passkeys. The data list includes plans for every project Cassix Station personnel have going on the drawing boards. Fleet court-martial will nail you on theft of military secrets, without appeal. You need me alive, boy. Unless you know enough to go into that system and monkey that file out of existence without leaving tracks."

Jensen felt shaky down to his shoes. He lacked the expertise to clear the encoded locks on the *Shearborn*'s software, much less to alter records on the other side. His helplessness galled doubly. In the event of a trial, the very ignorance that ensured his innocence would be impossible to prove.

"You're much too quiet, boy." Mac James shifted his weight with sharpening impatience. "Why do you think I've been so busy?"

Rocked by a stab of hatred, Jensen perceived more. "You sent that other skip-runner in, pitted me against him specifically to gain entrance to Cassix Station without leaving traces. The Indie contract on the kidnappers was only a cover."

A strained silence followed, broken gruffly by Mac James's reply. "A man lives according to his nature, you for pride and advancement, and Captain Gorlaff for his bets. That one buried his future permanently because he neglected to watch his odds. You can, too, boy. Or you can lift off Cassix and rendezvous with the *Marity*, where I can transfer that incriminating file without leaving traces in the system. I'll return Harris in a cargo crate. When he recovers from his hangover, he can fly you back to Commodore Abraham Meier for the commendation and promotion you both so richly deserve."

Jensen steadied his grip on the gun. His hand trembled, and his face twitched. A single shot would restore his inner pride but shatter his public career forever. Swept by rage, and by a desire like pain to see the skip-runner captain who had manipulated him end up cold and bloody and dead, Jensen shut his eyes. Cornered without recourse, he made his choice.

Commodore Meier stepped forward on the dais, and stiffly cleared his throat. "Each man lives according to his nature," he said in official summary. The medals in his hand flashed brightly in the lights of the vid cameras. "May others draw inspiration from the bravery and initiative cited here."

Jensen held very still as the precious medallion was affixed to the sash on his chest. Like MacKenzie James, he never gambled; there had been no allowance for doubt. A Fleet officer with a future might pursue a skip-runner to the death. The duel of wits would continue. Reveling in his promotion and his honors, the newest Lieutenant Commander in the Fleet promised himself victory at the next pass.

The Snare

Inspired by the painting
'The Wizard' by Don Maitz

The opening move was deadly because of its extreme simplicity. Iveldane caused one of the candles in the Wizard's private study to flicker out. There was no draft; the casement was tightly closed and latched against any intrusion of the starry night without. The Wizard raised no arcane defense. Mellowed, perhaps, by wine and smoke from his hookah, the enchanter, whose stare had once shattered mountains, and whose spoken word leashed earthquakes and stilled the raging seas of hurricanes, suspected no threat from a single, darkened candle. He glanced up, even as a mortal might, annoyed at the sudden invasion of shadow across the drifting trough of his lap.

Spindled with smoke, the spark-tipped wick glowed red as the eye of a demon, pinning the Wizard's gaze. Before he shaped a Command of Rekindling, Iveldane's snare transfixed his unguarded mind like a spearshaft, and held it.

Wind tore like laughter through the chamber. Flung headlong from its ensorcelled current of air, the Wizard's goblet shattered in a spray of glass and wine. Iron candlesticks toppled, scattering the carpet with necklaces of flame. The spellbook crackled, a tumbling wheel of pages, as stone walls wavered and danced in destruction's wild light. Bound, the Great Wizard of Trevior sat with blinded eyes, unaware of all but the voice of his antagonist.

"Long have I awaited this moment, *Master*!" Deep in his cave of ice and rock, Iveldane smiled. The winds of his summoning screamed in echo of his taunt, and fanned the white mustache and tailored robes of his enemy into profane disarray. Hapless as a doll in the hands of a cruel child, the Master of Trevior was unable to protest.

Iveldane's smile broadened. "Does my return from the prison you fashioned for me surprise you?"

He loosed his grip, slightly, allowing the Wizard enough will to reply. But the silence was disturbed only by the crisp speech of flames, and the Wizard did not imprint the inanimate with any message. Through the heat of his triumph, Iveldane sensed frost. It made him laugh.

Still, the Wizard said nothing. Iveldane borrowed current from the stars and banished the study with all its ruined comforts. For half an age, he had planned this. Spells spiralled and wove through his slim fingers. His dark brow shone damp with sweat. Presently, the Master of Trevior stood before him, bound in glassy chains of wizardry and ice.

"Do you fear me, Master?" The tone was mocking.

The Wizard's black eyes met blue ones without expression. "I fear only a past misjudgment." His words were calm as the sea's depths.

Iveldane felt his heart twist, but hatred did not shake his control. "And was a thousand years of agony confined in a volcano's fiery core a *misjudgment*?" Iveldane stared at his enemy, weighted with the bitterness and suffering of days past.

The Wizard bore his stony gaze, patient. "Was it?"

Iveldane's expression soured, and echoes of his laughter bounced off pillared shafts of icicles. "You'll answer, before I have done."

The Wizard bowed his head.

Iveldane's confidence wavered. An icy draft tumbled across the chamber momentarily raising gooseflesh on his braceleted arms. The ornaments hid scars left by fetters of fire, and that nod had been the same gesture which condemned him to torment ten centuries past. But this time, nothing happened.

He taunts me, Iveldane thought. Rage clamped his gut like iron. He called upon the earth, and dirt rose from the floor like a gaunt old hound, circling the Wizard's feet.

"I will seal you, living, into your grave, even as you did to me." Iveldane's whisper carried clearly over the grind of soil and stones. The Wizard made no reply, though that freedom had been left him. Once, with a word, he would have smoothed the earth to rest. Iveldane waited, then wondered why he did not. "I don't understand," he said.

The Wizard looked up. "You never understood."

Iveldane unleashed his anger. Dust rose in screaming fists of maelstrom. When it settled, the Wizard was buried wholly beneath a barrow of earth. Iveldane sat, with his chin on his fist, and waited for the Wizard to tumble the barriers that imprisoned him from the light. Yet he did not.

"You were once my Master, and my friend." Iveldane stared at the mound of rubble, and memory surged over him like the tide . . .

He saw himself as a boy again, frightened of the night and soaked by driving rain. The door against which he huddled, shivering, suddenly opened, spilling him awkwardly across a marble floor at the feet of the Master of Trevior.

"Why have you come here?" said the Wizard.

Iveldane looked up, and it seemed those dark eyes saw only the water which dripped from black hair onto the ragged cloth of his shirt. "My Lord, I wish to learn."

The Wizard's veined hand tightened on the door panel as he pushed it shut. "Do you think I will beat you any less than the smith you ran away from?"

Iveldane flinched. Yet his reply was bold. "My Lord, you are the World's Master. Should you beat me, then surely I will have earned it."

The Wizard looked abruptly away, and a small shiver seemed to grip his thin frame. "Remember this. The lesson of wisdom can be painful. And only one can be Master." Flat as dark obsidian, his eyes returned to the boy. "Do you understand?"

"Oh, yes, my Lord."

The Wizard extended a strong warm hand, and helped the boy to his feet. "Then let us start with dry clothes and warm soup."

You never understood. The words mocked, sharp as needles. Iveldane stared at the rubble which covered the Wizard who had uttered them, and felt the hair on his nape stir. He tried to laugh, but it felt wrong. "Never once did you beat me."

The earth was still.

"Instead you betrayed me. *Are you listening?*" The anguished words shattered into echoes against the glassy rungs of ice. When no answer came, Iveldane looked once more into the past . . .

"I have taught you all I know." Cloaked in the golden glow of candles, the Wizard stood with a shadowed face. "The time has come for you to leave me."

Iveldane raised eyes pale as frost. His hair glanced in the light like a raven's wing. "You are the World's Master. There is no place I can go where I will not walk in your shadow."

The Wizard spoke with sorrow. "Some things cannot be taught. If you have loved me, go, and learn contentment."

"That is a poor return for the years and the knowledge you have given me, Master." Iveldane knelt on the patterned carpet, unashamed. "Let me stay and serve at your side."

"Service is not your fate."

Iveldane looked up, and saw an old man with tears on

his face. His own heart turned in anguished response. "I beg you, let me stay."

Salt-drops fell like sparks in the candlelight. The Wizard cried out, once, in protest, before steadying his control. Then he raised his Mastery, and sure hands carved the air like ice. "There is only one reward I can offer for such loyalty."

The room crumbled out of solidity with a sigh. Iveldane felt himself lifted as though weightless. His sight blurred into blindness. All bodily sensation fell away, until his spirit seemed to stream across eternity like blown smoke. Held fast by shackles of wind, Iveldane made no attempt to resist. If the World's Master saw fit to imprison him, no skill he possessed would avail.

Air was a gentle jailer. Iveldane knew neither pain nor want, and his thoughts were his own, for the Wizard left him alone. He tests my love, Iveldane thought. Certain in his loyalty, he waited one thousand years with flawless patience. Yet the Wizard never came.

"Have you forgotten me?" Snatched by tireless currents of wind, Iveldane's appeal went unregarded. Doubts assailed him. He fought them, when they grew too strong. His beleaguered mind imagined the world swept by flood, famine, and earthquake.

"Disaster would keep my Master from me," Iveldane reasoned aloud, and he wept. "Free me, Lord. Gladly would I lend my strength to yours."

But if the winds carried the words to their Master's ear, he did not respond. *Perhaps he, too, is prisoner*, Iveldane realized. Desire for freedom arose within him like a wave. Tireless as the tides, it battered his patience until he could no longer endure.

Iveldane struck at his bonds. He struggled until his muscles burned with exhaustion, and the sweat of exertion chilled on his skin. The wind's whisper mocked his efforts. To silence it, he raised glittering webs of enchantment, and discharged them as blazing white wheels of fire. The wind swallowed his energies, scatheless. It would heed but a single master's word, and that one, the Wizard of

Trevior. But confinement had robbed Iveldane of reason. He fought, until weariness claimed him, then woke and fought again. Yet against his prison of air, all efforts were vain. Centuries passed. His passion cooled to listless despair.

Sucked clean of emotion, Iveldane lay passive. The wind gradually claimed the hollow place his thoughts had abandoned. Its sibilant voice filled his battered mind until sight and sound were forgotten, and former experience became shadowy and insubstantial as a dream. Iveldane merged with the wind, *became* the wind, and so inherited its secrets.

Years went by before that knowledge held meaning. Startled to tears, one day, by realization he held the key to his own freedom, Iveldane spoke with a tongue long unaccustomed to words. His bonds dissolved. The air turned around him. His feet struck ground and he stumbled, unprepared for his own weight, and landed on his knees in sand.

For one unbelieving moment, he knelt, blind with weeping, nostrils filled with the salt breeze off the sea and the sour scent of marsh grass. *The earth was whole, untroubled by the nightmares his captive mind had imagined.* Relieved, Iveldane raised his eyes to the sunlight, and saw the Wizard waiting for him on a rock-strewn rise a short distance away. The breezes toyed with blue-and-gold robes, rippling the sleeves like banners.

Iveldane rose, aflame with the joy of reunion. "My Lord, I am your servant, still." Naked and polished to slenderness by long years as the wind's captive, Iveldane crossed the sandspit.

The Wizard watched his approach with black, fathomless eyes, no welcome at all on his face. "I never doubted your love."

Iveldane checked, wrenched by sudden confusion. Elation drained from his heart, leaving terrible emptiness. "Then, my Lord, why did you banish me?"

The Wizard stared at the breakers, silent.

Iveldane bent and scooped a palm full of pebbles from

the soil at his feet. Their roughness scoured at his skin, as one by one, he cast them tumbling, into the teeth of the surf. "Did you take the idea from Maegrel?" Unwanted bitterness threaded his tone. "He did the same with his apprentice, apparently for sport."

"True enough." The Wizard watched the last stone's flight, the brief splash of impact drowned in the rush of incoming tide. "Can you name Maegrel's apprentice?"

Iveldane's hands hung at his sides, empty. Wind teased his black hair back from features stippled with sweat. "Does it matter?"

"Perhaps. He still lives." The Wizard's gaze never left the sea.

"You told me he killed his master." Iveldane's words were edged with self-doubt. But he did not add, *as I suddenly long to kill mine.*

The Wizard fixed unfathomable eyes on his face. "I know."

Chilled, shaking, Iveldane shouted back. "But I never *wanted* to challenge you! I was content with what you taught me. Did you think I would ask anything more?"

Still as stone, the Wizard said, "Do you recall the warning I spoke when first you came to me?"

"Only one can be Master." Iveldane shook his head, puzzled.

The Wizard glanced down at his hands and spoke a word. Flecked with chips of mica, a small pebble appeared in his palms. A quick, hard gesture sent the stone spinning in a high arc. Iveldane's eyes followed its plunge toward green, foam-laced waves.

"So be it," said the Wizard.

The stone struck with a splash. Water closed over Iveldane's head. Aware too late of the trap, he screamed protest. But shadowy depths had already claimed him, and the sea's chill embraced his flesh, unyielding. Iveldane's heart ached like an old wound. For uncounted years, salt-tears mingled with salt water . . .

• • •

Iveldane shivered free of memory's grasp. He stared at the mound he had raised, as though his eyes could read the Wizard's thoughts written on the earth itself.

"If you had been on the shore the day I won free of the sea, I would have left you," he said to the still air. "Instead, I learned hatred. You taught me, when I reached dry soil, and you bade the earth imprison me in turn. Tell me, *how does it feel?*"

Iveldane smiled, accustomed now to silence. "But it was the fire which came after that made me desire your death . . ."

For fire had been a cruel warden. Iveldane had needed every secret he had gleaned from earth, sea, and air for bare survival, and even that knowledge was not enough to ease his agony. Of all elements, flesh was least tolerant of fire, and the volcano in which the Master of Trevior had chained him was far hotter than any flame. Iveldane's screams had shaken the roots of the mountain. Desire for vengeance alone bound him to life. Ten centuries, he endured unimaginable torment, all for hope of the chance to trap the World's Master at his mercy.

But his strength had run out. Cursing, he had lost his battle, and flame had consumed him, utterly. Yet he did not perish. Possessed by the volcano's molten core, its lessons had scarred his soul. He emerged with mastery of fire, and an unquenchable passion to inflict punishment on the Wizard who had consigned him to torment . . .

Restless in his triumph, Iveldane released his binding spell. Soil slithered back, exposing the Wizard's torso. The Master's face was streaked with dirt. Grit had brought tears to his eyes.

"What a sorry sight you are." Iveldane rose and leaned close. "I haven't the patience to waste centuries for your secrets."

The Wizard stirred dusty shoulders. "Between us there are no secrets. I was Maegrel's apprentice."

"*You!*" Iveldane stared, and the ice cave rang again with his laughter. On impulse, he seized the Wizard's arms and, with cruel force, jerked them free of the earth. The Wizard blanched in pain. Yet he did not resist as Iveldane twisted his wrists and bared scars twin to the ones the bracelets covered.

"This, for loyalty?" Iveldane released his enemy and stepped back.

"No." The Wizard's voice caught. He paused to cough up dust. "Maegrel thought me ambitious."

"You returned and killed him." Iveldane waited, still as a serpent.

"To my sorrow." The Wizard spoke without bitterness. "It was not necessary."

Iveldane smiled with poisonous delight. "Do you plead with me for your life? I'm amused." Suddenly his expression darkened like a stormfront, and a sharp word left his lips. Fire rose, crackling from the torn earth. The Wizard screamed, even as his apprentice had screamed when the lava had seared his flesh. "Master, one day you will plead with me for death."

Iveldane turned his back on the Wizard's suffering and retired from the ice cave to more comfortable quarters above ground. The setting of the snare had taxed him, and though the Wizard's demise rang sweet in his ears, he wanted rest. Settling himself on a silken bed, he slept . . .

. . . and dreamed. Cold with horror, he saw the earth stripped of life. Trees cast shadows gaunt as skeletons over sere ground. Lake basins shimmered under mirage, dust-dry, and webbed with fissures. The air was poisoned by the stench of death. Pierced to the soul with unnameable pain, Iveldane opened his mouth to cry out. No sound came.

He fell upon the ground, dug his hands to the wrists in

ruined soil. Great, hoarse gasps ripped his throat as he shaped the commands which would call air, water, earth, and fire to his will. Emotionally flayed by the earth's torment, he stared as the sky wheeled above him, yet no response came. No living force answered; even the oceans were dry.

Crushed by despair, Iveldane wept. The soil drank his tears. Night fell, garish with stars, and a three-quarter moon rose, grinning like a skull. Iveldane covered his face with his fingers. The earth's wounds pained him as the fires never had. Wracked by inconsolable loss, Iveldane screamed at the empty sky.

"*Who has done this?*" The shout lost itself without echo. Rage flared in his gut. "Who has done this?"

"I."

Iveldane flinched at the sound of that familiar, hated voice. Slowly he rose to his feet.

Sure and unmarked in blue and gold, the Master of Trevior stood at his shoulder. "I have caused the death of the earth. Dare you return and avenge it?"

Iveldane stared into eyes as reasonless as a snake's. His shaking hands reached to throttle the pale, soft throat of his enemy. But the Master's form shimmered and vanished.

Iveldane woke weeping. Anger shook him like a storm-wind. He flung the coverlet from him with violence enough to tear it. Back, he went, to the ice cave, possessed by fury no pity could contain. Icicles flashed, prismatic in the flickering light, until his shadow quenched them. Captive still, the Wizard of Trevior writhed in his chains, tormented by a crown of fire. Iveldane banished the flames with a glance.

Coarse against sudden silence, the sound of his breathing mingled with its own echoes. "I am going to destroy you. *Do you hear me?*"

The singed head stirred. The Wizard looked up, his cheeks crystalline, awash with tears. "I hear." His voice was serene, even joyful.

The incongruity struck Iveldane like a blow. The great anger in his soul faltered and, dizzied suddenly, he staggered back. "Filth! Earth-murderer! As World's Master, how can you weep for joy?"

"That title is no longer mine." The Wizard raised eyes that were clear of deception. "You, as my successor, at last have delivered me from that responsibility, and the power with it."

Iveldane drew a harsh, sobbing breath, and saw it was so. Water, air, fire, and earth had each impressed him with their secrets, and the dream had shown him how deeply ingrained was the instinct to protect all that lay under his charge. Like a blind man given sight, Iveldane reached out with his mind, and saw the earth whole in the moonlight.

"Did you think I would punish you for nothing?" The Wizard spoke with such trepidation, Iveldane laughed and made haste to release him.

Dreamsinger's Tale

The spring grass grew long and lush in the glade, and a brook where peepers shrilled in annual courtship ran close by. There, Huntress Skyfire flung herself down, panting and hot after a long run through the forest. She drank and splashed cold water through her hair, then shed her bow and her spear and her sweaty, winter-musty furs and rolled onto her back. Mother moon peeped like a needle of bone through the leaves. Skyfire regarded its thin crescent and sighed, not quite content. Something was missing, lacking, *not right*. Hard as she ran, fast as she could shoot an arrow into fleeing prey, she could not quite catch up with whatever it was.

Her wolf-friend, Woodbiter, arrived at the clearing. Old now, and surly where he had once been full of antics, he had leaves sticking in his coat. With his ears canted back, he crouched in the grass, panting also. The breeze that wafted through his fur carried the scent of something dead.

"Rolled in a scent patch. Again," Skyfire sent. She wrinkled her nose in distaste.

Woodbiter regarded her with unwinking yellow eyes. "Go hunting now." The wolf's image held the savory taste of hot blood, the thrill and the kick of prey as his jaws closed and snapped the spine.

"No." Skyfire rolled onto her elbows, irritable as a she-wolf past her heat. "No." She was hungry, but hunger was not what drove her. She would go hunting, but not now, not tonight.

Woodbiter endured his elf-friend's gaze for the span of a heartbeat, then whined, rolled, and showed the pale fur of his throat to appease her aggressive mood. "Hunt alone," he sent. When the Huntress neither answered nor forbade him, he sprang up and slunk off into the forest.

Skyfire hammered her fist into soft spring soil and flopped with her chin on her elbows. The *not right* feeling persisted. Though she tried, she could find no name for it. This was no anticipation of danger, like the moment when the prong-horn's charge caught a spear-thrower off guard. Neither was it a feeling of threat, like the packs of human hunters who sometimes wandered too near the holt. Skyfire twisted two grass stems between her fingers. Decidedly, this was not even the faintly giddy feeling one got after eating too many dreamberries. She frowned at the brook, and watched the moon's broken reflection frown back. She could not say why she was here, lying idle in new grass when her belly growled with hunger. Well after nightfall, the tribe would be wondering why their chieftess did not appear to lead the hunt. Yet Skyfire made no effort to rise. She would not take up her spear. Some instinct as deep as earth urged her to linger.

She plucked a grass blade and chewed the stem, only to spit it out because it tasted sour. In the stream the shape of the moon rippled on as if nothing was wrong. The peepers shrilled in a forest that seemed touched by strange, waiting silence; not the quiet of approaching predators, but a sort of stillness that caused the hair to prickle. In that moment, with discontent sharp as a thorn in her side, Skyfire first heard the singing.

The melody touched her first, high and sweet and filled with the vitality of growing things. Skyfire tilted her head, tense and listening. She sniffed the air, but smelled no taint of humans. Belatedly she noticed that this song held none of the grunts which passed for language among the five-fingers. Perhaps in sound, perhaps in sending, this singer used no words at all, only notes laid out in brightness and light. Each lilted phrase filled Skyfire with a pure and innocent joy. Without quite knowing she had moved, she found herself on her feet. The song drew her as nothing in memory had ever done before.

Only the sternest habits of survival made her remember the spear, bow, and quiver lying in the grass. She paused to gather them up, though the delay made her ache. The sweaty fur garment she had shed no longer seemed important, so she abandoned it. Clad only in thin leather tunic and cross-laced boots, Skyfire slipped into the dark of the forest.

As only an elf or a wolf could move, she followed the elusive song through thicket and draw. Yet the singer eluded her. Between the black boles of oaks, over ferny hummocks and marshy hollows, he walked and left no marks. Neither branch nor briar nor deadfall seemed to slow him. Huntress Skyfire shook her bright hair in annoyance. She was considered a fine tracker, lacking only the nose of a wolf to unravel the most difficult trails. She hurried, silent and adept and forest-cunning, and determined as never before; but somehow, the uncanny song caused her native grace to abandon her. Scratched on twigs, scraped on thorns, she felt clumsy as a five-finger, and as foolish. Yet to stop or even slow down was to lose the music that even now filtered through a copse of saplings. The melody ran flawless as stream water, describing delight that bordered the edges of pain. Skyfire ran. Breathless, she twisted around tree branches and half tripped on roots and vines. Still the singer evaded her. His melody drew relentlessly farther ahead, until at length it became no more than the memory of beauty, the fading essence of dream.

Skyfire cursed and stumbled to her knees in moss. Tired, confused, and even hotter than before, she rubbed at scratches on her spear arm. The discontent which had troubled her earlier intensified, became a disappointment near to sickness. She jabbed at soft earth with her spear-butt. The silence, the terrible absence of song, left her aching in a way that knew no remedy.

Around her, night had begun to fail. Gray light shone between branches and new leaves, and birds awakened singing. Soon humans might be abroad, dangerous to any elf who foolishly stayed in the open. For once Skyfire did not care. Crossly she threw herself prone, her chin cupped in her fists. She did not move as the world grew golden with dawn, nor when the sun speared slanting through the boughs, striping her shoulders with warmth. Furious at her own folly, yet helpless to free herself of yearning, she lay and frowned until her head ached and her thoughts spun with hunger. The music pulled at her still. The memory did not fade before the *now* awareness of her wolf-sense; notes spilled and echoed in her mind until she wanted to weep, bereft.

Woodbiter found her at midday. The wolf had fared well on his hunt and his belly was gorged. He had dragged his kill beneath a fallen log, then urinated upon the place to mark it; the cache was not far, and still fresh. Yet meat would not assuage the emptiness left by the singer. Skyfire refused her wolf-friend's offer.

The animal sensed her discontent. He licked her eyelids in commiseration, and finally curled in the shade to sleep.

Skyfire left him there. Irritable and alone, she arose and retraced her trail from the night before. The path of her run was clear, a swath of torn leaves and twigs freshly snapped. Many times she had stepped carelessly on soft soil and left the imprint of her booted foot. Although she searched and sniffed, she found nothing of the singer. His melody haunted her. Once when she might have stopped to spear fish, his memory stung her haplessly onward.

In time, the daystar lowered and the birds flew to roost. Exhausted, and hopelessly in thrall to the singer's dream, Skyfire stumbled and fell. She caught herself short of a bang on the head; and there, between her hands, found the impression of a bare foot. The track had four toes, clearly made by an elf. Yet Skyfire knew at once that none of her own tribe had trodden here. Precisely between the hollow of toes and heel, there bloomed a flower entirely out of phase with the season.

Astonishment overwhelmed Skyfire, and her breath caught. For no reason she could name, she knelt by the blossom and wept. Then, as if the release of emotion had snapped the dream's hold on her mind, she acknowledged the sending from the holt which had sought her for some hours. Most oddly, it was Twigleaf, the youngest cub in the tribe, whose call reached her first. Skyfire returned reassurance of her well-being. Then, with weariness similar to the feeling of waking from dreams of escaped prey, she rose and returned to lead the hunt.

For an eight-of-days, the chieftess ran with the pack as always. The rough way of the Wolfriders and the song of their mounts as they howled before the hunt stirred her, made her heart lift and the blood race through her veins. Only now the challenge of survival seemed somehow less keen. The lilt of the song stirred within her at odd moments, like an echo never entirely lost. And as was her habit in the old days of Two-Spear's strife, Skyfire wandered often. Perhaps not by chance, she found her way back to the clearing. There, yet again, she waited for something she could not name.

This time clouds shadowed her vigil. Rainfall slicked her hair on her shoulders and dripped coldly down her back and groin. She shook herself like a wolf, licking irritably at the runoff. Long hours she listened between the patter of droplets over leaves, but no song reached her save the shrilling of peepers in the damp and the puddles. Shivering, saddened, but never quite miserable enough to leave, Skyfire finally dozed.

The song returned in her dreams. Notes tripped and spilled between thorn brakes where no rain fell, and the forest lay dappled with sun like high summer. In dream,

Skyfire leaped up and pursued. The song flowed like sending, and images swept through her sleeping mind. Though the singer used no words, his music spoke of other times, of taller, fairer elves than those who ran with the wolves. They wore beautiful, many-colored clothing. Beyond them Skyfire beheld strange dwellings, then stars sprinkled uncountably across blackness deeper than night. She saw suns that blistered her eyes, and moons silvery as the trinkets that humans cut from mussel shells. And yet there was sorrow beneath the beauty of this song. Woven through the strangeness and wonder of the images lay a memory of cold, like death. In the dream, Skyfire started. The stars and the moons abruptly vanished, and dark against the silver-ice light of new dawn, she beheld the singer.

He stood before her, clad in grey. A wolf of the same hue lolled at his side. The eyes of wolf and rider were eerily alike, deep and light as mist. But the elf-singer's hair was black, hanging tangled and unkempt down his back.

Convinced she had awakened, Skyfire surged to her feet, all grace and speed and anger. Nobody, wolf or elf, *ever* sneaked up on her like that, far less a stranger in territory hunted by her tribe and pack.

Yet even as she raised her spear and called challenge, the singer and wolf both vanished. Skyfire checked. The dream dissolved around her and she woke in reality, to chilly rain and daylight. Her breath came painfully to her chest. On the ground, where in the dream the singer's feet had trodden, the grass grew sere and dry as autumn. A single oak leaf lay caught between the stems, not the new soft green of spring, but colored red as blood.

Skyfire gasped. She brushed the dried grass with her hands and shivered. This singer of dreams was surely part throwback. The magic of the old ones ran deep in him.

The storm had split into broken clouds, and the leaves dripped sullenly by the time Skyfire returned to the holt. Most of the tribe lay in tree hollows, sleeping, but a few of the young ones tussled like wolf cubs in the shade. One just barely an adult watched over their play, her hands weaving baskets out of rush.

"Been stalking black-neck deer?" Sapling taunted. Her fingers stilled on her handiwork as she tossed back pale hair. "Or maybe something bigger than a deer stalked you? Looks like you spent the night holed up in a thicket."

Skyfire bent and snatched a rush. "Close."

"Barren hunt?" asked Sapling, quick enough to grab back her stolen green. Such teasing had been part of her life since she was a cub.

The chieftess shook her head, but the ravvit she had caught and eaten on her way home had not left her sated. The dreams and the singer were driving her to distraction. Even her wolf noticed her ribs, as if she was gaunt from the season of white cold. As Skyfire reached the tree which held her sleeping hollow, she sensed the concern of Pine, who sometimes lay with her after the hunt. She never confided in him, but the fact that she was troubled had been noticed. Yet Pine's embrace offered no comfort. Chilled and confused as Skyfire was, she did not wish the warmth of a lovemate. A strange elf walked the forest, one who belonged to no pack, and who owned depths not seen in cubs born for many generations. He was Wolfrider, surely enough, but different in ways not easily understood. Skyfire sensed trouble. If she told the rest of the tribe of the song-dreams and their maker, the wolf in them might precipitate an outcome that could not be controlled. Though pack ways and pack actions served well in matters of survival, Skyfire struggled to balance instinct against a drive that ran deeper than curiosity. She realized she must track down and confront this singer without help from the other Wolfriders.

The limbs which led to her hollow were smoothed with many climbings. Skyfire pulled herself upward out of habit, her mind preoccupied with unfamiliar concepts. Against her nature, she must plan, for the tribe must not suffer for her pursuit of the singer. She must lead the hunt through the night, and then in the gray hours before daybreak, slip away.

The hollow in the tree was dim and invitingly cool, but Skyfire did not sleep. Curled in her furs, her bright hair wound damply over her shoulders, she wondered how an elf could track a shadow. For the singer was shadow, a figure spun of dreams. In the depths of his gray-silver eyes she could easily become lost.

The mild weather of spring quickly gave way before the darker foliage and the stronger sun of summer. Like most elves, Skyfire abandoned use of her sleeping hollow altogether, preferring to curl up like a wolf in the dappled shade of a thicket, her body against cool earth. But while the winds stilled, and prey grew fat and plentiful, and the Wolfriders became sleek with easy hunting, their chieftess grew lean with muscle. After the nightly kill, she ran, until she could traverse the dense forest in silence at speed. She learned not to thrash through briars, but to twist and duck and dodge through the narrowest of openings without slackening stride. She practiced leaping over streams, from rock to fallen log, to banks treacherous with moss. Her feet became very sure; for the first time, Woodbiter had trouble keeping up.

"Gray-muzzle," she teased once, as the two of them lay panting in companionship in a forest glade. She licked the corner of his lips in the manner of one wolf showing affection for another.

Woodbiter's eye rolled and met hers. "Killed deer," he sent in wolfish reproach. Except for rank, distinctions were never made between members of the wolf-pack once a cub reached adulthood. A wolf either hunted successfully and held his own, or else failed to survive.

Skyfire slammed playfully into her wolf-friend's shoulder and tussled, rolling over and over upon the ground. As elves, her tribe handled life with little difference. Hardship made no allowance for individuals who were not strong. Such was the way of the wild. But as Skyfire wrestled with her wolf in the midsummer heat, she thought upon the singer's dreams. For the first time, she wondered whether

Timmain's sacrifice, which first mingled the blood of wolves and elves, might have been made in the hope of something more.

That night the hunt went well. Early on, Spearhand brought down a large buck. Then Skimmer and his wolf, Brighttail, flushed a herd of prong-horns. The Wolfriders leaped eagerly in pursuit. By the time the two moons lifted toward the zenith, there was feasting. Skyfire did not gorge on the meat with the others, but ate sparingly and wrapped a second portion to carry with her. Then, leaving her spear in Sapling's care, she tightened the strap of her quiver and settled her bow over her shoulder.

"Going?" sent Woodbiter. He licked his bloody muzzle and raised expectant eyes.

Skyfire returned the image of the clearing by the brook. By that the wolf understood she would spend another night running, or perhaps simply sitting by water staring at nothing. He chose to remain with his kill.

Huntress Skyfire twisted her red hair into a braid. Aware that she prepared to embark upon another night of wandering, her tribe-mates did not ask why. Neither did they try to go along, as once before they might have. Skyfire did not explain her leaving. If a wolf-chief wanted solitude, he drove off his subordinates with snarls, not affection. Skyfire could be as fierce in defense of her wishes. No elf in the tribe cared to provoke her wrath as Two-Spear had, on the day she had challenged him for leadership.

Yet the more distance Skyfire set between herself and the members of her tribe, the more determination deserted her. She paused, leaned against a tree, and rested her cheek against rough bark. She had heard no singing for many eights-of-days. All her practice at running and her nights of vigil had led her no closer to the strange elf than the time when the peepers called. Soon the forest would change. Frost and cold winds would strip the green from the leaves. The season of white cold would follow and the struggle for survival would force an end to her search. Recalling the marvels in the singer's dream, Skyfire clenched her teeth in frustration. Somehow she knew that if she failed, the lost feeling inside her would never be answered.

Accordingly, she tucked her bow more comfortably across her shoulders and began to jog. Tonight she paid no attention to landmarks, but traveled without purpose or direction. She might encounter humans, or even one of the clearings where they set snares for game, but this once caution deserted her. The singer's long silence drove her, aching, to recklessness.

Skyfire ran. The familiar paths, the known trees, the territory hunted by the wolf-pack, all fell behind. Breathless, weary, the chieftess would not rest. Deer started out of her path, and night creatures looked up from their hunting. Still she ran, while stars blinked endlessly between the leaves overhead. The earth jarred over and over against the soles of her feet, and her bowstring rasped blisters on her shoulder. Still the chieftess ran.

Her breath came in wrenching gasps. She did not stop. Not until her legs failed her and she tumbled headlong into old leaves. The musty smell filled her nostrils, and skeletons of veined stems caught in her hair. Skyfire rolled miserably onto her back. Her frustration skirted the edges of despair, but she was too spent even to curse.

She could do nothing at all but lie still and listen to silence until her ears stung under the weight of it.

In time her heart stopped hammering and her breathing slowed. Something stirred in her mind and she heard a faint drift of melody. Skyfire shut her eyes, uncertain whether her imagination might be tricking her as had happened so many times before.

But the singing grew stronger. The melody turned and interwove like a waterfall, intricate beyond understanding. Skyfire rose up on her elbows. Longing woke within her. Feeling tears burn behind her eyelids, she pushed at last to her feet. She did not feel the protest of her tired body as, once more, she started to run. The singer's dream enfolded her senses, drew her irresistibly like a moth toward flame.

Skyfire no longer saw trees, or the night-dark vista of forest. She ran through a waking dream of wide, open plains under cloudless sky. The stars seemed close enough to touch, and the wind held a bite of cold that burned her throat as she breathed. Scents of many descriptions filled her nostrils, intoxicating in their detail. Skyfire sniffed deeply. She realized that she ran with the senses of a wolf, even as Timmain had done generations in the past. Yet though her limbs might seem clothed in fur and her body that of a beast, still her mind was not entirely animal. The compassion, the gentleness, and the sorrow of her ancestors reverberated through her being. As she raced on four pads over the plain, she shared echoes of Timmain's thoughts.

Then the singer's melody changed. The dream of sharing wolf-shape faded and turned deep and sad and lost. The cold deepened. Snow fell, a whirling maelstrom of flakes that smothered the memory of summer or stars. Frost cut cruelly into flesh no longer clothed in the protective pelt of the wolf. Skyfire cried out, painfully rubbing fingers that were thinner, longer, and more delicate than those she had been born with. She experienced the past suffering of the first ones, and the crippling confusion of minds accustomed only to contemplation. Terror ripped into nerves she never knew she possessed.

She cried out, stumbled, and fell waking into the icy reality of a snowdrift. Cold shocked her back into memory of self; around her, the singer's melody sang of despair that approached madness.

Skyfire rolled until the end of her bow no longer hampered her legs. She shook icy flakes from her lashes and hair, and stood upright with a shiver. The music seemed very near, and it pulled at her heart without surcease. Around her the trees drooped under a hardened burden of ice. Summer stars shone faintly through the cold. Skyfire blinked. Unquestioning as a wolf, she shook off the muddle left by the chill and pressed forward. The snow deepened. Before long she labored through drifts that rose to her chest. But her efforts brought progress. The melody grew stronger as she went; the spell of the singer wove inescapably through her being. Whether she risked death, she would not stop now.

The way grew more difficult. The snow acquired a hardened, glassy crust of ice that cut at her fingers and toes. Skyfire was not dressed for such weather. Her flesh gradually went numb. She shivered uncontrollably, and longed for the stoic presence of Woodbiter at her side. Still, harsh as her own straits seemed, nothing prepared her as she scrabbled over the final rise in the snow and beheld the singer at last.

He sat with his head bowed over crossed arms, bare feet buried to the ankles in the pelt of his gray wolf. Black hair hid his face, trailed in unkempt tangles over shoulders clad thinly as Skyfire's. He did not shiver, though his fingers seemed frozen and bloodless as quartz. His song surrounded him with magic. Thick as mist, the spells he sang brought cold deep enough to crack stone, and grief enough to make the trees weep.

Skyfire hesitated as if struck by a blow. Then, before she quite realized she had reacted, she was running, sliding, flailing down the steep drift, to tumble breathless at his side.

The gray wolf looked up and growled, its eyes all silver-bright and wary. For once as brash as her brother, Skyfire dared its wrath. She recovered her footing and addressed its uncanny companion.

"Who are you?" Though she had not planned, her words came out as sending.

The singer looked up. Eyes identical to those of the wolf met hers, and it seemed for a breath that the earth stopped turning.

Then his song changed, flowed without break into sending. The melody itself framed answer, describing him as Outcast, wild as the bachelor wolf who runs with no ties to a pack. Skyfire, listening, heard a melancholy that made her spirit ring with echoes. The song described more than an elf with silver eyes, more than a hunter who roved alone. The chieftess of the Wolfriders heard silence more deep than sky, wind more free than storms, a spirit more solitary than the terrible moment of death. She knew then that she had been gifted with this elf's soulname, and in the depths of his silver-ice eyes she saw her own self reflected back at her.

"Kyr."

There, in an unseasonal enchanted snow, Huntress Skyfire became Recognized by an elf who was a stranger, and who conformed to no law and no pack. More terrifying still, the melody this outsider sang held all of the exhilaration, and all of the pain, and all of the twisted madness that the magic of the high ones became heir to on the world of two moons.

Even through the compulsion of Recognition, Skyfire sensed danger. The spell the song wove was not gentle, but filled full measure with remembered tragedy from the past. The effect was compelling enough to wound, and both she and the one fate chose for her mating were entangled in its threads. One of them must free the other, and of the two, the singer was most lost in his dream. Recognition offered no choice in the matter. Skyfire reached out to the singer, but never completed her touch. The gray wolf's warning became a snarl of rage and his muzzle lifted over bared teeth.

The despair of the singer's spell only hampered. In desperation, Skyfire sent to the beast, her image all strength without threat. The wolf did not respond as a pack member would. Mad as his outsider master, he rose and advanced on stiffened legs. Skyfire sensed the tautening of muscles beneath the silver-gray pelt. The wolf was preparing to rush her, and she carried no spear to defend.

Only her bow remained to her, hung uselessly across her shoulders; if she made the slightest move to free it, the stranger wolf would charge. Skyfire knew better than to attempt to flee. The spell slowed her reflexes and the snow would mire her. The wolf would sense her disadvantage. That would inevitably provoke an attack, and she had no desire to die with fangs sunk into her neck from behind.

She glanced to the singer, but no help awaited her

there. Snow flurried over his dark hair, and his eyes were mirrors of grief. Song and sorrow had overwhelmed his senses; his magic ran out of control.

The wolf growled again. It shifted onto its haunches. Aware she was out of options, Skyfire snatched for her bow. The string barely cleared her shoulder as the great beast sprang. He was larger than Woodbiter, and young. Skyfire raised the frail wood, tried uselessly to stave off his rush. Fangs closed over the shaft and splinters flew. Then the chieftess was borne down beneath hard-muscled weight and gray fur.

She ducked to protect her throat. Battered into snow, she rolled. The terrible jaws clacked over her head. The wolf pressed for another snap. Skyfire twisted and managed to jab a knee into the animal's ribs. The wolf snarled in rage and tried again. Once more she dodged its teeth. Her quiver banged into her thigh, spilling stone-pointed arrows treacherously over the ground. If she rolled in an attempt to throw the wolf off, she risked becoming impaled. Yet she had little chance if she hesitated. The wolf caught her braid in its teeth, slamming her head from side to side. She punched at its eyes, missed, and caught a glancing slash from a fang.

The wolf scented blood and attacked with renewed fury. In danger of severe mauling, Skyfire braced against its chest and sent, "Submission-fear-fury-submission." She hammered the beast's mind with her self-awareness, the irrefutable knowledge of her right to lead. She had challenged for dominance, and won. This stranger wolf must back down before her, or else kill, or be killed in turn. Such was the way of the wolves.

Skyfire gritted her teeth, the scent of her own blood strong in her nostrils. She knew no fear, only determination; this the wolf sensed. Its great heart faltered. Skyfire sensed its instant of unsureness. She twisted, used a wrestling trick and threw the heavier animal down. At once she went for its throat. Her nails caught its flesh and twisted, hard. The breath rasped in its throat. It lived now only by her sufferance. Her green eyes stared into ones of silver-gray, elf and wolf both equally savage and fierce.

Then the wolf went limp. Its lips stayed turned back, but it arched its neck to farther expose its throat. Skyfire gave the animal an extra shake to enforce her moment of victory. Then she backed off.

The air felt very cold. Grazed, disheveled, and bleeding from her slashed wrist, the chieftess licked at her hurt. She watched the gray wolf warily, but it rose with its tail down and settled on the far side of the singer. Only then did Skyfire realize that the terrible song had stilled. She looked around to find the black-haired elf senseless in the snows his magic had spun. But the dreams of the past which inspired him had dissipated. His awareness was dark as the night.

Skyfire shrugged her torn tunic back into place. Stiffly she regained her feet and went to him. His eyes were open and empty as clouds. Outcast he had named himself; but to Skyfire he was Dreamsinger, and would remain so, though he had no pack to name him. Slowly the chieftess knelt at his side. She cautiously extended a hand, and this time the gray wolf did not challenge. Her fingers bridged a gap of empty, wintry air, and touched.

His flesh was very cold. Skyfire sent thoughts of urgency into his mind, and could not reach him. His magic had carried him perilously far. He would return on his own, perhaps, but unless he wakened soon he might freeze. The possibility filled Huntress Skyfire with a new and uncomfortable dilemma.

The way of the wolf-pack urged her to leave. Survivors did not burden their resources; to be encumbered by the helpless was to invite a pointless death. Yet the dream of the singer had poisoned the familiar, pushed Skyfire's awareness beyond the limits of experience. Though taxed by the rigors of her night-long run, and shaped by the same wild laws which had arbitrated her dispute with the wolf, the chieftess hesitated. Skyfire found herself incapable of leaving the Dreamsinger to die.

Surely Recognition might cause such madness. Partially reassured, the chieftess caught the stranger beneath the shoulders. The gray wolf whined, but did not interfere as she half lifted, half dragged him over the heavy drifts. The Dreamsinger was slight, perhaps the same build as Sapling. Yet the Huntress was tired, and the snow hampered her steps. Leaving her arrows and broken bow, she labored over the ice with her burden until her feet stumbled beneath her. Her strength was long-since spent. Somehow she continued. In time the magic of despair fell behind. The stars overhead lay pale in the glow of dawn, and green ferns and moss cushioned her steps.

Skyfire lowered the Dreamsinger in a clearing and flung herself down by his side. Whether or not there were humans, she could go no farther. She curled on the ground beside the strange elf and slept. After pacing with uneasiness the gray wolf curled on the opposite side of elf-friend and buried its muzzle beneath its brush.

Huntress Skyfire awakened to song. Sunlight dappled her shoulders and eased the ache of her cut wrist; yet even summer's warmth seemed thin beside the joy in Dreamsinger's melody. The chieftess stirred, and found eyes of unearthly silver intently watching her. The black-haired elf seemed poised, as if for flight; only the ties of Recognition prevented.

Speech itself seemed an intrusion, a sour note against a magnificence of song that no living being might dare to spoil. "Come," Skyfire sent. She raised her arms toward him.

The outsider elf hesitated. Outcast, the song defined him, and a thread of sadness slowed the cadence.

"No." Skyfire smiled, for the moment as sure as bedrock. "Dreamsinger." Though the ways of the pack and the vision of dream might war inside her, the call of Recognition obscured them.

For a moment the fey elf did not move. All his years of wandering cast a current of doubt between them. Skyfire smiled, uncaring; and the pull of longing overwhelmed. The Dreamsinger answered the name he had been given and gathered Skyfire into his embrace. His song swelled

around her. For an instant she knew the wild joy of
Timmain running with her wolf-mate; then the pound of
blood in her veins overturned the dream. The notes of the
spell shifted afresh, transformed the clearing to a place of
new spring grass that was softly perfect for mating. Skyfire
had known the exertion and thrill of the hunt. She had
killed for food and for survival, and lived the fierce way of
the wolf-pack. She had howled in moonlight, and chipped
winter ice for drinking, and gnawed upon bones when her
stomach was hollow with hunger. The life of the pack contained all there was to know of death and survival. But in
Dreamsinger's arms the Wolfrider chieftess learned gentleness, and that one thing overturned all else.

Dreamsinger traced her many scars with light fingers.
His song spoke now of healing, and places where elves need
not kill. Skyfire heard, and ached with the terror of the
unknown. This dream which lacked the howl and the hunt
tore away the familiar, left her adrift without bearings. The
Dreamsinger sang of the past, lost forever, or of a life
impossibly far into the future. Skyfire caught her fey mate
close, for his body was warm and listening caused pain. Yet
little comfort came to her. He was the song, and his
strangeness brought conflict beyond bearing. The pull of
Recognition would not let her leave, not let her run and join
Woodbiter, and find refuge in the pack. She could not go; in
time she no longer wanted to. The Dreamsinger's strange
magic touched her spirit and wove irrevocable change.

After the mating he caught up her fiery hair and glo-
ried in the color, which promised both sunset and dawn. As
he braided the shining length of it, Skyfire looked up past
his head and watched a tree burst spontaneously into blossom. The scent made her languid and content, until the
Dreamsinger's spell changed key, as, inevitably, it must.
He belonged to no pack. As Outcast, he must leave her, or
risk the leadership she had won from Two-Spear at such
cost. Dreamsinger's music encompassed the brightness and
sorrow of that. Released from the drive of Recognition,
and caught in contention between ways, Skyfire pulled free
of his arms, unable to speak.

The aftermath of their joining was bittersweet. The Dreamsinger pulled on his ragged clothing with his back turned. Before the afternoon was spent, his grey wolf arose and slipped away with him into the forest.

Evening fell, and the moon rose. Skyfire sat amid drifts of falling petals. Woodbiter crouched at her feet, insistently proud of finding her; she had strayed very far from known territory. The old wolf's sides heaved as he panted, yet occasionally, in concern, he would turn his muzzle and lick at the cut on his chieftess's arm.

Skyfire scratched absently at his ears. She was hungry but had no inclination to hunt. The woodland silence oppressed her, filled her with a strange, numb emptiness that the way of the wolf could never fulfill. She would bear a cub to the Dreamsinger; such was the fruit of Recognition. But his song and his dream might leave her with more than offspring, if she was bold enough to risk leading the tribe into change.

For by the way of the wolf, Dreamsinger was Outcast. The magic of the high ones ran to madness within him. Rightly the earlier generations had driven him out, for compassion and dreams of peace had no place in pack life. Yet Skyfire had shared his visions. She had experienced the hopes of Timmain, and through them she understood that her ancestress had mated for more than the toughness and savagery of the wolf. The ancestress had wished to pass on hardiness and forest cunning, yet retain the bright dreams of the first ones. All of this had been lost over time. Skyfire's tribe lived only the way of the pack, and not an elf among them questioned why.

The chieftess rose restlessly to her feet. She drew on her boots, and blossoms fell like snow from her shoulders. She considered the cub she would bear from this mating. It might inherit its father's fey madness. By pack law, it also might suffer and be driven away into solitude. Skyfire flicked her braid back in frustration. By then she herself might not remember the song and the dream, for the wolfsong eroded the memory. This minute she perceived very clearly. If the tribe continued as it had, they would have nothing to offer their cubs but hardship and hunger and the changeable luck of the hunt. Something precious stood to be lost, perhaps without chance of recovery.

Dreamsinger himself held the answer. He wandered the forest in exile, hunting what he could forage, and driven relentlessly by gifts that had potential to kill him. Yet he had not died. His madness had harmed no others. Skyfire might bring him into the holt, and ensure the continuance of the dreams his songs inspired. But to do so defied pack law. For that the Wolfriders would challenge her, force her to fight and fight again until all had submitted to her will. Her chieftainship might be lost. She might be defeated by another, and earn death or even exile without hope of reprieve. The thought of sharing Two-Spear's cruel fate filled her with distress. Woodbiter sensed, and whined softly by her knee.

Skyfire stroked the wolf's head, but not to offer reassurance. "Find Dreamsinger," she sent.

The wolf hesitated. Sharply impatient, the chieftess drove him forward. She had learned a thing worth fighting for, worth even the risk of total loss. Elves might hunt with wolves, and share the hardships of survival. But Dreamsinger had showed her another way, neither elf nor wolf, but a glimpse of Timmain's wise vision. Skyfire chose change. She slipped through the thickets like the wild creature she was, her ears listening keenly for distant strains of a song she still could not distinguish between the sending of an elf, or true sound.

Triple-Cross

Lieutenant Jensen paced, spun in a tight circle, then hammered an angry fist on the chart table. Loose marker pins scattered from the blow, falling like micro-shot through furniture tight-knit as a battle formation. "Damn the man, what godforsaken plot could send him back to Guildstar?"

"Information, maybe," suggested Harris, who lounged with closed eyes on the wall bunk, his pilot's coverall in its usual neglected state of crumple. Quarters on *Sail* were far too cramped for displays of violent frustration; by now resigned to having sleep disrupted by his senior's obsession with the obscure motivations of a criminal, Harris chose not to fight the inevitable. "You can bet Mac James isn't making the run for any merchant's sake."

The model of a Fleet officer in a faultlessly fitted duty coverall, Jensen swore. Black-haired and classically handsome, he leaned on his knuckles and glared at his holo map of Alliance space, which hogged whatever paltry space their quarters had to offer. The display was crisscrossed with threads and speared with markers in three colors: blue for those sites the skip-runner MacKenzie James was rumored to have visited; yellow for a confirmed sighting, and red for any station or planet or interstellar vessel that had fallen prey to his penchant for piracy. Mac James being the most wanted criminal on Fleet record, the map was peppered red from end to end.

"Or else the source you bribed is selling you a line of crap," Harris added.

Jensen swore again. He smoothed back bangs razor-trimmed in the latest military fashion. "My informant isn't wrong. I pay another rebel to cross-check her."

Harris knuckled the orange stubble that roughened his jaw. He failed to open his eyes, or speak; but his silence on the subject spoke volumes.

"The two are not in cahoots," Jensen defended, hotly enough to send another pair of markers bouncing across the narrow aisle of decking. They fetched against the corrugated plastic of the shower stall, where the lieutenant irritably retrieved them. "My people don't even know each other, and since when does a Freer do business with a Caldlander without one sticking a knife in the other?"

Now Harris did sit up, incredulity etched across lines left by laughter and self-indulgence. "Damn, boy. You've been had. I know you're rich, and that you've dumped all of Daddy's allowance into tracking skip-runners, but didn't anyone tell you? Freerlanders never sell out on a comrade. Mac James has been named in their honor song since the day he jammed that surveillance station over Freermoon and knocked it out of orbit."

Jensen returned an arch look. "This Freerlander is the one whose ancestral burial grounds got slagged under nine tons of radioactive junk, direct result of that foray."

Harris flopped backward. "OK," he agreed in defeat. Jensen's back-up informant wouldn't be lying for gain, but hell-bent on bloody revenge. Harris wasted no energy wondering who else besides rebels his aristocratic senior had courted for access to Mac James's secrets. He shrugged one shoulder and said, "So your damnable pirate has business on Guildstar? So what?"

Jensen's brown eyes narrowed. Because it made no sense, he thought, slipping into one of those sudden, uncommunicative silences that claimed him when he contemplated the skip-runner captain whose activities pre-occupied him wholly since the Khalian wars wound down. Combat action was reduced to a minor few far-flung outposts, and the present best chance for glory and promotion remained the capture of MacKenzie James. And James, who was never careless, never forthright, and never in his life involved in honest trade, should have been anathema in a system as straitlaced as Guildstar. Half the merchants on the council there had suffered losses due to Mac's operations; his ship, the *Marity*, should in theory have been blown to bits the instant she applied for a docking bay.

Webbing creaked as Harris shoved to his feet. His pilot's reflexes spared him from stepping unshod on spilled tacks, but the near miss sent him muttering toward the galley cubicle for coffee, or beer, or the chocolate bars he ate after difficult flights that unjustly never fleshed out his middle; even his tailored dress uniform hung on him like a mechanic's coverall.

Jensen's lips thinned in distaste. Harris's sloppiness was tolerable only because he could fly the shorts off just about all of his peers. And if Harris resented his assignment on *Sail*, a three-man scoutship commanded by a lieutenant whose father had stonewalled all reasonable opportunity for advancement, the pilot was too lackadaisical to care. Jensen despised such lack of ambition, but kept his contempt to himself. Without Harris, *Sail* had no prayer of intercepting the *Marity*. Longingly, Jensen reached out and fingered the single green pin in the display. How would his pilot respond, he wondered, if he knew that Daddy's allowance had gone toward the spreading of false information? Would Harris file for transfer if he understood that the green pin marked a trap most painstakingly laid to entice the *Marity*'s master, precisely so that *Sail* could effect a capture?

But the *Marity*, damn her wayward, disingenuous traitor of a captain, appeared not to be buying; instead she was making a third run to Guildstar, decorously scheduled as the merchanter she assuredly wasn't.

Jensen loosened a clenched fist and retrieved a marker,

a blue one; with determined steadiness he imbedded the pin by the existing pair over Guildstar, then muttered, "It makes no sense."

Though Harris could overhear from the galley, Jensen felt no embarrassment. While other officers jockeyed for leave to visit wives and families, the lieutenant curried favor with Intelligence. He was first among the lower ranks to hear that the Khalia had been armed and financed by the Syndicate; the shock just beginning to filter down from above was that war was far from over. The heated issue now was location of the Syndicate's worlds. Weasel sources held no clue, spies in the most sensitive positions drew blanks, and the brass was reduced to screening hearsay in a vain search for coordinates. Jensen viewed the dilemma with an eye for opportunity. His passion to trap MacKenzie James took on increased importance: a skip-runner who trafficked in state secrets and whose record held multiple charges of treason would be acquainted with the Alliance's enemies. The Syndicate should be numbered among his customers. If James did not know their home system, he would have a contact, or a base of operations that would open a direct lead. To capture him, to claim the hero's honor for uncovering the turf of the enemy, Jensen was prepared to stake his name and career.

Lieutenant Michael Christopher Jensen, Jr. tapped the blue pin into the holo map, then considered another red one with a speculative frown. Mac James had pilfered plans for prototype weapons the Fleet had in classified research; the designs had not turned up in Indy hands, as everyone first supposed; where had James sold his booty that time? *Where?*

The blue pin mocked, by Guildstar.

"None of this makes sense, damn you to Weasel castration!" Jensen exploded, as though the arch criminal he hunted could hear his curse across space.

In the galley cubicle, surrounded by crumpled cups and a fashion magazine left by the ensign, Harris lifted doubtful eyebrows under a crown of red-gold hair. "Obsessed," he muttered to himself, and the coffee just ordered from the dispenser sat cooling while he rummaged under the mission's accumulation of debris after his illicit cache of beer.

In a dusty rebel settlement far beyond *Sail*'s patrol, a bar had been erected from slabs of modular siding filched from derelict stations and an abandoned colonial settlement. The corners did not match, and the sand took advantage. The floors were terminally gritty. In a side room, walled off by a fringed curtain, a Freerlander raised her cowl to veil a vicious smile. Her narrowed, desert-weathered eyes caught topaz light from a candle flame as she shifted gaze to the man who sat in the shadows. "The young officer was told outright, Captain. Guildstar, the time, the date. Everything short of your com codes, but the word is he hangs back, still."

A dry chuckle answered from the darkness. Pale eyes flicked up and glinted, while on the wine-sticky tabletop, a pair of hands scarred by coil burns flexed and straightened and flexed with an ease that, by the nature of such injuries, never should have been possible. Over the noise of the spacers' bar beyond the doorway, a voice equally grainy and grim observed, "Then the boy is not quite the brash fool he once was. No point in renewing the lease to that merchanter when this run's finished. I'll recall *Marity* when she makes port at Guildstar. Let out word that my next move will be those private sector interests on Chalice."

A chair squeaked as the Freerlander sat straighter, and a sigh issued from the hawk-nosed man wearing Caldlander harness who lounged opposite. After a black glance at the Freer, the Caldlander said, "But I understood the take on Chalice was worthy of a raid? Is it not risky to be baiting an Alliance scoutship on site at a real operation?"

"Well, Godfrey," drawled the man with the scarred hands. "If that's what it takes to get me access to a documented Fleet vessel, there's the ticket to the party. My mate Gibsen'd find the heat more welcome than bus driving guild cargoes, there's certainty."

The Caldlander made a disparaging sound through his nose; the Freer readjusted her cowl.

Both were cultural signs of displeasure, ignored by the skip-runner captain who stretched and rose, still in shadow. He half turned, scooped up a rattling collection of weapons belts and hiked them over his shoulder. Then he exposed blunt teeth in an expression that Freer and Cald both knew better than to mistake for a smile.

"Gentleman," said MacKenzie James in his boyishly amiable fashion. "Lady. If one of you kills the other after I leave, take my point, I'll gut the survivor like a fish."

No sound answered but a whore's raucous laugh beyond the doorway.

"Good," Mac James concluded. Still slinging the weapons he had, after all, never promised to return, he spun and ducked out, a large-framed bear of a man with a tread that incongruously made no sound. The door curtain slapped shut after him and left two enemies face-to-face over a wildly guttering candle.

"Damn his arrogance," swore the Caldlander. His fist slapped irritably against the hip that now held neither knife, nor sheath, nor pistol.

The Freer expressed her frustration through silence and a twitch of steel-nailed fingers. She found she had something to say after all. "If it were only his arrogance, neither of us would have come here, nor agreed to run errands to benefit some snot-nosed boy lieutenant."

The Caldlander stiffened fractionally. His eyes showed wide rings of white. "You suspect the information on Chalice is a setup?"

The face under the cowl yielded nothing. "The question is, does MacKenzie James?"

The enemies parted then, each wrapped in their own breed of silence. Days later, when Freer and captain were both beyond contact, it occurred to the Caldlander that Mac James's formidable cleverness might have fallen short. This once he might have overlooked the significance of a past action that had slagged a Freer ancestral memorial.

• • •

Sail emerged from the queer, deep silence of FTL on a routine run to deliver dispatches to Carsey Sector base. The capsule was relayed, another received to replace it, and in the six-sided capsule that served as cockpit, Harris snoozed in his headset, bored. Behind him, in the command alcove reserved for Lieutenant Jensen, *Sail's* third crew member slouched in the process of painting her nails. Sarah Ashley Del Kaplin, called Kappie by her deckmates, was short, whip-thin, and full-lipped. She had inviting, dusky skin and a deep voice, and she had taken assignment on *Sail* knowing that the lieutenant was handsome, but an iceberg, and that Harris was a bum who pinched. The pinches she fielded with equanimity, until they got too personal to ignore. Harris received a bruise he swore happened in a shower that was gravity stabilized, and the iceberg lieutenant was left to his romance with the machinations of MacKenzie James.

"Why's his nibs not out here reading off new orders?" Kaplin mused, turning her wrist to admire her nails, which this round were metallic lavender.

"Huh," muttered Harris. One elbow on the astrogation unit, he scratched his chest through his unsealed collar, then added, "The lieutenant will return to duty when he's finished housekeeping his map tacks."

A shout emerged from crew quarters, followed by what sounded like a war whoop. Harris shoved out of his slouch, and Kaplin swiveled around, her almond eyes wide with astonishment. "Did I hear that? Could this mean we've been assigned leave for the next tour?"

Harris grunted again. "Small chance. Jensen spends leave doing volunteer scut work for the recon boys."

Kaplin's groan was interrupted by Jensen's explosive appearance at the companionway. His rangy frame filled up the narrow opening; lit by the overhead panel, his face was flushed and his eyes overbright with excitement.

"He's done it!" the lieutenant shouted, waving a recent message com. "He's finally taken the bait."

The "he" needed no definition; nothing short of obsession with MacKenzie James could cause Jensen to overlook the crew member who usurped his command chair, the nail polish a calculated affront to his dignity.

From the pilot's station, Harris drawled, "Let me guess. We're going to go AWOL, maybe pay an unscheduled visit to Chalice? At least I presume all those messages coming and going between us and the private sector were not over an affair."

Kaplin watched this exchange, her nail brush forgotten in her hand. "If our boy is even capable of an affair," she muttered sotto voce.

Jensen failed to take umbrage as he crossed the cockpit in a stride. Risking an undecorous crease in his trousers, he leaned on the instrument panel cowling. This drew a frown from Harris, disregarded as the lieutenant plunged on. "No. We go under regs, by the book. *Sail*'s a scout and recon owes me a favor. Once we've placed these dispatches, I can get us an assignment to do a discretionary patrol sweep. Since the mines on Chalice are the juiciest operation the military has going with private business, they'd naturally need to be checked."

Harris raked his fingers through a rooster comb of red hair, then replaced his beret with its frayed Fleet insignia. "That'd work."

Only Kaplin insisted on particulars. "What's at Chalice for us?"

Jensen let her sarcasm pass. "Everything. I've been months setting it up. We're going to capture MacKenzie James and through him trace the home worlds of the Syndicate."

Kaplin raised pencil-thin eyebrows. "Oh? And what's in Chalice for MacKenzie?"

Smug now, Jensen smiled. "A trap. My trap. James thinks he's going to heist core crystals, ones engineered with the technology used to interface those fancy brainship modules with their hardware. But once in, he'll find out the booty was bait. *Sail* might not have all the latest tracking gadgets, but she's strong on gunnery. We're going to stand down the *Marity*."

The nail brush by now was thoroughly dry. Tossing it aside in exasperation, Kaplin flipped back ash-brown hair. "You're crazy. You'll get us all court-martialed."

"Or decorated," Harris interjected. "That's what happened last time."

That moment Jensen noticed the gaudy, nonregulation nail lacquer. "Ensign Kaplin," he rapped out. "One more breach of protocol on this bridge, and I'll have you confined to quarters." His voice did not change inflection as he resumed with orders for his pilot. "Harris, charge the coils and prepare for FTL. I want our dispatches delivered as if they were hot, and *Sail* on flight course for Chalice."

In fact the logistics took days to work out. On fire with impatience lest they miss their timing at Chalice, Jensen paced through *Sail*'s tiny corridors. He ran through his plan to trap *Marity* over and over again. Since the scout-ship's living quarters consisted of two bunkrooms, a galley cubby, and the bridge, his crewmates grew sick of hearing it. Harris escaped by closeting himself in astrogation to watch his library of porn tapes. Kaplin got bugged enough to argue.

Her fingers tapped the mess counter as she voiced her list of objections. "First, you took a helluva risk assuming those recon boys you brown-nosed could wrangle us an assignment."

"Irrelevant point," Jensen snapped. "We've got our papers and the assignment, both on target."

Kaplin shot a glance at the soup he would not eat because of nerves, and her next nail snicked against the counter. "Second, the explosive you had that dock worker rig in case your plans went awry could misfire."

Jensen gestured his exasperation. "Not if you know, as the rest of Chalice personnel does, that the box with the self-destruct is a dummy. The crystals inside are fakes, a decoy for MacKenzie James."

"Oh?" Kaplin's eyebrows arched. "You told *everybody* about your plot? Even the janitors? Hell, man, if you left things that wide-open, your skip-runner's deaf not to know it. His intelligence network's better than Fleet's, if he's got connections with the Syndicate. So who's fooling who on this mission?"

"Mac's best style is recklessness," Jensen countered. "And he wants those interface crystals very badly."

Kaplin threw up her hands, almost banging the dish locker in her irritation. "You're telling me nothing but insanity! Our success depends on MacKenzie James being quantum leaps dumber than you are."

Now Jensen grew heated in turn. "If you can devise a better plan, I'd sure be interested to hear it!"

The lilac-colored nails drummed an agitated solo on the countertop. "I can't," Kaplin said finally. "But God, we'll be lucky if our asses stay whole through this one."

The queer, intangible stagger that human time sense underwent through the shift from FTL came to an end, but confusion lingered. On re-entry to analog space, *Sail* seemed to hesitate and bounce, as if she were a plane engaged in a turbulent landing. Then something moving and metallic impacted her high-density hull with an awful, ear-stinging clang.

"Jesus!" screamed Harris from the pilot's seat. "We've dumped slap into a war zone!" He spun the spacecraft, tossing Kaplin and Jensen hard into their couch stations.

The lieutenant strained against the pull of vertigo and managed to punch up an image on the screens. Instantly his eyes were seared by the glare of an expanding plasma explosion. *Sail* had not entered a war zone; instead, the station logged as her destination had been detonated to a cloud of gases and debris. Harris responded, reflexively kicked *Sail*'s grav drives into reverse with a scream of attitude thrusters. Small fragments rattled against the hull. The gravity drives accelerated into the red, and buzzers sounded warning.

Jensen stared at the blowing burst of destruction that Harris labored feverishly to evade. What could possibly have gone wrong? he wondered, and his shoulders tensed in anticipation of Kaplin's acerbic, "I told you so, you arrogant, stupid fool."

But Kaplin said nothing, only sat with her face in her hands, caution lights from the recon unit a glare of yellow against her knuckles.

"Je-sus," Harris repeated, the Eirish accent of his childhood breaking through the more cultured tones he had acquired in air-tactics academy. A gifted sixth sense and instinct enabled him to quiet the drive engines; *Sail* described a smooth course just beyond the event horizon left by the explosion. "What now?"

Nobody spoke. None of the three in *Sail*'s cockpit cared to contemplate what might have been had their scout probe broken through FTL just half an instant sooner. Jensen looked at his hands, found them clenched whitely on the arms of his crew chair. Since he could not change the fuckup, he forced his brain to work.

And the obvious stared him in the face.

"Kappie," he said sharply. "Engage sensors, sweep the vicinity for the presence of other warcraft."

"What?" Overdue, the ensign's reproach was cutting. "Have you gone nuts? You set a live charge on Chalice station, and now you're after the culprit who blew it?"

Lieutenant Jensen repeated his command, his voice back under control. "The charge I had rigged was a contained net explosive. If anybody set it off, even accidentally, it might have burned one sector. Not the whole station. We're seeing the afterimage of a plasma bolt. *Now, make your sweep.* Our lives depend on it, because the enemy who manned the weapon is still out there."

"Could be renegade Khalians," offered Harris.

Nobody had time to suggest otherwise. An alarm cut across the cramped cockpit, one that signaled an inbound distress call.

Kaplin locked in on the signal. "A survivor," she called crisply. "He's in freefall with no life-support beyond a service suit." She listed distance and vector, then added figures for Harris to calculate drift factor. The human bit of flotsam moved with the debris from the station, no less a victim of the blast. "He's got a maintenance coding," Kaplin finished. "Probably a repair man who was caught outside when the charge hit."

"Set course for intercept," Jensen ordered. "By regs, we're bound to pick the fellow up, and maybe he can tell us what happened."

A pilot other than Harris might have protested; laying course through a high-speed, tumbling mass of debris was hardly the safest of undertakings. But Harris leaned over his console, a half-crazed grin on his face. As he began the maneuver, he relished telling Kaplin that she'd better not unbelt to fetch a Dramamine. The vector changes were going to be fast, and violent, and if she was going to be sick from inertia, better that than wind up splattered against a bulkhead.

The interval that followed became a hellish parody of a carnival ride. Harris alone found the gyrations enjoyable. He leaned over *Sail*'s console with his nose thrust forward like a jockey, every sense trained on the attitude displays, and his hands almost wooing the controls. The spacecraft responded to his measure, rolling, twisting, and sometimes outright wrenching a clear path through pinwheeling debris. Harris pressed *Sail* to the edge of her specs and reveled in every moment. His voice as he announced that the survivor was now close enough to grapple aboard sounded near as he came to elation.

Lieutenant Jensen issued orders through his vertigo. As Kaplin set hands to her couch belt, he told her to stay on station. "Keep the scanners manned. If we're not the only craft out here, I want to know it fast." Then, as if *Sail*'s cockpit were too small to contain his restlessness, he strode out to manage the loading lock and grapplers on his own.

In keeping with most scout craft, *Sail*'s utility levels were a warren of bare, corrugated corridors as poorly lighted as a mine shaft, and unequipped with simulated gravity. Experienced enough to disdain magnetic soles, Jensen made his way aft through the service hatch, hand over hand on the side rails. Although he had logged more space hours, Kaplin was more agile than he. She could zip through null grav like a monkey, never the least bit disoriented. Jensen's jaw muscles tightened. A lowly female ensign should not make him feel threatened; but thanks to the almighty wishes of his politician father, others as inexperienced had earned their promotions ahead of him. Kaplin might easily do the same, despite the fact she was apt to act flighty on duty, and her record held a collection of demerits.

The frustration of being continually passed over caught up with Jensen at odd moments. Intent on the injustices of his career, he drifted over the open-grate decking to the space bay, flipped open the grappler's controls, and slipped on the headset inside. He clicked the display visor down, powered up the unit, and initiated recovery procedure as if the drifting speck on the grid represented no castaway, but an enemy target in a weapon scope. Since Jensen held a citation for marksman elite, the mote of human flotsam was recovered in commendably short order. Jensen tossed the headset into its rack. Poised before the trapezoidal entry to the lock chamber, he engaged the space bay controls, then waited, his hand on the bulkhead to pick up the jarring vibration that signaled closure of the outer lock. His ears measured the hiss of changing air pressure as atmosphere flooded the chamber. Only greenhorns and fools trusted to idiot lights on the monitor panel. Electronics were never infallible, and there were prettier ways to die than voiding an unsuited body into vacuum.

The pressure stabilized within the bay. Jensen flipped off the manual safety and unsealed sliding doors through the innerlock. Inside the steel-walled chamber, the figure he had recovered drifted limply in null grav, clad in the bulky, ribbed fabric of a deep-space mechanic's suit. The elbows showed wear, the knees were grease-stained, and the tool satchels were scuffed with use. The hands in their fluorescently striped gloves did not rise to undo the helmet, and a second later, Jensen saw why. The face shield was drenched from the inside, with an opaque film of fresh blood.

Nausea kicked the pit of his stomach. He had not expected a survivor who was injured, or maybe dead. Hindsight made his assumption seem silly. The emergency tracer signal emitted by the suit did not necessarily trigger manually. The backpacks and tool satchel compartments were typical of a repairman's, and such gear often had a proximity fail-safe: if the worker wearing the rig accidentally came adrift from a workstation, the alarm would set off automatically. Jensen swallowed back sickness. He had seen death before, had once blown a man's brains out point-blank from behind. Now, duty demanded that he ascertain whether this suit contained a corpse, or a medical emergency.

Queasiness reduced to irritation, Jensen pushed off into the lock chamber. He bumped against the drifting figure, clumsily captured it in an embrace, and managed to hook onto the handrail before he caromed off the far wall. With one elbow crooked to maintain position, he wrestled the suited body upright, then flipped the clasps on the helmet.

As he lifted the face shield, the figure moved against him. A space-gloved hand gripped his waist from behind, and a hard object jabbed his side.

Probably just a tool appendage, Jensen rationalized, his pulse quickening. But the face behind the blood-streaked shield dispelled his last vestige of delusion. The lieutenant looked down into slate-colored eyes and an expression that held only ruthlessness.

"Godfrey, you boys are predictable," said the voice of MacKenzie James. The cheek in shadow beneath the face shield showed a smear of new blood, but the hold that gripped Jensen, and the arm that shoved what surely was a firearm against the lieutenant's side, were not those of a wounded man. MacKenzie James was bearishly strong, with reflexes not to be trifled with. Jensen had cause to remember.

Shocked by the skip-runner's presence and enraged to

have lost the upper hand to a castaway, the lieutenant fought to stay calm. "I presume you deep-spaced the man who owned the suit you're wearing."

The query prompted an insouciant smile. "Cut the crap," said James, his voice multiplied by echoes off of the lock bay walls. "If you've got any scruples about killing, they're faked." He shook back mussed brown hair and nudged the gun barrel in the ribs of his victim. "Unfasten my suit clips."

Jensen saw no option but compliance; if James decided to shed the bulky suit, a way might arise to seize advantage while his enemy was encumbered by the sleeves. Convinced that the pirate had tripped the charge in the bogus crate of brain crystals, and that an accomplice on *Marity* had seen the explosion and opened retaliatory fire on *Chalice*, Jensen talked in an attempt to distract his enemy's thinking.

"You'll never get away with a hijacking. *Sail*'s courses are automatically logged, and she runs under check-in protocols. All transmissions are coded and routinely traced."

MacKenzie James said nothing.

"Give yourself up, man." Jensen set hands to the last shoulder clip. "If our schedule is disrupted a millisecond, we're presumed to be boarded by enemies. We're tagged and targeted for armed search, with orders to be slagged on sight."

The clip unlatched with a click. James raised insolent brows. "Let go," he instructed. As Jensen hesitated, James swung his body and wrenched the officer's fingers. Painfully freed, Jensen felt himself spun around, his right wrist looped neatly in a tool tether.

The lieutenant struggled, tried to jab an elbow in his enemy's face. The move was both anticipated and countered; after years spent in freefall standing ambush, Mac James had mastered null grav to a fine point. He did little but shift one hip. The result provoked a spin as he and his captive drifted in tandem from the rail. Jensen's fast movement added vector that hammered him sideways into the wall. James was protected by his suit; Jensen, caught on the inside, got the breath crushed from his lungs, and a bruise on the temple that nearly stunned him. Weakly he clawed for the lock. If he could reach the control, he might signal and warn the bridge.

The tool tie on his wrist jerked him short and rebound slammed him backward into James. Jensen tried to fight. A punch that ineffectively dented suit padding was all he could manage before a kick in the groin killed his resistance. Amid the chaos of motion provoked by his shoves and thrusts, the tool tie looped his other wrist. Mac James controlled his random tumble. He shucked the suit, revealing blunt features and a pair of nondescript coveralls soaked like camouflage with bloodstains. Plainly the suit's original owner had died from exposure to vacuum. Left queasy by pain, and by the coppery sharpness of the droplets drifting in freefall that unavoidably got inhaled with each breath, Jensen cursed.

The gun barrel was no longer pointed at his face. James's hand on the grip was relaxed, even negligent as he loosened the neck of his coverall; this action was an effrontery by itself since Jensen was not fully helpless. His feet were left free to kick; but to do so in null grav without use of his arms was asking for a nasty crack on the head. Mac James understood that Jensen was experienced enough to know this. The skip-runner relied on that wholly, an arrogance his captive found infuriating.

Jensen cursed again. He despised the notion that a criminal could so easily guess his mind. He decided any effort was worth the inevitable concussion, but on the point of action, James caught the tool tie and jerked it like a leash.

Snapped in line like a disobedient puppy, Jensen wrestled with shoulders and forearms, half gagged by the taste-smell of blood. His struggles skinned the flesh of his wrists, no more; Mac James towed him expertly through the inner lock. Crimsoned, coil-scarred fingers tapped across the control panel. The skip-runner was no stranger to Fleet vessels, Jensen observed in bleak rage. The lock hissed shut, fail-safe seals engaged.

"You lost your ship, at least," Jensen managed through clenched teeth as he was dragged past the service access to condenser and drive-engine compartments. "I hope she was blown to a million bits as a result of your late misjudgment."

Mac James half turned. A glimpse of his snub-nosed profile showed a sardonically lifted brow. "Misjudgment? Godfrey, boy. I'm exactly where I planned to be, which is more than you can say for yourself."

Jensen returned an epithet, clipped short as he twisted to stop a nose dive; Mac James towed him through the access hatch into the upper level of the ship, and gravity slammed his shoulders into the deck grid. The breath left his lungs and his feet drifted stupidly in the gravityless well of the service corridor.

"Up," said Mackenzie James. The pellet pistol was back in his hand and fixed in nerveless steadiness on the vitals of his captive. "Move, now!"

An impatience colored the skip-runner's tone that only a fool would question. Jensen rolled, pulled his knees beneath his body, then flinched as his captor clapped a hand to his shoulder. He was ruthlessly hauled upright, spun, and marched ahead. The tool tie tautened, stressed his arm sockets without mercy, while the pistol nuzzled the base of his skull.

"Now," said James in his ear from behind. "We're going to the bridge. At the companionway, you will stop and instruct your pilot to set course for Van Mere's station in Arinat."

Jensen automatically began to protest. A shake from Mac James caught him short.

The captain qualified. "Your current orders permit you to act on discretion. And discretion, if you wish to stay alive, says *Sail* engages FTL for Arinat."

Aside from the weapon at his neck, curiosity urged Jensen ahead. That James knew the fine print on his orders was a cold and disquieting puzzle. "Why Arinat? And what's at Van Mere's except a trading colony for a remote agricultural outpost?"

"Quite a bit," James said uninformatively. Then, as if stating everyday business, he added, "The *Marity* didn't blow to bits along with Chalice. She's spaceworthy, and awaiting rendezvous, and will go under your escort through the security zone checkpoint to Arinat."

At which point Jensen knew searing rage. He had played blindly into an ambush. Months of intricate planning had led him to this: not as the hunter, but the trapped prey, forced to play puppet for the skip-runner MacKenzie James.

"Carry on, Lieutenant," the gruff voice instructed in his ear.

Jensen did so purely out of hatred. He swore he would find a way to turn the tables, to bring this pirate to a justice long deserved.

Skip-runner and captive reached the galley nook; beyond lay the companionway to the bridge. The hand that poised the gun at Jensen's neck tightened ever so slightly. Since Mac James was never a man to act by half measures, Jensen squared his shoulders. He stepped up to the companionway, faced through toward the cockpit, and crisply called out orders.

"Ensign Kaplin, discontinue your search pattern. Harris, I want this ship on a new course for Arinat. Plot FTL coordinates for the security zone checkpoint, and from there to Van Mere's station."

Harris shot out of his habitual slouch. He turned his head, stared at his superior officer with an insolence peculiar to pilots, and said, "You want *what*?"

The pistol nosed harder against Jensen's neck. He swallowed stiffly. "Harris. You're insubordinate."

"When isn't he," Kaplin commented with her usual flat-toned sarcasm. She shut down systems for travel and spun her station chair, in time to see Harris narrow his eyes.

"No," the pilot said, quite softly. "We've done too many assignments together for me to buy on this one. I'll set course for Arinat on one condition, *sir*. Step in here and show me both of your hands."

Jensen had no chance to warn, no chance to act, just one instant of crystallized fear as Mac James shoved him aside. The pellet pistol went off, a compressed explosion of sound. Jensen staggered off balance, heard Kaplin's scream, and knew: Mac James had gunned down his pilot, even as he, on a past mission, had killed the *Marity*'s mate. In his own way, but for different reasons, Jensen shared such ruthlessness. He was not shocked, but only whitely angry, when he recovered his footing and saw the fallen figure sprawled in the helm chair. The pilot's beret had tumbled off, and the fiery thatch of hair dripped blood. The long, lean fingers that had performed feats of magic at the controls were not relaxed, but twitching in an agitation of death throes. Mac James's pellet had taken Harris through the forehead. He'd probably died between thoughts.

A muffled sound across the cockpit reminded Jensen of his other, surviving crew member. Sarah del Kaplin looked sheet white; yet the makeup like garish paint over her pallor masked an unexpected depth of character. Scared to the edge of panic, she hadn't lost it enough to stand up.

Which was well, for the murdering skip-runner shoved onto *Sail*'s bridge and snapped his next orders to the ensign. "Lady, your training included flight rating, and you'd better know the material, because you're going to push that body off the helm and fly this vessel to Arinat and Van Mere's."

Kaplin turned a shade paler. She lifted wide eyes to her senior officer; and prodded by the gun in twitchy hands at his back, Jensen said, "Kappie. Just do it."

She returned a jerky nod, rose, and struggled with Harris's cooling corpse, her hands with their extravagant nail polish shaking and shaking, but able enough nonetheless. She sat in Harris's spattered chair and engaged instruments to plot the skip-runner's course.

MacKenzie James followed the figures that flashed on her board. The criminal knew his astrogation, solidly; that he watched over Kaplin's shoulder told more clearly than words that there were stakes to this foray. A hum pervaded

Sail's hull, followed by deeper vibrations. The coil condensers began their charge cycle in preparation for FTL, and as if the change in the ship's drive galvanized Jensen's thinking, it dawned that *Marity* had blown Chalice station deliberately, her purpose to hide Mac James's tracks.

"You've stolen the brain crystal interfaces," Jensen accused, his voice muffled by his own epaulette as Mac James shoved his face down and to the side, and manhandled him sideways into the hanging locker reserved for officers' dress coats.

James responded with a grin that had no humor behind it. "You helped make it convenient." He pushed down, ramming his captive into the dusty closet. "Chalice security was busily watching your box of rigged bait. Really, boy, I'm surprised. A man would expect you to learn not to keep on meddling beyond your depth."

Jensen winced as his elbow caught on the door hinge. Jammed on a nerve, he gasped, sweated, and vainly thrashed for purchase in an area too constricted for bodily movement. "Damn you," he grunted, before the fine silk of his officer's scarf was forcibly crammed in his mouth. James used a length of shock webbing to tie the gag in place, then shoved the door closed.

Jensen crouched in fetal position, his wrists lashed bloodlessly tight behind his back. Pressure against his cheek flattened his nose against his knees, and the toes of Harris's battle boots ground relentless dents in his buttocks. Unable to move, unable to speak, he still could hear. The dry tones of MacKenzie James instructed Kaplin to adjust her course; she'd missed a decimal point. The result, as James phrased it, would get *Sail* an unscheduled refit, since Van Mere's star had an asteroid belt that could skin the shields off a battle cruiser.

Jensen squirmed and managed to cramp his left thigh. He could not stretch to relieve the discomfort, but only sweat with the pain. The closet quickly became stifling, and somewhere between nausea and frustrated tears, he missed the shift to FTL. He knew the transition had happened when the cramp eased off, and he realized the vibrations from the condensers had subsided back to a whisper.

A light tread crossed the cockpit; not Kaplin's, Jensen determined. She tended to slap her heels down, result of a flirty, provocative hip-sway she habitually used to distract. Most men were not immune, but James would prove the exception. Jensen knew the skip-runner to be formidably focused in his actions. The steps paused, and the couch by the com station creaked.

"You'll tell me *Sail*'s security code schedule," James suggested in his gravelly bass.

Silence. Jensen squeezed his eyes shut and moaned. Kappie, he thought desperately, you'll go the way of Harris. He tensely awaited the shot.

"Godfrey, girl," said James. He sounded strangely tired. "Don't shake so hard. I only shoot on sight when somebody's fixing to kill me. Your pilot kept a gun in the pocket next to his jock strap, or didn't you know that?" A pause. "No, I see not. His whores shared the secret, and for a pitiful bit of change, they talked."

In the closet, Jensen drew a shuddering, sweat-stinking breath. He had not known Harris packed a pistol, never mind under that ridiculously baggy coverall. Jensen's worst nightmare had never allowed that James might run a network that extended so deep, into the back streets of who knew how many worlds. The haunts of pilots on leave were notoriously varied, and scattered as stars to scope out. That this criminal's interest had focused so intently on *Sail*'s crew was a most unsettling discovery.

"The codes," reminded MacKenzie James, his voice gone strangely steely. Above the subliminal hum of FTL, the cockpit beyond the closet seemed gripped in waiting stillness.

Kaplin gasped as if hit. "I can't tell you," she lied. "I don't know them!" Her bravery held an edge of hysteria.

Jensen braced for a shot that never came. The chair by the com console creaked again as Mac James shifted his weight. "Dearie," he said in a tone of deceptive gentleness.

"I'm running out of time. That means you talk, or I embarrass the brass higher up."

In the closet, Jensen frowned; and Kaplin's tremulous silence became underscored by James's quick tread, then the tap of fingers over the keys on what had to be the command alcove console.

"What are you doing?" Kaplin asked in a blend of fear and suspicion.

"Canceling our course coordinates," MacKenzie James replied. "We're going to stay in the Chalice system until a battle cruiser comes to investigate."

"You'll get us all blown to hell," said Kaplin with the acid bite she used to admonish her senior lieutenant.

"Very likely you're right." James left the command chair, and by the squeals of outrage that followed, Jensen judged that the skip-runner tied Del Kaplin to the pilot's station with his usual ruthless style.

There followed a wait, in which the skip-runner fixed himself coffee. In the protocols manual under the console, he found *Sail*'s security code schedule and ascertained the time for her next check-in. Then, with a style more flamboyant than Harris's, he spun the scout craft on a trajectory that blended with the expanding debris from the explosion.

Nauseated by vertigo, and jammed in the suffocating closet, Jensen felt a horrible, hollow lurch in his abdomen as the artificial gravity was switched off. More controls clicked in the cockpit as the skip-runner adjusted *Sail* for total shutdown, making her invisible to all but a tight-focus scan.

An hour passed, then two. *Sail*'s call-in was due in thirty minutes. Jensen sat, ears straining, to hear how MacKenzie James planned to handle the Fleet cruiser that was sure to arrive at any moment.

Kaplin must have been left facing the screens, because when the battle cruiser arrived, she spoke with tense satisfaction. "That's the *New Morning*. She's a flagship with an admiral aboard, and an escort fleet of six."

"Eight," James corrected. "Chalice got off a distress

torp." He did not sound upset, but crossed to the com console and rapidly began punching keys.

"You're going to beg amnesty?" Kaplin said, just missing her usual sarcasm.

"No. Personal phone call," James qualified. "To your senior, Admiral Nortin." A burst of static hissed across the screen, followed by the chime that signaled a clear transmission. James spoke crisply. "Ah, Admiral, I seem to have disturbed you in the shower?"

Jensen tried to picture his crusty senior officer in a towel or a bathrobe. Imagination failed. Nortin was always, and ever would be, square-shouldered, tight-lipped, and well-groomed, with a daunting row of medals on his chest.

In tones slightly rusty from surprise, the admiral answered, "Get to the point."

"Indeed." James paused for what had to be a nasty smile. "I wish to know the security codes for the scout-class vessel *Sail*."

"She's on reconnaissance assignment." The admiral recovered fast; already his words had recovered their customary bite. "Why *Sail*?" Then the admiral's voice became softly menacing. "You on her?"

James made no verbal reply; instead, his fingers tripped lightly over the console. A moment later, Jensen heard the click of the drive in the log tape reader.

The admiral's voice came back jagged. "Where did you get that film clip?"

"From an extortionist who wanted something much too big for his resources. He got killed instead. His tape collection, unfortunately, survived him. Now, I want *Sail*'s codes, and quickly, or the fact you took pay to hang back from engagement at Elgettin will be broadcast to the satellite feeds."

"It was never so simple as that." The admiral sounded suddenly very aged.

"It never is, sir." A false note of sympathy colored Mac James's platitude. He was, after all, committing blackmail. Jensen raged at the indignity forced on the admiral, as, over com, he heard the old man calling information from security.

Sail's codes came through promptly after that, and Jensen despaired as he confirmed the accuracy of each sequence. MacKenzie James had done his legwork with the efficiency that trademarked his career. He humbled large men and small with the same evenhanded ruthlessness. For his pains, the skip-runner captain had gained himself a scout-class vessel with open search orders. He could travel the breadth of Alliance space, or any of a half-dozen security zones, and not be questioned; the *Marity* could accompany openly, masquerading under military escort.

The effrontery of the piracy cut Jensen like a razor. He did not mourn for Harris. He felt only passing sympathy for his admiral's private shame; but for his own whipped pride and the certain ruin of his career, his hatred burned murderously bitter. Fury did not allow for limits. Crushed and cramped into a hole not fit for a dog, Jensen twisted his shoulders sideways and strained against the tool ties. He forced numb and bloodless fingers to open and close and grope for the nearest object to hand, which happened to be Harris's scuffed, old battle boots.

Two places the Eirish pilot wore those shoes without fail: on deck during combat, and off on leave, where his hobbies had been whoring and brawling. The toes were reinforced with steel caps, and Jensen sawed his bonds feverishly against the metal in the futile hope of fraying through high tensile mesh.

Activity continued on the bridge. MacKenzie James reset the autopilot, then, in a masterful orchestration of instruments, cross-wired the grav-drive regulators and the life-support emergency generators to charge the coils in a split-second burst of power. *Sail*'s banks reached peak capacity and transferred into FTL in one screaming instant of vertigo. *New Morning*'s instrumentation would have seen the surge, but not in time to evaluate whatever had caused the burst. To keep ends neat, they'd chart the anomaly as an unstable bit of debris from Chalice's fusion reactor.

Assured that *Sail* was safely away, James confined Kaplin to the stores locker behind the galley. Jensen missed the light-footed tread that returned to the cockpit, but not the change back to analog space, and the voice that activated the com and summoned the *Marity* to take station to *Sail*'s rear.

Mac James relayed instructions to his mate. "I'll escort you through the checkpoint at the security zone, as planned. Once in Arinat system, we'll separate. *Sail* will execute patrol patterns while you transfer the goods and take payment. We'll rendezvous afterward off Arinat nine, darkside of the satellite called Kestra. That's the only blind spot in the Syndicate's sensor network, and it's a damned narrow one. Misplace a vector, and we're vapor, so be careful."

As the skip-runner closed contact and restored *Sail*'s altered circuitry to reprogram his original course, Jensen paused in his attempt to free his hands. Furiously he combined facts, those he knew with others he'd heard. His final conclusion was chilling. For MacKenzie James inferred that the agricultural colony beneath Van Mere's was a covert Syndicate outpost, undiscovered by the Alliance and, indeed, unlikely to be, since Arinat system lay within the Molpen security zone that ships could not enter without passing a military checkpoint. The added inconvenience should have discouraged spies; but in a backhandedly clever sort of way, the compromised location made sense.

Who knew, and who had ever thought to look for sophisticated technology underneath three continents of crops? The secret was viciously guarded, since James had risked acquisition of *Sail* to have her in system for his transaction. If the Syndicate faction behind Van Mere's valued their skip-runner contacts lightly enough to blow them out of space after goods transfer, the wisdom of *Sail*'s presence made sense. On patrol, her sensors would detect explosions or plasma charges. She would be duty bound to report such abnormalities and file for investigation. The spies on Van Mere's would wish to avoid such attention in the interest of preserving their anonymity. Stations that traded with agricultural outposts rarely acted with aggression, and that profile provided essential cover.

MacKenzie James had indestructible luck because he unerringly planned for contingencies. As Jensen resumed sawing at his restraints, he had to admire the man's genius. Mac's operations had the feel of a grand dance, precisely timed, and disarmingly masqueraded as coincidence.

That *Sail* should be commandeered for treason was no sane ending to contemplate. The lieutenant leaned back in the cubicle, flexed his wrists, and groped at his bonds with his fingertips. The webbing was not the least bit frayed, and a tug to test the knots showed his efforts had only chafed skin.

A man who hated less might have quit. Jensen rammed his shoulders against the wall and relentlessly sawed all the harder. He persisted though his muscles cramped into screaming knots of agony. He cut and cut and cut the tool tie across the toe cap of Harris's boot through the hours of passage to Arinat. His hands went numb, and then his wrists and elbows. He kept cutting. *Sail* completed her transit, kicked out of FTL, and the web of the tool tie he'd been tearing at showed the faintest trace of a nap. He rested, listening as James refined course and opened contact in an unfamiliar language with his Syndicate contact on Van Mere's.

Orders were relayed, and *Marity* assumed position for the sale of her stolen technology. Core interface crystals took years to manufacture, and there were many, many bodies left crippled from the war that waited, bathed in nutrients, in the hope of future service in a brainship. Since crystals were unique, and the idiosyncrasies of each required a precise match with the consciousness of the individual they would be paired with, today's loss meant the death of hope for someone who valiantly clung to life in total helplessness. Jensen ran swollen, aching fingertips over the light fuzz on the tool tie. He acknowledged the sorry fact that he could never rip free in time to matter.

In the cockpit, MacKenzie James logged in *Sail*'s codes and established routine patrol at Arinat's. He set up a closed band connection with his mate on the *Marity*, and the core crystals came closer to changing hands.

Prisoned in the closet, Jensen shut his eyes. He reviewed every memory of Harris. There had to be a reason, besides steel toe caps, why the pilot insisted on a particular pair of boots whenever he flew into combat.

"Never catch me being lab rat for a Weasel," he had once confided over beer; Harris, whose whores had known he wore a pistol in a hip strap over his undershorts. Jensen reasoned furiously. The combat boots had metal-capped toes, but no ankle laces. It followed that Harris might have chosen the style to carry a knife in his boot cuffs.

Jensen strained to raise his arms, hampered as his elbows jammed against the back wall and the door panel. He lacked the space to flex and reach the boot tops only inches away from his wrists. He grunted, forced blood-starved muscles to contract. Using wall and door to wedge his shoulders, he raised himself inch by torturous inch and scrunched backward. He sat on the insteps of Harris's boots; while in the cockpit, MacKenzie James monitored the exchange of the crystals with a coolness that rankled the nerves.

Jensen groped, caught the left boot cuff between his knuckles. He pinched, kneaded, and crumpled the tired old leather, while his joints tingled horribly in complaint. He found nothing. Close to tears of frustration, he twisted at his bonds, forced his shoulders into an angle that all but flayed his back, and managed to hook the right boot. He found what he sought, not a knife, but a razor-thin strip of metal sewn between the seams above the ankle.

It took him a pain-ridden hour to work the implement free. By then utterly exhausted, he had to rest, his hands numbed lumps of meat, and his wrists scraped down to raw gristle. In the cabin, MacKenzie James wrapped up his transaction and gently set *Sail* on an outward spiral toward Kestra.

Jensen cut himself twice before he got the razor positioned against his bonds. He nicked the weave of the tool tie over and over, his hold precariously slippery with his own blood. The stubborn webbing gave way. Shivering, wretched with discomfort and relief, he wormed his arms into his lap and cradled his hands to his chest. He had to pause through an agonizing interval of time, until Mac James chose to leave the cockpit. Jensen dragged off his gag. He used the spoiled silk to wrap his gashed fingers, then, uncontrollably shivering in a cold sweat, he stole his moment to act.

The lieutenant tripped the catch to the closet and spilled unceremoniously onto the deck. His legs refused to obey him, and his manual dexterity was shot. Aware that he had only moments, he half dragged, half rolled his body across the cockpit to the weapons locker. More seconds were lost as he blotted blood from his hand so the security sensor could read his palm print. The lock clicked open. Not trusting his aim with a kill weapon, Jensen chose a riot pistol armed with stun charges. Then, scuttling crabwise, he positioned himself against the companionway bulkhead just as Mac James stepped in through the access corridor.

The skip-runner saw the opened closet and instantaneously jerked out his pistol. Formidably fast, he spun sideways, almost into cover as he punched the switch to shut the access hatch.

Jensen's charge nipped through the fast-closing panel and hammered the skip-runner in the shoulder. Nerves and muscles went dead and the pellet gun clanged to the deck. The barrel wedged in the hatch track. The door jammed, leaving a sliver of a gap; enough for Jensen to squeeze off another round.

Luck favored him. The charge caught Mac James as he leaned to kick free the jammed pistol. He grunted what might have been a word, then crumpled and sagged to the deck.

Jensen could not resist a crow of triumph. He might not have the *Marity*, might have lost the precious interface crystals to the enemy, but he had MacKenzie James. And along with the most wanted skip-runner in Alliance space, he could deliver the first definitive proof of a spy connection with the Syndicate. The wreckage of his plans at Chalice had not ended in failure.

The sweetness of victory and the sure promise of

promotion made his recent humiliation worthwhile. Gripping the stun pistol in his swollen, lacerated hands, Jensen pushed to his feet. He had details to arrange, a criminal to secure, and no choice but presume that the spies on Van Mere's monitored military com channels. He'd need to withdraw from Arinat system as if nothing untoward had happened, and initiate FTL before he dared call for an escort. *Marity* was still at large. The mate left on board would know James had encountered problems when rendezvous failed behind Kestra. Yet unless MacKenzie's man wished to broadcast Fleet connections and face reprisal from Van Mere's, he'd be powerless to pursue until too late.

Jubilant, drunk on his own triumph, Jensen cleared the companionway door. He gave the stunned body of his captive a vengeful, self-satisfied kick, then squeezed past to free Kaplin from the supply cubby. She could damn well reset their course log, since her infernally manicured fingers were probably not mangled to incapacity. As he stumbled on nerve-deadened feet, Jensen acknowledged that he desperately needed to use the head. He considered his ruined uniform, and wondered, between planning, whether his efforts to escape the hanging locker might have bloodstained his best battle jacket.

Well after the code check at 1700, Ensign Kaplin drifted cross-legged in the dimly lit corridor by the space lock. Unimpressed by Jensen's bubbling elation, and unconcerned that her hair needed fixing, she sullenly chipped enamel off a broken thumbnail. Her thoughts centered darkly around the admiral whose record was impeccable, but whose past was anything but. Her future in the Fleet would become deadlocked as a result of the tape she had witnessed. The lieutenant was a fool if he thought the captive held trussed in the lock bay was going to sweeten an admiral whose private shame had been leaked to the crew of a minor-class scout. As Kaplin saw things, MacKenzie James might never see trial; more likely he'd die of an accident, or someone would pull strings to set him free. He hadn't gotten where he was without connections in high places. His record of success was too brilliant.

Kaplin jabbed at her fingernail, plowing up a flake of purple lacquer. Jensen was an idealistic idiot, and Admiral Nortin a desperately cornered man; no need to guess who'd survive when the dirt inevitably hit the fan.

A discreet tap at the lock door disrupted the ensign's brooding. She started and looked up, saw the haggard face of MacKenzie James drifting by the small oval window. His hands were bound; he'd managed the knock by catching the pen from the bulletin alcove between his teeth and rapping the end against the glass.

"Damn," Kaplin muttered under her breath as her grip slipped and mangled a cuticle. She sucked at the scratch, pushed off from the floor grate, and, still cross-legged, peered through the glass. "What do you want?"

Other than a leak, she mused inwardly. If the stun drugs had just worn off, that's what most people wanted.

Mac James ejected the pen from his teeth. "Talk," he said, his succinctness blurred by echoes. He bunched his shoulders against the webbing Jensen had contrived to confine him. The result would have tethered a bull elephant, Kaplin felt, but hell, she was only the ensign. She unfolded elegant legs, set her shoulder against the lock, and lightly braced on the door frame. "Should I listen?"

James managed a grin. His forehead had somehow gotten cut during transfer from the bridge to the lock bay, and a bruise darkened the stubble on his jaw. "You might want to." He tossed back tangled hair and added, "I'd hate like hell to be left at the mercy of an admiral whose secrets were compromised."

Kaplin pursed her lips. "You're quick."

James's grin vanished. "Always."

The ensign considered her torn thumbnail, then elegantly unfolded her body and tapped the controls to her left. The lock unsealed, and a rush of cold air from the barren metal bay raised chills under her coverall. She shivered. "Speak fast. I'm not sure I should be listening."

"Be sure," said James. "I can get you reassigned. To another division, under another admiral, with a few less demerits on your record."

Kaplin regarded him carefully. Trussed hand and foot, his massive shoulders twisted back, James did not seem discomforted. His expression was much too confident. He watched, his eyes steely and level; as she noticed the scar over his right carotid artery, and as she lingeringly weighed the rusty stains that remained of a Chalice mechanic that patched his threadbare flightsuit. He was a man who had seen death from many angles. The possibility the next might be his own failed to move him.

"You'd have to free me, get me back to rendezvous at Kestra," he finished in a voice that was dry with disinterest.

A pirate should have owned more passion, Kaplin felt. The list of criminal charges did not seem to fit with the man. She thought deeper, while those gray eyes followed; her hand tapped involuntary tattoos on the railing. MacKenzie James, skip-runner, should have gunned the other crew down with Harris. His hold over the admiral was all he truly needed to commandeer *Sail* without questions.

As her oval chin rose obstinately, Mac James seemed to follow her reasoning. "I didn't kill Jensen because I need him. His obsession is a tool, invaluable because it's genuine. A man's hatred is always more reliable than the best of laid plans."

Kaplin narrowed her eyes. "Who are you," she demanded. "You'll tell the truth, or we don't talk."

Now Mac James studied her. He no longer seemed boyish, or hardened, but only unnervingly perceptive. "I take orders from Special Services," he said, his face like weather-stripped granite. "And my criminal record is genuine. I could be tried and convicted on all counts, and no pardon would come through to save me. I am legitimately skip-runner, traitor, and extortionist, and because of that, I have served as the Alliance's contact to disclose the motives of the Khalia and, now, the Syndicate behind them." A strange thread of weariness crept into the prisoner's voice.

He tried, but did not entirely hide a ghost of underlying emotion. "Sometimes it takes a bad apple to know one. And through *Sail*'s surviving officers, the Fleet is free to deal with what Van Mere's is actively covering. *Marity* is not involved, my cover is kept intact, and the Syndicate's best outpost is exposed to counterespionage before anyone inside knows they're compromised."

He was not pleading, Kaplin decided. He was appealing to her loyalty on a higher level; loyalty to humanity above her oath to serve the Fleet. She considered what he had not said, the threats he had not outlined: that *Marity* was yet at large, that *Sail* was still a long and lonely distance from the nearest battle cruiser or station, and that the Special Services branch of Intelligence often stooped to ugly tactics to free its operations from interference.

Fractionally, James shook his head. "Gibsen won't pursue. He's under my orders, and he won't break. Not to spare me from arraignment. The Syndicate outpost was always our target, whether I am sacrificed or not."

Kaplin chewed her lip. "Damn you," she whispered into the echoing chill of the lock. "What about the interface cores? And the outright murder of Chalice station?"

Now James lowered his lashes. His inscrutable expression cracked into a grimace of wounding compassion. "The cores we traded were genuine. The thirty pieces of silver, as it were, to confirm the presence of the enemy. And Chalice personnel, curse their bravery, defended their post with their lives."

Kaplin drew a shuddering breath. She bunched her hand and slammed the closure button; and the lock hissed shut, leaving the skip-runner and his haunted bit of conscience to the solitary chill of the space bay.

"Oh, damn you," Kaplin muttered. "Damn you to deepest hell." She needed a coffee, she decided; and every other habit that was ordinary to quiet a vicious inner turmoil. For the favor that MacKenzie James requested for the higher good of the Alliance was nothing short of mutiny. As she left her post and propelled herself through null grav toward the galley, she reflected that Jensen was going to dismember her.

Lieutenant Jensen snapped awake to the realization that *Sail*'s vibrations had changed. She was no longer traveling FTL, but powered by her more obtrusive grav drives. The lieutenant glanced at his chronometer, his worst fear confirmed. *Sail* had deviated from his chosen course and orders. He leapt from his bunk, jammed his legs into the nearest set of coveralls—Harris's by the smell of beer and sweat—and raced full tilt for the bridge.

He found the pilot's chair deserted. The course readout on the autopilot confirmed trouble well enough: *Sail* was currently under gentle acceleration out of the Arinat system. Directly astern, like a thing cursed, lay the cratered lump of rock some forgotten mapper had named Kestra.

Jensen was too enraged to swear.

He spun, plunged through the companionway hatch, and hurried with all speed through the service corridors.

He reached the lock to the space bay. A furious survey showed Kaplin drifting cross-legged in the chamber, twisting and twisting the shock webbing that once had confined MacKenzie James. She had been weeping. The mechanic's deep-space suit was gone, of course, along with the skip-running criminal who had killed its owner for hijack.

"My God, Kappie, why did you let him go?" Jensen's voice was a scream of unmitigated anger.

The ensign looked up, startled to fear. "Sir! He's Special Services, and on our side."

Jensen heard, and a greater rage crashed through him. His handsome face twisted. "Damn you, girl. He's the biggest con artist in the universe. You were *had*, and he was lying. You're nothing but his pawn, and a traitor." There would be an inquiry over Harris's death, Jensen's frantic mind understood. A trial would follow, and under investigation and cross-examination, the flimsy plot arranged at Chalice would surface and ruin his reputation.

The lieutenant ceased thinking. He reacted on the

reflex of a cornered animal, and hammered the green, then
the yellow, then the orange button on the console. The
lock door hissed shut, cutting off Kaplin's panicked
scream. Warning lights flashed, but the hooter that signaled a deep-space jettison never sounded. Kaplin had dis-
connected the alarm to release MacKenzie James for his
rendezvous.

For that reason, her pleas could be heard very clearly.
"Jensen! Listen to me! You're MacKenzie's best pawn, and
he knows it!" She launched away from the wall, hammered
her model's hands against the innerlock. "We could stop
James, both of us could stop him! Blow his cover with
Special Services, and he's lost his righteous reason to keep
skip-running. You didn't see his face, but I know. The
remorse would put him over the edge."

Jensen's lips stayed fixed in an icy half smile. Deaf to
pity, mindful of nothing beyond the ambition that was his
life, he ground his palm hard on the red jettison button.
The outerlock doors cycled open. Atmosphere vented outward, along with the corpse of the ensign who had dared to
turn triumph into failure.

Admiral Nortin's office on *New Morning* was sumptuously
large, but bare to the point of sterility. On the hard metal
bench by the doorway, Jensen sat in his dress uniform. He
kept his eyes straight ahead, resisted the urge to search the
impeccable white of his jacket for bloodstains the cleaners
had soaked out. He waited, rigidly correct, while the admiral's pearl-white fingers paged front to back, through his
report.

The words matched the circumstances closely enough:
Sail had happened across a raid on Chalice station and
picked up the trail of a skip-runner who had stolen core
intelligence crystals. The lieutenant in command had given
chase, followed the space pirate MacKenzie James to Arinat,
Van Mere's station. The log spool on the admiral's desk
held proof positive of a Syndicate spy post, in the form of a
recorded transaction between James and a covert network

on Van Mere's. *Sail* had maintained a standard patrol pattern, then pursued as the *Marity* made her getaway. Battle had resulted. *Sail*'s bridge had sustained severe damage, her pilot and her ensign dead in the course of duty. Jensen, sole survivor, had nursed his command back to base.

The admiral finished reading. He raised bleak eyes to the impeccably dressed lieutenant before his desk. He did not point out the unmentionable, that the log spool might hold proof of a Syndicate spy post, but events differed drastically from the report. Neither Jensen nor the admiral wished the particulars of that tape examined for documentation. Jensen staked his future on the surety that Nortin held the power to misplace, or alter, or erase, the flight logs and checkpoint records of *Sail*'s passage between Chalice and Arinat. Jensen balanced everything on an extortionist's secret imbedded within proof of his own crimes. Only the admiral's guilt could spare him from certain court-martial and a firing squad.

A minute passed like eternity.

The admiral's cragged face showed no expression when at last he drew breath for conclusion. "Young man," he said sourly. "For outstanding service, and for your discovery of a Syndicate spy base, you'll report for commendation, decoration, and promotion. Then you'll be transferred into Admiral Duane's division, and I trust we'll never need to set eyes on each other again."

Dreambridge

The axe fell and blood ran, not from living flesh but over treebark, to spatter across frosted ground. The unnatural warmth raised steam against the bite of wintry air, each drop a stark splash of scarlet against leaves left curled and frail by the season that prevailed in the earthly lands across the veil.

Far off in the borderlands, in a cottage under forest eaves never blighted by cold or steel, Kirelle awakened shivering in tangled bedclothes.

The dream, she knew, had been no nightmare to be shrugged off and forgotten upon waking. The bleeding tree would be real, though the mortal whose hand had wielded killing steel would bide unaware of his damage. In earthly lands no sign would show that this axe-wounded tree was something more than the mature offshoot of an acorn.

Kirelle sat up, wishing the soft scents of apple blossoms and pressed herbs could ease her gut-deep uneasiness.

A snowy owl sat perched on her windowsill.

The instant it saw her take notice, it flew, ghost-silent on spread wings. Mild air stirred through the space it left vacant, rustling the bundled herbs strung in rows from the rafters. The phials of potions and simples above Meara's work-table loomed in dim ranks on their shelves; useless, all, Kirelle despaired. If the trappings of an herbalist's lore held no remedy for an axe-stung tree, the deeper mysteries of the art could be called on for other than succor; this she feared as she crossed in trepidation to the window. Bird and dream would not have arrived by coincidence. Owls could read the future, and owls alone could cross at will from the borderlands that bridged like a ribbon between the fey realms and mortal earth.

Kirelle reached the sill, touched by wry thought of Meara, who had laughed when first asked why their cottage must lie in the thickest heart of the forest, an inconvenient distance from the village. *"There's a part of our trade, girl, that has naught to do with sick babes and dry cattle. Sure as rain falls, you'll learn wonders."*

Wishing the wise woman was not away to Eastling to attend a birthing, Kirelle saw a rider on a silver-gray horse awaiting below in the dooryard. Old and straight-backed, and elegantly mantled, his skin was dark as turned earth, the beard that bristled from under his hood a glint of pale silver by moonlight. Both hands were gloved in black. The air all around him seemed alive with owls, weaving like silent shuttlecocks through the warp and weft of the breeze.

The Wizard of the Forest, and none other, had come here to ask for some favor.

Oh, trouble had come, of the direst measure, Kirelle understood as she hastened to her wardrobe to dress. Little mysteries that othertimes would have evoked her delight failed to lift her foreboding, not the teasing play of the air-sprite that whirled a mild tempest of apple petals through the casement, nor the wakeful mocking bird that sang in the melodic tones of a lark. Kirelle hastily pulled on the patched hose and shirt that briar snags should have sent to the rag bin. Too fast for neatness, she brushed and braided her waist-length dark hair, then threw on her cloak, its thread spun by fey from the fibers of midsummer flowers. Lighter than down, warmer than wool, the fabric shimmered like twilight from palest blue to deep violet.

From her pantry, Kirelle snatched up her satchel and a seed cake sweetened with honey. She was no fey, to go without sustenance until touched by a whim for gay feasting. Neither was she entirely human, since the day she had been snatched as a changeling from parents she could not remember.

The Wizard of the Forest had once been human also, before he had been guardian of the border realm. His knowledge of the mysteries ran so deep only rock itself was any wiser. If he held any name beyond his title, it had been forgotten, or else, like the most ancient trees, through long silence words had lost all power to rule him.

Uneasy for the dream that had drawn his presence to her dooryard, Kirelle pushed closed the cottage door. The latch dropped with a clear chink of brass, and the silver-gray horse raised its head. Bells on its trappings trilled an answering chime as the Wizard reined around to face her.

His study felt distinct as a physical touch. Despite the mild lines that etched his features, the merciless strengths of his powers were too fierce to mask in serenity.

Overcome by the presence of portents too large for her skills to encompass, Kirelle gave way to impatience. "Why should you send such a dream?" she burst out. "Bleeding trees bespeak evil deeds, and no herbal of mine can heal such, nor ease the wrath of the fey when they learn that mortal steel has cut heartwood."

Motionless, the Wizard regarded her. His horse champed softly at the bit. Harness bells clinked in single notes, and the stars themselves regaled his presence in a thousand points of bright light. "You are most quick to say what you cannot do." Like his bells, his voice was rich in overtones, and his searching gaze never wavered.

Unsettled and out of her depth, Kirelle wished the wise woman who taught her might stand here in her stead.

"If Meara's aid was needed, I should be in Eastling, to fetch her," the Wizard added gravely. "And I had no part in any sending. Instead, I followed the dream's path, and that, of itself, led to you. The Eld Tree that holds the last link with mortal earth lies threatened. Can you know this and still refuse help?"

Sorry for her haste, and never more aware of her inexperience, Kirelle could not ignore the implications. When fey magic had knitted the borderlands that divided the otherworld realms from mortal earth, thin places were left in the fabric, some said for hope that mankind might someday outgrow their heedless ways, and that misunderstandings between races might be eased. Others claimed the fey still cherished mortal lands for their plangent and transient beauty. Whichever tale held truth, a chosen few Trees from the Eldforests were left bound to earth's soil as anchorpoints, and on such sites the veil could be crossed in the months of solstice and equinox. While mortal kind grew ever more estranged from the mysteries, such crossings were made less and less, and finally rarely at all.

Few could say when the fey had last ridden the wild hunt at midsummer. Except for the isolated foray to snatch a few changelings for mischief, the borderlands bridge through the veil lay all but forgotten. Only one Tree yet remained tied to earth, sorrowfully aged by the turn of time and seasons. If it died, the last link would be gone; fey mysteries would be lost to earth forever.

"You do see," the Wizard said gently. "A mortal with an axe has violated the last Tree, and the fey, when they hear, will cry vengeance. If blood-price is not met, their wrath might leave the worlds forever sundered."

Kirelle regarded the clearing that held her cottage, then the orchard, bejeweled with dew in the still, brief hour before dawn. She watched the windsprite dance amid shedding blossoms, and relived her irritation at the burrow the gnome had dug in his hope of stealing apples when they ripened. The chance that the powers that quickened these things might come to be unraveled tore at her heart like pain.

"How has this happened?" she asked the Wizard. "What disarmed the guardspells that should hide the last Tree from the eyes of any blunderer bearing steel?"

"Ah, wise lady, the answers I have are too few. There

was not one man, but three, and the owl I sent to turn their footsteps was shot down while in flight." The Wizard bent his head, grief in his eyes like hot sparks. "My brave messenger lies dead, murdered with as little thought as the axeblow that cleft the Eld Tree."

Kirelle could have wept then, for certainty. "My task is to go across and turn these mortals from their reaving?"

His hands crossed over his saddlebow, the Wizard regarded the silent flight of the companion owls still left to him. "The choice must be yours. My birds see the future, and they led to you. Since the Tree's cry for help chose you also, the mysteries themselves have their reason. But more than these borderlands lies at risk. If you cross, I intend to pass with you."

No need to belabor the dangers, that to step through the veil was to risk a cold exile: perhaps aging, surely death, if mishap occurred on the other side. Once the fey learned of the harm to one of their own, their anger would demand retribution. Blood-price would be asked that one of three mortals must pay, or the borderlands themselves could be forfeit.

"We must go. Time is short, and the crossing is most easily made at the site of the Eld Tree itself." The Wizard wheeled his horse, expectant that Kirelle must follow.

"I haven't said I'd go at all," she whispered. But reluctance could not unmake dire portents. Kirelle trailed along under the glide of the owls, pierced through with sadness and dread. The avaricious, sneaking little pranks of the gnomes in retrospect seemed joyfully endearing. Nothing she owned would have been too precious to give, to ensure safe return to her orchards.

Dank under shadow and the slow drip of dew, the paths that had led Kirelle to share in the wood's lore and wisdom tonight neither welcomed nor befriended. Breezes muttered through the branches to a tireless sibilance of leaves that whispered of driving men mad. In the past, when the worlds were still joined, to stray uninvited into an Eldforest was death, and sometimes worse. These trees were roused and aware, and although they had known no touch of cold steel since the veil had been raised to protect them, they remembered older times, and thoughtless humans. Outside the borderlands, an Eld Tree had been maimed by an axe. Although Kirelle had never trodden those lands ruled by time, or done aught but rejoice with growing wood, the forest in its anger, in the thick, stately flow of its sap, did not care.

Oppressed by unsainly hostility, Kirelle tightened grip on her satchel. Her voice shook as she crooned soft notes to reassure the trees of her harmless intentions. The Wizard chanted strictures of his own, mightier by far than any song of hers. But melody and litany availed nothing. Black boughs dipped low and laced the way like knotwork. Chill leaves pressed down like a shroud.

The gray horse snorted uneasy alarm and sidled as, gently, the Wizard addressed the trees. "Your rage is misplaced. Would you hinder ones who go to help?"

The forest paid no heed.

The rustle of boughs held no reply, and a brooding moment passed. Kirelle endured the scratching touch of twigs and the prisoning, chill kiss of leaves.

From somewhere near at hand an owl called; the Wizard's voice answered, steady and soft. To Kirelle, he added, "The forest has denied us free passage, and further persuasion will not sway it. Without the Tree's bridging powers, I can do nothing but raise raw force and send on one of us alone." He looked at Kirelle, clear-eyed and awaiting her decision; if she went on, she must brave the earthly world and three reaving mortals by herself.

But to stay behind was to remain here, trapped by the rage of the forest until the threat to the Eld Tree was righted. Fail in that task, Kirelle knew, and no path she could tread would be safe. The clearing that held Meara's orchards would be barred from human use. Without the small daily gifts that bought blessing, the apple trees would be choked out, root and branch, and the cottage torn asunder stone from stone.

In such things, the balance that ruled the borderlands

was unforgiving. Gifts of life and sustenance were never to be taken for granted.

"I will have to place trust in the Tree's dream," she finally said. "Let me be the one to go."

The Wizard bent in his saddle and offered three flakes of slate smoothed by the waves on the lake shore. "These talismans carry a dreamspell that can be tuned by your healer's gift. Set one in the hand of each mortal as he sleeps, and let the beliefs in his heart shape his fate. Once you've crossed, I cannot help. The Eld Tree must show your way back. My white owl will attend as your guide."

The appointed bird banked in a whispered curve and called, mournfully dusky and wild. Beyond that, the wood's hostile stillness remained unbroken. Not the ratchet of crickets nor wind in the leaves wished her well as the Wizard raised uncanny spells to bridge the veil, that twisting, intricate web of energies that divided earthly lands from the otherworldly realm of the mysteries.

Alan lay wakeful in the chill of a blustery winter night. It wasn't that his sleeping bag was too thin; he'd bought a good one, suited for subzero temperatures, when he'd thought he'd be hiking in the Rockies. As much as the cold was apt to bother him, his palms were sweating hot.

Raw nerves kept him jumpy and wakeful. Not good at lying, especially to himself, he could not deny that his years in the service had wrecked his appreciation for the wilderness. Not a truth he liked to admit; still less to the two others with him: Bill, all macho bluster, and Rafe, who acted the suave city sophisticate, but who'd die before letting anybody see he couldn't beat a jock at his own game.

Why was it, Alan thought bitterly, that male pride too often held nonconformity as a weakness?

He reached out for the hundredth time in an hour and checked the rifle gripped in his hand. Deer season—what a laugh. He found no joy in hunting animals, hunting anything, in sad fact, not since his time in the service. Then, killing had meant plain survival, until the mind grew sick on its own fear, and a man could grow to live for the unholy thrill of an enemy's blood on the ground.

Another man dead meant staying alive. Except those who came home found that life had somehow rearranged itself, and nothing of past importance had retained real meaning anymore.

Alan stroked icy steel and shivered like a baby. The safety on his weapon wasn't set. Recollection left him sweating, of being ripped out of sleep by flares and gunfire, and of the buddy who'd died because of a shot he couldn't return fast enough. The wind lashed at the trees, and a scratchy patter of leaves tumbled past. Alan tensed, halfway to a crouch with his rifle up, before he could stop himself and rationalize: this was the States, and rustling leaves here were just that, not an enemy stalking to kill.

God, he shouldn't be here. Never mind he felt obliged to mediate, to keep Bill and Rafe from destroying each other in a rivalry neither one would let wither. Twenty years since discharge, and, no use pretending, there were moments when his nerves were still peeled raw. Alan berated himself for not having sense enough to shrug off outworn high-school loyalties. He should've let two friends that time had changed and distanced thrash out their competitive egos on their own.

The wind blew, mournfully soft. The dressed-out carcass of Bill's trophy spun creaking from the rope that lashed it up. The owl that Rafe had winged just to even up the score would be bleeding somewhere in the brush, if it wasn't just as wastefully dead. Strung out with nerves, Alan couldn't bring himself to close his eyes, not without somebody on watch. To turn his mind from past horrors, he thought about Bill's indefatigable boast that he shot his trophies for the freezer. Everybody knew his wife felt sick at the thought of a dead deer.

Alan shifted, discovered himself checking his gun again, and cursed himself for a fool. Who cared whether or not he could face himself if Rafe and Bill were left alone to drive each other too hard? Both men were married; Bill had a daughter. The wives should have taken over the chore of being the influence that tempered. Sweating more, and hurting tense, Alan took a breath of frost-sharp air that turned in his fickle mind to the smells of steaming hot jungle, and sharp-edged anxieties of enemies that lurked in dank tunnels. He stared up at oak leaves to moor his slipping sanity, and to shove unwanted survival patterns into a past that refused to stay quiet.

Sometime after checking his gun for the two-hundredth time, he dozed and fell into fitful dreams.

The first step beyond the veil raised the sharp crackle of dry leaves, cause enough for Kirelle to stiffen in alarm when she had known nothing underfoot but lush moss. Then the air, equally strange, edged with frost and suffused with the underlying scents of rot and decay. This was the other side, where the wrong word or the mishandled chance encounter could doom the unwary traveler to life-long exile and death.

Kirelle paused, aware of the pull of the moon in her blood, of the wheeling swing of strange stars, and the slow, insistent aging that ruled all aspects of earthly life.

Curiosity filled her, too. She had been born here, taken across the veil as a changeling unknowable years in the past. Never before had Kirelle felt moved to wonder whether her human parents had grieved when the glamor left by the fey wore off, and they discovered an unbreathing bundle of twigs left in place of their stolen child.

A moment later, listening uneasily, Kirelle noticed the wood's appalling silence. Wind alone dared raise voice in this place. No crickets called, nor any night-singing bird. The missing, subliminal thread of harmony her art should have sensed from growing wood raised panic, until she realized: stripped branches and hard-edged, unsoftened moonlight were proper, here. This world went dormant for winter, its smaller creatures frost-killed or departed until the renewal of spring.

The only vibrant life within reach of Kirelle's senses

seemed to be the Wizard's white owl, that carved impatient circles as it waited for her to regain wits and purpose. Kirelle touched a sapling to borrow from its rooted firmness the assurance to brace her failing nerves. But her contact revealed something worse than dormancy; the young beech felt sluggish and dull under her hands, stupidly reft of its power of being and retarded from self-awareness.

Horror and pity sent her reeling a step back.

These earthly trees were mute, brutishly groping through soil and sunlight without the gift of wakening. No one had walked this wood for many years who understood how to nurture the spirit nature of wild trees.

Kirelle bit her lip, tasting tears. The anger of the fey would bring justice for the neglect and contempt that had befallen these sorry forests. But if the dissolution of the borderlands and the final separation of the mysteries was a punishment such thoughtlessness deserved, her own fate and the Wizard's freedom were now as deeply entangled.

Grown urgent at her delay, the white owl banked broad wings and flew. Kirelle stumbled to follow. The ache in her assumed the proportions of despair, that the threatening presence of three reavers permitted her no interval to rouse these trees to awareness.

Against the mute void that heartlessness had allowed this wood to become, the true-song of the Eld Tree rang in solitary splendor against the far distant chime of the stars. Long before the white owl swooped to alight on the mighty oak's branches, Kirelle could sense its power. Although leaves, trunk, and branches embraced the earthly world, the taproots of this Tree bridged the veil and sank deep into borderlands soil.

Yet reunion with the familiar brought no sense of rejoicing. The Tree's muddied anger all but stopped Kirelle's breath. Sour wind tugged her cloak hem and stirred the hair that twigs had raked loose from her braid as her healer's gifts picked past raw rage to bare the thread of stark pain underlying. A moment later, as the late rising moon sliced torn clouds, she saw the gleam of the axe left struck in striated bark.

Even from several paces off, the steel raised an ache in her bones. Fully as hurtful was the blood reek of the stag, thanklessly killed, then gutted and lashed to a branch by a rope that creaked in the wind. Other unidentifiable odors dizzied Kirelle's senses as she made herself close the last steps.

And there they were, three forms sprawled out on bare ground and wrapped in bright-colored bedding that to Kirelle's eye looked light and fine-woven as silk. They smelled of woodsmoke and damp leaves and the animal tang of dried sweat. No aura of savagery warned which had cut the Eld Tree, or which had slain the Wizard's owl. Asleep, the men looked innocent and ordinary, in their way as dumbly vulnerable as this world's unloved trees. Kirelle saw nothing she recognized as a weapon beyond the axe, though other steel things whose use she could not fathom riddled the site of their camp.

Touched by a strange surge of pity, Kirelle shivered. The axe blade in any earthly tree would have roused no uncanny reverberations. But with the Wizard left trapped by the Eldforest's ire, her healer's preference for mercy must not lead her to risk that the fey's cry for vengeance be balked from finding expiation. The talisman stones must be set, and their dreams be given rein to unravel three minds into nightmare.

The nearer man slept in a sprawl, one powerful arm clenched over his chest, and his legs entangled in his bedding. He breathed in the rhythm of untroubled rest and never stirred as Kirelle reached out with shaking fingers and tucked the first stone in his palm. Softly, silently, she engaged the powers of her art to sound his intents and make a weaving of his vulnerabilities.

Bill Farlane leveled his rifle. Equipped with the finest telescopic sight, he aligned the crosshairs on the buck. The moment came back in perfect clarity, from the clean bite of the wind to the winter-thin patch of sunlight that danced on the deer's dun pelt.

He held his breath to steady his aim, squeezed off the round like a caress—then felt the triumph in his gut freeze to horror as the deer dissolved, replaced before his eyes by his daughter's pink-and-blue parka.

No!—his thought too late. Already the report of the rifle spat its flat crack through the wood. Crows exploded into raucous, indignant flight. Pink acrylic showed a blossoming stain of red, and a pitiful three-year-old body crashed headlong into sun-dappled leaf mold.

"Nice shot!" Rafe said, his personal brand of sarcasm making even praise feel like insult.

Bill straightened, mouth opened to cry Sallie's name.

But to his utter terror, his heartdeep cry of grief emerged as banal conversation. "It was a nice shot, darned if it wasn't."

Those words, he thought wildly, *they'd been said over a deer.*

But no buck lay in the clearing. Only Sallie, dreadfully bloody and still. The rifle still warm in his hand had shot her cold, and like some ugly, played-over script, Alan's voice was repeating, "Well, fine. You've bagged your trophy. For the love of mike, go in quickly. Make sure the shot was clean and use your knife if it wasn't."

Bill screamed in impotent silence: *That's my daughter.* Yet the words stayed mired in his head. His shoulders set for a satisfied swagger, he ejected the spent shell and laid his rifle against a tree. Locked into actions that denied his raw grief, reft of all power to stop himself, he saw that willpower and muscle, all of his prideful strength and competence were going to do him no good. He was going to rise, going to walk, going to kneel down by his little dead daughter, and dress out her body as he should have done the killed meat of a deer.

While Rafe said something ordinary and Alan gave a meaningless reply, Bill felt himself rise from his stalking crouch and heft his new knife in his hand. The first step toward Sallie's body tore him to inward shreds; he knew, oh god oh god, he knew that the feel of soft, white skin, the drum-leather punch as the blade sliced through flesh, the steaming blood as the abdominal cavity opened, was going to sear him from sanity . . . *God, oh God, Sallie, NO!*

The huge man curled into a ball, tearing pitifully at his bedding. He sucked breath after gasping breath while his stubbled face twisted in anguish.

Kirelle fought back tears and guilt, aware as never before that her healer's instinct to mend in this place might tempt her to irrevocable folly. These were reavers, whose actions threatened ruin to the borderlands. Their misguided feelings could not be permitted to matter. Kirelle fished the second stone from her satchel and approached the next man, the one with the gentle face who lay with his cheek neatly cradled on one elbow. By appearance, he seemed the most harmless of the three, with his fine, pale hair, and the glint of a linked gold bracelet circling one elegant wrist.

Feeling the sting acutely—that Bill had bagged a deer he should have seen first—Rafe lounged in bed and relived the frustrated moment when the owl had chanced to fly past. His reflex reaction had made up for the lapse, as he'd ripped off that snap shot on impulse.

He shut his eyes, revelling in the satisfaction he'd felt as the bird tumbled out of mid-flight.

The snooze alarm's buzz erased Rafe's faint smile. Lord, he should have had his tail in and out of the shower ten minutes ago.

Worried over the financial summary he was expected to present, that was in order as far as notes went but needed fleshing out before the meeting, Rafe slugged aside designer bedclothes and stopped in shocked surprise. His hands were smeared with fresh blood. On the sheets by his pillow lay an owl's feather, broken and wrung and blotched scarlet.

Four-letter words were inadequate. His first thought, that he'd be late for the board meeting, was belatedly followed by the incongruity of the gory feather. He hesitated, unwilling to come to grips with the weirdness, that a dead owl could enact some spooky sort of vengeance.

The concept was just too bizarre.

Unwilling to lend credence to hallucinations, Rafe plunged bullishly on toward the bathroom.

But his hands as he turned on the shower were still maddeningly, scarletly drenched. The fancy's irrational persistence left him ticked enough to plunge into the spray while the water was still icy cold. Through subsequent shivers and gooseflesh, he refused to note the color of the water that swirled down the drain. Blast if he'd be sorry he'd shot some worthless owl.

He killed the water, snapped a bath sheet over his shoulders, shaved, then made a paranoid inspection of his knuckles. There had to be a cut he hadn't noticed.

Nothing. He dug out a clean shirt and dismissed the distraction as he hurried through the motions of dressing.

The blood appeared again as he snatched up his briefcase. Frantic, he dropped the expensive leather handle before the stains soaked in. The case hit the hardwood floor with an echoing bang and fell over as he dashed to the kitchen for a dishcloth. His thoughts on his presentation all scattered, he dabbed ineffectively at the blotches left on his briefcase. Predictably, they didn't come out.

He'd have to spend the bucks to buy another one.

A harried glance at his Rolex showed he was now irretrievably late. The report was going to have to be presented in its current, raw state, no credit to his months of hard work. Annoyed by life's unfairness, Rafe snatched his overcoat from the closet and ran.

He got no farther than his apartment door before his fingers became drenched in blood again. An explosive curse ripped from him. This time, he'd managed to spatter his shirtcuff into the bargain. Back in the bathroom, hands under the running water: *this has to be a nightmare*, he thought. Raggedly nervous, he reached to straighten his

tie, then recalled his wet fingers and jerked short. The last
fool straw in this messed-up morning was to look as if he'd
dribbled breakfast down his front. With a sour laugh at
himself, he grabbed briefcase and overcoat, rushed out of
the apartment and sprinted into the parking lot. He
unlocked his BMW, breathless and feeling pig stupid, and
hopeful the fresh air might steady him.

Probably stress and anxiety had caused his mind to
play tricks.

But when he jabbed the car keys into the ignition, the
fresh blood was back again. Damning, slippery fingerprints
smeared on everything he touched. Choking back sobs of
frustration, he saw another mangled owl's feather float down
and settle on the dashboard.

At that moment Rafe fully understood: he was not
going to handle his meeting; he was in fact going to lose
his job. The money and prestige and quick thinking upon
which he had secured his success were not going to save
him. An owl shot down for a moment's stung pride had
marked him, and the crime was going to blight his life
forever . . .

Kirelle sat back on her heels, saddened by what she had
learned. The two reavers she had dreamspelled were just
thoughtless, prideful braggarts, ignorant rather than evil. A
stag and an owl had died to no purpose, and for that, she
must see two mortals driven from the wood with incentive
not to return. The last of the three, by default, must have
been the one to cut the Eld Tree. He must be left bound in
sleep to even the balance when the fey arrived to demand
blood-price.

Bent with the stone cupped in her hands, Kirelle composed herself to discharge that last unpleasant duty. Beside
her, the blond man with the costly bracelet moaned in the
deep throes of nightmare, and the third reaver snapped out
of sleep.

Silent, he was, and blinding quick. His explosive surge
threw off blankets to bare the moon-caught gleam of hard

steel. Breathing fast, his grip on his weapon bone-white, he swung to take out the intruder.

The near proximity of cold metal had already stung Kirelle to inadvertent recoil. Her braid tumbled down across her shoulder, a slash of dark against the fey-woven shimmer of her cloak.

The reaver sucked in a breath half-strangled with surprise and managed, just barely, to curb his reflex to kill. "A girl!" He shifted onto one elbow, stiff with unfriendly suspicion. His weapon continued to threaten as he snapped off an emphatic question.

His accent was unmusical and clipped, the words too rushed for understanding. Kirelle shook her head, while his attentiveness dissected every inch of her. She saw his moment of reassessment: that she was a woman, if small and otherworldly, and not some briar-scraped child dressed in tatterdemalion rags. His eyes stayed mad nonetheless, empty as smoke over water. If Kirelle had expected him to be ugly, he was not. Reaver he might be, and patently vicious, but he was neatly made. In body and feature he had as deadly a grace as one of the fair folk themselves.

Kirelle stared at him, undone by fear and unsure what to do next. Beside her the blond companion ensnared in spelled dreams started hoarsely and raggedly to sob.

The man yanked back in a flinch at the sound, and Kirelle snatched the chance to try retreat.

His left hand shot out and caught hers, and painful strength caged the half-enspelled stone between their shared grip.

Kirelle cried out, aware of the danger, but utterly unable to tear free; and so it passed that the dreamsnare unfurled and meshed with two minds and two hearts.

For a second, all senses upended. The mortal man beheld himself through borderland eyes in a spinning rush that made him gasp. The slaughter of a deer and an owl became re-rendered as pittance before his own most thoughtless axe-blow, so innocently motivated, a plain measure of safeguard to stow edged steel so that nobody should blunder into an unsheathed tool after dark. Torn headlong from mortal heedlessness, Alan saw blood well from heartwood. He felt its pain shake the silence of winter night to disharmony, then knew the deep, subliminal thunder of an Eldforest's awakening to rage. Full knowledge of his deed wrung from him tears of abject despair.

At the same moment, Kirelle, helplessly torn from her roots, felt herself seared by the murderous war that had plundered the joy from a lifetime, horrors that had tortured and killed, an unconscionable destruction of land and life that had left this survivor half-unstrung in time of peace. The ways of mortal earth had nigh broken Alan's spirit, Kirelle saw. Least-likely reaver of the three, it was he whose blood would be called to right the balance to placate the wrath of the fey. The irony cut, as her healer's perception further revealed that the hurt in him cried out for reprieve: that after years of misery, his heart had raised its answer: the desperate strength of his need had unbound the arcane defenses. The Eld Tree of itself had shed secrecy, to invite this man across the veil.

"You," she gasped, as the firestorm of images thinned and finally released her. "It was you who invoked the great mystery."

Alan freed her hand, head bent and shaking. "I didn't know."

"That's not entirely true." Kirelle sighed. "Your heart led you better than you realized."

Reminded that moment of the gun still clenched in his hand, Alan snapped on the safety and cast it aside in distaste. His gaze, light as smoke, flicked across her. Then he got up. Still terrible in grace, he strode away from his sleeping companions to draw the offending axe his blow had left wedged in Eld oak. He ran light hands over scarred wood until his longing burst out into words. "Show me the way to cross the veil. Your borderlands are more beautiful than dreams, and what life I lead here has no meaning."

"You can't know what you're asking!" Kirelle said, moved to desolation by his plight. "Your steel has harmed the last Eld Tree on earth. Across the veil, the blood of

your deed will draw the forest's wrath and mark you out
for fey vengeance."

He stood, resolute in the calm of his conviction.
"Then let me answer there for my ignorance."

His words fell with an uncomfortable, sharpened clarity upon a night that abruptly seemed changed. The deep
shadows went suddenly, painfully harsh-edged, and the
moonlight seemed alive with vibration.

"Veil magic." Kirelle gasped, her dread overridden by
a piercingly musical voice. "Debt must be answered for,
here and now!"

Overhead, the Wizard's white owl raised wings and
exploded into flight as Kirelle whirled, the mortal man
along with her.

Around the trunk of the Eld Tree stepped a rangy,
graceful figure magnificently clad in green and gold. A
black lacquer bow adorned with river pearl crossed his
shoulder. Beneath hair the glossy dark of a raven's wing,
his eyes shone a lucent silver gray. No crackle of sound
betrayed his step as he crossed the carpet of dead leaves.
The sightly beauty of him made the earthly air seem to
burn and shimmer with his presence.

The mortal man by Kirelle's side gasped aloud, his
deadly fast reflexes turned stupid and still by the uncanny
arrival of the fey.

Kirelle had never owned courage; old Meara often had
chided that unsettled nerves made her tart. Before the fey
could raise voice to claim blood-price, she found herself
crying useless protest. "Your kind had abandoned these
woods. Who is to blame if spells of guard set so long in the
past have thinned to the point where one man's need could
wake the mysteries? Alan's act was without malice. His
desire was only to protect."

The fey regarded Kirelle in all of his bright, cold arrogance. "Price must be paid, nonetheless. Steel has cut an
Eld Tree, and blood must atone for blood. It is true
enough the guardspells have weakened; thus I am sent
here, to unmake the last link in the veil."

"Why claim the one man whose heart could touch an

Eld Tree?" Kirelle begged, piercingly torn for a failure that could not save the Wizard's borderlands, nor spare one innocent life. Her gesture encompassed the two men asleep on the ground. "There are other mortal reavers whose interests are the more callous."

"Two lives for one?" The fey raised his brows, perhaps prepared to strike a bargain, until Alan reached out and caught Kirelle's wrist, his fingers coldly unsteady.

"Wait. I forbid this."

Years and reason and counseling had never satisfied his guilt, that chance had granted him survival when others more worthy had died. Blundering through life without faith or clear purpose, this time he could not walk away. To the fey, he insisted, "If it's true and I've offended, I will give what is asked."

"No," Kirelle whispered. "You will yield up nothing. Your death will not win reprieve, nor will it save the last link. The mysteries will be cut away from your earth, and our borderlands will perish along with them."

The fey regarded her, narrow-eyed. "What does any of that matter? Earthly folk care nothing for Eld ways. The mysteries, to them, are just tales, and true magic a beauty forgotten."

Which was, perhaps, the real reason why the veil's guardspells had slackened, Kirelle thought. The mysteries themselves might have reached out to a mortal to thwart further shrinking of their boundaries. She knew now, beyond doubt, why she had been the one chosen to receive the Eld Tree's dream. "Your complaints could be changed," she said quickly. "These woods are not dead, nor unfeeling, but only numbly asleep."

"You would stay, then, and waken them?" The fey laughed, his mirth a sword-sting of mockery.

Kirelle swallowed. One word, one act, and she would be trapped for a lifetime. She glanced at the mortal beside her, felt once again the unquiet pain that tormented him, the creative potential this world's works had taken and twisted and ruined. "Let this one go," she begged, knowing the borderlands could ease him. At last, her own will was certain. "I will stay. This wood will have me as guardian, and the old mysteries will be quickened anew to nurture and guard the Eld Tree."

"A life for a life," the fey agreed, unsmiling in acknowledgment of the pact. "Your mortal shall have his reprieve. He may cross back with me to the borderlands if you remain here in his place."

Dawn threw gray fog over the campsite when Bill awakened from his dream. Gasping and sweating as if he'd been running for his life, he glanced up, saw branches half blurred in dawn mist, then loosed a sharp, breathless laugh. Nightmares, he thought, overwhelmed by a wash of relief; only nightmares. For a second, on waking, he'd actually believed he'd shot down and gutted his own daughter.

The vision remained acidly vivid. Bill pushed onto one elbow to reaffirm that the trophy he'd dressed was a buck.

The shock hit like a slug in the gut: for there was no deer, *only Sallie, hanging by one ankle from a bloodstained length of rope*. Behind her, clad in a cloak that looked cut from no earthly sort of cloth, a tiny woman stood with the wind blowing through her dark hair.

Reproach in her eyes as biting as frost, she spoke before grief could unhinge him. "Go. Take your trophy, and upon your heart's blood, may you never kill again for your vanity."

Weeping with fear, shaking and weak at the knees, Bill scrambled out of his sleeping bag. "I can't do this," he gasped. But the woman's eyes gave him no quarter. More frightened of her than of losing his last hold on sanity, he rummaged underneath his jacket, found the knife he'd stripped off the night before. Half blind with tears of remorse, he reached up and cut his daughter down. Sobbing deep in his throat, he wrapped her slack body in his sleeping bag, then clumsily smoothed her blond hair.

His hand brushed fur, cold gray fur, then the unyielding tines of an antler. In his arms, cradled against his bare chest, lay the blood-rank carcass of a buck.

Bill looked up, too shocked to be angry, but the woman who had threatened him was gone. Unsettled by feelings that every move he made was being watched, he spilled the wretched carcass upon the ground, packed up his gear, and fled without a backward thought for his forsaken companions.

Left alone at the campsite, Rafe roused to a spill of winter sunlight and the rustle of foraging birds. No apartment, no office, no report due, he understood in a flood of rising spirits. He thrust his arms from his sleeping bag to stretch . . . and froze, half crippled by chills.

His hands were running with red blood. He started up in panic, then all but retched as he blundered across the stiff, feathered corpse of an owl that someone had left dumped on his chest.

His scream tore apart the forest silence.

The small woman who watched him went unnoticed until he ran out of breath. She stood over him, uncanny and bitterly accusing. "You will go," she said clearly. "Kill no more for your ego, and the death of the owl will be forgiven."

"Who are you?" gasped Rafe. But he didn't want an answer, not really. He just needed out of here, as fast as he could throw on clothes and jacket.

Afraid for his sanity and survival, he abandoned his expensive gear and fancy rifle where they lay. Without pause to look for Bill or Alan, he raced headlong to his car. Sweaty, panting, and shaky, he waited until he had the engine running before he dared to check whether the blood was gone from his hands.

Under the Eld Tree, in a morning wood emptied of reavers, Kirelle regarded rank after rank of sunlit, sleeping trees. Amid a litter of meaningless camping gear, she sensed the soil beneath her feet and listened to winds that had long ago forgotten speech. She found no regret in her heart, but a strange, eager joy for the task that lay ahead of her.

Rapt as she was, intent upon the needs of the forest she had adopted for her own, she did not hear the silent beat of wings. The owls that flew widdershins around the Eld Tree went unnoticed as they flocked and finally settled to roost in the branches over her head.

The first she knew of the Wizard's presence was the merry chime of brass bells. She spun, surprised, as he reined his gray horse to a stop and regarded the oddments of gear the reavers had abandoned when they fled.

A smile carved his face. "Did you think to bring back the mysteries to mortal earth on your own?"

Kirelle laughed. "I didn't think at all, but only chose as I must."

She moved to the Wizard's side, pleased that they would waken the wood together, and knowing that borderlands magic would one day come to bridge the veil and restore the lost link between worlds.

"Alan is with Meara, and safe," said the Wizard. "Anyone lacking a healer's compassion could have left him unjustly condemned as a reaver." The secretive smile behind his silver beard turned ruefully reminiscent. "You may not have known, but my guardianship began with an inadvertent slight to an Eld Tree. When our labor is complete, and the wild hunt returns to ride these earthly fields, I much doubt your exile will be permanent."

Song's End

The wolf's jaws snapped shut with a sound like the crack of new ice. Deadly teeth slashed nothing but empty air, and the beast's frustration could be felt, hot as the spurt of fresh blood. On damp earth barely one stride distant, Huntress Skyfire rolled and evaded the edge of the stone knife which stabbed down to kill her. Breathless, sweating, bleeding from three previous challenges, she scrambled into a crouch and leapt while her opponent recoiled from his lunge.

On the sidelines the wolf whined. Its lips lifted into a snarl, and its haunches bunched, quivering. But this combat was a thing between elves. The pack was forbidden to intervene.

Skyfire struck her attacker solidly in the chest. He overbalanced, and both of them rolled with the throw. The knife grated against dirt. Skyfire took a knee in the ribs; air left her lungs with a grunt. The scent of her opponent filled her nostrils as she gasped a fresh breath. His odor carried a tang of fear. This, because she had bested two stronger challengers before him; those defeated had not lingered to watch her fight again. Both had retreated to the wolf lairs to lick wounds and nurse resentment.

Skyfire caught the new challenger's knife-hand and

bore him down in swift and merciless attack. Fright made him dangerous, even desperate. The chieftess clung grimly as the Wolfrider thrashed beneath her. Anger lent her tenacity to match his fear. She barely felt the blows as he kicked and punched to win free. She twisted the wrist in her grip, felt the sinews tighten. Bone grated beneath the pressure of her hand. While pain distracted her opponent, she kicked away the knife, and sought his throat.

Abruptly the Wolfrider went limp under her hands, chin lifted in submission. Skyfire released his wrist and neck. Wearily she gathered herself to rise, to turn, to face the next of the challenges that had inevitably followed her return with the Dreamsinger to the holt.

Only that morning, she had shouted to the first dissenters who crowded round. "He is an elf, and a Wolfrider, and by the Way, I say that he stays in this tribe by right!" Now, in her exhaustion, the words seemed still to ring in her ears.

At some point during the second fight the Dreamsinger had faded into the forest. With him had gone the scent of dreamberry blossoms, and soft south winds of spring. His leaving changed nothing. Wolfsong gripped the tribe like lust, and the open outbreak of rivalries had upset order within the pack. Skyfire barely noticed Rellah's hostile glare. These fights made distasteful work, since the challenges themselves were an indulgence of wolfish instincts. That Skyfire did battle to temper those same instincts mattered little. Bites and wrenched joints and knife wounds demanded exhaustive concentration and energy drain, and Rellah had none of Willowgreen's natural gift. Still, with the healer gone away with Two-Spear's exiles, only Rellah remained to fill that responsibility. She carried on with a learned knowledge of herbs and bandaging, and an uncompromising sense of duty, ancient as she was.

"Dreamsinger," Rellah sent, "is spell-blind, mad. Not worth this bloodshed, desist."

Skyfire refused the reprimand. Scuffed, stinging, sticky with the blood of conflict, she shook back tangled hair and snarled.

Rellah failed to flinch; and that lack of reaction by its very incongruity raised Skyfire's hackles. Prompted by distrust, she spun, her snarl changed to a growl of rage. The sudden movement spared her. She took the knife thrown by treachery from behind in the shoulder instead of the heart, where it was intended.

"Murder!" screamed Rellah. "A curse upon Timmain for mingling the seed of the beast in our children."

But Rellah's outburst reflected only ignorance, and anger at things she could never understand. Skyfire gripped her shoulder, hot blood dripping through her fingers, eyes narrowed with a rage only Two-Spear might have equaled. This assault had not arisen from the blood of the wolf; pack hierarchy was a discipline ritualized to minimize deaths. Stealth, subterfuge, attacks calculated to catch the victim disadvantaged were subleties reserved only for the taking of prey.

Ready now to kill out of hand, to discipline in the manner of the pack, the Wolfriders on the sidelines crowded around the offender. They caught his hands and feet, splayed him helpless upon the ground that, wolflike, they might rend him limb from limb.

First in their longing to tear out his throat was Huntress Skyfire; yet she did not. She shivered and overran instinct and kicked the nearest of the scufflers, who happened to be Skimmer, with her boot. "Stop! Let him go." When others were slow to listen, she jerked the knife from her flesh, then dove in and hammered them all with her fists, her elbows, her knees, and sent the offenders rolling away in surprise. Dizzy now, and caked with clinging dust, she glared around the circle of her following. "No elf must die."

She remained upright until the knife-thrower had shambled to his feet and fled ashamed from the circle. Then the dizziness took her, and she staggered . . .

. . . and awoke, sweating in noonday heat, to scratch at a scar that seemed endlessly to itch, and to wonder just why this dream should return to trouble her. The tree hollow was stifling. Skyfire brushed damp hair from her eyes. She rolled for a breath of fresh air, and as her hand brushed empty space, realized. The Dreamsinger had left her. In the dance of moons since the fights had ended, this was not like him.

A chill roughened her skin, a premonition of something amiss. By reflex, Skyfire reached out with her mind for her mate.

His sending cut her awareness, sharp as a knife's edge with danger. One with his mind, she felt a blow strike his shoulder, then a sensation of falling, falling; and then pain, sudden and shattering and violent. She recoiled in shock, and slammed hard against the tree wall. Her mind rang with the Dreamsinger's sending, and the last, whispered syllable of her soulname.

"*Kyr!*" Her own scream snapped the link. "Dreamsinger!"

She scrambled in a rush from her nook. Down the tree limb she slid, without bothering to reach for handholds. Bark scraped her skin. When she reached the main trunk, she leapt outward.

And re-experienced the rush of the Dreamsinger's fall for an instant of shared memory.

Then she struck ground. Rolling, banging into roots and the detritus of last year's leaves, she reached out to recapture the link. She received not the smallest spark from the Dreamsinger. Where once the air itself sang in echo of his magic, emptiness remained. The song, the life, the vitality, all had ceased in a terrible, smashing fall from the heights.

Skyfire fought her way to her feet. He was dead; she knew this beyond doubt. The wolf-pack sensed the kill through her distress. They gathered already, restless to dispose of the remains. Such was the Way, and not a thing Skyfire would forbid. Her mate was beyond help. Reason more dire than sentiment caused Skyfire to spring into action. With the weight of the Dreamsinger's cub heavy within her belly, she broke and ran from the clearing.

Only Sapling saw her go. But though Skimmer was soundly sleeping, and Pine was busy with a lover, and Owl absorbed by another of his enigmatic weavings, Skyfire's emotions cut through with an urgency that would not be denied. One by one the Wolfriders arose from their hollows, or abandoned the thread of their activities. In silence they gathered to follow their chieftess; of them all, only Rellah was obliged to ask where to look.

The ravine lay in the direction of sun-goes-up from the holt. Trees did not grow near the rim; only the toughest lichens could garner a foothold upon the jagged, flint-black rock that stabbed like teeth through the soil. Below, the stream carved a course like knotted thread, frayed at intervals into waterfalls that threw drifting curtains of mist. The sound of water tumbling and frothing over stone had fascinated the Dreamsinger. Many an afternoon he had lingered above the ravine, perched on an outcrop with his feet dangling.

Now Rellah stood on that same formation, her hide skirt pinched in nervous fingers, and her skin roughened by the moist chill that eddied off the falls far beneath.

"The Dreamsinger's song is ended," she said. Unlike the Wolfriders gathered at the site, she avoided looking at the shadowy forms which darted like ghosts along the streambed. Years had done little to accustom her to the ways of the wolves. The fact that the mangled rag of flesh and bone that had once been a living elf was now only meat to sustain the pack revolted her. Curiosity alone brought her to the scene of death. The attraction for many of the others was similar. But Skyfire was not among the few who clustered with Sapling out of concern.

Apart from friends and Wolfriders, the chieftess knelt on the earth at the forest's edge. With a diligence that brooked no interruption, she examined the ground for sign, and found none. Now, more than ever, she missed the companionship of Woodbiter, who had hunted his last ravvit soon after the coming of the green season. Without the guidance of her wolf-friend, Skyfire could not unravel scents too faint for her nose. That such clues existed only fueled her frustration. Here she could smell the rancid leather track of a sandal, and there, clinging to ferns, the musky hint of sweat; just enough to know that an elf other than Dreamsinger had recently trodden this path. But the subtleties escaped her. Precisely *which* elf Skyfire had no way to determine.

Absorbed by the problem, the chieftess did not look up as the rest of the Wolfriders began to disburse. Sapling slapped her shoulder in sympathy, and Pine offered condolences. She acknowledged both with a nod, but made no move to return to the holt. Rellah's insistence that companionship might ease her grief was ignored.

"He was mad," the older female said in her infuriating, superior way. "His presence caused dissent, and if he chose to end his life, the whole tribe is better for it."

Skyfire arose then, so suddenly the taller elf started. Pale with anger, the chieftess said, "*Kyr* did not choose to die."

Rellah recoiled a step. The Huntress's wrath was a palpable force, dangerous as the wolf crouched to spring. The first elf dared not argue, but retreated quickly, breaking into a clumsy run just beyond view in the forest.

Skyfire heard her departure as a noisy crashing of sticks, an inept intrusion that rankled upon nerves already overtaxed. Lips drawn back into a snarl that was all wolf, the chieftess returned to her task. She quartered the ground in relentlessly widening circles until twilight stole away the light.

Summer night fell, loud with the voices of crickets. The water crashed down its course, misting the air, and dew beaded the rocks over the precipice where the Dreamsinger had fallen. Huntress Skyfire straightened, aching in ways that had nothing to do with the fact she had spent hours on her knees. She perched in the niche her dead mate had left vacant, eyes closed in misery. No longer would the trees wear blossoms out of season, or brambles blaze with the colors of autumn during spring.

The Dreamsinger was gone, his magic reduced to a memory. Only one legacy remained: the cub in Skyfire's womb quickened and steadily grew toward its birthing. As much for that unborn life as for her own grief, the Huntress could not let the father's death rest. The tragedy that had overtaken the Dreamsinger might one day happen to his offspring; as surely as she breathed air she knew that another elf had dealt the blow that precipitated the fatality. The act was a poison, a danger hidden as a snake among the tribe; a Wolfrider's mindset was trusting by nature. The Way of the wolves had no analog for murder.

Skyfire kicked irritably at the moss-caked stone of the ravine. To search out Dreamsinger's killer posed almost insurmountable problems. The sending she had shared in the instant before annihilation had shown no face; just the roughness of the hand that pushed, and the terrible plunge, and the pain. A wolf might unravel the scents, but by now the trail was cold. The tribe had crossed and recrossed the paths to the ravine, and Skyfire's own search had further obscured the evidence. Even without these complications, no other rider's wolf-friend could be trusted to investigate in her behalf. Pack members who bonded to an elf owed their first loyalty elsewhere. Should her request fall on a tribesmate who was involved, or in sympathy with the killer's cause, she would learn nothing but lies. Dreamsinger's madness had been feared, distrusted, and at the last resentfully tolerated because she had fought and bested every Wolfrider who had dared to challenge his presence. But dissidents remained, too timid or too crafty to fight. Of the many who had licked wounds in defeat, some might whisper for retribution. Factions lingered yet from the days of Two-Spear's chieftainship; Skyfire sensed them at the hunts like tangles in the continuity of the pack. Though most Wolfriders were not capable of intrigue, any one of them might be led by conspiracy.

Half lost in his song and the visions woven by magic, the Dreamsinger had never thought to take precautions. For that, Skyfire blamed herself. From the head of the ravine she listened to the howl carried out in her mate's memory. She did not return to participate. Alone on the height that had killed, she listened, straining to determine which voices were missing, and which sounded uncertain.

Her suspicions knotted uselessly into confusion. The howl for the Dreamsinger ended quickly. His brief stay with the tribe had largely been misunderstood. Skyfire alone had been able to temper his madness, and see beyond to the shape of Timmain's dream. Only she had seen promise of a future where the gentleness of elvish heritage might coexist with the hardy cunning of the wolf. Yet now, with one who murdered magic at large among the tribe, that future and that dream lay threatened.

Night deepened. The two moons lifted over the trees; light through the leaves dappled the forest floor, and touched the rocks at the precipice with a glint like dagger steel. The larger of the moons led the dance, silvering the spume which veiled the head of the gorge. The place where the Dreamsinger had fallen lay lost in black shadow. Brooding, sad, and uncertain what to do, his grieving mate shook back her bright hair.

"Which of us wished you dead?" she asked the empty air, the faces of the moons, the soft sigh of the wind. Only crickets answered. Their song of summer's plenty held nothing to console an empty heart. Restless with loss and frustration, the chieftess cursed.

At the sound, something at the forest's edge started back. Alarmed, Skyfire ducked low in the niche. Carelessness made her cross. She had been as trusting as her mate to linger here, and certainly as foolish. Now the rushing water at her back held threat enough to raise the hair at her nape. She carried the Dreamsinger's cub. If she could sense its gift of magic as it grew, so might others; so might the killer who had destroyed its father. A push from the same hands might send her to share his death. Memory of that plunge and the agony of its aftermath returned with a force like premonition. Skyfire shivered.

Cautiously she hugged the stone. A leap to safer ground might provoke a retreat; already this elf had proved his lack of courage. Yet she chose a more dangerous course. If she could tempt an attack, make her situation seem more precarious than it actually was, she might emerge after a scuffle with Dreamsinger's killer held captive.

But time passed, and the tunes of the crickets continued undisturbed. Skyfire listened until her ears ached. The forest night revealed nothing. At last forced to conclude that the movement had been an illusion born of grief, she raised her head and looked.

The angle of the moons had changed, plunged the trees in deep shadow. Yet the dark beneath the branches was not empty; there shone a pair of silver eyes, eerily identical to the Dreamsinger's.

Skyfire gasped. At the sound, the eyes flashed and turned, lost in the forest's dark. Shaking now, and fighting tears, Skyfire scrambled up from the precipice. She rested her cheek on cold rock. Her mate had not turned spirit to haunt her; she had seen only his gray wolf, who shared the color and intensity of his eyes. While the rest of the pack retired to sleep off gorged bellies, this one restless beast sought a master who would never hunt again.

Deprived of Woodbiter's company, and robbed forever of the Dreamsinger's mad passion, Skyfire longed to reach out to the wolf, to sink both hands to the wrists in his luxurious silver pelt. She wanted to weep in his warmth, and then to run, fast and strong, into the heat of the hunt.

"Song," she called, though she knew the wolf would not come. Wolves who lost elf-friends did not bond to another tribe member; so said Owl, who sometimes, after dreamberries, remembered such things.

The appeal of Huntress Skyfire to her Dreamsinger's wolf brought only a flash of white brush as he turned and retreated into the trees. For a moment, she almost let him go.

Reason why she must not snapped her mood of brooding heartache. Skyfire started up from the rocks. Her brow furrowed with a determination the rest of her tribe knew better than to cross. Song was more than a wolf who had lost a master. He was the key to the identity of Dreamsinger's killer. For that one name, Skyfire was willing to undertake any difficulty, no matter how impossible.

Huntress Skyfire raced into the forest. The wolf fled ahead of her. Running hard, she glimpsed his form as a flash of silver through the glades where the moons' light struck through. She heard him as a rustle of leaves, the scrape of claws on stone, and the soft, disturbed breath of air as he sniffed his back trail for pursuit. Song was fleet, young, and clever enough as a hunter to have survived through the Dreamsinger's exile. Yet he was not a maverick by nature; he had challenged for position, and won acceptance in the pack that ran with the Wolfriders. Skyfire had fought him once, in the course of helping his master. She had gained the victory, but Song's submission had not cowed his spirit. His trust would be troublesome to earn, and time was of the essence. The Huntress understood enough of wolves to know that she must win Song over at once; otherwise loneliness would drive him to identify irrevocably with the pack.

The two moons lowered with the coming of dawn. Shadows turned vague and gray under the trees, and in that uncertain light, obstacles became difficult even for a keen-sighted elf to discern. A wolf, with better sense of smell, had less disadvantage. Song unavoidably drew ahead. Grimly Skyfire held to his trail. Exhaustion blurred her purpose; threat to her unborn cub merged with grief for her Dreamsinger. As she drove each tired foot into the next stride, the silver wolf who darted like a wraith out of reach came to symbolize the mate she had lost. If she could only catch up with the beast, if she could once touch its fur, something of the compassion she had learned through love might be recovered.

But Skyfire's persistent desperation won no ground. Song's intent to escape became all the more frantic. He did not understand the Huntress's motives; his strongest memory of her had been a fight, after which he had been forced to yield to her will. The wolf had let her run at her Dreamsinger's side out of submission, not goodwill. Now, with the master gone, Skyfire's pursuit keyed nothing but a primal instinct to flee. Years spent with an exile lent the wolf cunning: he was not habit-bound to any territory. Where a pack-raised beast would keep to familiar trails, his run a wide loop around a chosen area of forest, Song ran straight cross-country. He might not anticipate every twist in the terrain, or fallen log, or stone outcrop. He might be slowed by unexpected roots, or avoidance of a thicket too dense and tangled for running. Yet the Huntress who followed was equally disoriented; the safety of the cub she carried made her uneasy in strange country, where men might prowl, and unknown terrain lead her into danger. Eventually her two legs must tire, and then Song could slip like a shadow into the wood to seek out his own kind.

Still, Skyfire had spent most of the summer season hunting without any wolf-friend to bear her weight. Spring's crop of cubs had already been weaned when Woodbiter died, and those that were inclined to partner an elf had already bonded. Aware her predicament must extend through the next turn of seasons, the chieftess had hardened to compensate. She did not quit, but continued, stumbling and pushing through the brush, until long after dawn. The sun blazed high overhead when at last she threw herself, panting, in a glade.

Song was footsore as well. His belly was empty of game, and his sinews too spent to hunt. Tail drooping, nose low, he sniffed out a small cave beneath an outcrop. There, he curled up and slept to recover his strength.

Although Skyfire was too weary to run, stubbornness would not let her quit. She tracked Song's footprints through last year's leaves, a briar thicket, and over the moist bed of a stream shrunken down to a trickle by summer. The heat of midday wore upon her energy, and hunger nagged her belly. Soon, for the sake of the cub she carried, she must stop for food and rest; but not yet. The impressions of Song's pads told of a stride no longer fluid. The wolf was tired also, and not so urgent in his flight. Presently Skyfire observed that his path began to meander, as he searched for a lair to take cover.

She paused then to wipe sweat from her face. If she found the wolf before he woke, she had a chance.

The cleft was situated beneath an outcrop of moss-caked stone. Spring water pooled nearby, protected by a stand of trees. Song's marks were plain in the mud by the bank. The darkness between the rocks held the warm scent of his fur. Certain the wolf had laired there, Skyfire retreated from the area with the care of a seasoned predator. She left no unnecessary scent, and made not a whisper of noise. Song must not awaken and discover her presence too soon.

The Huntress knelt at the spring and drank her fill, then wove a snare for small game. She retreated after that to wait. The sun on her back made her drowsy, yet she battled the lure of sleep; if she succumbed, and Song left while she rested, she would lose him. He had run too far through the night, well beyond the territory of the pack that ran with the tribe. This part of the forest was hunted by wolves unfamiliar with elves. Song would be forced to fight for a place among them, or move on as a loner who spurned others. His memory of the Dreamsinger's companionship would fade quickly, and Skyfire knew that success must depend on prompt action.

A ravvit jumped squealing into the snare. Huntress Skyfire started out of a drowse, shaken by the fact that sleep had taken her unaware. Quickly she studied the light. The sun's rays slanted just slightly lower; her attention had lapsed only minutes. Stretching stiffened muscles, the Chieftess arose and drew her dagger. She killed the ravvit with one deft thrust, but resisted the instinct to gorge. With the blood of fresh game on her hands, she set out to share meat with Song.

Her approach to the grotto was cautious as before, but the slight increase in moisture as the day waned made the scent carry. Blood-smell aroused the sleeping predator from his dreams of chase and the hunt. Skyfire heard the click of claws on rock as the great wolf bounded to his feet. She felt the gust of his breath as he sampled the air, then greeted her presence with a low growl of warning.

The Huntress froze instantly, ravvit flesh dripping between her fingers. She made no further move, but waited at the entrance to the cleft for Song to consider her gift.

The wolf made no effort to advance. Skyfire accepted his ambivalence in stride; she had expected no less. Wolves were distrustful by nature, and interactions between members of a pack were rigidly dictated by rank. She had bested Song, and by tradition, he could fill his belly only after she had gorged and lost interest. To share food without regard for hierarchy upset the order Song understood; and things not understood were to be feared.

Skyfire sensed the wolf's uneasiness. She held firm, even as his hackles rose, and a snarl furrowed his muzzle. Shining gray against the dimmer gray shadow of his head, the eyes of the wolf never left her.

"Song." Skyfire put sending in the word. She offered reassurance in place of uneasiness, warmth in place of cold, food against the pain of hunger. She promised joy, and life, and the heady thrill of the hunt in full summer.

Song's snarl intensified. He remembered the past fight. That had ended with his throat bared to her mercy. His instinct was submission, but the close rock walls confined him, cut off his escape if this Huntress pressed her proven superiority against him. The ravvit promised nothing. The smell of its blood only drove the wolf to frustration, for he was hungry, yet dared not feed. Enraged by conflicting instincts, Song crouched on the hair-trigger edge of a spring.

"Song," Skyfire whispered. She shifted her weight slightly to ease a cramped leg; and that small movement tripped the balance.

Song lunged. Wild with fear, crazed to escape, he leapt for the elf in the entryway.

Skyfire could have dodged aside, let the wolf brush past to win freedom. But the name of the Dreamsinger's killer was a threat more dire than mauling. Her tribesmates must not run with a murderer unknown in their midst.

Tired, and slowed by hunger, Skyfire met Song's rush with braced feet. His weight slammed her, hips and shoulder, and his jaws snapped closed on her wrist. The pain was terrible. His teeth ripped down into muscle, and grated with bruising force against bone. Skyfire yelled, in part to distract him, but also to vent the shock and the agony of a wound that wrung her mind with faintness. Just enough awareness remained for her to hammer a fist at the wolf's gray eyes, Dreamsinger's eyes, shining now with the lust to tear and kill.

Song released her before the blow fell. He would not risk his sight; nor could he entirely forget his former defeat at the hands of this same elf. He had attacked, but she had neither given way nor succumbed to fear; either reaction would have invited further aggression. Yet since the elf met challenge with a savage intent to fight, Song backed down. Snarling, he lowered his brush and retreated to the farthest cranny of the lair.

Skyfire knelt, her shoulder pressed weakly to cold stone. The ravvit lay where it had fallen in the dirt between her knees. She cradled her injured forearm in her hand, wrung dizzy by the odors of fresh-killed meat and new blood. Somehow, through pain, she clung to her purpose. She must not leave the grotto, must not permit Song an opening to leave. The safety of her unborn cub depended on her steadiness now.

Teeth clenched, Skyfire worked off her tunic. She wrapped her wrist to slow the bleeding. She knew from past mishaps and remembered scoldings from Rellah: slashes were the least of her worries. More serious were the narrow purple punctures which cut deep, but did not drain. Without herbs to draw out the poison, these were sure to fester, slow her with sickness and fever until she lost her strength and died.

Dreamsinger's fall from the cliff had been a much cleaner end.

Skyfire squeezed her eyes closed. Such thoughts had

no place, except to obscure one fear behind another far more dire. She had but one purpose: to win the murderer's name from Song before her tribe's future came to grief. Cautiously the chieftess shoved to her feet. Her shoulder scraped the rough stone, but she needed the support to rise, to stand straight as if she still had spirit to call challenge. Let Song once gain the impression that she could not fight, and the contest of wills was lost. At the slightest hint of helplessness, the wolf would attack and press for victory.

With a low growl of warning, Skyfire carefully, so very carefully, stepped back. She waited then, though dizziness skewed her balance. Song did not react. Skyfire clung to the stone. She thought of the Dreamsinger's music, now forever stilled; the anger that went with that memory helped to support her through another step, then still more slowly, another. Song watched, but offered no aggression.

Beyond the mouth of the grotto, the sun shone red in the treetops. The heat had eased, but Skyfire sweated in discomfort. Left no other alternative, she knelt at the entrance to Song's lair and trailed her injured forearm in the spring.

The icy water eased the ache and cleared her head enough for her to notice the emptiness in her belly. The meat dropped in the lair was lost. As twilight fell gray over the forest, she heard the sharp crunch of bones in the jaws of the wolf who had bitten her. Song had grown bold enough to appease his hunger on the ravvit. Skyfire wondered how long before he became restless, or desperate, or thirsty to the point where he challenged once again for his freedom.

Darkness brought stars and heavy dew. The sultry heat of day gave way to light breezes; frogs croaked in chorus with the crickets. Skyfire lay and listened to the night woods, her wrist soaking in the spring. Pain would not let her sleep. Light-headed with exhaustion, she reviewed each member of the tribe in her mind. Most were friends; all but the very oldest were forest-cunning, wise, and dependable in the hunt. All had shared through lean times, and bickered over trivia when there was plenty. True enough, there were factions, brittle tensions left over from Two-Spear's time. But the turn of the seasons had dimmed the old distrusts. Skyfire had taken pains never to show favor; always in council she had listened to any rider who spoke out. The fights over Dreamsinger's presence had caused the only open dispute since her chieftainship began.

Skyfire curled her fingers in the current, and winced. The pain of the bite had not lessened. The swelling had increased to the point where she could not effectively grip her knife or spear. Even the simple snare she had woven that morning lay beyond her dexterity. The Huntress rested her sweating forehead against the earth. Help and the holt were beyond call. Yet even the threat of starvation could not turn Skyfire from her quest. That the hopes she had discovered through Recognition should be left at risk to a murderer offered hurt far worse than any wound. Song alone held the answer; only the wolf could reveal which friend, which Wolfrider, which elf under her trust still harbored enough hatred to deceive.

New day dawned humid and close. Birds flitted from the treetops to drink at the spring, but Skyfire could only follow their flight with her eyes. Song was awake and pacing. Fretful herself, Skyfire tried and failed to find a more comfortable position. Her arm had swollen to the point where only the icy water in the pool offered any relief. Her pain could be tolerated as long as she kept the wound submerged.

By noon, the sun fell full on the rocks. Song lay panting in the shadows, eyes fixed ceaselessly on the elf who kept him penned. Skyfire dipped water from the spring in a fold of her leather tunic. She offered to share with the wolf, but Song declined with a growl; irritable, restless, he arose and paced his prison.

Skyfire sweated with her back against the boulders. Reflections off the water hurt her eyes, and the wind which gusted through the treetops rushed unpleasantly against ears that rang with fever. Sickness only increased her determination. Periodically Skyfire checked the lair. Sometimes she saw the Dreamsinger's silver eyes, watching in silence from the grotto. Other times she saw only a silver-pelted wolf, vicious and surly with frustration.

"Who killed you?" she raged in delirium.

The wolf flinched away from the sudden croak of her words; the Dreamsinger refused to give answer.

Skyfire tossed fitfully. She dreamed in the throes of fever that fish with the teeth of predators came to gnaw at her hand. She awoke, screaming with pain, and faced the fearful certainty that her arm had festered from the bite. Rellah was going to be angry; except that Rellah and her bags of smelly herbs were too far distant to help. The thought somehow seemed funny, that the sour old female might wind up scolding bones. Skyfire laughed outright, while thunder growled, and a late afternoon storm showered rain on her head.

Lightning flashed, throwing white-edged reflections into the lair. The Dreamsinger's eyes followed her, shining gray in the shadows. "You're dead," Skyfire muttered, mad with torment and fever. "I will die, your cub will die, and an elf who kills other elves will shelter like a snake in the pack."

Her ravings were absorbed by forest stillness. Twilight darkened around dripping trees. Skyfire lay on her back in the mud, talking to stars that shone through sooty drifts of cloud. They did not bring her Sapling, as she asked; neither did they intercede to prevent the dream that racked her over and over: a staggering step into air, and a fall that ended in blood and pain on the rocky bank of a stream.

Night deepened, and another sort of darkness blanketed Skyfire's thoughts, until even suffering lay beyond feeling.

She awakened, ice-cold, and shivering uncontrollably. Night had gone gray with new dawn, and the wind carried promise of heavy rain. Skyfire opened her eyes. Weakly she attempted to sit up.

Hard hands shoved her back, crashed her bruisingly

onto stone. The impact shot pain from her injury clear down her arm to her shoulder. Shock knocked the breath from her lungs. Through a sucking tide of darkness, she saw a face, and tangled hair, and a raggedy, leather-clad elf. His features were familiar. Through dizziness, Skyfire strove to remember.

"Stonethrower?" she murmured; and vertigo fell sharply away before memory. This elf was an outsider, an exile, not among the faces of friends who shared the howls at the holt. Fear followed, thick enough to choke: Stonethrower had gone off with Two-Spear, his parting words an oath of undying vengeance for the plight which had befallen his chief at Skyfire's hands.

"You!" said Skyfire, recognizing through touch the memory of a sending that had ended in a fatal fall. "It was you who pushed my mate from the ledge!"

Stonethrower did not speak. But the flash of the stone knife he raised above her body offered answer enough. He had returned only to kill her.

Skyfire rolled clumsily aside.

"Whelp of a starved she-wolf!" Stonethrower jerked her back. "You won't escape. You've strayed too far for sending to reach the others. They'll have no warning from you when I return and kill them, one by one, until there is no tribe left."

Strong and cruel and crazy, Stonethrower caught her hair, twisted her head to bare her neck to his knife.

Skyfire thrashed. Her reactions were muddled from fever, and sickness left her too weak to evade the blow. Still, she fought. Aside from threat to her tribe, her death would take the life of the cub within her belly, and the legacy of old magic bequeathed by the Dreamsinger might perish unborn. Frustration, grief, and an overwhelming sense of terror shaped a cry to a mate who was beyond all answer.

"*KYR!*"

Skyfire's sending framed the Dreamsinger's essence, just as Stonethrower struck downward.

A leaping streak of silver flew between. Song launched

from the cave mouth with a growl of animal rage. He recognized the smell of his master's murderer, and Skyfire's sending rang over and over with echoes of the Dreamsinger's presence. Song's sense of loyalty blurred. He leapt for the hated attacker, bristling with a rending lust to kill.

Stonethrower sensed only movement; then the great wolf's charge overtook him. Committed to his thrust at the chieftess, he barely turned his head when the silver male's weight knocked him down. Jaws found his exposed throat and closed over gristle and windpipe with force enough to crush. Stonethrower dropped the knife. He never heard the splash as his weapon sank in the spring. His heels battered uselessly into stone as the wolf's jaws tightened and worried him, shaking elf flesh until the last scent of life was extinguished.

In time, Song tired of the corpse. He dropped it a short distance off in the forest, shook his pelt straight, and returned to lap at the spring. Once his thirst was satisfied, he raised his dripping muzzle and sniffed the dawn air for game sign. A moan from behind made him turn.

The she-elf lay where she had fallen. The hand outflung from her body smelled overpoweringly of hurt. The wolf whined. A presence was missing from his side. Restless now, Song trotted a few steps back and forth. The scent in his nostrils meant trouble; the hunter who should partner him lay wounded. Drawn by the mystery of pack instinct, the silver creature stepped close, crouched down, and began to lick the still fingers of the elf-hand.

He still worked at the task past sunrise, when Wolfriders burst from the trees.

"She's here!" called Skimmer to the others. Rising wind and clouds heavy with rain served only to increase his concern. "Our chieftess is hurt. Sapling, run and fetch Rellah."

Song poised, ready on an instant to run, to abandon the tie so tenuously forged in the night. But a familiar pack surrounded him, and the habit of companionship was strong. As the Wolfriders hurried to succor their chieftess, Song raised his head. Holding ground at his elf-friend's shoulder, he growled challenge to any who might dare to interfere.

The Renders

Stars flecked the sky when Jaiddon reached the headland that sheltered the town of Fisherman's Cove from the sea. Every turn in the deserted road showed the Pattern which secured all Shape on the Isle of Circadie against the Void. Delicate as knotted gilt thread in the failing light, its interlocking tracery of force was visible in the veins of the leaves, the curve of the hills, even the dry sand of the shoreline which stood against the tireless rush of the sea.

Beyond the headland lay a scene of devastation. As though smashed by a fallen sky, the town lay splintered in ruins. The sight struck the breath from Jaiddon's lungs. Not even the boats in the harbor had been spared. The beach glittered with the silvery, crescent corpses of a skipjack's dismembered hold. Smooth sand lay sundered by a ragged gap that passed clean through the shore. Ocean swells rolled through the breach, unimpeded by shallows or shoreline, and on the other side, the land where people had once raised homes lay twisted beyond memory of patterned Shape.

Jaiddon could count the bodies. Trained since childhood, he could see the snarled remains of the patterns that held their spirits in life.

Air sobbed into his throat. Renders had undone an entire town as though its existence was no more solid than morning mist. Jaiddon hardly felt the path beneath his feet as he stumbled over the dunes. The Renders had gone on into the hills. Their trail would not be hard to follow, marked as it was with wreckage.

Anger and hatred gripped Jaiddon in the shadow of that levelled town. Would all of Circadie be undone, as Fisherman's Cove, until her tortured rings lost power and slumped into the sea? Jaiddon bunched the hands whose promise had set him against the Renders into fists. Perhaps if he released the solidity of the ground where the cursed beings stood, he could drop them into the deep. Certainly, that had never been tried. The Masters, all, were bound by oath to preserve the Pattern.

Jaiddon showed his teeth in an expression not quite a smile. He might wear a Master's Colors, but he had sworn no such oath.

Over and over, he was impressed by Circadie's vulnerability until, half blinded by tears of frustration, he was sorry he had not refused the Master's request.

He still found it difficult to believe the bedridden cripple he had faced that afternoon was the Master Shaper of Circadie. The Master whom Jaiddon had always known was a tall, ruddy man, black-haired and full of humor. His hands had been strong and capable, nothing like the warped, skeletal claws Jaiddon had seen trembling on the coverlet. And the face! Jaiddon flinched with horror at the memory of features deformed beyond all recognition.

Yet the eyes in the deep, crumpled sockets had opened. They were still yellow, not yet devoid of the life that once shaped the cycles of Circadie with such enviable confidence.

"I am blind, Jaiddon, though within, I can still Shape your memory," the Master said. The light eyes closed. The ruined face smoothed as an image of a white-robed, barefoot novice with sparely muscled bones and hair the color of brass formed behind seamed lids. "Jaiddon, there are Renders in the land."

The Master's words drove a sharp spike of fear through Jaiddon's thoughts. Few could stand against the power of Renders, outsiders whose disbelief could unravel Shape like a tear in knitted wool. Not even the Pattern of Solidity, foundation of all Circadie, was secure against the destruction such a mind could unleash. Blind and deaf to all but Reality, two of them had once blundered through an entire forest without perceiving the fragile power that held its existence against the Void. Everything they touched was destroyed, reduced in a moment to the flotsam from which it had been created.

"The Renders number three," the Master Shaper said, snapping Jaiddon's paralyzed shock. "They are shipwreck victims, dazed and delirious with thirst. Megallie thinks they are mad. Certainly, they are strong, stronger than any Render who has ever challenged the Solidity of Circadie. We are desperate, Jaiddon. That is why you have been summoned."

"But my Lord!" Jaiddon stared with fresh horror. "I barely passed my apprenticeship a fortnight ago!"

A nightmarish parody of a smile touched the Master's withered lips. Jaiddon felt his heart twist in response.

"Years and experience have proven useless against these Renders." The Master Shaper spoke with difficulty. "Varna, Loremistress of the Pattern, lies dead. Myself, they have broken. I can no longer Shape even a child's toy. Circadie is dying. I place her last hope in your hands."

Tears spilled sudden and hot down Jaiddon's cheeks. He was glad they could not be seen by the man in the bed. "What can I do that you could not?"

The Master was silent for a long while. "I do not know," he said at last. "You are young. Your training is incomplete. But you are talented beyond all that have gone before, so is it inscribed in the Pattern of your hands. It is my hope, all of Circadie's hope, that you, with your untried, unchannelled power, might find means your forebears missed by the wayside. I realize I am probably asking your death. Yet, I ask. Will you face the Renders, and challenge their Reality with Shape?"

Jaiddon stood like a statue. Sunlight spilled through the window and branded a square of warmth in the sweat that chilled his back. He was afraid. Once as a child he'd had a cut that would not stop bleeding. It had been Shaped to health, but the man, the Master whose hands had wrought against the Void, lay dying of a Render's touch. Jaiddon swallowed again, and spoke.

"My Lord, the Renders will have me anyway. I may as well meet the Void in their path."

But the blue tunic and white shirt of Mastery given him after his audience did nothing to ease his self-doubt. For all his alleged talent, Jaiddon could not even read his own lifepath. His peers had laughed often over that.

Black as oblivion, the Renders' path ran northward. Jaiddon could sense its presence without sight by the utter lack of resonance beneath his feet. Here and there, his step struck solidity, and he recognized the harmonics that answered. They were Megallie's. Newly appointed Loremistress in Varna's stead, she had been mending, perhaps after seeing the Master Shaper comfortable.

Her work had been cursory, her touch, unerring. Gazing downward through the darkness beneath his soles, Jaiddon saw where a Grand Axis of the Pattern was laid bare. Megallie had fused it, perfectly. He could not repeat her work. Years of training lay ahead before he dared attune to a major ring, far less forge one complete.

Jaiddon cursed. His earlier plan was no better than a foolish dream. Having seen the original Pattern of Solidity after which all others were formed, he knew himself incapable of breaking even its simplest curve.

Jaiddon moved on. Anger drained away and left a rocky bed of despair.

The Renders lay in a hollow beneath a tangle of scrub thorn, asleep. Jaiddon came upon them so suddenly he nearly fell into the ditch their unbelief had torn through the fabric of the ground. There were three, as the Master had said, opaque bodies dark as blight against the Patterned perfection of grasses fired like crystal by starlight. Even passive, the Renders' Reality radiated threat like a breath of cold.

Jaiddon shivered and fought revulsion. His ancestors had once been formed of substance, as these Renders were, but generations of Shaping had transformed them gradually away from Reality. Cast upon the sea as exiles, they had delved among the mysteries of the mind and the illusory laws of sorcery, and in their fusion, developed the art of Shaping. Circadie was raised above the waves through generations of effort. Ring upon ring of power, joined and interlaced, held its soil dry above the tide. From that framework, the Shapers of Circadie forced tiny allotments of wood, metal, and stone to serve the needs of many.

The Pattern and the Shape that was Jaiddon would not be visible to the Renders when they wakened, just as the grass, the trees, and the soil did not exist through their senses.

Jaiddon groped through despair for an action, any action, that might halt the Renders' terrible course. He knew from memory each passage from the ballads that described past encounters with their kind. But such facts were useless. The Master Shaper had charged him to abandon precedents. Jaiddon pressed damp palms to his temples. If Circadie and the people who inhabited it could be made visible to the Renders, their disbelief might weaken, diminishing their ruinous effect upon the Pattern.

The simple act of enforcing the shape that surrounded them would not suffice. That had been attempted already without success. Jaiddon decided instead to inscribe the Pattern directly upon the minds of the Renders. Surely even Reality's logic could acknowledge and accept the laws of solidity and allow Circadie existence.

Jaiddon took a last breath, unmindful of the thornbranch that hooked his sleeve. Substance never yielded its Reality easily, and a Render was a living entity, self-aware, and defended against intrusion. Prepared for struggle,

Jaiddon closed his eyes and reached out for the thoughts of the Render who lay nearest. Had his training been complete, he would have known the Pattern of Solidity represented the framework of madness to the mind he sought to Shape, but he had barely won his novitiate, and in ignorance, he touched.

Contact opened a blind abyss of unreason. Jaiddon broke into sweat, strove to hold firm against a Reality whose nature commanded Shape to go molten and flow formless into the Void. It seemed as though his Pattern of existence would be crushed to powder beneath the weight of the Render's mind. As the first tremor of dissolution crept through the fibers of his body, Jaiddon cried out. So this was what happened to the Master! Panic thundered through the gaps in his being, twisting reason into a hard knot of terror. Jaiddon tore free.

He was drenched, shaking, and the echo of his scream seemed reflected in the quivering stars. Shocked by the enormity of failure, Jaiddon did not pause to review the nature of what he opposed. Instead, he flung himself recklessly into a second attempt. This time, he shaped fear into a bastion of support.

The Render flinched beneath his touch. He stirred and moaned softly as Jaiddon began to inscribe the primary axis of the Pattern behind his thoughts. As the secondary axis was begun, his protest became louder. Jaiddon tasted sweat on his lips. If he slipped, he would die. With remorseless determination, he bent the will that opposed him and fused the first of the seven rings of power.

The Render shot bolt upright and yelled. His companions roused at once, and the force of their waking thoughts threw Jaiddon from his feet.

"Sweet Jesus, Alaric, what ails you?" said one of the Renders sharply.

Alaric shook his head and shivered. "I dreamed. Mary Mother, I dreamed I saw grass and trees, land."

"Ye're mad, man," his companion said. "There's nothin' here but ocean, and this silly boat afloat on it." He thumped his hand. Circadie shuddered in recoil. Bushes, soil, and a nearby boulder frayed like overstressed fabric, and vanished.

Jaiddon dragged himself to his knees, numbed beyond thought by the heaving dark that bloomed at the Renders' touch. He had failed. Though the effort left him weakened, he had to move clear of the Render's blundering presence and think of something else. Slowly, he rose.

The motion caused Alaric to whirl, eyes widened in panic. The incomplete Pattern within his mind allowed him partial sight of the Shape surrounding him, and he yelled hoarsely. "Almighty God, there's a ghost!"

"Alaric, ye fool! Ye'll have yerself overboard!" A companion jerked him back by the shoulder, then fixed a flat gaze upon the spot where Jaiddon stood. "No ghost there, man. Nothin' but sharks 'n' salt water."

Unbelief struck Circadie like a stormwave. Shape shattered to fragments before it, land and the life it harbored flung piecemeal into the yawning dark of the Void. Jaiddon cried out as the ground under his feet came unbound. Every skill he possessed fought to hold his being complete against a rushing tide of ruin. Loose pebbles and soil slipped like lost hopes through his fingers as he tumbled between debris toward the restless ocean beneath.

His fall was broken by unyielding blue light; a bar of the Pattern itself laid bare. Deformed like wax touched by flame, it had not yet parted beneath the stress of the Renders' unbelief. Jaiddon groped for handholds in the riven earth, dragged himself upright. Dizzied and confused, he forgot caution, and the moment his head appeared above ground level, Alaric screamed again.

The other Renders restrained him with difficulty. "'Tis the devil's work, surely," said one. "A clear case of possession."

Jaiddon dragged himself clear of the ruinous gap. The word devil meant nothing to him, and with uncomprehending eyes, he watched the Render who had spoken kneel over Alaric.

"Christ deliver us," he said. "I never thought I'd perform an exorcism for a soul in an open boat."

More strange words, and the chant that followed was in an unfamiliar language, as well. But its effect upon the Pattern was instant annihilation.

Half a hill exploded soundlessly into oblivion. Jaiddon screamed. The Void rose to engulf him. He felt light, insubstantial as ash. The breeze off the sea blew through the rifts as the Render's strange ritual unbound the force that held him complete. Trapped in a rushing vortex of wind and dark, Jaiddon suddenly longed to see the disbelief that was destroying him take Shape. Shape could be opposed, and on the heels of thought came insight.

He had always been ridiculed as a dreamer, unable to master his own imagery. What if he broke precedent, abandoned control and coupled the result with his lifelong training as Shaper? Jaiddon cursed and laughed. Poised on the edge of dissolution, he threw his wild imagination free rein. It seized upon the darkness that gnawed him and clothed it with pictures. Though they reflected unrelenting nightmare, Jaiddon patterned them and gave them Shape.

Circadie flowed and changed at his bidding. Plant, soil, and twig mirrored the fabric of his images. Fast as thought could unreel, Jaiddon found himself in an alien place of red haze. The ground turned to ash beneath his feet, littered with the Shaped symbols of the Renders' disbelief, among them every desire, hope, and motivation that founded it.

Jaiddon stepped carefully between the glancing sparkle of gem stones, jeweled goblets, and the dirt-gray bones which were his reshaping of the Renders' dead senses. He had no understanding for much of what he patterned, nor was he given time to seek it. Jaiddon waited to see which form would seek his death.

They came as demons, three of them, savage and thoughtless as the unbelieving minds they represented. Starved, naked, and crowned by bleached shocks of hair, they moved through the shadowed haze of imagery, eyes sultry as candleflame, and forked tongues tasting the air. Jaiddon knew immediate fear at the sight of them. But their Shape was comprehensible. It could be opposed.

Bending, Jaiddon scooped up a fistful of ash and

placed his will upon it. Form broke and ran fluid at his touch as he repatterned Shape to match desire. Controlled, that which seconds ago had been ash assumed the outline of a longsword. Jaiddon tested the balance, then grimly inflected the pattern of tempered steel.

The weapon in his hand warmed. Its rough surface acquired the glassy bluish sheen of the forge. Jaiddon shivered with impatience. The change would take too long. The demons had sensed his presence, and with a hiss like a water kettle, two of them charged. The patterning was not yet complete, but Jaiddon had no choice. He raised his blade to meet them.

The demon that rushed at his throat was impaled. It screamed and wrenched. The half-finished sword snapped off near the hilt. Jaiddon fended the second one away with his forearm. Teeth and nails tore like knives through cloth, then flesh.

Jaiddon bashed himself clear with his knee and thrust the demon back with the jagged remnant of his blade. It sidestepped and spat. Jaiddon turned with it. The fallen one writhed underfoot, treacherously close. Nearby, the third crouched, watching with a baleful yellow eye.

"Render!" Jaiddon forced the word around the terror that gripped his tongue.

Nimbly avoiding the steel, the demon attacked, slashed, and twisted clear of Jaiddon's riposte. Thin furrows opened in Jaiddon's arm as it struck. Blood soaked through shredded silk shirt. Fear made the breath rattle in his throat. Circling, feinting, he survived two more rushes. Sweat stung his eyes. The demon was still unmarked. The third crouched, still, to one side. Jaiddon knew he was finished when it chose to fight.

Raising his free hand, Jaiddon shaped in glowing lines that portion of the Pattern that sealed its final Solidity. The demon hissed in fury and sprang for Jaiddon. Patterning broke with an aching flare of light. The creature bore him down. Hot breath scalded his skin. Fangs mashed his shoulder, and the demon's nails gashed at his side and back. Jaiddon battered unsuccessfully with his hands. Dizziness whirled his head. All would be lost in a matter of seconds. Aware of nothing but the final darkness that closed over thick as water to drown him, Jaiddon threw himself into a last, desperate attempt to Shape.

He wakened, choking. Water and blood had soaked his hair and clothing. Callused hands shook him.

"Death, 'e looks like the sharks been at 'im," said a voice from above.

Jaiddon opened his eyes, blinked. He lay in a boat. Two strangers stood over him with faces bearded, gaunt, and peeling from overexposure to the sun. He struggled, craned his neck, and tried to see over the gunwale.

"Easy, lad," said the man. His fingers tightened on Jaiddon's shoulders, making dizziness flood back. "Ye come near to drownin'. Best stay still a bit an' catch yer breath."

Jaiddon closed his eyes and wrestled despair. He had fallen into the hands of the Renders. Why was he not dead? Where was Circadie?

"Let me be," he said softly as soon as he could speak. The hands fell away.

Jaiddon sat up, gripping the boat with bloody fingers. His body burned like fire, it was cut in so many places. When he stared outward, a triple image assaulted his eyes. If he looked with a Shaper's perception, the hills of Circadie appeared, churned and distorted where the Renders' thoughts had warped its form. The Pattern of Solidity glowed through, serene and blue where it remained whole, black and gapped where the Renders had broken through. On top, pale and insubstantial as a ghost's drawing, moved the heaving, restless shoulders of ocean swells that stretched in endless ranks to the far horizon.

Jaiddon fell back, suddenly weak. In his last moment of awareness, he had sought to Shape himself a form beyond the Void. He should have died. Instead, his dying act had transformed him close enough to Reality that the Renders could perceive him. When the sun rose, his flesh would cast shadow, as did all Substance.

Jaiddon dared a look at the Renders. Two stared at him with eyes that bore the haggard stamp of hardship. The third lay grotesquely sprawled and still in the stern. Jaiddon recognized the Render he had inflected with a fragment of the Pattern. Remembering, also, the demon that had fallen beneath his sword, Jaiddon drew a painful breath and spoke.

"What happened to Alaric?"

The Renders started. One of them blanched with fright.

"Dead," said the larger of the two. "'E woke up raving an' died. It was madness that done for him, but how did ye know his name?"

The other Render started forward and shouted. "He knew because Satan sent him! Didn't he appear at the moment of Alaric's exorcism?" He pointed an accusing finger at Jaiddon. "You come from Hell, your purpose to tempt us from faith. God will punish us for bringing you aboard."

The large Render spat. "The devil, Chaplain? Do ye smell brimstone?" Laughter followed, but it was forced.

Jaiddon raised himself onto the seat in the bow. Dizzy, sick, and weak as he was, it was evident the Renders distrusted his Reality. They might kill him, in their misunderstanding. Jaiddon thought quickly. Though he knew nothing of Hell, the devil, or exorcism, they were obviously powerful images to the Renders. Perhaps even these might be Shaped to advantage.

"I did not come from Hell." His voice startled both men. "I would help, but if you have no faith, I am powerless."

"Christ have mercy," said the Chaplain.

Jaiddon ignored him. "You suffer greatly from hunger and thirst." Both men stared, speechless. Jaiddon plunged ahead and hoped their confusion would last long enough to weaken their disbelief. "Fetch me a container. I will provide you with food and drink. Then give me your oarshaft, and I will Shape you a sail to carry wind, that you may return to the land you desire."

The larger Render laughed. "Would ye make miracles, lad?" He rummaged among the floorboards, and after a moment, extended a wineskin. "Ye've got my faith, what there is of it."

"Fill it with seawater." Jaiddon's eye fell on the Chaplain. "Do you have faith?"

The Chaplain swallowed and crossed himself uneasily. "I pray four times daily."

"Pray, then." Jaiddon accepted the dripping wineskin. Its rough leather stung his torn flesh unpleasantly, but that did not deter him. Every kitchen drudge in Circadie knew how to pattern the salt from the water they drew to wash their pots. This was the simplest form of Shaping, and it took Jaiddon the space of seconds. He copied the Chaplain's motion over the wineskin for effect, and offered it to the Renders. "Drink. If you have faith, you will be refreshed."

The larger Render pulled the stopper, peeling features stiffly expressionless. He raised the wineskin to his lips, filled his mouth, then swallowed greedily. When his thirst was eased, he knelt before Jaiddon in awestruck silence while the Chaplain, also, drank his fill. . . .

The tale is still told, in dockside taverns, of how a chaplain and a deckhand survived the wreck of the ship Saint Helena by saving a holy man from the teeth of a shark. In turn, he rewarded them, changing seawater into cheese, bread, and wine by miracle. There were witnesses who observed the two tacking into the harbor, their sail the bare shaft of an oar. The holy man was not with them. He was said to have left the boat by walking on the face of the sea.

Somewhere, over the horizon on the isle of Circadie, Jaiddon's ballad is still sung. It tells of a young novice who took a Master's Colors to defend the Pattern of Solidity from Renders, and how he accomplished his purpose and returned, bleeding and weary, the only Shaper since the Founders to cast a shadow.

No Quarter

The laser hit burned through the *Kildare*'s shields
and vaporized the aft attitude jets in an instanta-
neous burst of explosion. The ejection of debris
and gaseous propellant created recoil that the damaged
system failed to counter.

On the bridge, in the act of rising to visit the head,
Commander Jensen was spun sideways into the com console. The impact left more than a bruise. Over the stabbing pain of cracked ribs, and through the high-pitched,
excited curse from the pilot on helm duty, the officer
assigned charge of the *Kildare* strove against a mind-
whirling onrush of vertigo to muster the necessary attitude
of command.

"Damages?" he gasped on an intake of air that was all
he could manage, being winded.

Across a narrow aisle banked on either side with
instrumentation, the ensign still strapped in his seat recovered from surprise. "Aft attitude thruster's gone, sir, portside. Also the rear screen sensor. Burnt clear out. Hull's
intact, but we'll need the engineer's report to know if it's
stable."

That explained the horrible dizziness: inertia, not pain.
The *Kildare* tumbled from the hit, her guidance units

unable to compensate with one quarter of the system blown
out. Left gray and disoriented from his own hurts, Jensen
fought the buck of the deck and crashed back into his command chair. "Find out if she's stable," he rapped out in reference to the hull. Then he glanced across the gloom of the
V-shaped control bridge toward the silhouette of his still-
swearing pilot. "Get this hulk back under control, fast."

The pilot, the fair-haired son of somebody's father in
the Admiralty, was nowhere near as good as the rating
sewn onto the starched sleeve of his coverall. Neat to the
point of fussiness he might be, but his hands were slow,
and his touch, far from unerring. Trembling, he fumbled
the controls.

Whiplashed by a second round of inertial force all the
more aggravating for being unnecessary, Jensen shut his
eyes in forbearance. The last pilot he'd been assigned had
been a sloppy son of a bitch when it came to appearance;
but he could by God fly. *Kildare* rolled, bucketed, lurched,
and finally wobbled out of her tumble.

By then the young ensign had recovered his curiosity
enough to voice the obvious. "Damn, Commander, who
would be firing on us out here?"

Jensen ignored the question until after he had queried
his one competent bridge officer, a wary middle-aged
woman named Beckett who'd been born without the
instincts of motherhood. "Gun crews intact, sir, and your
engineer gives the drive systems a tentative okay," she
answered in her husky baritone. The sandy hair pulled
back from her forehead emphasized bushy eyebrows, and
square, oversize front teeth. If homely appearance had stifled her social life, Beckett poured her frustration into her
work. She'd already confirmed the engineer's next check.
"Dak's testing the coil regulator for signal overload, but
adds it's an outside possibility."

The laser hit must have grazed them, Jensen determined, and concluded further that if their shields had been
breached, the attack weapon was more powerful than any
small vessel should pack. Still, reassured that the main
drive systems of his vessel apparently remained intact,

Commander Jensen stared across an undecorated expanse of grate flooring to the junior ensign who had questioned inopportunely; a boy so fresh from his Academy training that he still wore his *hat* on the bridge; hunched in earnest over his board, the kid had a clear, pudgy complexion that ran to acne, and ears that stuck out from under spikes of silvery fair hair. He was currently gazing, rapt, at the image of drifting fragments on the main analog screen.

"I thought I asked you to check on the status of our hull?" Jensen snapped, pained by more than his ribs. He resisted an impulse to blot sweat from his brow, then silently pondered the self-same issue. His ship was a converted yacht, a rich man's toy hastily revamped for Fleet service in the face of threat from the Syndicate. She was armed more for scout duty than defense; and with her untried crew and recently promoted senior officer, Admiral Duane had stationed her as far from any probable site of action as possible. Why *had* the *Kildare* been fired upon? And by whom, when they were just a patrol sent out for observation, in case the battle that currently centered around Target proved to be a feint?

"Beckett," Jensen said belatedly, "initiate a scan."

The communications officer nodded her leathery face, eyes underlit by the scatter of lights on her board. She did not belabor the point that she had done so, long since, but the blown aft sensors left her blind to near half of the analog grid.

On the bridge of the *Marity*, by appearance a hard-run merchanter, and by trade a skip-runner ship, a bearish, blunt-featured man scratched at the mat of chest hair through the opened neck of his coverall. The flight deck of his vessel was too cramped with instrumentation for a man of his size to stretch. This did not seem to trouble him as he turned deceptively lazy eyes to the mate who worked the console beside him. "They found us yet?"

Slender, elegant as an antique rapier, *Marity*'s mate, Gibsen, turned his head with a half-raised brow. Framed by a vista of illegal electronics and signal lights of alien design, he said, "No. And their pilot's a kid who can't fly."

In the half gloom of *Marity*'s flight deck, MacKenzie James didn't speak. On the graying side of thirty-five and muscled like a wild beast, he made no move. But the corner of his mouth that lifted toward a smirk said "incompetent" more plainly than words. His scarred hands stopped their scratching, and his gravelly, basso voice phrased orders with a sparseness that hinted at exasperation. "Forget subtlety. Show them."

As if blowing the hell out of the ass end of any Fleet ship hadn't been questionably unsubtle, Gibsen set tapered fingers to the controls and tweaked.

The *Marity* changed position.

Which meant Beckett, bent yet over a console set for a fine-screen search, suddenly got an eyeful of side vanes and struts where a second ago her instruments had shown emptiness. The impossible happened. She got flapped, screeched a startled oath, and jerked back before she thought to step down the magnification. "Dammit to hell with a hangover!" she repeated, sounding more like her gender than she ever had. "We're being messed after by a goddamn merchanter."

"What!" Jensen half sprang from his command chair, then sank back with a grunt of pain. Plagued by echoes of his own startlement reflected back at him by bare, metallic bulkheads, he went suddenly cold to the core. The only "merchanter" he could imagine near the site of a major battle against the Syndicate would be the *Marity*, command of the skip-runner and criminal MacKenzie James. "Get me a registry number," Jensen snapped through stabbing discomfort. "Or lacking that, scan for specs."

Beckett read back the requested information in her usual sexless voice.

"*Marity*," Jensen confirmed. And his manner held an edge that his crew had never known.

• • •

On the dimly lit bridge of the *Marity*, the mate Gibsen raised baleful hazel eyes to his captain. "Mac, they aren't minded to be sportsmen, this morning. The portside plasma turret is rotating our way."

"Beats hell out of being overlooked," Mac James said laconically. "Now give 'em something to chase."

Gibsen's narrow features lit in a grin, red-tinged by the lights of his console. "Lead them on by the nose, you mean." His delight did not fade through the split-second interval as he played his controls with a touch his Fleet counterpart aboard *Kildare* would have sworn on his scrotum was wizardry.

Beckett patently refused the belief that the *Marity* was anything other than a hard-used private hauler; she argued loudly up to the point when her screens displayed a maneuver that should by *Marity*'s aged specs have destroyed the integrity of her hull. Caught midsentence in denial, the com officer paused, closed her heavy jaw, then recited the formula that outlined the effects of inertia upon the *Marity*'s supposed limitations. "Bits," she finished heatedly. "We should be looking at flying bits of wreckage."

Cracked ribs prevented Jensen from rounding on her in a fury. As a result, his instructions to his pilot came out with unintentional control. "Tail her. And set our coils charging for transit to FTL. If *Marity*'s going to jump, we jump with her, or blow our coil condensers trying."

"Bloody hells, Commander, whatever for!" interjected Beckett. "We've an assigned post, and despite the provocation, I see no reason to abandon our position."

Jensen moved a foot and swiveled his chair toward her. He glared the length of the bare, functional bridge compartment. "Are you questioning my direct order?" he demanded with a rage that burned entirely inward; his face stayed deadpan, and his eyes, unflinchingly level.

Beckett's rough complexion reddened. "I question unreasonable judgment." Nonplussed, her huge hand flicked the switch that assured her words would be monitored and incorporated into the ship's official course log.

The fresh-faced ensign beyond her followed the exchange with an interest that could damn, if the issue ever came to court-martial.

Frostily stiff, Jensen said to his pilot, "Carry on, Sarchev. Follow the *Marity*."

Later, when the craft of MacKenzie James initiated FTL, the *Kildare* followed suit.

"Hooked," murmured Gibsen when the queer hesitation in human time-sense passed, and the darkness of FTL settled like a hood over both of the *Marity*'s analog screens. "Your boy commander's taken the bait."

On the adjacent chair, which had a tendency to leak its stuffing out of several haphazardly stitched rips, Mac James turned his blunt-featured face. Red-lit by the array of the *Marity*'s instruments, he showed the smile of a sated predator. He flexed his coil-scarred fingers with the method of old habit and murmured, "After the tangle we made of Jensen's plot at Chalice station, did you ever think that he wouldn't?"

Gibsen lounged back in his crew chair, his long-lashed eyes deeply thoughtful. He did not say what he felt, that the more you messed with a man's obsessions, the more dangerous he was likely to become. The corollary required no emphasis: Jensen's hatred of MacKenzie James was no longer rooted in sanity.

On the control bridge of *Kildare*, Communications Officer Beckett whacked a ham fist against her thigh. "You're crazy, and a goddamned danger to all of us."

Jensen regarded her outburst with no other reaction beyond a blink. "Question my authority one more time, and I'll see you stripped of your rank."

His total absence of passion was all that made Beckett back down. Surrounded by taut stillness that gripped the two other crew members present, she looked down and fiddled a few adjustments on her board. The next instant the chime that signaled departure from FTL sounded across silence.

"Short hop," murmured *Kildare*'s pilot, and the next instant everybody on the flight deck had their hands full.

The engineer called in to report a power failure in the main drive. "Coil leakage," he said tersely. "No way of predicting the stress crack that caused it. But FTL's a closed option until the system's been drained and patched."

Even as Jensen drew a pained breath to express his annoyance, Beckett delivered worse news: their precipitous flight after *Marity* had landed them all but on top of the leading edge of a war fleet.

"Identify," Jensen snapped back.

The greenie ensign did so, in tones surprisingly steady. "Syndicate, sir. On a projected course toward Khalia." He would have added the pertinent facts, concerning numbers of dreadnoughts and formation, but Jensen's next order prevented it.

"Where's *Marity*?"

"Sir?" Now the ensign's voice did quaver. Naively inexperienced, and fearful of questioning a senior officer, he added, "We should inform Fleet Command, sir. The skip-runner's presence is secondary to the defense of Khalia."

"Mac James's presence indicates involvement with the enemy," Jensen replied with a patience he did not feel. "Now find me *Marity*, fast, because in case you've forgotten your notes, draining the coils means we'll be without shields. We're a sitting duck right now for a trigger-happy skip-runner, and that's our first concern."

Almost in defiance, Beckett stabbed at her board. The analog screen flashed in response and gave back an image of scuffed paint and rust-flaked vanes, and the faded letters of a registry code that the years had weathered unintelligible. "She's off our bow," Beckett added sardonically. "Close enough to be in bed with, and right where we have no weapon to bear, and where our attitude control systems are too perfectly crippled to maneuver. That's not luck. I'd say this was a prearranged trap."

She did not belabor the point that *Kildare* was well within range to be detected by the approaching fleet. Despite the fact that she was a conversion from the private sector, *Kildare*'s weaponry specs readily identified her as a Fleet vessel. In seconds rather than minutes the *Kildare* and her crew of seven would be nothing better than a target.

The particulars of that dilemma had scarcely registered when a voice horned in through the security net that should have kept *Kildare*'s com bands shielded from outside interference.

"Commander, I'd say your survival options are limited to one," came an intrusive drawl that made the skin on Jensen's arms roughen to gooseflesh. He knew the inflection, would recognize that grainy timbre anywhere for the voice of MacKenzie James. "Unless you'd rather get slagged by a plasma charge," the skip-runner captain continued, "I'd advise that you surrender your vessel unconditionally to me."

Jensen's jaw muscles knotted. The moment held clarity like a snapshot, preserved in time by preternatural awareness of the bridge compartment, with its gray drab walls flecked with lights thrown off by the controls, and set in that dance of shadow and reflection, the faces of his officers, all staring. The pilot wore a stupid expression of surprise; the set of Beckett's outsized jaw showed cynicism; but of them all the greenie ensign was worst, with his wide-eyed, choked-back fear that implied utmost faith in his commander's ability to produce a miracle.

Feeling the stabbing ache of his ribs and a gut-deep hatred that made him shake, Jensen licked white lips. When he did not immediately speak, the voice of MacKenzie James elaborated.

"Boy, you'd better decide fast."

"Damn you," Jensen cracked back, though with no channel open Mac James could not hear.

Beckett said nothing. The ensign looked near to panic, as his awe of his superior officer became shattered before his eyes. Only *Kildare*'s pilot managed the wits to speak. "The skip-runner could be bluffing. He's got no protection, either, and the whole Syndicate fleet is bearing down."

Which was not only naive, but stupid, Jensen raged inwardly. MacKenzie James never backed himself into corners, except by clearest design. This skip-runner had sold Fleet secrets to goddamn Syndicate spies, and since he was uncannily reliable when it came to trafficking classified material out of the Alliance, the enemy dreadnoughts bearing down on Khalia were unlikely to advertise their presence merely to take out a contact likely to be useful against the Fleet. Nor would they blink at a prize ship stolen from an adversary. Wise to the ways of the skip-runner and determined to stay alive to best him, Jensen gave the only answer that left him any opening.

"I surrender the *Kildare* and all her crew to the master of *Marity*, without condition." Through the heat of his own humiliation, Jensen was aware of his ensign trying desperately not to cry, and a glare of vitriolic contempt from Communications Officer Beckett.

Mac James's pilot had the hands of a monkey when it came to dismantling a control board. His narrow, sensitive fingers could reach and unhitch and disconnect circuitry behind narrow, cramped panels that by rights should have invited curses. Gibsen whistled, oblivious.

The sound set Jensen's teeth on edge, as did the quiet, deliberate voice of Mac James as he commandeered a communications console as yet unmolested by Gibsen's tinkering. It did not matter to *Kildare*'s former commander that the skip-runner, of his own volition, was following through with the duty first urged by the baby-faced ensign now bound and gagged in the back bay of the flight deck. That the message torp bearing word of the Syndicate fleet's vector toward Khalia was fired away under Commander Jensen's own codes did not matter; that Admiral Duane would receive the communication in time to give Fleet forces the edge in the coming battle to preserve the Khalian planets did not matter.

Jensen's mind centered on one thought.

MacKenzie James was a criminal. He did not act out of heroism, but only callous self-interest. If he wanted Khalia defended, that could only be because the two-faced Weasels who'd surrendered made a healthy, lucrative market for traffic in illicit weapons. Gunrunning being second only to state and military secrets on the list of Mac James's transgressions, *Marity* would be involved to her top vanes. Jensen stared at the stubble of hair that furred the crown of the skip-runner captain's head, just visible over the com station. Hatred and rage had both given way to a patience unforgiving as stone.

Tied to his own command chair, unmoved by Beckett's grunts of discomfort from the corner where she lay bound alongside *Kildare*'s ensign and pilot, Jensen waited in motionless tension like a snake coiled before prey.

Gibsen muttered a query from behind an opened cowling.

"Gun turrets next," Mac James said in drawllessly succinct reply. "We'll want the coil regulator and the magneto banks, but leave life-support intact." The salt-and-pepper crown of hair disappeared briefly as Mac James leaned forward to toggle a switch. His next instructions to his mate were buried under a drift of garble from the com, most likely cross-chat on a Syndicate command channel.

Jensen ground his teeth.

Gibsen straightened with his hands full of circuit boards; and the foreign speech paused in an inflection that framed a question. MacKenzie James answered in the same lingo, and the response that came back was mixed with laughter.

There followed an infuriating interval while Gibsen and his skip-runner captain stripped the *Kildare* with sure, no-nonsense efficiency. Jensen found the pain of cracked ribs less intrusive than the pain of humiliation. He sat, strapped helpless on his own flight deck, unable to face away from the analog screen somebody had carelessly left operational—the screen that showed the passage of the Syndicate fleet bound to attack the planet Khalia, dread-noughts and their fighters arrayed in formation like some grand, silent procession.

A few of the behemoths winked their running lights in salute of the *Marity* and her latest act of sabotage against the Fleet.

Blackly murderous, Jensen chafed at the lashing on his wrists. He considered a thousand ways to kill the skip-runner captain MacKenzie James, all of them lingeringly bloody.

The Syndicate fleet departed, leaving the black of space on the analog screen. Hours passed. Jensen's hands were numb. His full bladder became a torment. His wrists stung and his shoulders ached, and his ears had long since stopped hearing the thump and bump, and the hiss of flushed air from the lock belowdecks as the *Kildare*'s heav-ier components were off-loaded to the hold on board *Marity*. The tap of footsteps coming and going ceased, replaced by one incongruously light tread recognizable as that of MacKenzie James.

At the entry to the bridge he paused, and called instructions to his mate and pilot. "Go back to *Marity* and power up the coils. Syndicate's about reached Khalia by now, and when they find Duane there to give a hot wel-come, I want to be gone from this system."

Gibsen said something that rang with cheerful sar-casm.

Then MacKenzie James strode across the metal floor plates, rounded the central bulkhead that divided the rear half of the bridge into two compartments, and ended by looking down at the commander still strapped to the cen-tral crew chair. He studied Jensen with an intensity that unnerved. For once, Mac's coil-scarred hands were still. A faded, much creased coverall covered his muscled shoul-ders, the cuffs unhooked and turned back where they'd bound at sinewed wrists through the hours of hanging in the wreckage waiting to spring the trap. Although the only one of *Kildare*'s original crew without a gag, Jensen waited for the skip-runner to speak first.

"Boy, the message torp giving the Syndicate war fleet's vector to Khalia went out under your codes. For that, your brass might overlook the fact that you were careless enough to get your ship boarded and stripped. If you've got the guts and the glibness to lay your story right."

Jensen regarded the captain he reviled with every fiber of his being. His career standing did not trouble him. That concern would arise later. Now, only one question burned to be answered. Staring into an expression like chipped granite, Jensen asked, "Why should you send that message torp? You're not a man who does favors on principle."

MacJames gave back a rogue's grin that harbored little humor. "Who else could have done the job and been ignored through the passage of the entire Syndicate attack fleet?"

Unsatisfied, Jensen said nothing.

The coil-scarred fingers flexed, one by one in succession with the familiarity of long-established habit. Mac James qualified on a note of dubious sincerity, "Say I didn't want Khalia scragged."

"Did it have to do with your market for illicit weapons?" Jensen demanded, burningly fierce.

The most-wanted skip-runner captain in space awarded his adversary a half shrug of dismissal. "You have one outstanding asset, boy. Your thinking is simplistically accurate."

Since the comment was the last that Jensen might have anticipated, he was left without ready rejoinder.

Untouchable, untraceable, and infuriatingly confident, MacKenzie James turned on his heel. He stepped off the stripped bridge of the *Kildare* and departed through the lock for his transfer back to *Marity*. Moments later the same accursed analog screen showed the skip-runner ship's departure.

Yet the last word came over the com channel the captain had deliberately left open.

"You have no propulsion system, no firepower, and no

communication or navigational equipment left aboard," observed the blunt tones of Mac James. "However, in the aft console where message torps are stored, you'll find one Gibsen left behind. That should be sufficient to see you rescued, when the fight winds down over Khalia." A moment later the skip-runner captain added an afterthought: "Oh, yes, and your engineer, is it Officer Dax? He's locked in the emergency escape capsule. You'll want to let him out. Apparently he pissed off my mate some, and the air supply in the capsule was left off . . ."

It was Cael, one of the laser crew, who worked out of his bonds first. Lanky, sallow, and looking as if he'd worn the same coverall for a week, he arrived on the bridge in an excited gush of talk. "Can't find Dax," he said breathlessly as he cut Jensen's hands free. "Damned skip-runner must've abducted him, or killed him, or something, because he's not in any of the compartments. Jesus, you should see what's happened down there. Ship's got no guts left, I swear. Stripped down to her coils, which leak, and are useless anyway."

"Cael," said Jensen, standing stiffly due to discomfort and an icy vista of fury. "Kindly be silent and cut your fellow officers free."

The next thing Cael chose to cut was Beckett's gag, which from Jensen's point of view was a mistake. She never did keep her mouth shut.

"You won't get away with this, Commander," she said, between hawking sour spittle from her throat. "That message torp to Fleet won't bring you farts for a citation, because I'm going to see you burn. You surrendered a Fleet vessel to a goddamned skip-runner, saw her stripped to her pins without a fight, and now you think to profit by it? Guess again."

Slapped awake from his obsessive desire to see MacKenzie James dead and rotting, Jensen simply stared at her. He did not notice the looks given him by the ensign, nor the baffled curiosity of the gunman who paused in his ministrations to the pilot. In a tone of velvet quiet, the commander said, "Carry on with your duties. I'm going down to free Dax."

Jensen strode coolly from *Kildare*'s bridge. From the moment he rounded the bulkhead, his crew burst into excited talk, but he did not hear. Sprinting full tilt for the access hatch to the lower level, he thought only upon how to save his career. Beckett was an unanticipated problem. Damn her for having no ambition whatsoever. Damn her for being a stickler for protocol. Old for her post, she'd probably never been promoted because the officers she'd served under hated her.

But deep down, Jensen knew that Beckett was only a fraction of the problem. Even if the other five members of the crew went along with a falsified story, how long before that greenie ensign or that all-thumbs pilot talked over their beer?

Involved in furious thought, Jensen hurried on.

Around the bend, past the gutted remains of the drive compartment, Jensen nearly collided with the other member of his gun crew. "Rogers," he said, trying not to wince at the stab of pain from his cracked ribs. "The rest of the crew are on the bridge. Join them and wait for my return."

"Aye, sir," said Rogers, his corpulent, ruddy features showing no curiosity at all. Cael often said he only came alive under his headset, with a live target in front of him.

Just then, Jensen was grateful for one crewman who was content with a stolid outlook. He ducked down a side corridor that narrowed into a tube. The light panels were out, lending a gray, echoing ghostliness to a downward plunge into dark. *Kildare*'s conversion had been too hasty for aesthetics; her gratings were blessedly bare. Jensen found the access panel by feel and tapped out the security code. A panel hissed open. Striped black and yellow, and glinting with reflective tape, the last remaining message torp rested untouched in its cradle, exactly as MacKenzie James had said.

Jensen lifted it out, grunting at the pain as cracked ribs protested the exertion. He hefted the capsule to his sound side, but found the effort a waste. The strain on the muscles called on to hold his body erect against the off-balancing weight hurt him just as much.

Breathing with all the tenderness he could manage and hating the fact his eyes watered from the effort, Jensen inched his way back down the access tube. He'd have to cross the main bay, which was probably unlighted, and that was the moment he'd be vulnerable if any of his crew chanced to stray from the flight deck.

The lights proved to be on, which was infinitely worse; Jensen felt exposed as he crossed the open expanse. His hands shook, and his fingers left sweaty prints on the reflective strips of the message torp. He pressed on, toward the shadowed alcove with its reflective emergency emblem.

The escape ejection capsule's lock cracked open with a faint hiss and an escape of stale air. Grunting despite his best effort as he ducked, Jensen pushed his way inside, the message torp tucked across his knees. He elbowed the plate that would light the interior, and saw what looked like a bundle of rags in one corner. The seeping red stains in the cloth belied that assessment.

Jensen set down the torp, shifted, and light from the overhead flooded over his shoulder to reveal the engineer, Dak, bound, gagged, and rolled up in a shivering ball. The knuckles visible through the strapping on his hands and wrists were grazed, and he had a gash on one knee, an elbow, and the curve of one acne-dotted cheek. His eyes, which were blue and bugged out, swiveled in surprise at the sight of his commander. He moaned something that had the ring of obscenity into his gag and thrashed determinedly at his bonds.

Preternaturally aware of the access hatch gapped open at his back, Jensen whispered urgently for silence.

"Hostiles are still aboard," he lied as he stooped over the battered engineer. He began with the wrist bonds and whispered into the ear that poked over the edge of the gag. "We're in very deep trouble."

Dak flexed his freed hands and gave Jensen a wide-eyed

look of sarcasm. His first words, as his gag came loose, were "No kidding."

Jensen let some of the anger he felt toward MacKenzie James leak into his voice. "Crew's all dead. Without quarter."

That shut Dak up, fast. Sealed in the escape capsule, he'd had no clue as to what had befallen. He stared in shocked horror as his senior officer continued.

"They spared me so they could pump me for security codes and information," Jensen fabricated. He paused, made a show of staring at his hands, which were abraded and raw from his constant twisting at the ties that lashed him to the crew chair. "I talked some, mostly as a ploy. The skip-runners thought I was scared and didn't view me as a threat. They tied me less carefully than they might have, and I managed to work free." Now Jensen raised his eyes and stared ingenuously at his engineer. "We need to blow the ship," he confided. "Take out those skip-runners before they have a chance to use my codes against the Fleet, or to make off with *Kildare* as a prize."

"They were going to leave me to suffocate!" Dak burst out in a fury.

Nervelessly, Jensen played along. "No doubt." He allowed a moment for the unpleasantness of that concept to register, then gently prodded for what he wanted. "I need you, Dak. We're stripped of all energy sources but that cracked coil unit, and somehow we need to destroy *Kildare*."

Dak's face grew thoughtful, almost boyish as he considered the problem. "Shouldn't be too difficult," he surmised, his knobby fingers tapping his agitation. "The crack's making the unit unstable anyway. All we need to do is play a current through it. Should create a critical imbalance on short order." He ruminated for a moment, chewing his lip. "Trouble is, once I start the sequence, there won't be any fail-safe. *Kildare* will explode, and nothing we do could stop the process."

"You'd rather die at the hands of the skip-runners?" Jensen said brutally.

Dak shrugged. "Rather not die at all, truth to tell. But I guess this is our best chance."

Jensen settled back with a show of relief that was not entirely feigned. "I'll see you commended in my report, for courageous duty to the Fleet."

For a moment Dak looked wistful. "My mom would appreciate that. If we ever get through this alive."

Jensen nodded. As his back settled against the console of the escape capsule, he made a point of wincing over his cracked ribs. "I've brought a message torp," he said thinly. "When you get back from sabotaging the coils, we'll launch the capsule without engines. If we're lucky, drift will carry us clear before the skip-runner notices. When we know we're away, the torp will call in a rescue."

At the crucial moment Dak's childish face looked uncertain. "I hate to go out," he allowed. He dabbed at the gash on his knee and made a face. "That damned skip-runner's mate fights dirty."

Cloaked in the icy air of command, Jensen held back a sigh. "I won't remind you of the need to keep out of sight."

"I don't ever wake up their husbands," Dak admonished dryly. "Be sure of it, I'll be *damned* quiet." He folded his awkward assortment of limbs, slipped past, and sauntered off into the main bay with his lips curled in a nervous grimace.

Left alone in the stuffy confines of the capsule, Jensen readied the panel for takeoff. Mac James had left all the systems operational, which was well, for he had no intention of leaving the *Kildare* by drift. He'd go under power, and fast as he could manage, and he'd watch his command blow from space. That his crew were to die without quarter caused his hands to shake only slightly.

He'd weighed his options and decided without regret. The ghosts of a greenie ensign, and that dried-up bitch Beckett, a gun crew, and an incompetent pilot would not haunt him half so much as a career despoiled by court-martial.

That Dak had to be duped was a pity. The kid was a gifted engineer. . . .

● ● ●

In a cubicle office of Special Services, a thin man with a dry complexion thumbed through the report. The lines that described Jensen's story were straightforward enough—that *Kildare* had been commandeered by the skip-runner MacKenzie James, her crew murdered without quarter, and only her commander kept alive, for purposes of interrogation. With his vessel taken in tow to rendezvous with the Syndicate fleet, Commander Jensen had contrived escape, fired off the warning message torp to Admiral Duane's fleet, then arranged to scuttle *Kildare*. He had been rescued from his escape capsule, forty-eight hours after the battle off Khalia, in battered condition with several cracked ribs.

Cloth rustled as a short man seated in the corner shifted his weight. "The boy's lying outright. Mac James never kills unnecessarily."

The thin man's silence offered agreement. He thumbed the corner of the report for a moment before shuffling the pages straight.

The short man felt moved to clarify. "The security codes on the warning torp were Jensen's, but Mac James's personal cipher was appended. I say he's still alive, and that Commander Jensen destroyed his ship to hide evidence detrimental to himself."

The thin man stirred at last. "MacKenzie James is undoubtedly still alive. But the promotion to captain that's coming to Jensen cannot be stopped without blowing Mac's cover. With the Syndicate families being the threat that they are, I'm reluctant to call down a public hero. The people need the morale boost. And Mac's far too valuable a contact to waste just to bring a murderer to trial."

"Let it pass, then?" the short man concluded.

"No." The word held the hardness of nails. "Give Jensen a file in our records. He might prove useful someday."

That Way Lies Camelot

The May sunlight that fell through the window was serene enough to trigger a violence of resentment and hurt. Lynn Allen hurled a sodden, crumb-gritty sponge in the sink and ran her fingers through hair that fell thick to her shoulders, in neglected need of a cut. Childless, still single at thirty-three, she held little enough in common with a younger sister whose pretty, homey kitchen reflected family cheer at every turn. And what could anybody say to comfort a sibling who was divorced, a mother of three, with her eldest just barely twelve and lying in a coma, not expected to last out the day?

Words failed. Despair raged in like flood tide.

Wretched with the helplessness that overran them all over Sandy's terminal illness, Lynn blinked and roused and wiped damp palms on her jeans. She tried to regroup, to recover a grip on the immediate, while at the end of the gravel drive outside, a school bus slowed to a grind of gears; stopped to a squeal of brakes.

The front door banged.

"Damn it!" Raw with exasperation, Lynn repeated the same check she'd completed five minutes earlier. There'd been no forgotten books or sweaters in the breakfast nook then; she hadn't overlooked a misplaced brown bag lunch. No dab hand with kids, she'd thought she'd done miracles to get her nephews out the door on time for school without their incessant bickering firing her temper.

In typically eight-year-old smugness, Tony hollered bad news from the hallway. "Dog pen's empty, Aunt Lynn! Grail's run off again."

And the front door, left open, wafted air strongly scented with bursting pre-summer greenery. The patter of the boy's running sneakers diminished down the porch stair as he raced headlong toward the waiting bus.

"Damned stupid flea-bag of a mutt!" Lynn clenched her fists, feeling sloppy and out of synch in clothes more suited for weekend picnics. The dog's timing couldn't be worse; and worse, couldn't be helped. He would have to be rounded up before he finished dining from the neighbor's upset trash cans, and nosed out more original mischief that would incite some busybody's complaint to the county dog catchers. Ragged already from grief and exhaustion, Ann was shortly going to be coping with the funeral of a son. Given hassles with the insurance company over hospital expenses worth more than her house, the last thing she needed would be another fine for an unleashed pet.

The dog was Sandy's, after all. Obligation to a child, who could not be spared by all the torments of modern medicine, would invoke motherly sentiment by the bucket. The scrofulous yellow hound, with its torn ear and its ridiculous shambling gait, would be redeemed. An ounce of common sense suggested the creature should be better off abandoned to be humanely destroyed.

Through the window, washed in early, blinding brightness, Lynn saw Tony's neon jacket disappear inside the doorway of the bus. Brian, just ten, had boarded already. One problem less, with the boys off her hands; which left the damnfool dog. Lynn moved mechanically to the closet and snatched the first jacket to hand, an anorak that was baggy and grease-stained enough to have belonged to Annie's ex. She grimaced and pulled the thing on. It felt worse than her face, which any other day would have been tastefully made up for her work as design manager for a New York advertising firm.

But her job, as well as the tacked together appointments she called a social life, had been wrenched to a halt by Sandy's relapse. The event had impelled her to acts of insanity: to cash in her unused vacation time and leave the office in a hair-pulling rush.

Her boss's shouting troubled her yet. "There might not be any job here for you, whenever the hell you get back!"

And her reply, as filled with female bitchiness as any chauvinist could wish, to find fault for firing her later: "My nephew is ill, and I'm driving to New Hampshire to help my sister. If you've got a problem with that, then take my resignation in writing, sideways, down the first orifice you can reach."

She'd slammed the office door upon a thunderstruck, stupefied silence; and although she'd stayed absent for a month and sent no word, nobody from the firm so much as phoned.

Presently on her knees in the silvery pile of Annie's living room carpet, Lynn smothered a halfway hysterical laugh. Just now the convolutions of high-pressure employment seemed a picnic, beside the daily management of young boys, and keeping tabs on one alley-bred mutt. She scrounged under the coffee table, careful not to upset the empty pizza box with its cache of stale crumbs, and stretched to rescue her sneakers. These had somehow been kicked so far underneath the sofa they were wedged against the back strut. Grunting other inexpressible frustrations in epithets over the dog, she sauntered across waxed wooden floors and expensive orientals to the doorway, still open and decorated with a wreath that had Easter eggs wired in withered sprigs of hemlock.

The decoration had stayed up, forgotten, in the crush of concerns that followed Sandy's sudden onset of infections and the ugly, inescapable diagnosis that every agonizing scientific remedy had bought little more time, and no cure.

Lynn crossed the white-and-green-painted New England porch, squinted through light that hurt, and dissected the muddle of shade cast by a privet hedge whose wild growth reflected the absence of a husband. Though the fence wasn't torn, and the wire gate on its sagging hinges was still wrapped shut with chain, the dog's pen stood deserted. The infamous Grail had departed on another of his happy gallivants.

She sighed. Grail. What a stupid name for an ungainly mutt that loped like a roll of discarded shag carpet, propped askew on four legs. A creature nobody would have wanted, in right mind or not; but as a shambling stray towed home on a length of twine that showed signs of its salvage from the gutter, he had not been easily refused. Not when his plight had been championed by Sandy, who had sneaked outside unseen, still shaky and pale from the effects of his chemotherapy treatments. The huge eyes and gaunt face of leukemia in remission had overturned practicality, which would have been fine if the idiot dog had been content to enjoy his good fortune.

But the mongrel was friendly and brainless, and possessed by a penchant for wandering. He chewed through ropes, dug under wire fences, then progressed to other escape methods as unfathomable in their art as Houdini's. It had been grandfather Thomas who had called the creature Grail; the name stuck because of his young owner's obsession for Arthurian legend, and for the hours the whole family spent in Godforsaken searches that seemed as regular and futile as crusades.

"Do us all a service and charge in front of a delivery truck," Lynn grumbled to the creature's absent spirit. She kicked a stone and hiked after its savage ricochet down the drive. Over the grit and sparkle of gravel left mounded by the melt of last season's snowdrifts, she rounded the hedge toward the neighbor's yard.

Charlie Mitchell still wore his bathrobe, sash and hem flapping as he ill-temperedly chased down a bread wrapper caught by the wind. The trash can stood righted amid a chewed litter of The Colonel's colored packaging. Obviously

Grail had feasted and departed. Poised to beat a quick retreat, Lynn moved too late.

White hair askew and pajama cuffs grayed from the dew, Charlie pounced on the plastic. He gave a crow of triumph, swiveled around, and realized in embarrassment that his antics had been observed. Flustered by his unaccustomed burst of exercise, he called in carping irritation, "Damned dog lit off for the woods an hour ago! Get wise and buy him a chain, can't you? It's illegal to shoot dogs out of hand in this state. Or by God, I'd have loaded my shotgun and blown the mutt to the devil."

Lynn choked back excuses that a chain had failed already. Grail's brainless skull was narrow like a snake's, and collars slid off him like so many layers of shed skin. The chain, hacked off a foot from its swivel clip, now fastened an equally useless gate. She produced a polite apology for her sister's sake, and returned in resignation toward the house.

Inside, cut off from the gusty freshness of bursting azaleas and tulips, the rooms were sun-washed and silent. The waxed antiques and stylish hardwoods seemed too warm with life, their expensive comforts disjointed by a wider setting of tragedy. Lynn gritted her teeth unconsciously as she passed by Sandy's room, with its counterpane bedspread and clutterless floors, all too painfully neat. Unlike Tony, who slept like a hot dog in a bun, Sandy tended to rip his bedclothes off wholesale and leave them tousled in heaps. Photos of medieval castles lined the walls, as well as an old poster, lovingly framed, from a stage production of Camelot. The books and toy knights were not scattered across the rugs, nor arrayed for a charge against Saxons. They sat ranked in rows on the shelf, helms and ribboned trappings dulled by a layer of soft dust. As if Sandy's boisterous presence had been subdued, reduced already to a shadow that diminished the vibrance of his memory. Lynn pressed a hand to her mouth and hurried the length of the hallway, her track automatically bending to avoid the clutter of the younger boys' toys.

But the desk in the corner of the master bedroom offered no haven at all.

Lynn sat, elbows crackling in stacks of envelopes that showed not a curlicue of Annie's idle doodles. The mail lay as it had come, unopened, or else torn apart in fierce bursts, contents rifled for information. North sky through the casement blued the oblong, windowed cellophane; the return addresses of medical labs and oncologists, printed starkly in thermographed typefaces only preferred anymore by doctors, lawyers, and funeral homes.

Off to one side, bent-cornered and half buried, lay the unsent application for the charity that granted the wishes of terminally ill children. Only the blanks that related to Sandy's condition were filled out; the doctors' signatures meticulously collected in heavy-handed, near-illegible scrawls. The last sentences, in defiant schoolboy printing, requested a visit to the Round Table of King Arthur. After that, unfilled lines stretched in rows. The memory still cut, of the aftermath, with Ann driven to the edge. "My God, Lynn. Sandy's old enough to know that a trip to the past is impossible!"

At this desk, in this chair, Ann had sat white-faced over the pens and the papers gathered up from the kitchen table. She wept in despairing exasperation that the one wish her boy chose to long for was beyond human resource to fulfill.

Later, around the rubber-soled tread of busy nurses and the unending interruptions of hospital routine, they tried to coax Sandy to reconsider. Donated funds could send kids to Disney World, let them play with circus clowns, allow them to meet famous rock stars, or tour the set of a movie. But sending a boy back to King Arthur's court was just not a practical aspiration.

Too thin, too pale, his scrawny hand clenched on the wrist that had bruised red and purple from too close acquaintance with needles, Sandy stayed adamant. He would see Camelot, or go nowhere at all.

Lynn swore and blinked back tears. It wasn't as if they couldn't have sent the kid to a Renaissance fair, or a summertime re-creation staged by the Society for Creative Anachronism. Yet Sandy scorned the idea of a staged joust. He wanted real chivalry, and swords that drew blood, as if the savage bright danger of a legendary past could negate the horrors he endured through his illness.

"You know," he confided to his mother, "men got hurt in Arthur's time, and suffered wounds, and it was for a *cause*. Knights died for other people, Mom. I hurt, and I'll die too, but nobody will be better or get saved."

A boy's view: more than just desire, that leapt reason's restraint and became dreaming obsession. The tissue of tears and salvation for him; agony to the family he'd leave behind. Ann had pulled a tissue from her purse, blown her nose, and put the subject behind as best she could. She gave Sandy a hug and insisted it probably didn't matter anyway, as grants to bring joy to terminally ill children usually were awarded to cystic fibrosis cases. Leukemia, these days, was considered the less devastating disease.

Not Sandy's aggressive form, this was true.

Battered by platitudes that even the child could sense were meaningless, Sandy never complained. Colorless as the pillows he lay on, his features made over into an eerie, premature old age by the hair loss caused by his treatments, he had comforted his mother by pretending most diligently to forget.

Now, stung to useless fury by this fortitude, Lynn plowed aside the paper clutter that mapped a child's last month of life. She grabbed the phone and jabbed numbers fiercely.

The line rang once. Ann answered. She sounded beat to her socks.

Lynn made a failed attempt to sound cheerful. "Still there?"

A wrung out sigh came back. "Still there. At least he still shows breathing and a heartbeat." A pause, as Annie roused enough to take worried notice of the time. "Did Brian miss the bus?"

Lynn blinked faster, and felt tears trace hot lines down her cheeks. She could not, so easily, brush away the vision in her mind, of Sandy lying lost in a sea of adult-sized sheets, his wasted form diminished by the monitors and the tubes, overhanging his bed like modern-time carrion vultures awaiting his moment of death. "Brian and Tony are at school, and fine. I called because Grail's got out."

An interval of shared exasperation. "That dog. He's probably picking the chicken bones out of Charlie Mitchell's trash. You'd think the old coot would spend a few bucks and buy cans with lids that fit. The ones he hangs onto are a lunch invitation to coons and every other passing animal."

"Grail ate the trash already. Now he's run off to the woods." The unspoken question dangled—should Lynn abandon the mutt and drive to the hospital, or embark on a cross-country bushwhack?

"You'd better find him, I suppose." In the background, over the faintly heard tones of a nurse and a doctor conversing, Ann said, "Just a minute." A muffled roar as her hand smothered the receiver. She came back, tiredly resigned. "There's little enough to do here, anyway."

"Hang on," said Lynn. "I'll join you soon as I can." She dropped the receiver in its cradle, swearing like a sailor, because at that moment she hated life. She ached from sad certainty that Ann wanted her off to find the dog because even now she held out for a miracle. Outraged motherhood would not accept that Sandy's final hour must happen soon. He would not wake up, recover, and come home; but as long as life still lingered, it was unthinkable to Ann not to have a dog waiting, to bark and lick Sandy's hands in greeting.

"Damn, damn, damn," said Lynn, her eyes now dry to her fury, and her insides clenched in misery. "There ought to be a law against mothers outliving their children."

But there was no law, beyond the one outside the window, in cycles eternally unaffected. Nature wove all of spring's fabric of rebirth, in the flight of nesting barn swallows, and in the sunlight falling immutably gold over maples crowned with unfolded leaves.

Lynn shoved up from the desk, returned to the

kitchen, and dug through the clutter of children's drawings and coupons for the spare ring of keys. She locked up a house made cozy for living, but that echoed empty as a tomb. She slammed the door, set the dead bolt, and crossed the back yard to the woods in a blaze of targetless anger.

For Ann, and for Sandy's memory, she'd find the blasted dog.

Grail was the sort who tore up great grouts of earth with his hind feet just after he defecated. Assuredly no tracker, Lynn nonetheless could not miss the divots chopped out of the grass and raked in showers across the patio as evidence of Grail's blithe passage. A smeared print or two remained in the mud by the swing-set; these pointed unerringly into the shade, and should have been companioned by the sneaker treads of a young boy, were it Saturday, and Sandy not mortally ill.

Lynn crossed the dried weeds that edged the sandbox. Dandelions pushed yellow heads through the stalks of last year's burdock. The woods lay beyond, and through them, well trodden by young boys, was the path that led to the fort they had built out of sticks. The birches threw out new leaves, pale lit in sunlight as doubloons. The path was strewn with the drying wings of fallen maple seeds, and snarled mats of rotted twigs. If a dog had passed, nose to ground on the scent of a possum or hot after the tails of running squirrels, no sign remained. The path dipped toward the stream, the soft, moss-grown banks speared by unfurling shoots of skunk cabbage, and ranked on drier soil, the half-spread umbrellas of May apples. Across the narrow current lay the fort. Lynn paused. Naturally the water was high at this season, last summer's stepping stones washed out or submerged.

A fallen log offered the only crossing and an exercise in balance not attempted since childhood. Hesitation over a patch of wet bark cost her a slip. Lynn splashed knee-deep in a sink-hole. One leg of her jeans, one sock, and one expensive designer sneaker became as icily sodden as her mood.

Hating Grail with fresh energy, she sat, and skinned the rest of the way across on her fanny. The far bank was reached without mishap beyond a torn pocket and sadly tattered dignity.

Longingly she mused upon clothing that was pastel and fluffy. The smell of the oil-stained anorak made her feel off, and if the staff in the office were to see her, their worship of her unflappable grooming would suffer a shock beyond salvage. Well, they could all perish of missed deadlines, Lynn thought venomously, and she smiled as she arose and dusted off particles of bark.

Winter had not been kind to the lean-to that comprised the boys' fort. Snow load had caved in the roof. One wall sagged inward, and the wooden shield on which Sandy had sketched his make-believe coat of arms rested on the ground, weathered bare of poster paint. The unicorn lay dulled to shabby gray. A rusty can contained water, black leaves, and assorted bent nails. Beyond a snarl of moldered string and a burst cushion, a trash bin still held whittled sticks, imaginatively fleshed out as lances. Sad pennons decked the ends, cut from old pillow slips that dampness had freckled with mildew.

Nowhere, anywhere, was there sign or sound of Grail.

Lynn sighed and sat down on a boulder. She listened to the chuckle of the stream, wiggled toes that squelched in the wet sneaker, and finally undid the laces. Her hands got chilled as she wrung out her cuff and her sock. The gravel and mud ingrained in the knit she could do little about; too depressed for annoyance, she hoped the stores still carried laces to coordinate with last year's fashion colors. She shoved her wet calf to warm in a patch of sunlight, and cupped her chin in her palms.

A catbird in its plain gray squalled outrage from a maple. Lynn watched its discontent, abstracted.

How foolish to feel sloppy in jeans and no makeup on a weekday. Now adorned in mud, bits of bark, and dead leaves, her own problems seemed dwindled to insignificance. The man she'd hoped would become serious, who'd never phoned through to Ann's to inquire; the silly stresses abandoned at the office; her boss's tantrum at her leaving; all these seemed reduced, re-framed in the triteness of a sitcom.

By contrast, Ann's efforts at handling the pending loss of her boy seemed unapproachable; as pitiless and futile as a modern-day search to define the true Chalice of Christ. Everywhere one turned lay Sandy's memory; and where recollection had not trodden, new things cut the heart no less fiercely. The awareness never ceased, that this sight, or that fresh experience, could have stirred the boy to delight.

For two years, he'd had so little, between the doctors and the treatments, and the jail-like isolation necessary to shelter him from infection.

Lynn slapped her wet pants leg. Days like this, under spring sunshine with the hope ripped out from under all of them, she felt like suing Almighty God, that He would allow a little boy to be born, solely to suffer anguish and die. New-age philosophies and spiritual metaphors simply ceased to have meaning, when Sandy had sat straight with pencil clenched in hand, demanding impossible wishes.

His own way of asking, perhaps, for something the healthy otherwise took for granted. A fit of rebellion, that life, for him, was as unreachable a dream as a quest in historical legend.

That moment, the rusty, deep-throated bay that was Grail's split the woodland stillness. Jolted to recovery of her purpose, Lynn jammed on her shoe and stood up. The sound came again, from upstream. She jogged, her wet sneaker squishing, and hoped the mutt hadn't flushed a deer. Grail might run dead crooked, his hind legs flailing crabwise a foot offset from his forepaws, but he could go on tireless for miles. As the damp sock wadded up on her heel and began instantly to chafe a new blister, Lynn determined she was not going to chase that dog one step further than her breath lasted.

That promise she broke in sixty seconds.

In the ten minutes it took to track Grail down, she raked one arm on a briar, and ruined her other sneaker in a slithering step across a pit of black mud between swamp hummocks.

The sight of Grail gave no cheer.

He was wet, had been rolling in something nameless and noisome, and his coat was screwed into wiry ringlets like an Airedale's. His butt was raised, burr-coated tail waving like a whip, and his snout was jammed to the eyeballs in the cleft of a half-rotted stump.

Lynn flagged back to a walk. "Grail!"

The dog yiped, inhaled mold, and loosed a forceful sneeze into the stump. The beat of his tail increased tempo; beyond that, her summons was ignored.

Lynn walked up beside him. "Grail," she snapped. "Unwedge your face and come here."

Moist brown eyes rolled in her direction. Grail gave another muffled bark.

"I damned well don't want to share in your hunt for snails!" Lynn reached out, twined two fists in the dank ruff, and pulled.

Grail's hide rolled like bread dough, gave and peeled back until his bones seemed suspended in a bladder. She dragged him stiff-legged out of the cleft, and wondered belatedly whether he had a skunk or a muskrat held cornered and angry inside.

That possibility shortened her temper. Manhandling the dog like an alligator wrestler, Lynn hauled back from the stump.

"Bless my buttons and whiskers!" piped a voice over Grail's frustrated whining. From the inside of the stump, somebody waspishly continued, "It's long enough you took then, silly dog, to heed the plain voice of reason."

Grail yapped. Lynn started, and all but lost grip on his hair as the animal scrabbled frantically forward. Jerked off balance, her uncut bangs caught in her eyelashes, Lynn glimpsed the absolute impossible: a little brown man about three inches high stepped smartly out of the tree stump.

He had red cheeks, and chestnut whiskers that unfurled like frost-burned moss over a green waistcoat buttoned with brass. He wore leather boots, tan leggings, and a rakish cap topped with a jay's feather. At sight of Lynn, he shrieked in high-pitched anger.

She had no chance to stay startled. Grail tore out of her hands in a snarling bound, and as the man skipped backward in agile panic, rammed his muzzle back into the cleft with staccato, hair-raising yaps.

Knocked to her knees by the fracas, Lynn sat heavily on her rump. "Jesus Christmas!" She wasn't in the habit of having hallucinations; particularly ones of muskrats looking like little brown men who wore green waistcoats and talked. Where paired-off folk made decisions by compromise and committee, she had learned, living alone, to call her shots as they came.

She scrambled up out of the leaves and hit Grail in a shoulder tackle. He bucked, he heaved, he whined in piteous protest. After a lot of scratching and flying sticks, she managed to drag him aside. She then placed her face where the dog's had been, and, ignoring Grail's muddy nose as it poked at her neck and ear, looked into the dim cranny with its rings of old fungus and spider webs.

She almost caught a stick in the eye, one with a brass-shod tip, brandished by the furious little man. She yelled at the scrape on her cheek. He stumbled back with raised eyebrows, cursing in a language she'd never heard.

Certainly he was real enough to draw blood. Lynn dabbed at her face, while the man stepped back. Apologetic, he tucked his stick under one jacketed arm and spoke. "Ah, miss, so it's you." His skin was seamed like a walnut shell, and his eyes upon her might have been merry had he not been bristling with indignation. "It's a wish you'll be wanting, I presume. Though far likely it is I'd rather treat for my freedom with the dog."

"That can be arranged." Sourly, Lynn licked a bloody fingertip, and swore.

Pressed and heaving at her shoulder, Grail sensed her shift in attitude. He rammed in for another go at the stump, while the little man hopped and shrieked.

"Wait! Wait! Lady, I misspoke myself, I did truly. Pull

off that dog, do please. For your own Christian conscience, let me go."

Damp, dirty, and possessed by a sense of unreality that yielded an irritation equal to her captive's, Lynn said, "Why should I?"

The little man folded his arms. He puffed out his cheeks, looking at once diffident and crafty. He shuffled his boots, whacked his stick against the walls of his wooden prison, and finally faced her. "Well," he conceded. "There is the wee matter of a wish. You do have me caught, not so fairly, mind! But it's trapped I would be, I suppose, if you slipped your hold on that hound."

"And so I get a wish?" Lynn suppressed a rise of hysterical laughter. The strain, the surprise, the total weirdness of what was taking place smashed her off balance in a rush. "I need no wishes granted," she said tartly, and finished, defiantly flippant, with the thought uppermost in her mind. "It's Sandy's wish needs the attention."

"Ah!" The brown man sighed. He sidled, leaned a shoulder against the stump wall and frowned with a bushy furrow of brows. "A sick boy, it is, who begs a visit to Arthur's Round Table?" He gave a cranky shrug in reply to Lynn's astounded stare, and his anger swiftly melted to sad compassion. "You do know, miss, that yon one is soon to die."

The grief hit hard and too fast, that even a supernatural figment in the form of a finger-sized man could know and be helpless before incurable disease. Lynn choked back sudden tears.

The man strove quickly to console her. "Ah, miss, it's not so very hopeless as all that. Just hard. You ken how it is in this creation. Every living creature must choose its time and its place. Such is the maker's grand way. Your boy, now, Sandy. If he's to have what he desires, somebody's going to have to convince him to change his mind." The stick moved and slapped boot leather in reproof. "Somebody being me, no doubt. That's hard work, just for a wish. Hard work." He pinned her again with dark, restless eyes, his annoyance grown piquant as she opened her mouth, perhaps to ridicule; surely, foolishly to question. Humans did that, would in fact spit on good fortune when, like Grail, it bounded its way through their front door.

"Be still, now," snapped the man. "Let me think! It's my freedom I'm wanting, and yon's a muckle hard course you've set me if I'm going to fix a way to win it!"

With that, the little fellow deflated, plumped himself down, and set his elbows on his knees and his chin in cupped palms, to ponder the gravity of his dilemma.

The boisterous Grail had against all his nature grown still, and Lynn seized the moment to take stock. She unlocked her hand from the dog's neck, reawakened to discomforts both mental and physical. One pant leg was icily soaked. She had sticks and leaves in her hair, an astonishing departure. But these upsets paled to insignificance before the fact that she could exchange conversation and bargain with a creature that by rights belonged in the province of fairy tales.

After the briefest cogitation, she concluded that her nerves were too worn from the strain of dealing with Sandy's illness. That was enough to wrestle without battling further with a situation that confounded logic. Either the creature in the stump was a pixie or a leprechaun, or something else of that ilk; or else she was irrevocably crazy.

The truth in the verdict was unlikely to help Sandy, either way.

The next instant the matter resolved itself. With no warning, and a blinding quick movement, the little man shot to his feet and bolted for the opening in the stump.

Illusions didn't bid for escape. Lynn ducked to block off the cleft, and collided shoulder to shoulder with Grail's snarling lunge to achieve the same end.

The combined effect startled the little man back with his hands palm out in supplication. "Mercy! It's crushed by your blundering about, you'll have me. And unfairly, too I might add, since I've figured a chance for the boy to have what he's wishing."

Grail whined doubtfully and rolled his eyes.

Unwilling to credit the mutt with intelligence, but

touched by the self-same distrust, Lynn glared down at the little man. In vindication for bruised dignity and a growing sense of the ridiculous, she was determined to extract satisfaction, even if the next moment she woke up, rumpled in her bedclothes, to discover the whole event a silly dream. "You tried to get away," she accused.

The brown man sulked. "What if I did?" He crammed chubby hands in the pockets of his waistcoat and started with agitation to pace. "I'm caught still, and trying desperate hard to remedy that unfortunate mistake!"

Grail snarled, as if the creature might be lying. In a blend of acerbity and sarcasm that was her way of fending off what could not in conscience be taken seriously, Lynn sighed. "You don't look to me like a man keeping his half of a bargain."

The little fellow winced, then looked affronted. His roving carried him over a blackened acorn cap and across the musty confines of the stump. Removed from Grail's muzzle enough to feel secure, he stopped and folded his arms, booted foot tapping. "Is it so? And what are you thinking? That meddling with a boy's dying, not to mention playing hob with a time frame that passes through legend, is easy? Wishes, which you human sorts almost never bother asking, are grueling business!"

Sore from stooping, Lynn eased her knees by leaning a companionable arm across Grail's rawboned shoulderblade. Noisome wet fur was no substitute for upholstery, but the touch of an ordinary animal had become a necessary comfort. She looked a great deal less disgruntled now than her captive, which brought the shrewdness of her management background to the immediate fore. If she was going to play the fool and talk extortion with a fey being inside a rotted stump, Sandy may as well have a crack at the benefits. "Then, to go free, you'll have to show me some results."

The tiny man sidled; a sly grin tipped up one corner of his mouth, and he stroked at his wiry fall of whiskers. "It is hard work I'll be going off to then, lady. To fix your boy's wish, truth to tell. For that you'll be having to let me out."

He stepped in brash confidence toward the daylight that shone through the cleft.

Lynn's outraged, "What?" tangled with Grail's sudden snarl. The pelted muscle under her shoulder surged as the dog rammed headfirst and growling into the opening in the stump. A scuffle ensued. For a moment, the animal's bulk obscured sight of what transpired within.

Then Grail's tail whipped straight. His buttocks heaved and he backed up. Clenched in between rows of bared teeth, the little man swung from his waistcoat, his arms waving, his terrified shouts thin as a bird's cries over the growls of the dog. The stick whipped the air to and fro, shining like a little brass pin, and about as uselessly effective.

Lynn spared a moment for sympathy, mostly for the fact that the little fellow was probably perishing of dog breath. Discounting his clothes, the rest of him was unmarked, however much his shrieks suggested otherwise.

"Put me down!" he screeched. "Oh, lady, for pity, I can't be fixing wishes as a dog's snack. Surely it's wise enough you are, and merciful also, to be seeing that!"

Lynn set her jaw and said nothing.

Grail sat, lips peeled back and trembling above his victim. The little man kicked in agitation. "You need me to make arrangements, don't you? Well, true it is I can't *do that* sick with beast stink and prisoned inside a stump!"

"How do I know your word is good?" Touched to acerbity, Lynn sat down to set her head level with Grail's. She fingered the damp cuff of her jeans. "Really, if you're going to be trusted, I should go along as observer, to be certain the terms of Sandy's wish are fully met."

The man's arms fell to his sides with a faint slap. His whiskers drooped. He hung like a mouse from Grail's jaws, a forlorn morsel with a fat belly that strained at his rows of brass buttons. "I'm not lying. Spit on my luck if I am."

Grail's brown eyes held level with Lynn's, imploring canine prudence, and oddly, knowingly, infused with a wisdom no dog she'd ever known had possessed. A queer chill shot through her. In a dark, unbreached corner of her mind, conviction grew, that the dog's purpose was and always had been to find such a tiny man, and take him captive.

But of course in cold logic, that was ridiculous.

Pressed unbearably against the realities of a child's terminal disease, and faced by unspeakable suffering and now the bitter ending of Sandy's life, Lynn found reason a poor arbiter. Hope and superstition this moment seemed infinitely more kindly. Grave, supremely detached from the ongoing cruelties at the hospital, she sighed. To the tiny man she said, "That's not good enough."

"Bother and fiddlesticks!" cried the man. Jostled by movement of the jaws that prisoned him, he rolled widened eyes in trepidation.

Grail looked befuddled, as if his nasal passages had sprouted an itch from too heady a scent of the supernatural. The little man observed this, growing alarmed. He evidently understood that in canines, heavy sneezes often ended with an unkindly whap of muzzle and teeth against the ground. "I'll show you the results in a dream!" he hollered in sharpened anxiety. "It's not so simple, you'll appreciate, with a wish involving more than one party, and one of them with scarcely an hour left to live. You're wasting time!"

"I think not." Punched inside by reminder of Sandy's condition, and sorry for Ann, waiting alone and unsupported for an ending her heart could not encompass, Lynn held hard to the last fragment of detachment still left to her. "That's not good enough. Dreams can be manipulated, I must assume, or the dog who holds your coattails would be satisfied. Grail hasn't seen fit to let you go."

"You'd have me set the Sight on you!" howled the man. Dangling, he managed to look irked as he folded his arms across his chest. "Well that's another wish!"

Lynn glowered levelly back. "That's no wish, but proper surety."

"Ah, it's hard, hard in the heart, that humans can be, you female sorts most of all." The man waved a miniature fist. "An unchancy business it is, always, dealing with modern-day mortals." He unlimbered a wrist to wag a finger, cuff buttons flashing like pin heads. "You folk muddle about wide awake, most times, with your dreams the most living part of you. Did you know as much, you'd fare better." When this diatribe left Lynn without comment, the brown man fixed her with a glare that made her tingle. "Well, it's not *my* part to adjust your mortal ills and your muckle mistaken thinking! Very well, miss. As you wish. If you're the blundering sort who sets no stock by dreams, it's the Sight you'll get, to witness my part in the bargain. But sorrow you'll find, and weeping too, when you long to be quit of the gift afterwards!"

This was delivered in vindication, not warning, for the little man raised his hand and flicked his fingers, as if to splat water in Lynn's face.

She saw no physical projectile. But something struck her forehead just below the hairline. A golden bloom rinsed her eyesight, a painless dazzle that flared and faded, and left her senses momentarily encapsulated. As if a bubble had been spun around her consciousness, she felt as if physically suspended.

She raised her head, gasped; the wood she knew was altogether gone. No skunk cabbage grew; no May apples. The ground was a living carpet of shining myrtle. She breathed a chillier, more fragrant air; the trees all about were old oaks, huge towering crowns shafted with midday sunlight. The ground fell away, toward a clearing floored in ivy and moss, and sheltered by water-channeled outcrops.

Little men that lurked in stumps were one thing. This, a forest setting more appropriate to a page of medieval romantic illustration, was too much.

Lynn opened her mouth to cry out.

"Be quiet, fool woman!" The little man rapped her fingers with his stick, which caused her a violent start. "Wake him up, and you'll spoil Sandy's wish!"

Muddled, unable to re-orient herself, Lynn whispered, "Wake who up?"

Apparently the little man and the mongrel dog had made their peace, for in course of a wild search, she located him, seated in his spit-dampened waistcoat, astride Grail's thick ruff. The brass-tipped stick now pointed toward something a ways off in the undergrowth.

Lynn peered through twining runners of ivy, and saw what looked like bits of basket woven out of sticks. Closer scrutiny revealed a young man, black-haired and high-browed, and barely past his boyhood. He appeared to be asleep. A cheek as innocent and clear-complexioned as a peach rested on uncallused knuckles. His limbs were well made, though delicately muscled, and over his simple tunic he wore what looked to be shoulder pads and breast plate all woven out of willow fronds and twigs.

"My God," breathed Lynn.

The little man bristled. "Not God!" He went on to snap in an undertone, "Just the magic you've demanded of me, and no more."

Lynn could not quite stifle awe. "Who is he?"

"Your Sandy will know." The little man clapped his palms together in a silent explosion of fey power.

Lynn's hair bristled. A jolt hammered through her that rocked her awareness to its root. She blinked, shaken by its passage, and then stopped, slammed cold still, by the sight of Sandy standing barefoot in his hospital gown. He stepped forward and paused, eye to eye with the creature on Grail's back.

The tubes, the needles, the paraphernalia of medical science that inadequately sought to prolong his life had all gone. Bruises remained, under his eyes and on his arms and in the hollow of his shoulder; the stitchery left by weeks upon weeks of IV needles. He still looked sick and thin, all knobby white limbs and a neck that rose frail as a stem. His eyes shone sunken and huge, haunted yet by the shadows of his suffering.

"Sandy!" gasped Lynn.

But he did not look at her. The little brown man addressed him and his ears seemed sealed to other words.

"You'll be knowing who that is, lying there?" The stick twitched toward the sleeper, and a hand miraculously tiny twined in a fall of chestnut whiskers.

Languid as if sleepwalking, Sandy turned his head. He regarded the young man in his bed of ivy and moss, and a yearning transformed his face with life. Incandescent in delight, he almost laughed. "Perceval!"

"You'll be knowing the legend, then," prompted the fey man who had brought both together, the sleeping young man and a dying boy's spirit, to a woodland Lynn could not place in any ecosystem known to modern earth.

"Of course I know." Sandy's excitement broke through his weakness, made his thin voice ring with derisive joy. "Perceval was son to a rebel king, thrown down by King Arthur's justice. He was raised in isolation by his mother in a far off tower. She hoped he would become a priest, and escape the fate of his father, to die in battle. But when from a distance Perceval saw some knights riding, he was struck by the sun on their armor. He asked what sort of creatures they were, for their beauty left him in awe. His mother, afraid he would leave her to take up fighting and bloodshed, told him he had seen angels."

"And so lost him," the little man picked up, as Sandy's enraptured recitation trailed off. "For young Perceval replied that there was no more worthy quest than to follow God's angels to heaven." The little man cracked a smile filled with crafty sharp teeth and inclined his head toward the sleeper. "Well, so you're seeing," he confided to Sandy. "Yon lies Perceval, who set off wearing armor he wove out of sticks, that he could be as like unto the saintly hosts as possible until his reunion with them should be fulfilled."

Sandy knotted bony hands together. He gazed in admiration at the young man, whom he knew would go on from this clearing, to win his place at Arthur's Round Table and be one of the chosen few who would glimpse the Holy Grail. Drinking in details for sheer delight, Sandy stared: at the fine, shiny dark hair, unblemished in health; at the unstained innocence of the face. He looked at the hands, palms soft and unmarked; at muscles too delicate to have done much more than hold books.

The hero worship in his look became marred by dawning doubt. "He's a wimp."

The little man said nothing.

Sandy's study encompassed the wrists that lay lax in the moss, unmarred by even a briar scrape. Troubled sorely, he swung around and glared in accusation at the little man. "You lied. That can't be Perceval. He doesn't at all look like the sort who would go for hard rides and bloody fighting."

And Lynn, understanding a thing, held her breath, while the little brown man answered him reasonably.

"You're part right, my boy. But I never lie. That's Perceval, there, and you've spoken the heart of the problem, his and yours. For within the next hour, your two fates must resolve. You will be greeting God's angels, and he will wake up to discover his 'angels' are earthly clay in the form of tough-mannered, battle-trained knights."

"Oh!" Sandy stepped back, his soul laid bare by longing. "If only we could change places!"

"Said is done!" cried the little man, and he clapped his hands with a crack that shattered the stillness.

Sandy vanished.

Birds started up from the trees, and the young man in his armor of sticks sat up, a look of raw startlement on his face. He raised his arms, stared at his palms as if flesh, bone and nerve were appendages that belonged to a stranger. Then he looked wildly about until his gaze found and locked on the little man. "You've done it!" And he smiled as though all the world had been reborn between his two hands.

"So I have." The little man laughed and pointed westward through the forest. "That way lies Camelot, young Perceval. Fare you well, on all your quests, until the last, until the day you sight the Grail."

Lynn came back to herself, with Grail's tongue dragging and dragging across her cheek. She sat in soggy leaf mould, one shoulder braced against a stump whose cleft was now empty.

She shivered once, violently; in distaste she pushed off

the dog. For once, Grail gave over his affections with deference to the person being mauled. He backed off, sat, and looked at her. His tail whacked up a storm of forest detritus. His expression looked inordinately pleased.

Lynn shivered again. Chilled by uncanny experience, and also by her soaked shoe and pants cuff, she looked about, as if expecting the woods to be somehow momentously different.

They were not.

May sunlight slashed the trunks of the birch trees like knife cuts limned in gold; the catbird's mate sang at her nesting, and two squirrels ran scolding in a territorial squabble through the bursting leafy crowns overhead.

It did not seem a day for miniature men and bright wishes. Neither did it seem any more appropriate a time for a twelve-year-old boy to lie dying.

Lynn cursed. Whatever had befallen her, be it illness, hallucination, or stark raving madness, she had an obligation, now that Grail was found. She must hurry on to the hospital to lend her support to Ann.

That moment, ridiculously, she recalled she'd neglected to bring a leash. Grail seemed to need none, creature of obscure contradictions that he was. For the first time in his miserable life, he came when called. Apparently content for once to follow, he frisked at Lynn's heels all the way back to the house. More surprising, he stepped meekly into his pen at her bidding; and once there, lay down, nose on tail, to fall asleep. He looked like an old string mop, stiff-curled as if dried in ocher paint.

Lynn left him. Inside the house, her intent bent exclusively on the logistics entailed in joining Ann quickly at the hospital. Shoes, one muddy, one damp; dirty jeans, oil-stained anorak; all flew off her into a heap. She wanted a shower, but settled with splashing cold water on her face. Too pressed to fuss over details, she snatched khaki slacks, a silk blouse, and a tailored jacket from the closet. She had dress for success down to reflex, and her thoughts she held firmly to practicality, until the first cog slipped in her regimen.

She realized she'd left the shoes that went best with the jacket in the city. Her desperate self-control fled.

Frowning, frantic not to think, and still barefoot, she dug her makeup case out of the bathroom and parked in front of the mirror. Trivia refused its role; would not keep her preoccupied. She froze through a moment of silent struggle; to focus on anything and everything onerously ordinary, that she not be overset to disturbance over what had or had not occurred out in the wood.

Tiny men, and brown thoughts; she was as much in denial of Sandy's straits as webbed about in the peculiar insanity Grail had lured her to tread. Dangerous ground. Better to debate her choice of lipstick.

She rummaged through her cosmetics and selected a shade of cover-up to conceal the nick on her cheek. Then she glanced up at the mirror. And stopped dead.

Where her own features should have looked out at her, she saw instead a different view. Ann, seated in her untidy cardigan with her back bowed and her face in her hands, beside a bed in a hospital room.

"No!" Lynn shoved her knuckles against her mouth in denial, even as memory of the little man's protest mocked her. *If you're the blundering sort who sets no stock by dreams, it's the Sight you'll get, to witness my part in the bargain. But sorrow you'll find, and weeping too, when you long to be quit of the gift afterwards!*

The ache in her died to a whisper. "No." But the deathbed view of her nephew bound her senses, as vitally real as if she were present at her sister's shoulder.

No recrimination, no fear, no sense of disorientation or disbelief could tear her attention from the body, supine under white sheets. The pastel hospital gown betrayed by its lack of wrinkles how far removed from life and movement lay the consciousness that delineated Sandy.

Lynn choked a breath through her tightened throat, then stopped, even breathing suspended.

For the motionless boy on the bed sighed slightly and opened his eyes.

They shone, blue and enormous in the subdued, artificial

lighting of the hospital. Dark as marks in charcoal, his brows sketched a puzzled frown. Too weak and emaciated to do more, he regarded the sterile white walls, the plastic pitchers, the raised side rails, and the IV line dangling at his shoulder as if he had never in his life known such sights.

He looked as if witness to marvels.

Lynn caught her breath in a gasp. She knew like a blow, that *this was not Sandy, looking out through the eyes of his face.* She stood, frozen and trapped before the vision of a perfect stranger residing in Sandy's failing flesh.

The boy noticed Ann at that moment. Perhaps he heard her stifled weeping, or was drawn by her forlorn posture as she convulsed in silenced grief. He raised the hand not burdened with needles, dragged limp fingers across the sheet, and gave her a brushing touch.

Ann started up as if shot. "Sandy?"

He blinked as she caught his wrist. "My God, my God," she cried in wonder and jagged-edged joy.

He looked at her. The familiarity of the gesture tore at Lynn's heart for the fact that he had no cowlicks left to tumble brown hair across his eyes.

Because of that, she and Ann both saw: the boy's hollowed features were lit from within by a burning, unearthly rapture. "Lady," he whispered in an accent that sounded gallant and antique. "You must not weep for me. It is promised. I go on to God's glory, to meet His most beautiful angels."

The fingers in Ann's chilled hand tightened one last time, and the spirit, lightly held, left the flesh.

Lynn came back to herself, gripping the sink too tightly. Wild-eyed, her own face stared back from the mirror. The pinprick cut showed livid against her pallor, and her chest ached as, in tears, she recovered herself with a cry.

A strange, exalted exhilaration possessed her, snapped at once by sharp grief at the jangling intrusion of the telephone.

She stumbled out to reach the hallway extension.

"Lynn?" said Ann's voice as she answered. "It's over. He's gone, just this minute." She paused for a wondering breath. "You wouldn't think it, but it happened beautifully. He woke up to tell me . . ."

Words failed her, and Lynn couldn't bear it. "He's gone to meet the angels."

Startled, still drifty with shock, Ann came back in surprise. "Lynnie, how could you know?"

Lynn crouched, weak-kneed, and steadied herself on an elbow that ground with real pain against the baseboard. "Never mind," she answered. "It doesn't matter."

But it did; the uncanny proofs remained with her. Into old age, the fey man's gift of Sight never left her; and Grail never wandered again.